GOING WEST

by the same author

PLUMB
MEG
SOLE SURVIVOR
PROWLERS
THE BURNING BOY

Going West

MAURICE GEE

faber and faber
LONDON · BOSTON

First published in 1992
by Faber and Faber Limited
3 Queen Square London WC1N 3AU

Phototypeset by Wilmaset Ltd, Birkenhead, Wirral

© Maurice Gee, 1992

Maurice Gee is hereby identified as author of this work
in accordance with Section 77 of the Copyright,
Designs and Patents Act 1988

A CIP record for this book is
available from the British Library

ISBN 0-571-16832-9

6 8 10 9 7

Acknowledgement

This novel was written with the assistance
of a scholarship from the
Queen Elizabeth II Arts Council of New Zealand.

Jack Skeat's Notebook: 1

He was born at New Lynn in 1930, with Amalgamated on one side and Crum on the other, and died in 1988, out past Tiri in the Hauraki Gulf. He was the author of nine books of poetry and a small amount of fugitive and occasional verse. He had two wives, two daughters and two sons; but his first wife (who is mistaken) told me once, 'He never married.'

How comfortable it would be to leave him to his memoirist, Elfin John, who sees 'a running fire of brilliance' over him. We need all the brilliance we can get. John fills his book with jokes, occasions, parties, *bon mots*. Even I, the other John (the Jack), say something smart now and then. The poet falls over on a flight of steps and bleeds into the cup of his hands. 'Does anybody happen to have a wafer?' Jack Skeat asks.

We don't need any more of that sort of thing. I know jokes the Elf can't tell because he wasn't there – he wasn't there most of the time – but I'm not going to put them in unless they do more than raise a laugh.

Born 1930, died 1988. Those years contain him, and contain much of me. Is that why I take on this task? I want to write my own life, not his? I'm tired of being a satellite, author of one bad book? I want my magnitude observed?

Jack and Rex made a binary; and if I was a dark star, well, I had more weight. (You see now why my book was bad. Never mind. When I get down to it this stuff will go out.)

Notes, comparisons: We were both born in 1930, he in New Lynn by the brickworks and I in rural parts, west and north: a small town in the orchards. My father was a solicitor with a good country practice and my mother a lawyer's daughter, who passed her life in social isolation. No one in our town, not the vicar's wife, not the schoolteacher's daughter, was good enough. She locked herself in our garden, behind our gate, and never went out, and never let in anyone who might attempt to know her. As for my friends: 'The butcher's son! The engine driver's son!' I must keep boys of that sort out on the footpath.

I must keep Rex out there. His father was a brickie. A hooligan, a boxer, a better on racehorses. He taught me how to lead with my left and cross with my right. I stood beside him while we peed in a hedge and the amount that came out of him would have filled a bucket. I wondered how he had ever managed to get his wife. She would have been good enough (almost) for my mother if she had not married him.

Les Petley's wife. Rex's mother. For one night she was my mother too. Clever, sad, graceful, beautiful. The adjectives tumble out like bubbles from a pipe but all they do is float around her head.

Wasted. There's one that doesn't float.

Leave her. Leave Lila Petley for later on.

Territories, places. West of Auckland, out towards the ranges. Purple evening hills with a sunset like an open wound. We both knew that margin to our world, Rex from New Lynn, I from Loomis.

I must beware of false weight and too much primary colour; and of the pastel shadings of nostalgia. My verse – my early verse, before I chose cleverness as a better way – was disfigured and denatured by pink and blue, a wash, and bloody red and midnight black. I'll have, I'll try to have, none of that. (And not have too much cleverness either – open wound!) Rex was never troubled in that way. He seemed to have no mess in his head, none of the human mess simmering and stewing in me. Large plain movements Rex had, a tilting and intersecting of planes. Or was that later? And before? In any case, simplicity and largeness. Mess in abundance, though, in his daily life.

Westward the ranges. Naked beaches on the other side; mile-long combers crashing in. Auckland city lay in the east; opulence and commerce, bright lights, sin. Rex was put out once to find that I too weighed those places in that way.

We had a north-south axis as well, but that comes later.

From Loomis to Auckland there were three ways:

2

1) The green and yellow ABC buses, straining up the white concrete road to the edge of town – where farms opened out, with a long view over the harbour, past Pt. Chevalier and the sugarworks, to Rangitoto pale and uneasy in the distance. (What a lot of weight that island, that mountain, has to bear. The city's claim to greatness often seems to rest on it.) The road ran down Waikumete Hill, with acres of grey gravestones and white crosses on the right, and over the little hump at the bottom, and up the equal hill on the other side. Oh the plunge into the valley in the ramshackle bus. Was it death (those thousand grinning skulls underground) or was it sex? The twin slopes opened out like thighs, with a little hump there, pubic mount. (It will be said that I steal this from a Petley poem but, for the record, I pointed out the likeness to him and he dressed it up.)

Then New Lynn and the brickworks, Amalgamated and Crum: black open sheds stacked with orange pipes, chimneys with iron ladders up their sides, and once in twenty years a steeplejack on top. We crossed the Whau creek – mud and mangroves – where country ended and the suburbs began. Avondale, the racecourse, and Pt. Chev., the asylum. You might see loonies walking in the grounds. ('Not loonies, Jack,' Lila Petley said, 'people who are mentally ill.') Past the golf course and the zoo and Western Springs stadium where the midget cars raced on Saturday nights (Frank 'Satan' Brewer), and up another hill into Grey Lynn, and there the city proper, Karangahape Road along the ridge. Then a plunge down Pitt Street to the wharves and terminus and a glimpse of Queen Street as you went by. That was my most frequent way. Forty minutes from the Loomis orchards to white liners sailing from the bottom of the street. Queen of streets. And forty years and more from that time to this and still the excitement comes on me.

The question is, of course, how did Rex Petley feel about it?

2) By train. From Loomis station the track ran straight for several miles, with straggly town on one side – Ah Lap's grocery where you could buy Chinese ginger in jars, the Scout Hall, the Anglican Church, the jam factory – and vineyards and farms on the other. Then the line began to curve and the impression one had was of worming into Auckland. It went up inclines and through cuttings, and you saw a grey fringe of cemetery overlapping the hill, and the

lumpy end of the ranges on the other side. New Lynn, round the back of the shops, across the front of Amalgamated. The house where Rex Petley lived until he was eight stood hard against the line and I think I saw him once before I knew him, sitting cross-legged on a pile of sleepers, watching as the train eased through a railway gang. Rex with hanging adenoidal mouth. That can't be right. Perhaps he was yawning. I envied him his place on the warm stack of logs.

Once across the spindly bridge there was no creeping, you stabbed like a knife. Avondale, Mt. Albert, houses tumbling one against the other, iron roofs in a frayed quilt of reds and greens; and Morningside, Kingsland, with Eden Park mown like a lawn waiting for the big match Saturday; then the prison, an English castle, with the quarry where the prisoners broke stones, and Auckland Grammar standing above, its Kublai Khan buildings in the sun and boys in navy-blue kicking footballs high. What happened when a football went into the quarry? Newmarket Tunnel, with men's cigarettes in the dark, and kids making ghost yells, and the smell of sulphur – and once in there, the big kids said, a Seddon Tech boy rooted his sheila and they both had their pants pulled up and were sitting as though nothing had happened by the time the train came out the other end.

At Auckland station the ramps made you run and the echoing big hall threatened you and you felt that you might travel up or down instead of along, by slanting, sliding ways or by the plucking of a Hand, and hear a big final Voice. The dusty straggling walk along to Queen Street ended that.

The bus had the cumulative magic of the known, the train odd bits of drama and a back view of things. The third way was the one I liked best.

3) Tram. You got off the bus in front of the undertaker's in Avondale and walked back twenty yards to Rosebank Road, where the red and yellow car hummed softly at the bottom of the hill. But always I felt danger: those shining grooves and bacon-slicer wheels. Peril is a better word. The motorman released the rope, manoeuvred the whippy pole, set the grooved wheel on the overhead wire. He took his place in the box in front (the tramcar had two fronts and two backs), woke the lovely throbbing underfoot, eased the lever round,

and we were off, grinding up the single track and lurching through the curve on the Y. When the seats filled up you gave yours to a lady and stood on the platform with the road rushing by at the bottom of the steps. You leaned out when the pole broke loose and watched sparks flash and heard them spit as the motorman eased the wheel back on to the wire. High speed along the flat into Mt. Albert, with a grinding and hissing from the wheels and a swaying in the car that was barely in control. Up the hill through Kingsland, along Symonds Street, past Grafton Bridge where the suicides jumped into the cemetery in the gully, along Karangahape Road, and then the stomach-lurching right-angle turn and the dive down Queen Street, past the town hall and the Crazy House and the Civic, to John Courts and Smith and Caughey and Milne and Choyce. Off at the zone there and through the traffic, the city's heart. That was why I liked the trams, they set you down in the middle of things. (And while I remember the zones, those narrow concrete islands in the street, Rex used them in his poem 'Passing Through' and some readers have failed to understand zone as an actual thing. It's the safe place between the slicing wheels and the butting cars, but not a place one can stand about in. By the time he has finished with it, of course, it comes to mean any number of things.)

Why do I do this? Why start? I have no need of discovery. Isn't that what I am leading to? Not simply memory but the ordering that is a kind of invention? Looking at things I haven't known is likely to prove fatal to me. Danger. DANGER! Here I am, sixty, retired with a sigh of relief, fresh and ready for the rest of my life. The things I'll do: I'll read, I'll sport, I'll travel, I'll drink two glasses instead of one and maybe I'll even smoke cigars. All that waiting for me – and what do I do? I shine my torch back into the dark. Stupid bugger! Don't go there.

On the other hand I'll have a great time. That sort of great time one has in battles and affairs. One's at risk and terrified and alive. And if I come out minus a limb or with some part broken or diseased? I really don't want that. I want no trouble; and I can't stand pain. I want to be happy, I want some slow-paced fun. I've always said there's ten good years in there, sixty to seventy, and that's where I'll take my reward. I want to go to Greece again, not back to Loomis. I want the Castalian spring, the hill of Kronos. I want Tuscany, the Danube, the Dordogne, I've dreamed of them. Is my way to that – this? Must I run the gauntlet? And maybe plunge off a cliff at the end? And never reach that great old ruined Europe I've promised myself?

Rex is saying to me, 'Why go there, mate? Everything you need is right here.' That is his true authentic voice.

I'm not going to do his childhood. All I'll do is make a chronology, a catalogue. The dates, the places, the people, the circumstances. And nothing circumstantial as evidence. No evidence, in fact. I won't even quote verse, although I'm in a better position than most to say what he invented and what connects with his experience. I can guess too, better than Elfin John, at all the things that lie between. But I won't do that. Rex hated biographical raking around in his lines. I'll say what I know, that's all, and let him speak for himself.

'The deepest springs of his poetry.' That's where John Dobbie claims to go in his first chapters, and he gives us a sensitive small boy, full of pure responses to leaf and cloud and bumblebee and bubbling stew etc. Would you like to know all the things the Elf has him 'nakedly handle with his lovely mind'? Page 11. Here goes: a broken bottle in the grass; baby eels wriggling in the slime; skeletons of spiders in their webs; bent-pin fish-hooks; steaming woollen socks above the stove; blackbirds breaking snails out of their shells; sparrows mating; wetas in the dunny; slaters; Maori-bugs, their stink; a naked swagger in the waterfall; ice in the horse trough; used frenchies under the bridge; clean washing on the line; the tea-tree prop; Dinky-toy roads carved in the bank; the doughboy; boiled cabbage; date roll; bread-and-milk; the News from London; BB guns.

John could go on but he won't. These things are 'gateways into innocence'. I think they're images in poems. As for their significance, who couldn't make a similar list? Getting them into poems, that's the hard thing. And John, to his credit, knows that. But he will go on about 'the creative mystery'. He's better later on when he tells jokes.

Rex, indeed, was a sensitive boy. I've seen him pick a flower up from the pavement and put it in the shade under a tree. I've also seen him throw grasshoppers into a spider web; and rescue some of them just in time. As for those used frenchies, he washed them out and blew them up and knotted their ends and floated them on Loomis Creek. We bombarded them with green apples. Great fun. John, they're 'the Armada with swollen sails'; not the flax-stick boats with paper sails we made. The poem doesn't say what you think. There's a sub-text reading sexual disgust.

I'm the one who knows and I won't tell.

Dates and places. 1938. Loomis school. The new boy says, 'Rex Petley, Miss.' I'm jealous of his name. My own is sissy and ridiculous. John Skeat. I try to make my school friends call me Jack.

Rex. Wrecks. And it means king. Petley though is sissy. Mother's pet. Teacher's pet. It will make a useful weapon if I need one.

I'm not going to keep on like this. Tomorrow I'll turn up different things. And the next day something else. Rex as milk monitor. School bellringer. It's like watching soup in a pot – here's a pea rising, here's a bit of carrot, here's some leek. If I'm to do it I need to be governed by an idea, something that will enable me to select. So: poet. But which comes first, the poet or the man? And both, of course, are prefigured in the boy. 'In the lost childhood of Judas' etc. I'm happy to leave that game to someone else. I want the spiritual two-backed beast, Rex/John. We both of us, didn't we, strove to see last things? (I don't mean the Four.) And both of us believed that in this world of appearances the proper task of poet and of man was to find those things one could fix with a Name. And both of us (Jack Skeat early, Rex Petley late) gave it up.

That is to simplify. But it does provide me with an idea. And it gives me a place to stand.

Image: two amoebas vainly trying to swallow each other up. I'm not sure I don't prefer dark star.

The healthy working of many of my parts is gone for ever. There's nothing to be gained from complaining. Mirrored in a shop window, I'm pleased with what I see. Desiccated follicles, all right, my hair falls out, but I wash what's left of it with Johnson's Baby Shampoo and it keeps some body and stirs nicely in a breeze. At sixty I have to be pleased with that. I stride along, I'm boyish. Who's to know the circulation in my right foot is poor, making it colder than the left? It's not important when I walk. It only bothers me at night but I warm it up by covering it with my left calf. Heat transfer, I like the economy, using one part to bring another up to scratch. The trick can be used to cure mental ailments too. That almost feverish nocturnal activity of the mind is treated with images of sea and yellow beaches. I put myself to sleep on yellow beaches. The warm sea lifts me up and floats me out.

Mind has never caused me too much trouble. I keep control even when pressures are extreme. I've raged and screamed with jealousy and frustrated ambition – who escapes? – and have thought myself not capable of loving – a condition that made me wordy and declarative for a time (only to myself) and made me think of suicide too. But in all this I sat on my shoulder watching me, and I (which I?) was never lost, in any place either dark or open to bright light. I've always had myself watching me. I watch in orgasm. True. In all explosions there's a small still place and my tiny other self is there. Perhaps I'm mad. Perhaps, on the other hand, I'm sane, and that is why.

Rex may have been mad at the end. He never had, I think, a watching self.

I meant to keep Rex out of this discussion.

Looking at Him

Jack Skeat cannot keep Rex Petley out. Even his stratagem of counting his ailments is bound to fail. For all his boasting about control and the little Jack who sits on his shoulder he cannot free himself from Rex. It's clever of him too – he is a very clever man – to rush headlong at the problem. By that I mean write Rex's life. Or if not life then memoir of his friend. I hope he manages. I hope it works. While we wait for that an objective look at the man may be of interest. His appearance (and decay) will serve as a starting point.

Jack is of middle height but some people believe him tall because he stands so straight. As a boy he slumped (and moped – puberty turns some boys into zombies) until his mother threatened to have a board fixed to his shoulders to hold them back. She believed in straight shoulders, a firm handshake, and looking people straight in the eye. These things signalled inner health as well as good breeding. Jack was terrified of his mother. He knew she would have the board fixed if he did not stand straight – so back went his shoulders and they've stayed back ever since. And although he has always made a point of questioning popular wisdom – did she know it was popular? – he believes uncritically in the hand, the eyes, the shoulders.

He does not believe in good looks, they're accidental. He has an undistinguished face: there's too much here, too little there, too much nose and forehead, too little mouth and chin, to make it pleasing in a conventional way. Too little bone under the eye. And too many teeth – that's the impression – in too little space. I'd like to say, 'Ah, but you do notice his eyes.' It's true, you notice them, but if you're a man and you're meeting him for the first time the reason is because they won't back down, they hold yours longer than is natural. He learned his mother's lesson too well. Jack Skeat will not drop his eyes for fear of being taken for a weakling.

It's a pity about this willed boldness because when he forgets he

9

has a range of thoughtful and tender expressions that many people find attractive. His anger is attractive too. Sometimes it verges on the comic, which he's not bothered by – not bothered for long. He would like to be able to frighten people but knows he would hate it after a while and would apologize in the end. He works his anger out in imaginary witty sharp exchanges and scores complete momentous victories and picks his victims up and dusts them down when it's all over.

These eyes: green, uncertain, innocent. Surprised, uncomprehending, even though Jack Skeat believes that all the crimes and cruelties we can imagine have somewhere been committed, or will be. He cannot understand; will not accept; and remakes our human nature in an, oh, momentous exchange. This gives him lines of painful concentration round his eyes. It has made him interesting, for a time, to several women. It decides people, as they get to know him, that he's not so undistinguished after all, not so plain.

He has a stringy neck and a sharp Adam's apple. Emotion makes him swallow and the little elevator moves to the bottom floor and up again. 'I know when you want me,' his wife said. 'I don't listen to what you're saying, I watch your throat.' He tried not to swallow after that, but sometimes found it useful to invite her in that way.

He likes his wide shoulders. When he was a young man he practised spreading them and fancied that from the back his torso had a cobra shape. He felt venomous, desirable, dangerous. He kept his arms locked in front when putting on that display, which helped conceal the smallness of his hands.

There's a pompadourish roundness in his middle parts. (Pompadour, he knows, has to do with hair, but somehow the word has attached itself elsewhere.) Chest above, legs below, they're masculine enough, there's jut and edge, a muscular containment, nothing slack. But he sometimes feels less than masculine physically, and suspects a genetic betrayal. It's too trivial to worry about, but enough to provoke a compensatory swagger now and then: another betrayal.

Jack is not the self-doubting person this account begins to make him seem. He has a strong sense of his own worth and a good many victories, both private and professional, to his credit. If he plays them over, in detail, it's for pleasure, not to reassure himself. But he does know he might have done better and when he's tired is inclined to berate himself. Chances lost cause him aches not unlike those in his joints. (Hips, shoulders, elbows, finger joints trouble him. A test has shown the presence in his blood of the antigen for ankylosing spondylitis. He's older than most people are when they get that disease but he won't escape – so he believes. It's a likely answer to his wish to be exceptional.)

Joint, articulation, point of transfer: Jack has trouble. (It's his mind I'm talking about now.) Either the angle is too sharp or there's a dislocation and the message, memory packet, is stripped of significance or falls back and is lost. It worries him more than he admits to his wife. He admitted to her, several years ago, that he thought he was getting a brain tumour. The left side of his head had a way of going numb. She touched him with her fingers, each side of his head, cool and firm. 'Jack, you've got a dent along here. You silly man, your glasses are too tight.' He wears his glasses looser today, the dent is gone, the left side of his head feels fine. But inside, what is happening there? No touch, no 'silly man', will cure that. Recent things – names, meetings, bits of news, addresses – get lost and won't come back. He no longer says, 'I read a marvellous book the other day,' until he has the title and the author's name in place. On the phone last week he could not remember the name of his street. For a hideous moment he was lost in the universe. Then it came. 'Sorry about that. Dropped the phone. Deane Street. Forty-one. You'll have to give the gate a boot, it sticks.'

There's a dreadful name he knows but refuses to say. He read an article that claimed water might help. He drinks six or seven pints a day. (Pints beat litres, miles beat kilometres, into his head. He sometimes calls a ten cent coin a shilling.) It doesn't do his bladder any good because, down at that end, his prostate is enlarged. (This time he's early.) He turns with relief from brain to prostate. Peeing, flicking, dribbling out another teaspoonful, he grows furious about waiting lists. Fifteen months he's been on his and now that he has shifted to Auckland has probably gone to the back of the queue again. He has no medical insurance, doesn't believe in it, he has paid his taxes all his life and taxes can look after him now. He could find, if he had to, the three thousand dollars for a private op – but he won't. He'd rather get up five times a night, and pee like a woman

11

for the last bit, than pay for something owed him by the state. His wife calls him a miser and hints that he's afraid, and sleeps in a separate room so she won't be woken all the time, but on this issue Jack won't budge. No! End of discussion.

He suffers from allergic rhinitis. Attacks are brought on by changes in temperature and, possibly, house dust, and, possibly, apples. One day he means to take some tests. In the meantime he keeps putting garments on and taking them off and closing windows for the draught and staying out of the way when his wife shakes the mats. He does his share of the housework – cleans the toilet every Saturday morning, scrubbing on his knees, virtuous – but he won't do anything that raises dust. Now and then he swears off apples but they're his favourite fruit and he soon goes back, especially when the Cox's Orange are ripe although he suspects that these acidy ones also bring a rash up on his chest. He treats that with a herbal cream and tries to clear his sinuses with drops and inhalations. They don't work too well and during his attacks he wakes in the morning with his mouth like a vacuum cleaner bag. His worst fear, his private nightmare, is being gagged by a burglar and not being able to breathe. He'll fight knives and sawn-off shotguns before submitting to a gag. Now that he's in Auckland, in the muggy heat, he's afraid his rhinitis will get worse. There are more burglars in Auckland too.

His mental health, he claims, is good (leaving that brain trouble, which is physical, out of it), and his willingness to examine his moral health helps it stand straight. Many people are not aware that there is such a thing as moral health. Too close an examination doesn't do it any good though. Jack, retreating, uses the ugly metaphor 'picking at scabs'. He would like to deny responsibility for the damage he did other people when he was young but he won't take that easy way. If Kurt Waldheim can be called to account after forty years – not that Jack has anything like that to answer for – and the line of responsibility traced back, then those who believe it legitimate must submit to their own private trial. Jack does. 'I'm guilty. I did it.' But none of his offences is chargeable and there's no sensible way of punishment now. Embarrassment punishes, but it annoys him too and obscures the point of tracing back. After a while he leaves his past alone but has a sense of having tried and sometimes of having done well. As for today – he does not think he damages other people today.

In religion he's a humanist and he is stern-minded in his belief. There's a roundness in humanism he enjoys. Natural man is trying to get out, increase his claim, and Jack will allow some of that; but not too much. He's not ashamed of the animal in our nature (finds it human) but insists that mind is more characteristic. Mind, he explains, arguing at the door with Mormons and Jehovah's Witnesses, doesn't it excite you? Think of where we've come from. Out of the slime. And where we're going. 'God' encloses things so much. I'm an explorer. He is ashamed afterwards – ashamed of his over-dramatic claim and of his failure to find arguments. He can do better than that. But even when he sits down to think he finds he can't. Nevertheless, as surely as any Christian, Jack Skeat knows.

Atheist? He won't wear the label. It's a way of sneaking God in. Original sin? He won't buy it, it revolts him. Divine? He finds the idea unpleasant. Saviour? What a human defeat. And so on. Evil, though, brings him up short. There are things he can't find any other word for. How he wishes he had a better mind and was able to do some exploring there. Sometimes he confuses evil with madness and finds it hard to separate the two. Evil, isn't it willed? And madness? well . . . He does not like this blurring of edges, and thinks defensively, It's religious territory, I'm not going to lose my self-respect, I've been there once. But there's no temptation to go back.

He's not being strictly truthful in saying he was there. More than bodily presence is required. I was just a bum on a seat, Jack explains. As soon as he was able to break free from his mother he got out. She was, in any case, not much more present in church than he. Jack believes he has a spiritual life, there's no other way to explain the workings of his conscience, but spirit is a human possession and is therefore, so to speak, in the canon. Spirit never touched his mother at all. She was in church for propriety's sake.

Now Jack's out of it and finds his way without a guide and he does feel like an explorer at times. He sometimes feels in danger because of his mental weakness. Things lie all about to pick up and examine but one has to be able to hold them first and he drops them all the time. Calling out their names won't bring them back. He tries.

Freedom, he says. Spirit. Conscience. Good. And evil of course. They slide beyond his reach. It's easier, more comfortable, to think about death. That has an effect impossible not to see. Bodies rot. Death is a fact. It has a way of leading on to life though. Where has life gone? What's the spark? And consciousness, where is that?

Although he's not equipped for this Jack is desperate to understand. At other times the mystery elates him. Death, he knows, will get him in the end. Then he'll understand. Or not. The idea of oblivion can excite him.

He's elated by the inescapability of death.

On the Map, in the Marriage

Neither has the sense of having come home but each is contented and feels about the new house, this will do. It would not have satisfied them once. Jack had promised himself a house by the sea – 'It's not just a view I need, I need to hear the waves' – and Harry had wanted a 1910 villa to do up. They had once made an offer on a villa in Worser Bay where the salt spray in southerlies would rattle like hail on the window-panes – it rattled on the day they inspected the house, the trees thrashed, wind boomed in the ceilings – but someone else saw it and offered more. Harry shed tears over that and said it was like losing a baby. Now, thirty years later, they're contented with a house built in purple brick, two storeyed, semi-detached, on the sunny suburban slope behind Castor Bay. The gulf waters are calm, the yachts stand straighter. Rangitoto slumps in the middle of the view.

Harry, who has never been Harriet, is Auckland born and Auckland raised. Thirty years in Wellington have modified her view of her home town but not weakened her attachment, 'blood attachment', to the place. She is rarely extravagant in her language – makes a thing of being neat and cool – but lets herself boil over now and then on the subject of belonging in a place. 'Roots,' Harry says, without a blush. The house and suburban Castor Bay, they are not home, but the city on the isthmus, and the wild west coast out there, and the blue gulf in her view, and the beaches and the mangroves and the mud – Harry belongs.

Jack Skeat is pleased for her and full of sympathetic recognitions. He starts to feel that he too has come home. It is not second-hand, it's strongly felt, it belongs to Jack. But his view is complicated by his overstrong sense of his wife. He watches her, he loves her, but uncertainties prevent an easy view of everything he sees that she sees too. When she gazes out there is it the candyfloss clouds that make her touch her lips with her tongue or is it Rangitoto waiting to

15

explode? Does Harry taste sugar or destruction? Jack would like to know. After thirty years she puzzles and excites him. He wants to see with her eyes and wants her to see with his, believing there's a union they haven't known and are capable of; more capable than they have ever been, for their fineness in unspoken understanding improves, even though much of their congruency is lost. They do not even age at the same rate. Nor do they both still have a career.

Harry has claimed the upstairs sitting-room as her studio and is happily at work there on her part of the new book – an unnecessary book in Jack Skeat's view – she and Jo Bellringer are putting together. (With a girlishness that embarrasses Jack, and makes him suspect some dark concealment at other times, they call each other Ms Pictures and Ms Print.) Jack agreed to the ripping-up of the carpet and the cork-tiling of the floor; to the stripping of the wallpaper and painting in matt white of the walls; to the fitting of a skylight in the roof to bring alive the south-facing room. Harry's new eye outstares the sun and the sun's eye watches over her patient building (happy building) of stems and leaves and petals for Bellringer and Edwards: *Weeds and Wild Flowers of New Zealand*. He has told them to reverse it. Wild flowers and weeds should be the order. That's elementary psychology. Harry agrees but Jo Bellringer, on the principle of chief (and female) begetter, will not agree. Jack also feels that the author order should be reversed, Harry's part being much the more important. Her skills, her art, her sensibilities, bring alive the mere botanical knowledge Jo possesses. But Jack keeps quiet. The alphabet is on Jo's side, along with precedent. There have been three Bellringer and Edwards books already.

He finds it inhuman that his wife's collaborator should be so indifferent to him. There's no injured vanity in his dislike of the woman, it's philosophical. All things human require notice.

He works in a tiny windowless hole under the stairs. 'Hole' makes no judgement on the place. He likes the feeling of being enclosed. The slope of the ceiling, which he duplicates in his torso as he leans at his work, puts a weight on him like moral compulsion. Jack explores, backwards, inwardly, and will describe exactly what he finds. Nevertheless it's something less than inclusiveness he attempts. He will choose to go up or down and left or right. He's not going to breathe rarefied air or advance in caves where he has to wriggle and slide. He's not afraid of guessing or invention and will probably attempt some of each – is not afraid of ugly things he'll come on in that way – but he wants to avoid cleverness, which is a way of holding at a distance. Jack wants to see close, Jack wants the truth. He would like it to be significant truth.

Already he discovers that pomposity is his vice.

The doorbell rings and it's Jo Bellringer. 'Hi,' Jack says – one of several modern idioms he's mastered – and stands aside, pointing at the stairs.

'Nice day, Jack,' Jo says, lumping by. Her remark is enormously negative – it negates him – but Jack no longer tumbles down the hole she digs for him.

'Lovely,' he says, standing his ground. She is lovely in her heaviness. He loves her round forty-year-old buttocks, never still. He wants to take them in two hands and feel in them her mounting of the stairs. He loves her chest, her red and tanned sun-tormented chest and her bean-bag breasts and her sun-scorched hair and her round eyes – they never blink – across whose surfaces he moves but does not move. Of all the women he can't have Jo is the one he wants the most. It's lust after an object. She turns him into nothing so he has no compunction about turning her into that. Jack does not want to make himself alive for Jo. It has got to the point where that would spoil things.

He points her at Harry and watches her out of sight, then goes back under the stairs feeling neither diminished nor unhealthy. He hears Jo call his wife's masculine name. They are, he thinks, a thoroughly ambiguous pair. And now that Jo is Harrying Harry there, and throwing her botanical weight around, and laying her blunt finger down on drawings too delicate for naming, Jack, in his hole, begins to find his human weight withdraw. It's a familiar consequence of lusting after Jo. Victory is hers, every time. Now he feels he must admit to being a little sick. In this one area. It's very specialized, very narrow, and does not affect his overall health.

He spends an hour writing; and some time thinking, some time dreaming. There's a fuzzy edge between the two. He feels an attenuation there, a state of new being that can't be held, but he stays long enough to feel his understanding thrown like a blanket –

no, thinner than a blanket, a sheet – over all things human. It's spurious, of course, he realizes that almost at once, but the state is interesting and would repay study by someone with the knowledge and the skills. They would have to take into account that until a few months ago Jack was a busy and important man. He had a staff of fifty-four and a budget of 9 million, he reported to a Minister of the Crown. The larger study would have to be retirement – the loss of habits and habitat; loss of importance, narrowing of the self. One becomes, Jack thinks, a man in a hole under the stairs, occupied with internal workings.

His mother would have said to that, Get out into the garden and do some digging. He hears her voice, sees the imperative in her eye, and when he has noted it he'll get out, he'll take his spade and turn the good earth over and break it with a hoe and plant some broccoli and radishes. Jack will do as he is told. And he'll enjoy it.

His mother is merely his agent now.

'Jack,' Harry calls from her window, 'will you run Jo to her car? She got a puncture and she came by taxi.'

'Where?'

'On Lake Road.'

'Is it fixed?'

Jo's head appears, squeezing Harry's out. 'I dropped my keys off at a garage and they're doing it. But I'll get another taxi, it's all right.'

'No you won't,' Harry says.

'Give me a minute to finish this row.'

He trickles radish seeds into the furrow and palms earth on top and pats it down. 'You come too,' he says to Harry in the kitchen. 'We'll get a Chinese take-away.' Domestic easiness between them makes Jo uncomfortable, and sometimes seems to hurt her for she'll scrape her ribs or hips with her fingernails and blink her eyes as though at a muscular contraction. Jack enjoys his advantage. He grins at her. 'My turn to cook. We were only having ham.'

Harry has gone pink: a girl invited out. She asks Jo (and explains): 'Why do take-aways always sound romantic?'

'And improper,' Jack adds. He has Jo defeated, and aware of him, and feels no desire for her at all. 'OK, let's go.'

With Jo in the back seat, tightly strapped (Jack insists although she's mutinous), they drive to Castor Bay and over the hill to Milford.

'Remember the salt-water baths?' Harry says.

'And the Pirate Shippe?' They've asked each other these questions before, recently, but this is for Jo – to somehow include her, on Harry's part, and push her further out, on Jack's. 'We used to go to dances there. Round the top of the harbour in Rex Petley's old man's truck. A dozen or so of us on the tray, singing nice clean early fifties songs.' He smiles at Jo. 'We had to go down on the beach for a woo.'

'That was before my time,' Harry says.

'Woo. What amazing language.'

'Wasn't it pashing?'

He's pleased with her. 'She knows,' he tells Jo.

'It's the garage by the lights,' Jo says. 'Harry, I just remembered, *hophomyrtus bullata*, there's a little gully full of it just off the road to Whatipu. I'll get a branch for Tuesday.'

'Yes, you told me,' Harry says.

'Will you have *obcordata* done by then?'

'Well, not the berries,' Harry laughs.

'I know that.' Jo is cross. She has put herself at a disadvantage, playing his game; and Jack is anxious to be out of it.

'This one?' – pulling off the road and stopping at the back of petrol bowsers. 'I'll fill up while you get your keys.' He puts in twenty dollars worth of unleaded, which gives him a little glow of virtue (sometimes it seems wimpish and he has to restore his manliness with a show of efficiency at the self-service pump).

Jo comes back with her mended tyre held like a wreath. 'They put the spare on. Now I'll have to change this one back.'

'I'll help. We'll do it straight away.' He wants to show how good he is at practical things.

'I'd sooner do it at home, thank you.' She drops the tyre in his boot and wipes her hands on her handkerchief. She is busy saying Jack is nothing again. He smiles at her and opens the back door.

'In you go. I'll let you off the seat-belt.'

They drive along Lake Road and find her little tin-can Deux Chevaux. She fits herself in and putt-putts away. 'Poor Jo,' Harry says. The plain car suits her. 'I wish there was something we could do.'

19

'Well, there isn't.' Jack makes a U-turn and drives back the other way. Jo gone is Jo switched off for him. 'Time for the lake?'

He thinks, driving down to the shore, that he could put his foot down and they'd dive into the water and sink hundreds of feet in the cold crater, the maar – and lie there drowned, side by side. It's a fantasy born of contentment. He is happy with Harry, he's touching her, and he wants more closeness.

Black swans glide and wind-surfers skid and houses glitter richly in the trees.

'That one,' Harry says.

'Not unless Bellringer and Edwards write a best-seller.'

'How do people get money? I mean real money.'

'I don't know. You married the wrong man, love.'

'The woman is just as likely to make it today.'

'You'd sooner be painting *morphotis bullata*.'

'*Hophomyrtus*. Yes, I would. All this is unreal.'

'The swans are real. The explosion was real. This lake could go up again one day.'

'The whole of Auckland. We should have stayed in Wellington.'

'For the hundred year earthquake,' he says.

Harry shivers.

'Cold?'

'No.'

'Under threat?'

She shivers again. This time it's theatrical. 'From all sorts of things.'

Jack laughs. 'Jo and all those Latin names? Come on, Chinee take-away.'

'Let's have fish and chips.'

'That's not like you.'

'Then we can take them up the top of North Head.'

'You really do want to get blown up.'

'I wouldn't care tonight. The world can end tonight and I won't care.'

He thinks about that as he waits in the fried-oil smell of the shop. Harry is a mystery. Is he ever going to know her? She becomes familiar, then recedes, and turns half round and there's a new aspect he hasn't seen. How does she do that? She has turned so many times nothing should be unfamiliar now. How does she remake, how does she new-feature, the part that's turned away from him before she, twisting unexpectedly, lets him see? He carries the hot packet out to the car. It seethes with heat and flavour and he hands the dangerous thing to her and feels he has paired like with like – and this is revolutionary, for Harry, it's her trademark, is cool. That is why it had been proper to think of deep down with her in the lake. Heat is improper. Is Auckland going to make Harry combust?

I love my wife, he thinks, as he drives to North Head, but the emotion is not grounded in any certainty of who she is.

'What's the matter?'

'Don't get grease on your dress.'

She has opened a hole in the end of the packet. A little gust of heat and steam escapes. Harry puts her finger in, withdraws it with a yelp; keeps on trying, worms a pale chip out.

'Give me one.'

'You'll crash the car. I hate pale chips.' But she smiles at him and huffs, 'Delicious,' round the hot chip in her mouth.

Jack drives up the steep road to the top of the hill and parks in the yard by the gun emplacement. It's years since they've eaten fish and chips in a car. The smell is appetizing and disgusting. They lick and grab and gulp shamelessly. The windscreen steams up and she rubs it with her hand.

'The sea's gone hollow.'

'Let's get out.'

They walk across the asphalt and sit on a grassy bank.

'I wish we had a nice cold bottle of wine.'

'Or some beer.'

He shakes crumbs of batter into a corner and offers them. Harry compacts them in two fingers and a thumb, and hunts the last few pieces with her tongue. Astonishing. She looks as if she's washing her face with the greasy paper – his neat and cool and artistic wife, with her cropped hair and buttoned wrists and her middle-aged skirt. She licks the salt.

'I love salt,' she apologizes. She has a taste for all things savoury, and, too, things creamy and sweet; but love, that's overstatement: what she loves is the occasion. He's happy with it himself but a little uneasy. Harry can be dangerous when shifting, momentum can suddenly die and she'll swing back, remove herself entirely from his knowledge. He points at the sky, the clouds, Rangitoto darkening, to prevent it. He mentions the warm wind and touches her cheek for its temperature and finds it cool. Delight, mental and sensuous, makes him swallow and turn away.

Harry giggles. 'Not here.'

Jack is afraid. She's very seldom naked, they're seldom as naked as this. He wonders how much of it is Auckland. Auckland is spread out, unashamed. They sit side by side on one of its volcanoes and 'extinct' is not a word he wants to use. The sea, the sky, the ranges, are passive, but they make an eloquent shout. Is Auckland going to change Jack and Harry just when their lives have settled down?

Jack does not want to be disturbed. He has things neatly in their place. But some have never been fixed, although for many years they have been still; and they want to move – they're moving now.

Rex Petley shifts about. Harry shifts.

Jack Skeat cannot keep himself in place.

Notebook: 2

When we started out as poets Rex refused to theorize, while I never got beyond the 'need to discover truth', which was 'the moral role of poetry'. I had no aesthetic and nor had Rex. He would not even talk about practice. I remember him saying that he liked nouns – and his are solid, undressed, plain (leaden at times). I believed in solidity too but I fell prey to adjectives (they still won't let me go) and I thought myself mature and stern when I cut them down to one. But stone was stone for Rex and clay was clay, and that's the way it remained all his writing life. To me he seemed to have no flair. 'Load every rift,' I said. But his poems made a census of the streets he found himself in: official, neat, local, contemporary.

Mine, by contrast . . .

'Good stuff, Jack. I like the way you colour it all up. And then, bang, the big generalization. Good stuff.'

I waited for him to go on, but Rex had lied as far as he was able.

'Hey, they'll have to shift that 'ess' to the back of your name.'

The joke failed to match the event. He held my lovely first work in his hands. Now what he must say was a serious 'John Skeat'.

'You beat me, you bugger. You're the one who's laid the bloody egg.'

That was better. That diverted me. Until I thought about it later on it was enough. Then I understood that he'd said nothing. All he had done was understand me. Rex had changed the points and sent me off on another line.

My book, of eighteen pages, was published by Serpent, Wellington. It was called *First Fruits* and came out in 1949, with crooked print and a stapled cover and an apple, ill-drawn, on the front. For a couple of months I played the part of teenage poet. Rex Petley nodded and kept quiet. In our fifty years of friendship he was unkind to me in many ways, but he usually left my verse alone – a strawberry mark, a crossed eye, a stammer, not to be used.

23

Merv Soper too, the Serpent, was kind. He was in Auckland on a visit, staying in Epsom with Leon Pittaway, a history lecturer at the university, and a poet himself; a pianist, a socialist, a tennis player, a wartime army officer, an astronomer, a family man and a great lover – Leon Pittaway, self-styled Renaissance man. I trembled in his presence, I stammered when I spoke, and I hung at his shoulder, looking up (he was six foot four), on that first meeting, waiting for his sign that he had read *First Fruits* and thought it good. 'Well pleased' was what I wanted, with a laying of his hand on my shoulder and a smiling down, benign, resigned. But he gave me nothing. He took me for another of his daughters' hangers-on, and sideways, long-armed, pushed his glass at me to fill in the kitchen – 'Lager, boy,' – and took it, when I brought it back, without even the glance you'd give a waiter; kept on talking to his honours students ranged in front, a bed of annuals gazing up at him, open-faced. (One of them is a cabinet minister now but in 1950 they were five foot nothing, it seemed to me, and none had poems to his credit, or any future.)

I slunk off, slunk about, looking for Rex, looking for Merv Soper. Closed groups and squared-off backs were everywhere, and conversations I had no confidence to enter. Parties of that sort – I went to quite a few about that time – where the talk was of things that I should know but hadn't got around to finding out about yet, and the talkers more clever than I could be, and so many of them glamorous, men and women both, in the sense of interfering with one's perceptions and one's judgement, and so magnifying themselves – those parties made me ache with longing, and shrink with insufficiency too.

I found Merv Soper sitting on the back steps. He was like me, he was worse than me. Parties terrified the Serpent. He was the most timid and rabbity person I have known. Merv had to be alone to find his opinions, in company they fled away and left him capable of only nervous ha-has and oh dears and golly gosh. In letters he could write, This seems sub-standard to me, and, I'd advise you to throw this back, but say a line at him and it was all gee-whizz, ha-ha, amazing! Merv was a civil servant, a ministry clerk; a man with a passion for good verse (his judgement went astray now and then) and a determination to publish it. He bought an old handset machine and set it up in the toolshed of his house in Grant Road, hard up against Tinakori Hill. He was no fine printer. Merv inked too light or dark and his lines ran crooked. But there, single-handed in his tilting shed, he published *Serpent*, his magazine, from 1947 to 1955, and kept a generation of young poets from despair. Now and then he'd do a little book like *First Fruits*. Rita Bullen published with him. So did Laurie Sefton. And John Dobbie took up six pages of *Serpent* with a Dylanish piece about his green youth in Helensville.

These poets, in their memoirs, dismiss Merv. He was useful for their juvenilia. They soon moved on to *Landfall*, and Pegasus and the Caxton Press. John Dobbie makes the point that Rex never published in *Serpent* – and he draws, in an aside, a picture, meant to be funny, of Merv busy in his toolshed like the greaser in the engine room of a coastal tanker. The point he is making is that Rex was a poet for the world.

Merv Soper died in hospital in 1955. He had been at a party in Kelburn. (I saw him unhappy and alone but I had Harry Edwards by that time and all I did was cadge his tobacco and papers to show her how neatly I could roll a cigarette.) Wellington is a crazy town of a hundred thousand steps, they tumble down the hills from street to street – and perhaps Merv tangled his feet on the flight beside the bridge in Upland Road. Or perhaps the wind was trying to be friendly and thumped him too hard on the back. Someone found him curled around the trunk of a tree, where he had crawled. He died on a trolley, in Emergency; and nobody carried *Serpent* on. If you wanted your manuscript you had to go to Grant Road and hunt in the shed. Rita Bullen left a single red rose on the machine – at least that's the story she put about. When I mentioned Merv to her several years ago she told it again, but insisted that Merv had lived in Hataitai, under the hills. He was, she said, the oddest little man, the way he popped out now and then and stood around blushing and then scuttled home to his burrow. But of course he had some value, in his way. One red rose . . .

'God, he was a bore. Even hearing his name makes me want to yawn.' John Dobbie.

No John, Leon Pittaway was the bore, Merv was just harder work than you or I could manage. There'll be nothing more written about him, although one or two libraries hold files of *Serpent* and will keep them till the paper falls apart. So let me put down that I sat with Merv on the steps at Leon's party and rolled a cigarette with his fine-cut Greys and he told me that my book was in quite a few shops on sale or return, but New Zealand poetry didn't sell and I mustn't expect . . . In that moment I knew I was not a poet. It came like a vision: my proper size. Was it Merv – diffident, provincial, amateur – turning as I turned and holding a mirror up to me? I said to myself, I can't write. The knowledge was not fixed from outside but was a new part opened and at once occupied.

I handed back his pouch and rolled the tobacco in my palm, enjoying its smell, and I remember saying, 'It's all right, Merv.' I felt a weight lift from me and my body levitate and I wanted to cry out with relief at being free. I need never suffer again the disappointment of not finding the words that would take me to the place where I wanted to be. Falling short had already set a frown on my face and would have sent me through life with a blurred eye and a limp tongue. Now I was freed from the pointless struggle. My lightness floated me across the lawns. I smelled the mown grass, I saw the kissing couple, I slid with the cool fish among the lily stems – and I did not have to write a poem. It was like being told that the lump is benign.

Merv's spectacles gleamed in the light. 'Leon wants me to publish some poems by his wife.'

'Are they any good?'

'It's hard to say. I'll need to take them home with me. Ha-ha.'

'Has Rex Petley sent you anything?'

'Rex Petley?'

'That's him there.' Walking up from the back of the section with the youngest Pittaway, Alice, his future wife.

'Does he write? He looks more like an All Black breakaway.'

'Breakaway, that's right. But he plays for Loomis Senior B.'

'Golly.'

'He doesn't let anyone read his poetry.'

Merv nodded in approval. That sort of poet made his life easier. 'Is he any good, do you think?' If he was, Merv needed to know.

'Rex is good at most things,' I said.

*

26

He was even good at being honourable. In the truck going home I said, 'How did you get on with Alice?'

'I like her. She's bloody intelligent.'

'Meaning she said no.'

'It ain't your business, Skeatsie. How about you and El Snako? He going to do another book?'

'No.'

'Why not?'

'Because I'm not giving him one. I've stopped writing poetry, for your information.'

Rex looked at me so long I put out my hand and steered the truck back into line.

'Did Merv Soper tell you to stop?'

'I told myself.'

'Leon must have got at you. I wouldn't take any notice of him.'

'Other people don't make up my mind. You and Celia Pittaway can take over.'

'Celia doesn't write. Does she?'

'Everybody writes. They're bleeding poetry all over the place. Thank God someone's got the sense to stop.'

And I must stop pretending that I remember every word of our conversation. We talked along those lines, I told him I renounced poetry and I made it sound like a declaration of self, a step from shifting on to solid ground; but in fact I did not know why I found myself in this new position, or exactly where I was – all I knew was that I had rid myself of something I had no need of. I won't say it didn't hurt. I valued poetry. I wanted to feel the need – but felt instead the lightness of looking into a future more widely open than it had been.

Now I can say that writing made me smart. It increased my cleverness; but only about those things I believed I should feel. So, in a way, it softened me. It reduced my intelligence, which is a moral intelligence in its essential workings. I nearly finished that with, Alas! But no, not alas, for although intelligence of that sort limits and hampers me in my progress, and makes me insufferable and vulgar at times, it confers clear sight – just now and then. Without those moments I would be nothing. Without them I would have no path to follow and no Jack Skeat with me on my way.

The pumped-up poetry I had attempted and the sort that bleeds all over the place were two of many kinds, I knew, but I confined my argument to them as Rex and I drove home that night. I moved towards my reasons for giving up. I said that I wanted to be useful and keep my eyes fixed on what was right. This was nothing new. We had had this conversation several times before, and Rex would agree that usefulness must be an aim, though how one was to identify it puzzled him, and right – right behaviour – must be tried for, although other people's 'carry-on' usually spoiled it.

I wonder how much he laughed at me. He must have known that I would never be the friend he needed. I was seriously, fatally, under-equipped. He swam like a fish in waters of speculation I had no awareness of, sliding among weeds that broke his line, that turned him about and tangled him and floated him, panting, belly up – I'd better stop this. I was all set to go on about the lovely flowers on the surface, in the dawn or starlight, that he saw in his state of distress, but good heavens how far these tropes remove one from the truth, which must be stated plainly if one is to see it close; if it is to have its natural weight. I must be careful not to let Rex become more or less than he was.

Yet I'm approaching him indirectly, through the effect he had on me. Why is that? I can't escape him yet I seem not to be able to say: he was six foot and a half an inch and had a bold nose, perhaps too fleshy, and an angular forehead, heavy-boned. Fortress head. It made one think that what he kept inside must be worth protecting. Blue eyes looking out, alert for danger. Ears with a generous curl and Plasticine lobes that turned bright red when he was angry. Mouth and jaw – what can I say? – too thin, too heavy? By whose standards? And for what? I don't subscribe to an ideal physiognomy. All the same he did not please in his mouth and jaw. Some people said he was ugly, others strong-looking, striking. No one said handsome – a word used of me once or twice when I was young.

Anyway, I've managed it, the description. Forced myself. It's much the same as the one in John Dobbie's book, although John is kinder on the whole. He says Rex had fiery eyes, and eyes of icy blue, and he brings the two into a nice accord. I won't argue. Rex gave the impression of burning coldly at times. But 'impression' – that's him through me. And it makes him more than he was. I don't want that.

In the truck I felt large and felt him small. There have been a good number of occasions like that. I'm one of the people who fought back. So I went on about usefulness, and the empty room and sinking swamp of poetry – used both of those, made eloquent by a passion part aggressive, part defensive. He kept his eyes on the road; down Waikumete Hill, over the hump, up past the graves. Away over farms the city shone. Sky and ranges, two dimensional on the other side, made sharp invasions of each other, hills pressing up, sky pressing down. We swooped into the valley where we lived, left and right on the concrete road, and it seemed to me that I came like a saviour; one who would be loving and stern.

'People are so bloody hopeless.'

'What are you going to do about it, Skeatsie?'

'You wait and see.' I would bring them forms and moralities, and fix a straitness on them, and show them simple ways – simple and pure. It would be nothing beyond human reach but would not be easy. I held Loomis in the palms of my hands.

Are such things common? It is not an illumination but nor is it delusional entirely. Let's say it's part of growing up and those who miss it fail to occupy all our space. I do not mean to praise myself. One needs to be facing the right way, one needs to be alert – to have been alerted. I have to thank my father for that; and blame him, as well as myself, for constrictions in my understanding. Spirit and imagination make uncertain halting steps in me.

My father presents himself, a rare event. If I do not welcome him he may never come back.

Diffidence was his mode of conduct. He had a little smile, a drawing in of his mouth at the corners, that qualified each remark he made. Remember Walter Skeat is insignificant, it said. His success as a solicitor owed something to it. He gave sound advice but seemed to allow his clients to find it for themselves. They came from his office glowing with their own cleverness. My father was the clever one though.

He was clever in his marriage. He offered all their shared ground to my mother. That way he managed to survive – that way he flourished, modestly, in corners she could not be bothered to occupy. He kept many secrets. He kept his cleverness secret, and he kept secret what he loved. I write of him in this formal way because he loved order, formality, he put bounds on nature by holding it in a web of limited responses. Nothing broke in on my father, nothing roared in his ear or flashed cruelly in his eye. (You see how it makes me write of him – 'ear' and 'eye' instead of 'ears' and 'eyes'.)

He had been religious in his youth, with some degree of warmth, I believe, but when I knew him well enough to talk to, in my mid-teens, two or three years before his death, he had shed all purely Christian belief. The Church was important in two ways – as an institution preserving forms and as the custodian of a morality.

Talking to my father was not easy and it did not happen frequently. I had to knock carefully at the door, not too long, not too loud, but firmly enough to let him know the person standing outside was his son. He would take fright at a need too plainly expressed. But it was part of his code that a father should talk with his son and advise him of his duties, and of satisfactions he might take. Dad warmed up after a cool beginning. He sometimes even called me Johnnyboy.

'Measure your wants, Johnnyboy. Never go after anything in an ungentlemanly way.'

That was a precept. He lit his pipe for precepts and puffed for punctuation and emphasis. His dry lips made little popping sounds.

'John, I'll say this' – pop – 'the man who chooses the easy way is setting off' – pop – 'in the wrong direction.'

I listened earnestly and thought him wise. Now and then a loop of saliva was dragged between the pipe stem and his mouth and I averted my eyes while he dealt with it. Dry lips, ideal for precept-making; but inside he was like the rest of us, moist, impure. It troubled me – and I was troubled too when he spoke of his Englishness. I thought him boastful, silly, self-satisfied. The English had been great, perhaps still were, but the war just won was ours as much as England's. Dad spoke of 'the yeoman virtues', 'the bulldog breed', 'hearts of oak', and was speaking of himself. He was drunk on his Englishness and to me, a puritan, he became unclean. I did not care for enthusiasm in my mid-teens when anything not in strict control seemed lurching in the direction of sex. Tell me about conduct, I wanted to say, and the moral code, and narrow paths, the strait gate, the gentlemanly way, the *manly* way, and our duty to subdue the blood. How do I stop thinking about girls and doing things to them in my head?

And he, as though recognizing my need, would put himself at a proper distance from us both and talk as I wanted him to.

I liked my father sitting well back, behind his pipe. He gave a polar balance to exigencies that weighed me down. I'm not going to be more precise. Young manhood (womanhood too) is full of tortures, we're all put on the rack, and nothing new is added if I describe my sufferings. Any youth's hard time will stand for all.

'There's something not quite right about a pun,' my father would say. He did not like anything that broke out of bounds. Metaphors. Apostrophes. Statements of intention. Disliked storms. Hated sunsets when the sky went bloody. Blushes, belches, farts, made him blush. Ejaculations, I have no doubt, became distasteful to him. But Dad, I'm not here to take the mickey. I think I had some luck in having you.

A moral sense need not be confining. I have travelled many places in mine and had strange adventures on the way. Dad would not have liked some of them. He would have been appalled to find me holding Loomis in the palms of my hands. But by that time he was dead. And I had travelled crookedly – discovered language, dabbled in sex, begun my lifelong friendship with Rex Petley. I had broken into fragments and started on my lives. But I retained my moral sense; and I keep it in my baggage still. It has given me huge amounts of trouble. Without it I would scarcely exist.

My father's death was uncharacteristic. That private man died in a public place and he died practising a vice. I've thought about the word. It was a vice. It went against the tenor of his life.

Every Friday he travelled into Auckland on business and came home by the 6.15 p.m. train. My mother and I did not meet him. We were not a family for that sort of thing. There were ceremonies in our lives, of sitting down to dinner, of leaving for church, of saying good-night and good-morning, but none for happy greeting after absence. From our house on the rise overlooking the creek I watched the train chuff along the track into Loomis. It whistled at the level crossing by Ah Lap's. My mother used that as a signal to lay the table. At 6.35 p.m. Dad walked up the drive with his Gladstone bag. He went upstairs to wash the grime of Auckland off himself. We sat down to dinner at 6.45. Nothing out of the ordinary had happened in his day.

'And you, my dear?'

'Nothing.' (Once a broken water-pipe had flooded the kitchen but workmen had fixed it and our daily woman had cleaned up the mess.) 'Nothing at all.'

'John?'

'Nothing.'

'Everything running smoothly? Good.'

Until an October evening in 1947. Our local constable stood at the door with the Gladstone bag held on his chest. My mother understood in a flash. She silenced him and showed him into the parlour, which was the proper place to hear bad news. We learned that Dad had fallen getting off the train and struck his head on a trolley and had, it seemed, died instantly. The policeman was appalled. His face was drained of colour and he was ten years older than when I'd seen him last, standing in the foyer at the pictures, keeping an eye on the Loomis hooligans. Death without meaning was out of order. My mother agreed, but thought it none of his business to state more than the facts.

'There was no drink involved, Mrs Skeat.'

'Well, of course not.'

'But he did get off before the train had stopped.'

'Are you sure?'

'He did it every Friday night. At least that's what the station-master says.'

My mother thought that impossible and I agreed. My father dismounting from a moving train: it made a fracture almost as great as his death in our ordered lives. It spread a blush, a warmth, over my greyness. (How these metaphors go on!) Colour invades my father's life. A pool of blood lies on the station platform. I see his judging eye, its calculating sparkle, as he leans from the step and waits his moment. Asphalt speeds beneath his tilted sole. His hand is on the rail and signals of release are at the ready in his brain. His Gladstone bag swings in his right hand and his pipe, cocked upwards from his smiling teeth, duplicates the angle of his hat brim. Every Friday, 6.15 p.m. His secret life. He calculates the speed, he makes his leap and starts his run; goes even with the train a dozen steps, with smacking soles; and reaches the ramp down to the road at a walking pace; raps his pipe out on the corner post; and damps himself; starts his walk along the pot-holed footpaths of Loomis; twenty minutes to our front door; and nothing out of the ordinary has happened in his day.

His judgement failed him on the evening of his death. He let go his hold a second too soon and hit the platform moving too fast. His legs could not keep pace with his upper body, which leaned further forward as he ran until it lay parallel with the ground. Too late he dropped his bag and flung his arms to protect his face. The trolley was drawn up to meet the goods van. He tried to jerk his head out of line but the corner of the tray punched a geometrical hole in his frontal bone.

'Blood on the station platform' comes from Rex's poem 'Incident', which describes a bit of mid-European violence in the 1930s. There's also a broken pipe and a Gladstone bag. I'm not sure Jews carried Gladstone bags but I'm pleased my father's death was useful to Rex. An irony, an ugly fact, known only to me, is that Dad 'really couldn't get too keen on the Jews'.

Morality does not crumble, it's shown to be horribly imperfect, that is all. Like our other attributes it wears a human face.

I can let Dad go now. He knocked and I let him in and we've reached agreement on my inheritance: his lesson, his death. Though one is misshapen and the other mysterious, they have become a part of me. They don't, of course, make me what I am, a multitude of other things comes into the sum. But they are – what? – they're formative.

Thank you for your lesson, Dad. Thank you for your death.

Rex drove down the blind street to his parents' house and let me out at the drive. It was after midnight but I wanted to walk home. Somewhere between Rex's street and my mother's house I would find a place, beside the creek, under the sky, where I would be able to stand and examine myself – walk around Jack Skeat and find what he was made of.

I closed the gate behind Rex and heard the truck grind away to its lean-to shed beside Les Petley's workshop. When the motor died, when the door slammed and Rex had gone into the house, I heard the creek sliding over the rock ledge by the swing-bridge. This creek, Loomis Creek, runs through my boyhood. It flowed in a shallow gorge beside the town, turning left and right along the base of low hills on its southern side. In the shade, under the banks, pools lay green and slow and bottomless. I swam in them but never dived deep. All through my boyhood I was afraid. I skidded over them with shallow strokes and hauled myself out on the mossy rocks; or I crossed lying on my back, kicking hard, with face and organs sheltered by my bony parts from whatever it was that lived on the oozy bottom.

Loomis Creek ran parallel to my family life. I was never sure I would be safe.

The creek is in Rex Petley's poetry. It's one of his stock symbols, which stops working in his later poems. It is just a number he paints in. But in the early ones I read his fear, I read my fear. I find joy and terror penetrating each other and I'm with Rex on our common ground.

I gave up my chance of exploring the creek when I finished with poetry. Yet it made a gift to me that night: it gave me Rex's mother, Lila Petley. I must put that differently. It gave me Lila Petley and she was never simply Rex's mother again.

The old swing-bridge, with fencing-wire sides and twin foot-planks, crossed from the end of the blind street to a path skirting an orchard and a swamp. I loved the way it bounced. You had to time your steps to cross without losing the beat. (It was poetry.) But I had hardly set my foot on the planks than her voice called, 'Is that Jack?' She was sitting in the middle of the bridge with her legs dangling through the wires. The shock of finding her there produced distortions. She came from the night and was ethereal, she had no substance; and she came from the creek, with darkness, mystery, terror all about her. It went away as I stepped out on the elastic boards. I became afraid of not knowing how to behave if I should find Lila Petley mad. To sit on a bridge after midnight, wearing a nightie, smoking a cigarette; to say, 'Isn't it a lovely night? Come and sit with me' – that was surely on the edge of madness and I would not be able to handle it.

'Hello, Mrs Petley, are you all right?' with a squeak in my voice; bending to see if the shine on her cheeks – oh my God! – was made by tears.

'Yes. Don't let me frighten you,' wiping her fingers on the bones that made her face – it was a lesson of the night – beautiful. She touched my wrist with dampened fingerpads. 'These are old tears, Jack. They're years old.'

'I'm sorry.' I've always been ready with that response, and it's genuine, but people will take it that I'm accepting blame. Even Lila Petley, on that night –

'It's not your fault. It's nobody's fault. Do you want a cigarette?'

'Thank you.' I sat beside her. I dangled my legs. I rolled my second fine cut Greys cigarette of the night. 'You don't see many women – many ladies – who roll their own. I don't mean that you aren't . . .'

She laughed. 'I'm not though. I never wanted to be. Would you want to be a gentleman when there are so many things . . . ? I don't think a poet can be a gentleman.'

'I'm not a poet any more.'

'Who says?'

'I've given up.' I looked at her and was honest, although drawing dishonestly on my cigarette. 'I'm not good enough.'

'Who says? Rex?'

'No, me.' I shrugged. 'It's not important. There's other things I want to do.'

She asked what those might be and I could not answer. It was true I hungered for a way that I might follow with a sense of being right, but I glimpsed, I almost tasted, an adulteration there; of propriety, of comfortableness, of being safe, of being gratified. And I knew how much I had wanted to write good poems, how much I had wanted to recognize things and describe them; and I knew my inadequacy. I seemed crippled to myself. For a moment I talked nonsense to Lila Petley, using words I had earned no right to; and she was disappointed in me. My disappointment in myself – no, my sense of

35

being bereaved, of having lost part of myself – overwhelmed me. I began to cry. So I was the mad one on the bridge and mine were now the cheeks that shone with tears.

Lila Petley knew how to handle it. She dropped her cigarette in the creek and put her arms around me and let me cry.

She must have comforted Rex in that way when he was a child. I had never had it (and I never had it again). I snivelled and sobbed and Lila put her mouth on my hair and rocked me and made soothing sounds. I wonder now how close she came to making love with me. My tears wet her breasts, her loose hair fell on my cheek – and she was naked underneath her nightie, and was naked in her feelings too. Love-making would have been a natural step; the planks would have made a lively bed. But I did not even think of it. I had no nature in me and I saw her as old. I moved away and she released her arms; perhaps it was the other way round. In any case, we stopped our touching. I wiped my face with my handkerchief, while she reached backwards for her tobacco and rolled a new cigarette.

'Want one?' She handed me the tin. I gave her my handkerchief to dry the wet patch I had left on her and then gave her my jacket, which she said thank you for and pulled on over her cotton nightie. 'Warm,' she said. 'It's funny finding other people warm.'

I dropped my flaming match into the creek. 'I'm sorry I cried. It's nothing to cry about.'

'It must have been or you wouldn't have.'

'I don't think I'll set up goals any more.'

'Be like Rex. Just recognize the place you're going to.'

'Where's that?' I must have sounded resentful to find him ahead of me again for she touched my arm and said, 'Oh, Rex's place. You'll have to ask him. I don't think it's where you'd want to be.' There's nothing wrong, she seemed to say, in being Jack Skeat – as long as you recognize Jack Skeat. I tried to show her I had done that, by talking about my need to find a meaning and point a way; and Lila was polite, she listened and said, 'I hope you do it, Jack.'

'I will.' But unconditional statements float in space and sometimes one doesn't know which way is up and which is down. 'You were crying too,' I said, to catch hold of her and steady myself.

'Yes.'

36

'What about?' I came right way up and seemed her equal in experience. 'You said old tears.'

'Oh, people dress things up. In words, you know. I was just crying because of things I haven't done. It's fairly common. It happens all the time.'

'Out here? On the bridge?'

'I spend a lot of time here. When everyone's asleep. I love the bridge.'

My own attempts at remembering employ dreaming and passivity; evasions, side-stepping, a circular approach; and various tricks of association. But this is all by way of getting there. When one is inside and engaged, when one is lost, then violence and tenderness take over. You run towards your discovery, you punch with fist and knee, and you spring back with a cry of shame or disappointment or despair or fright. You ram holes in events, you twist and stretch and let them snap into wrinkled shapes. You knock bits off, you try to fix bits on, forcing matter into places already occupied. And you stare blindly into multicoloured light; or stare with a comprehending sight at figures with a bit of colour here and none there, with a shining cheekbone, with a crooked tooth, with a high turned shoulder, with a red wet eye – all denatured by your understanding. You are there. You're central there. It's your tooth that is crooked. It's your eye that is wet. And that convincing cry of shame that meets the event, flashing back in time, is your own, and the edge of despair on it comes from your knowledge that you'll never get away.

Then, of course, there is tenderness. Thank God for it. How could we go on if we were not tender to ourselves? We long to lift up the girl or boy, and wash his face for him and brush his hair, and send him out, propel him with a firm hand on his back towards the consummation that he missed; correct his mistake; bend his mind from error, from its shrinking and its over-eagerness, and help him be present and exact – and how one comes, all the time, on the fact of the matter standing in the way. But tenderness is not only wishful, tenderness is ointment for the wound. One spreads it on and soothes for a moment what soon goes back to being incurable. Momentary victories of love, as real as hand or eye or mouth.

Lila was tender to herself. Perhaps I was the agent for that. She

37

was, I would guess, most often violent as she sat on the bridge while her family slept.

The facts of it are ordinary, I won't go into them except to say that she was the girl who, in her eagerness for love, married a man overflowing and bursting with life who wanted only renewable daily gratifications. A common story. These women (these men too) travel down a long road. They stand and watch themselves going away. Motion is jerky, like a movie stopped at every tenth frame; and at every stop their size is reduced. Longing does not die, it never quite dies, but it can turn ugly or turn sour; can turn them into martyrs, drunks, bullies, invalids; into public figures; it can kill them early or prolong their lives. It drove Lila Petley to her bridge. She was lucky. The creek, flowing under, flowing on, answered some of her need.

She gave me her life as a present. There's a magic element in this. And though it's only seeming it will do, will more than do – it has lasted all my life. If I were forced to explain I'd say, she offered me herself like a quartered apple and she has been whole for me ever since. No fragmentation, no breaks. I fit her together easily, the unifying agents are her love and pain. Girl; wife; mother – and a fourth, unnameable; a fourth thing that she might have been.

All lives have this part. I generalize easily, moving from Lila Petley to that knowledge as though it's the shortest of steps. I hear her common story and witness her common pain. Any one of the stilled frames will do to set an easy progress in motion that carries me to: That's the way it is – as unstrained, as natural, as breathing. Girl in her school uniform, standing in front of the art shop window where her Plasticine model of a witch and her cat are on display; woman at her washtub, a bar of yellow soap in her hands, while her husband makes a crown of soapy froth on her hair; and now he's drunk, ah yes, and now he's been fighting, and he comes around the doorpost, out of the night, with a grin on his bloodstained mouth; and the children hug and kiss, and they cry and fight, and they get their measles and whooping cough, and they get their hidings – and it goes on, until Lila Petley is a woman on a bridge, crying in the night for the Lila that she might have been. This is not, remember, the whole of her, this small hours self. But it's the whole of her while it lasts.

We smoked more cigarettes and she dropped a flaring match into the creek and we listened to the water to see if it had rhythm in its flow. She said that she could feel the cold on her bare soles.

'What's the time, Jack?'

I angled my watch into the light. 'Half past two.'

'Golly,' she said, climbing to her feet.

My jacket stored her bloodwarmth. I crossed to the far side of the bridge as she went back. Our steps made a fractured bounce and threw us off balance and I heard her half bad-tempered laugh. She had had enough and wanted her bed, and so did I. I ran along the path by the swamp and padded in the white dust of the road and up the silent lawn by our shell drive – leapt a cannonball shrub – and let myself in at our back door.

'John?' My mother's voice from her room at the top of the stairs.

'Yes.'

That was all. Her light went on as she looked at the time, and went off sharp. She had armed herself but would wait until morning to challenge me.

I lay in bed and held Lila Petley in my hands.

My mother too had a life like that. So did I. I shivered in my cold sheets at the knowledge.

Addendum: In one of Rex's unpublished poems, unearthed by the Elf, a woman sits at midnight on a bridge. She smokes a cigarette and drops a lighted match into the water. The poem is called 'Woman' and it isn't very good. It looks for a subject it can't find. There's a warp in it of half-formed accusations of betrayal.

Betrayal of whom? By whom?

The woman is alone. She wears a man's jacket round her shoulders, which manages simply to be odd.

Going West

He's aware that it's wider now than a search for Rex. Many figures have a place in the tapestry. What they are up to he can't tell. But it's likely to stretch around the room; with Rex and Jack appearing all the time. Rex and Jack up to many tricks. Not all their tricks. Accuracy, strict inclusiveness, makes him yawn.

Jack is aware he wants to win. Flights of arrows, severed limbs; he will use his cunning and his strength. Charity and kindness may very well turn into weapons too. And how valuable will truth turn out to be? Truth, as a weapon, will change shape.

He takes a rest from it and finds that the ordinary day makes his tapestry fade. He's grateful and wants never to go back. Harry works as long as the good light lasts, with her metronome head turning from her sample to her brush and back again. The shadowless world on her page makes him sad.

'It's not like that, you know.'

'Go away, can't you see I'm busy.'

'Take a rest. Come for a drive.'

'No, Jack. Go and dig in the garden.'

He carries up toast and anchovies and a mug of instant soup for her lunch. With an 'ooh' of fright she lifts them further from her work. The tiniest mark will ruin it. He thinks of her, unfairly, as outside time, just a perfect eye and hand, inhuman. Her little smile and thank you do not bring her back. They could be for anyone.

Jack eats by himself in the kitchen. He goes upstairs and takes her plate and mug and washes up, and drives to Mt. Eden to visit his mother. Across the bridge, along by the marina, up the fly-over, down the motorway – he makes these passages by preposition, relating himself by a new angle to each new world – and comes to the back of the mountain and the women sitting round the room. He passes into it through a valve and is assailed by odours of leakage and decay. He's ready for them, pushes them aside, and smiles toothily as he steps up to his mother. She is ready too, how quick she is for a woman whose mind is gone, and she draws away from his hand.

'So it is the devil. I thought it was the devil coming.'

'No Mum, it's me. It's John.'

'Don't touch me. You've got poison on your hands.'

'No, see, they're clean. Clean fingernails. I brought some Eccles cakes for you.'

'So you want to poison me with Eccles cakes now.'

'I don't want to poison you, Mum.'

Why does he keep on trying? His cakes and fruit and flowers have been sprayed, injected, dusted, with Flytox and Slug'em. There are pellets of strychnine thumb-pressed into his scones to look like dates. Rat poison, arsenic: her poisons are traditional. She covers her mouth so he cannot slip them on her tongue.

'Harry sends her love, Mum.'

'Did she bake those? Take them back and make her eat them.'

'I bought them at a shop in Takapuna.'

'How much do you pay them to poison me?'

He has read enough on paranoia in the aged to know that the family, the children – a son will do if no daughters are available – are the ones usually chosen as the paranoid pseudo-community; in other words, the plotters. Sometimes he thinks hatred, fear, courage, counter-attack, are a game she plays; but knows in his heart that they are real. He's impressed by her dignity. He sometimes feels that when she dies the police will find arsenic hidden in his house. But he wants to love her, and now and then he comes close to it. The emotion gets lost in sentimentality. Would he turn her into a little smiling white-haired lady waiting to die? 'Eccles cakes. How kind you are to me.' He doesn't want it. But he doesn't want this accuser either. Tall in her chair. Strong in her arms. See the way hatred makes her eyes clear.

'I'll put them in your room.' He always does that. The nurses say she eats them greedily, not knowing any longer who they come from.

The corridors seem rubberized, her room is like a rubberized extension. He puts the cakes on the cabinet by her bed. Last week's chrysanthemums stand in pale good health beside the ragged trio, *Roget, Concise Oxford, Pears* (1965), held in lacquered bookends from her own mother's house. Although she never opens them all she wants to know is held in there. She wants plain information and plain words. He doesn't ask where her bible has gone.

Jack straightens the coverlet on her bed. He sniffs the room. She's sometimes incontinent, after her stroke – that little stroke that warns of a bigger one (the stone-breaker's hammer poised above her head) – and yes, the smell underlies floor-polish, vase-water, laundry soap from down the corridor. Her father and mother, in oval wooden frames, seem to smell it too; and Jack says, 'It'll do you bloody good'; then remembers that they lived old, and died on rubber sheets in a home. He draws his breath in sharply. Will it happen to him? Is loss of bladder and bowel control locked in his genes?

Standing by her bed, he runs through his escape plan. When the time comes, when the signal is unmistakable – he's unsure of what it will be – he'll say goodbye to Harry (she will outlive him not just because women do, or because she is six years younger, but because her appetite for full shares and her belief in justice are stronger than his) – say goodbye and kiss her, put forty years into a simple kiss, and say he's driving north for a break, but she'll see the south in his eyes and will understand. Not stop him though. That, by then, will be the agreement. He'll go down the island at a careful pace and cross on the ferry from Wellington (a look at old haunts there, will that be a part of it?). In Picton he'll turn west; follow the curving tarseal, purr up the saddles, and in the Graham Valley he'll wait until no cars are in sight, and make his brave and sneaky left-hand turn into the pines; drive on needles on the forest roads; then on tracks, with grass and gorse and bracken scouring the chassis; and stop by the little cress-choked stream (have a nibble of cress) at the foot of Mt. Duppa.

He will park the car carefully. It is Harry's now. Up he'll go on the zigzag track, and there'll be last pleasures all the way – of limestone, moss, honeydew, bush robin; the pleasure of putting one foot before the other, professionally; of touching the old, damp, indifferent trees; of sucking a last barley sugar and drinking from his water-bottle filled at the last stream. He comes to the top. Huge land. Huge sky. The bare-headed mountain welcomes him, and although it is only three thousand feet it's his Everest, climbed solo and without oxygen.

There's a little basin with a grass floor in the boulders. Standing in it, he can see the long wooded ridge to the Doubles and the Dun. South and east the Richmond Range, Richmond and Fishtail, with the Kaikouras rising behind. And north and east the Pelorus, the Rai Valley and the Sounds. Swing west – the Arthur Range, the Owen, with the sea making bites into the land. Jack completes the circle. When he lies down the rocks lean inwards and close it off; angled blocks, warm in the sun.

He found the place ten years ago with Harry. They ate their lunch and dozed for an hour, and when he woke, full of life and drifting easily, he said to her, 'This would be a good place to die.' 'Shhh,' she said, and touched his mouth with her forefinger; dozed again.

Jack Skeat does not abandon discoveries.

He will put his daypack on the grass. He'll sit on a boulder and watch the sun go down. He'll eat, keep it simple, bread and cheese (Esrom though, his favourite) and olives, and perhaps one slice of smoked salmon, and drink the last of his water, or maybe just a sip of white wine, and then he'll relieve himself in the trees because he doesn't want to make a mess in his sleeping bag. He'll tidy up. He'll take his boots off. (What about his socks? Should he save some water and wash his feet?) Whatever his last thoughts are he'll think those. Then he'll gulp his terminal cocktail, a single swallow, 'Skol!', and climb into his bag and zip himself up to the chin. He'll keep his eyes open and watch the stars. Presently Jack Skeat will die.

It's most attractive, but he can shoot it full of holes. There are moral ones, and medical, and even aesthetic. To begin with, who will find him? It might be a child. Jack sees him – her? – running eagerly on the mountain top, full of achievement, mind open wide; and there he is, corpse in a sleeping bag. He hears her screaming, sees a wound go slashing across . . . Or, if that's too much of a chance, and too much terror, just to spoil someone's day, mark with death someone's happy climb, he does not want that. A note left at the car, under the wiper like a parking ticket . . . but suppose some fit young man . . . and runs up the mountain . . . helicopters him, they pump him out . . .

Being found, being dragged back, these are problems, clearly.

43

Some deep cave is called for, where he'll never be found. But caves are not to his taste. He wants a hilltop and the sky; and he has considered the hills above Ngaio in Wellington, along from the television mast. Lie in a sleeping bag and drink his cocktail there, with the city on one side and the Ohariu Valley rolling away – sheep and horses grazing and magpies chortling in the dusk. Some early morning whisper-jet pilot will be the one . . . Flight ZK14 to Control . . . a body on the hills west of Kaukau . . . There's a nice impersonality in that. No child will scream.

But magpies, won't they peck out his dead eyes? They'll shred his lips and ear lobes before the pilot sees. And wild pigs on Mt. Duppa . . . He cannot think of it. And then there is not being found. If no one comes up that road and he lies for weeks . . . Leave a letter with his lawyer, to be opened at a specified time? Complications!

But Jack won't give it up, he's wedded to it. He will escape, even if it's in his own bed, with Harry sent away for the night; even if he has to creep into his hole under the stairs and uncork his bottle silently. A note thumb-tacked on the door while she colours berries in her room . . .

They have been members of the Voluntary Euthanasia Society for nine years. With her it's philosophical. She doesn't know how personal it has become for Jack. He wants to live long, and means to die when he is no longer in command. Why shouldn't he anticipate it as a pleasure? He cannot understand how such a simple thing brings so many worries. Logistical, medical. Where to get the stuff? 'Terminal cocktail': he doesn't have a clue what it may be and the term conceals his ignorance. But how much time is left for jokes? Jack is sixty.

One day he'll have to go and ask. Does nine years membership entitle him? How will they know he does not want it for a murder?

Perhaps his mother smells his obsession on him. Perhaps she is demanding her own death.

He shifts the Eccles cakes to her pillow and goes into the corridor, where he takes the long way round, rubber-stepping like a male nurse. Rooms flash by, with women in barred beds – hollow-templed, hollow-cheeked – and men propped in pillows, sleeping open-mouthed, with their big hands on the coverlet. Why do the old men stay in their rooms? Have they had enough of women? There's too much nakedness in the dayroom. The men are clothed in reticence and patience while the crazy women squabble on.

He hears one yelling from the toilets. 'Help me, I've been kidnapped.'

'I haven't had any dinner for three days,' another cries. He goes in and peels her a banana. She plays with it and makes it ooze between her fingers. Jack finds a towel and tries to wipe her clean but she puts her shoulder up and plasters squashed banana on the wall. Then she smears her arms with it and smiles delightedly. Should Jack call a nurse or get out before one comes? He doesn't know who will be punished, or how.

'I'll find a nurse for you' – but there are none in the corridor, and when he finds a wardsmaid, bottom jutting from the laundry store, and tells her there's a lady in Room 9 with a squashed banana, the girl laughs and walks the other way. 'You should see some of the things they squash.'

Toughness is a way of getting by. He does not think it will do for him. He cannot face his own death without stars and dreaming; cheese and wine.

His mother is drinking tea in the dayroom. She's smaller now she does not have to sit up straight for him. If he approaches she will spit out her cake and empty her teacup on the floor. Jack goes away. He reaches high and punches the code that opens the door; and nods at the speed he does it with. When he can't dial numbers, when he can't remember who's who in a book, then will be the time he'll have to worry. Then will be the time to get in his car and head for – wherever. Before they take his licence away. Before his knees and hips give out. Before he can't remember any more he's planned his death.

The wind and sun restore belief in it and he is able to forget. He blows on his horn as he drives away. It means goodbye to his mother but he hopes the other old ladies will think it is for them. He feels free and generous. He feels that he has faced her maturely and done the little bit that he can do.

He drives to the top of Mt. Eden.

So here he is standing on a hill. If he can't make it to Duppa the crater in this one will do. Half a million people all about but here is a

45

place where he can lie alone and see a fringe of trees and the sky – and perhaps, as he fades, a city face that looks down and does not get involved.

There are Japanese tourists in the crater. They slide on the grass as they scramble out, shrieking like birds. He approves of them; of their unbreakable foreignness. It gives him a stance to take, on top of his own hill. They pass, they click their cameras, they get in their bus and drive away; and here Jack Skeat stands, where he belongs.

The other cones rise to shoulder height: Mt. Wellington, Mt. Albert, One Tree Hill. Several smaller ones come up to his waist. Over the water North Head and Mt. Victoria squat back to back and Rangitoto, silver-grey, rises from its glittering moat. Crenellated, Jack thinks; but the word comes out of other histories. The shape of Rangitoto, anyway, is so familiar that he has no need for adjectives. Let it be. And while you're about it, get rid of moat.

Harry is over there, under the eye set in her ceiling, working in her two dimensional world. Harry is set at an angle. She'll come out, they will stand face to face, but not today. He lets her go and turns to the west. Another harbour glitters, five miles from the one at his back. Mud and mangrove creeks reach into the city from two sides. It would be easy to make them meet. Then ships could steam through Panmure and Otahuhu and two hundred miles would be saved.

Jack moves his finger. It is done. The Pacific Ocean meets the Tasman Sea. He is impressed. Only a true Aucklander can do that.

What he is doing: he is keeping his uneasiness at bay.

Black lands. Navy-blue. Earth-brown. Clay-yellow. Ochrous. Brackenish. Brackish. Creek-green. These are words he chooses for his west. That west out there that makes him uneasy because it is where he grew up and where a part of him still belongs. He wants to leave no parts lying around.

Down again, along, through, into. Here is Loomis under the hills. A glass and tile front, traffic lights and carparks and people. He wants the town of empty dusty streets and broken hedges. It's in behind and a long way back. He drives down the shopping streets and turns left into industry and commerce – where once a little square-built jam factory had stood – and passes through a district of panel-beating shops and coal and firewood yards and boarded-up stores until, at a straggly line, Loomis is residential. It's Polynesian too, and he drives carefully. There was only one Maori at Loomis school when he was there. Now, he has read in the *Herald*, a third of the pupils are Maoris and Islanders. Women in muu-muus talk on a lawn. Youths with dread-locked hair stand around a stripped-down motorbike. He's anxious that they shouldn't notice him. They are foreign, he is foreign – who owns the point of view? He sees how his presence in this street, his clothes, his car, his language, speech, habits of mind, can only provoke. Is there any part of Loomis he can claim as his own? And backwards-claiming – what can it signify in the Loomis-1990 world? He feels that he is doing something vaguely indecent.

He drives on all the same, and goes down a hill into a neighbour-hood that seems pakeha. Across a concrete bridge where once a wooden . . . Along the road, beside the creek where once . . . Unseemly word; 'once' prevents, doesn't it, good mental health? Yet it creates a country, it's a territory in his brain. Jack declares his right to go there.

He parks, he locks his car, he tries to find his old swimming hole. The creek is opened up. It's as if someone has forced two hands into the gorge and pulled it wide. The creek lies in the sun. It never did that except at midday. But it's dirtier and meaner. That is natural. The water in the hole is yellow-green. It has a rotting vegetation smell in place of the eel smell he remembers. There's nothing for him here, no folding together of now with memory. Jack sneezes once and turns away. He climbs back to the roadside and finds two youths looking at his car. They must have come down from the houses over the street. One wears a league jersey and the other a cotton T-shirt with the arms torn off. League is threat. Torn off is threat. Jeans. Boots. Shaven heads. Beer cans that gurgle in unison.

'Lost something, mate?'

'No, no, I'm just looking around.'

'Good idea to lock your car round here.'

They have seen him do it. Jack blushes, half in fright. 'It's just a habit.'

'Good idea. Might get your stereo knocked off, eh?'

'Ha ha ha,' the other laughs.

'I was looking at the creek,' Jack says. 'I grew up in a house along the road. I used to swim in the pool down there.'

'Yeah?'

'Fifty years ago.'

They cannot comprehend fifty years. All the same they soften. They have drunk enough beer to make them sentimental. 'I had a raft there. When I was a kid.'

'Yes?'

'We piled the rocks up, eh? We made a real big pool.'

'It's a good creek,' the other says. 'I learned to swim down there.'

'So did I,' Jack says, although it's a lie. He learned to swim at Cascade Park. 'There were great big eels.'

Their eyes swing on to him. It's plain the eels have gone. He had better be careful not to make his creek better than theirs. But he's moved to find they have a creek at all. He is moved that it's still alive.

'It's deeper than I remember.' Another lie, but a gift to them.

'She's deep, all right. There's a pool up there you can't touch the bottom. I used to try.' The league jersey youth turns away. He's as moved as Jack.

'Have a beer, mate,' the other says.

'I'd better not. I'm driving.' He's envious of someone diving deep in his creek and wants to ask the young man what he found down there. He stamps his foot on the road. 'When I lived here this was all gravel and dust.'

'Musta been a long time ago.' They are not interested in the road. They walk to the creek edge and look at the water. 'Good creek.'

'Thanks for talking to me.'

'No sweat.'

'I'd better get along the road and see my old house.'

'Remember to keep your car locked.'

'Ha ha ha.'

Nice boys, he thinks as he drives away. He wants to keep them simple; doesn't want to look at their lives. That way they don't interfere but share the creek. He goes around two bends and finds a grassed area where there had been a field of gorse. He never penetrated it and never came to the creek that way. Now he can walk down and stand on the rocks by the water and make out a bike frame and bottles in the mud. He can turn and run his eye up the slope and over the road and get a partial view of the house he had lived in for the first twenty years of his life.

Partial because although the row of pine trees is cut down two new houses stand where the summer-house and the rose garden used to be. He sees the old front porch and door framed between decramastic roofs and hardiplank walls. The curving drive is gone – where is the curve, where is the contour, that stand for the times he got away? Running down the drive, leaning on the curve, bent him out of her world into his. Now there is a right-of-way between wire fences, running from the road to the door. There would have been no escape on that narrow way.

Jack sneezes four times. (It's nowhere near his record of nineteen, brought on by the smell of animals in the Wellington zoo.) He blows his nose on tissues and wads them in a ball, which he fires at a cairn of stones on the far bank, and hits it square. That gives him the confidence to look at the house again. It was built in 1927 for the newlyweds and the mortgage was paid off in 1947, several weeks before Walter Skeat made his fatal dismount from the train. They had their twentieth wedding anniversary there, though no one celebrated or even mentioned it. Dorothy Skeat – had anyone ever called her Dot? – stayed on in the house until the mid sixties, when she sold it for a very nice price and bought a home unit in Epsom. Jack had last seen the house as she moved out: four-square and substantial at the end of its white-shell drive.

Now, the letterboxes say, it is divided into flats. 126A,B,C,D. How can four families, even four couples, fit in there? Another question – what made the Skeats think they needed so much space? Four bedrooms, two bathrooms, two living-rooms, a dining-room, a study, for three people? It only started to make sense when you understood that each of those three people lived alone.

Jack and Rex sneak up on Mrs Skeat where she sits in the summer house drinking tea. She is the white squaw and they are Indian braves, bare to the waist, with seagull feathers fixed in elastic round their heads. Jack carries a bamboo bow with an arrow on the string. Rex has a tomahawk ready in his hand.

Nine-year-old boys rustle and whisper when they creep. These two make no noise. Rex's tomahawk is real. He ground the edge in his father's workshop. One way or another, he will take the white squaw's scalp. As for Jack, he is ready for his mother to die. Putting an arrow in her throat transforms them into love.

He sneezes again, four times.

And Mrs Skeat saves herself by speaking. 'Why can't I be dead? I want to die.'

His first thought is she's practising lines to use on his father. 'I want to. I want to' – and now he knows she's speaking to herself. He puts his hand on Rex's arm and jerks his head, let's go – making one of his feathers fall out. Rex obeys. His face gives nothing away.

Behind the house he says, 'What do you reckon she meant?'

'Nothing.'

'I've got to go anyway.' And he goes. They both know that talking to yourself means you are mad. But they learn more than that. Jack learns his mother's desperation, her other face, and although he never sees it again he knows it's there, behind her mask. And Rex – does his silence, from that day on, mean pity or contempt? Or has he carried something else away? Does he get the thing he needs and not have to come back for more?

John Dobbie says: 'It is strange that Rex Petley's idea of "real class" seems to go no further than a summer-house and a rose garden and a lady in a wide-brimmed hat, drinking tea. Where did he find these properties? Perhaps in some movie. It certainly could not have existed in the Loomis of his youth . . .'

Jack's eyes and nose are streaming. His tissues can barely keep pace. Atchoo! Atchoo! A woman cycling past cries, 'Bless you.' He is grateful. As often as not Harry will say, 'For God's sake go in the other room.' His marriage sometimes seems to him an intricate device of honesties and concealments. But the whole of his parents' was concealment.

He does not want to think about it any more. Coming to Loomis is a mistake. And how does Rex Petley get in? Jack shakes him from the fabric like a cockroach. He gets a litter-bag from the car and picks up the tissues he has dropped. The one over the creek will have to stay, although he feels guilty about it now. All the same, if anybody's germs belong in Loomis his do.

He drives back to Auckland by way of Waikumete. Less pine reserve, more graves. And down, up, down, up – no mistake, it's sexual. Young men do get some things right.

His sneezing stops, his sinuses settle down, but Harry can see he's had an attack.

'Was it your mother?'

'I think it's the disinfectant they use.'

'How was she?'

'Mad, as usual.'

'Why do you bother going there?'

'She enjoys it. It's like a thriller. You know, the murderer arrives but she's too smart. Think of the adventure she's having.'

'Where else did you go?'

'Drove around. Looked in the shops.' Loomis concealed.

Loomis is before Harry's time.

Notebook: 3

Rex wrote no autobiographical pieces. Although he stands hidden
'in many a poem' (the Elf's favourite phrase), when you locate him
he's fully clothed and rarely front on. But Dobbie is clever enough to
recognize that the images of small town, country school, kitchen,
workshop, creek the early poems are full of make a kind of
autobiography. He points them out, makes sure we understand that
this is no imaginary country, then lets the poems speak for
themselves. That is sensible. The corrections I would make, though
large in number, bring no significant change to the reading. All
right, the armada on the creek, the woman on the bridge, one day
perhaps I'll point out those, but it's of no importance that the
chestnut tree in the school grounds overhung the dental clinic not
the boys' lavatory or that Mr Warren not Miss Hoyle was our teacher
in standard four.

Future biographers must consult me. I'll satisfy myself that their
idea of Rex is not inflated before I tell them what I know. No
'burning eyes', please; no 'eagle-like clarity of gaze'. It's true that he
gave the impression of being bright-eyed. His rather heavy face –
heavy in the chin, heavy (one might almost say fat) in the nose –
seemed to shed some of its bulk when he became interested in some
person or thing or event: an effect of the liveliness in his eyes. And
then – I'll concede this to 'the making of the poet' – a look of
stupidity would take its place. (I've seen his father boot him in the
backside – 'Wake up, stupid.') His eyes turned dull as some process
went on in his mind: the cementing, I would guess, of a new thing
into place. All his brightness had gone inside. Is that too romantic?
I'm determined not to overvalue Rex.

'There is a multitude of Petley stories,' says the Elf, 'and some
must be taken with a grain of salt. But one who knew him better than
most was the minor poet and future National Archivist, John Skeat.
His importance as "best friend" in the poet's youth cannot be
overlooked; although, inevitably, Skeat trailed behind – indeed,

who would not have? They met in 1938 when Les Petley, spiralling downwards in those difficult times, shifted his growing family westwards from New Lynn to the depressed little town of Loomis under the ranges. The friendship began at Loomis school, matured on the creek that meanders through the town – school, town, creek, that fertile ground of future images – and continued, on and off, for the rest of Petley's life. Unfortunately I have not been able to consult as freely as I would have liked with John Skeat . . .'

You wanted to dress Rex up, that is why. I made you behave sensibly. And you punished me by trailing me behind, and calling me a minor poet too. I'm no poet, that's inaccurate. I was a versifier for a time. Now I'm the keeper of certain memories and I'll let them out as I see fit.

Rex Petley, as a boy, was open, attractive, ordinary. He was good with his hands. He built flax-stick galleons, he sharpened toma-hawks, with an instinctive knowledge of form and proportion, of when to press down, with how much weight, and how, at what angle, to touch one thing against another for the transfer of energy. These abilities must have helped him when he wrote. His poems are neatly made and are full of balanced energies. One can join the poet with the boy by more than Loomis images. But I prefer simply to state the facts.

He was the oldest child in a family of eight. There was a stillborn daughter too; and a cousin, a boy, lived with the Petleys for a time. Rex always had a bed to himself. His next two siblings were girls, they had to share, and perhaps that helped make Melva a loud and robust girl and Dulcie secretive. (Perhaps not.) Rex loved his brothers and sisters, of that I'm sure, for a largeness came on him when he was in their company. He seemed to gather them in by a sudden increase in himself, the way a drop of water creeps at smaller ones and swallows them. His brothers and sisters made him serene.

His mother and he had a more difficult love. She did not strain at improving him, she just kept up a soft relentless pressure. Even her liveliness was part of it. She gave him little calculating looks to see if he had been increased. It seemed strange to me that a mother should talk with her son in such an eager way.

Lila Petley took a batch of scones from her oven. She put them on the kitchen table on a wire tray, tapped one with her finger, smiled at their shape, and covered them with a holey tea-towel. 'So who does your Mr Warren say is better than Paul Robeson?'

'Someone called Jeeley. It's spelt like giggly. Tenors are better than baritones, he says.'

'Perhaps he doesn't like negroes.' She gave him a look.

'He says they can sprint fast because they've got long legs for running away.'

'Perhaps he's frightened, Rex. Of people who are better at things than him.'

'He says women shouldn't be allowed out of their kitchens.'

'Does he now? What do you think?'

'You've got to get out, Mum. You've got to hang the washing on the line.'

She gave the sidelong look again. 'Cheeky! And keep your hands away from those scones.'

'Just one, eh? I like them hot.'

'No.' She guarded them, eyes bright. He ducked, he feinted, she shrieked, he yelled, they wrestled. Embarrassed, I sidled round the doorpost on to the porch. There were giggles, laughs, scuffles, inside, and Rex came out with two buttered scones and gave me one.

There's nothing 'difficult' in this; but it seems to me that Lila Petley was trying all the time, even when she was being simple, even when she appeared to forget herself. Was she consciously making Rex? Later on, when he was a man, she had a way of speaking dismissively of him, but that might have been because her job was done.

There were difficulties of another sort with the father. When Les Petley was angry he hit. When he was disappointed he kicked gates open and slammed doors. He groaned, he shouted, he lit rubbish fires in his garden and threw old boxes on from yards away. He kicked the heads off thistles, he beat the mats on the washing line until it collapsed, he lined up beer bottles and threw half bricks at them, or dropped them in the creek and bombed them from the swing-bridge as they floated under – Rex and I joined him in that. When he was happy he ruffled hair. He threw his children up to the ceiling and caught them as they came down and swung them between his legs. He dislocated Melva's shoulder doing that. He hugged and kissed his children. He even kissed Rex.

Les Petley was a dangerous man. His rages and his love could injure one. The first time I saw him he was digging in his garden. I knew from the way he thrust his spade in and beat clods with the back of it I should not go near. My new friend Rex and I were passing a football back and forth on the lawn. Then we did droppies over the washing line. I understood the need for care. The ball must not go on the garden. Rex understood better than I; but Rex was flirting. He needed to go right to the edge. The ball slid off his foot, spun out of my reach, bounced on the edge of the lawn and ran across the digging into the plants. It snapped a pumpkin flower off its stalk.

Les Petley, breaking earth with his hands, did not stand up. He monkey-scrambled to the plant with a readiness, an inhuman speed, that transformed my world. I was suddenly in a savage place. 'I'll – get – you.'

It started as speech but ended in a roar. He ripped out a tomato stake, swung it so the plant attached to it went flying over the tankstand, and charged at us. I thought he was coming for me and I screeched and flung my arms to save my face, but he went past, brushing me so that my whole side seemed to burn, and went for Rex. Rex did not wait. He had been beaten with razor-strops and belts and willow sticks but not yet with a tomato stake. Perhaps he thought Les meant to spear him. Rex ran. He went down the path at the side of the house, rattled across the front lawn among dried-out hydrangeas, jumped the front fence, just out of Les Petley's reach, and made for the bridge. He must have seen at once that his father would cut him off for he made a sudden turn, gave a screech like mine, and ran for the manuka at the far side of the turning bay. Maybe he meant to climb them, or break through the gorse around their trunks and reach the paddock; but once more he had no time. He turned and went head first, slick as a weasel, into the drain that carried storm-water to the creek. His white soles vanished down the hole. His father whacked at them as they disappeared.

Now it changes. This must have been the pattern of Les Petley's life. Games with Melva; Melva's joint goes out. Murder Rex with a stick; then save his life and carry him inside in your arms.

He flung himself down. He reached into the drain to drag Rex out. 'You wait, you little bugger.'

Rex said, 'Dad.' A muffled voice.

It turned Les Petley round. It changed his world as suddenly as he had changed mine.

'Dad, I'm stuck.'

'Wait on, son.' He reached in again. He strained until his face, hard against the edge of the pipe, went plum-red. His mouth gaped and I saw his molars. He told us later on that he had touched Rex's sole with his fingertips. 'Christ, I could've tickled him, but I couldn't grab hold.'

'Dad, I'm scared. Dad. Dad.'

'Don't move, Rex. Don't make any noise, just stay where you are.'

'Dad.'

'Quiet, son. You'll use up all your air.'

He ran back to the house. He was over the front fence like a negro and round the back. I thought he had gone for help and I kneeled down and said into the drain, 'He's getting the police.' I saw the soles of Rex's feet like cardboard cutouts. The pipe was not much over a foot wide. I don't think, with my shoulders, I could have gone in, but long thin Rex had weaseled in all right. He had got stuck where the drain bent to the creek. I thought if I could wriggle along and take hold of his ankles Les Petley could use me like a rope to pull him out; and I started to suggest it as he ran back. He knocked me aside. He had his spade, caked with garden soil, and he flung himself flat again and yelled, 'Lie still, Rex,' before attacking the clay around the drain.

I have never seen a man in such a frenzy. He was like a competitor in a coal-shovelling race. Lila Petley had run out from her kitchen. Melva and Dulcie, Austin, Gareth, Verna, Joy, and the youngest girl, always known as Tweet (names I did not learn until later on), came from their scattered places in the house and on the section as though sucked by a force to the mouth of the drain. Joy and Tweet howled. Lila Petley, in her apron, with her face as white as flour and her mouth a black stretched O, held them glued to her, one on each side, as Les Petley dug.

A spadeful of clods hit me in the ribs and made me hop back from the family. Les had half a yard of yellow clay to break and fling aside. The pipe, from Crum brickworks, had flared lips, it made a hungry mouth, and when we saw its glossy skin uncovered in the earth we understood how far out of our world Rex had gone. Melva raised her head and howled louder than Joy and Tweet. The family swayed in unison, left to right and back again, in a wind of grief I could not feel.

Les Petley put his cheek on the ground. 'Rex? All right? I'm coming now.'

'Da-ad,' the pipe breathed.

He lifted the spade over his head. I heard a rush of air into his lungs. Down came the blade on the body of the pipe. Chips sprang out and cut my face. I shrieked and touched and pulled bloody fingers away. Two stitches from the doctor later on, and hard words from my father to the Petleys – but no one took any notice then. He struck again and the pipe caved in. Lumps of it rattled in its interior. Les Petley hooked them out, one red hand like a bulldozer blade; and struck and hooked again, until we saw, unbelievable, the twin neat soles of Rex's feet. Lila Petley threw her children off and rushed at them. She hooked her fingers on his ankle bones. Husband and wife together, they pulled Rex out. He seemed to stretch, worm-like, and I hear a pop as he comes free. They rolled him on to his back and looked down – all the Petleys – at his drowned face and cemented eyes. 'Rex. Rex.' They all said Rex. He opened his eyes but did not see. Their pupils shrank. Their irises reflected the sky. He drew a long coming-back-to-life amazing breath. Les Petley lifted him and Lila hugged his head and they walked inside. The older children ran to open the gate and the younger ones came behind holding whatever parts of their mother and father they could get.

I felt my cheek, I saw my blood again and I ran home, thinking it might recommend me to my parents. But that's another story . . .

When I saw the Petleys next day Les winked at me. 'He's a bit of a tiger, your old man,' and Lila touched my cheek and gave me a cookie. They let me come to their house although my father had forbidden it. They included me in the rescue and nodded their heads as I explained how Les could have used me as a rope. 'You know, that might have worked.' He took me out on the lawn and showed me how to lead with my left and cross with my right, and reckoned I would make a better boxer than Rex. I saw that he did not believe it though. He taught Rex punches he never taught me.

*

57

Les did not go to the war but those years were violent ones for him. He spent some time on Manpower, building gun emplacements (this when the Japanese came in) and barracks and garages and equipment stores, and he worked for a while helping erect a US naval hospital. Almost every week he was in a fight. He needed to show he was not afraid.

He was in prison for a month for hitting an army officer who spoke to him as though he were 'some bloody hick private. I showed the bastard. He was spittin' bits of teeth out like confetti.' Another time he fought an American sailor, a Golden Gloves champion, on a piece of wasteland in Freemans Bay, and 'flattened the black bastard', although his own face was cut up fairly badly in that fight.

John Dobbie sees all this as 'gladiatorial'. Les Petley is 'a raging bull of a man whose combative instincts were passed on, in more acceptable forms, to his eldest son'. He allows Les no mental life. He's condescending about the Zane Grey novels he read; portrays that taste as an addiction, like beer and tobacco, and knows nothing (so I mustn't blame him) of the Wild West games we played in the scrub patch at the back of the house and down the steep banks of the creek. All the Petleys, Lila too, joined in. I had to play the villain, chasing the girls (to do what?). Les and Rex hunted me and shot me and my speciality became falling down dead in spectacular ways. We used wooden clothes pegs, jammed together, for six-shooters.

I captured Dulcie once and tied her hands with twine and hid her in a tea-tree patch at the edge of the creek. I had become a reader of Zane Grey too, although I could not take the books home, and I knew that when the villain got the girl he tore her blouse off and a blush mounted over her breasts – or was it spread downwards from her throat, I can't remember. Anyway, the hero always got there in time and beat the villain to the draw and wrapped a covering blanket round the girl. I knew all that. So, I think, did Dulcie, although she was only nine. She smiled at me shyly, and I blushed. Her rescuers were close but she whispered, 'Quiet.'

'Jes' keep yore trap shut, wooman,' I replied, very tough; and Les and Rex and Melva, who would not play the girl, came bursting through the tea-tree and beat me to the draw, and I rolled down the bank into the creek. My most spectacular death yet. It made me very popular with Les.

As villain and outsider I could not help introducing sex into the game. Rex saw it. 'You better not try anything with my sisters,' he warned.

'Course not.' I substituted death for my other longings, which were not very strong in any case – were curiosity more than desire.

Les rescued Lila from me one day – we chatted about schoolwork as we waited – said, 'Gotcha, girl,' and picked her up and carried her inside over his shoulder. The bedroom curtains whizzed across. Melva and Dulcie grinned at each other. Rex went off to the bridge and dropped stones in, and I went home. I thought I would not go to the Petleys' house any more. But I was back in the afternoon, couldn't keep away, and there was Lila working at her stove and Les sawing firewood with Rex at the back of the section. They had a record for getting through a log and Melva counted seconds – 'One, Buckingham Palace, two, Buckingham Palace, three, Buckingham Palace, four' – as they tried to break it. No one seemed concerned by what had happened. Parents doing that! I could not forget, I have never forgotten. And Lila, in her kitchen, sweetly humming, her china-white ears showing through her hair; while Les sweated at his log and blew his nose into the grass.

I went home again. I said to my father (with his pipe), 'I suppose only some people know what being good is.' He agreed. 'You have to work at being good and keep your feet out of muddy streams.' Dad was little help to me on that occasion. I'll confess to loving Lila, in a confused way, and believing myself finer than Les. He seemed a Zane Grey villain most of the time. How could someone pure, like Lila, go with him?

He took up football again, although he was forty, and was sent off for kicking the referee. I could note down a hundred things like that: finishing off a run-over dog with his crowbar – 'Someone had to bloody do it' – falling off his bike drunk and being led home by Joy and Tweet – a hundred things: swimming underwater at Cascade Park, across and back, all the way; carrying two bags of cement, one on each shoulder, along a narrow scaffold two storeys high – but then I'd seem to agree with the Elf that Les Petley had no mental life.

59

He (the Elf) is not malicious or even judgemental. He is, in fact, benign, and then evasive. He wants Les to be a character so that he can be put aside. He does not really want to talk about him. 'Beginnings are a puzzle,' says the Elf, 'and what one owes one's parents can rarely be determined in cases like this.' I'm forced to agree, but I can't allow Les to be dismissed.

Putting things together was his passion. He worked with his tongue out, then he ate his lower lip. After the war he did very well as a bricklayer, he even employed two or three men. He added a bedroom to the house, he renovated the kitchen, he put in hot water and a flush lavatory. 'The happiest day of my life,' Lila said. He built a workshop at the top of the slope by the creek and bought the little Willys truck Rex borrowed for dances at Pt. Chev. and Milford and Swanson. Often when Rex arrived home Les would still be working at his inventions.

They were never fine things, but they were not crude. He made a hoist for lifting bricks and mortar. It was powered by a US Army surplus electric motor and I saw it working on several jobs in the main street of Loomis when the new shops were going up. One day he dismantled it and fitted the motor to his latest invention, a machine for making concrete blocks. It powered a vibrator that settled wet concrete in moulds. 'This is going to make us rich,' Les boasted. But first he had to make it perfect. Perfection was the better part. The block machine, too long for the workshop, lay in the yard, with one end against the fence and the other overhung by Lila's washing, while Les worked on it in the late afternoon. At night the children took turns standing by with a torch. If its beam wavered Les would roar; and when he had got some part right he would hug them.

Rex, and sometimes I, mixed concrete in a mixer turned by hand and poured it into a barrow and wheeled it to Les, who tipped it neatly into the moulds. They lay end to end, and in a later model side by side, on a chassis floating on springs. The vibrator was geared for a slow beginning but soon built up a fine turn of speed, and Les ran along with a bucket and trowel, topping up the moulds as the concrete settled. In a factory machines would do that, he explained. When the concrete was set he stood at one end of the machine, with Rex and Lila or one of the girls at the other, and swung the chassis on its hinges and laid a neat line of blocks on the grass. I felt they should be steaming, they looked so much like loaves. All the Petley children clapped.

Les made a second chassis for hollow blocks, then patented his machine and took it, broken into parts, round the concrete manufacturers – Humes and Winstones and smaller firms. He demonstrated it in a dozen places.

Was I the only one who knew Les would never be rich? Rex believed he would be. He believed the Petleys would live in a house with a swimming pool. But I was not in the family and I knew that Les would always ride home drunk on his bike and Lila peg washing on the line.

The big companies were not interested. They were getting mass production going on their own. The smaller had no money to put up. Les's machine lay rusting in the grass. For a while he talked of setting up his own factory but he did not have the money either, and nor did he have the interest. He wanted to invent and make a killing and live well – he wanted, Rex told me once, to own a good jumper and win the Great Northern Steeplechase. But I saw him at work in the torchlight, with his tongue out, and I'm sure he wanted, just as much, to build perfect machines.

One day he dragged his block-moulder to the bank and tipped it into the creek and bits of it are probably there today. He made nothing on that scale again. He built an extension ladder but there was nothing new in its mechanism. When he was retired – and still in the little house in the blind road with Lila – he turned a bit of extra cash by making wooden toys. They were solid and were put together well, but Les Petley's spirit was not in them.

I believe Rex owed as much to him as to Lila. Rex too worked with his tongue stuck out. That – or so it strikes me – is the classic way when one is matching part with part and working functions out and devising pressures and setting balance up. No one will deny that Rex's verse is well made and startles frequently with new-found uses for old properties. There's boldness too and daring and facing-up, left hook, right cross – and now and then, when everything seems lost, there's a bull's roar and a wild swing.

Let's not leave the father out.

*

I see the Petleys in a kind of dance. Each one makes his or her steps perfectly. There's a rightness in the measure even when hidings are dealt out. Rex found his meaningful pattern in family, in the interweaving of habit and acceptance and love. Even his father, violent and sentimental, fitted in; and things outside – my mother in the summer house for example – provided the necessary tension against. They made the dark the Petley light burned in. This simplifies and formalizes. But I read the poems and I know. I look at the boy, Rex, and I know. I have seen him come in dirty from the playground, or smelly from some piece of brutality on the creek – spearing an eel, beheading it, and hammer-throwing the body home through the paddock for the fowls (have I mentioned that the Petleys kept Black Orpingtons?) – come into the kitchen and hug his mother unselfconsciously and, almost like a lover, jerk the ribbon in her hair so the brown mass of it tumbled down. He made no pause between the parts of his life but passed in and out with no thought. Later on he saw them as parts and used them to describe himself. Others see his profile. I'm the one who knows enough to turn him face on.

Remember that piece, it's in half a dozen anthologies, about the boy who sits his younger sister on his shoulders and runs with her across a swing-bridge? The steps must be kept in time with the bounce. The metaphor is easy to see. A small miscalculation, one wrong step, and over the wire, into the creek, out of life, they go. (He puts it better, I trail behind.) Have you wondered why, although they reach the other side and the girl-child howls with terror and delight, there's a sense of foredoom, of grieving, in the poem? The children are not named; but I was there, I saw it happen, Rex and Joy. He never wrote about Joy's death, which happened three years later. He wrote about the two of them on the bridge, that was as close as he could come, and it's close enough. John Dobbie thinks the title 'Joy' stands for the emotion and it puzzles him why the poem is equivocal.

Too much dared: out of life go Joy and her cousin Bert. But there was also 'the thing that cannot be allowed for', as Rex puts it in another poem.

*

Joy was like Melva. We used to call that sort of girl a tomboy. Everything Bert could do she could do as well or even better. Although they spent most of their time together I do not think they liked each other much. He came to live with the Petleys in 1947. His father, Les's brother, had died in the war and his mother married again. Bert and his stepfather . . . it's an old story. So he came to Loomis and for two years competed hard with his age-mate, Joy.

Their rivalry helped kill them. It happened on the other creek, on the other side of Loomis, by the domain. It was late spring, 1949, two or three weeks after Lila and I had talked on the bridge. As they drowned a cricket match went on. I was not there, I played tennis not cricket, but Rex, with his quick eye, was fielding in the slips. The swimming hole lay in an elbow of the creek, a hundred yards away through old-man manuka. A dozen children and a few adults were swimming in the cold water, keeping near the bank, when Joy and Bert set out, like Les Petley at Cascade Park, to swim across and back underwater. She had bet him he would not make it. On the far side, under the bank, they tangled in a barbed-wire fence washed down in winter floods and although Bert thrashed up several times Joy never surfaced at all.

I wasn't there but I can see parts of it very well: men in white running through the trees; Rex in sodden muddy whites unwrapping wire from his sister's throat.

He never talked about it. He never wrote about it. And I won't speculate. Look at his poems; all of them.

Notebook: 4

The try-scoring boy, the six-hitting boy, the boy top of the class, the boy who knows how to manage teachers. The savage boy, the solitary boy. The boy who dismounts from the train before it stops and doesn't have the sensitivity to suspend that practice for a day or two when my father dies. The boy who gets off at New Lynn station and starts the long walk home along the track because he doesn't feel like school that day. There are so many bits to choose from and no organizing principle I can find. Although his poetry points at his life, if you can recognize the finger, not all of his life points at the poetry.

It seems that way to me, but perhaps it's only seeming. Do I know Rex well enough? It's possible to suppose that if one tiny bit had worked out differently – let's say his encounter with the girl whose name I forget, at Orewa beach – his poetry would have been different too.

I'm bound to tell that story, because it portrays a Rex who does have the sensitivity . . .

We went to Orewa for a week, over New Year, four of us, Loomis boys, Mt. Albert Grammar boys, with our tent and our groundsheets and our blankets, our baked beans and beer, our frenchies and our troubling virginity. I'm not going to write of attempts and failures and consummations, sex is private, and nothing would induce me to go into detail. All that I will write down is that I came away from the holiday no longer troubled in that way, and very pleased about it, and pleased to find in myself no need to boast – I had thought I would be boastful – while Rex came away a virgin still. But he too had found something unexpected in himself and was satisfied with what he had achieved.

Les Petley dropped us off in his truck and drove away winking, and we pitched our tent on our allotted site on the other side of the toilets from the family part of the camp, and set out looking for adventure: Rex Petley, Jack Skeat, Tony Jameson, Mark Bunce. We thought ourselves interesting, manly, attractive; but I stand at a distance of forty years and realize how ordinary we were. We were not even especially noticeable. There were bands of young men more accomplished than us in noise and cheekiness all over Orewa that year; in the camp, on the beach, at the nightly dances. They outnumbered the girls three to one, and the girls were mostly with their families. One had to work in those days and have a lot of luck.

I won't bother with the dances, they've been done many times. See, for example, Rex's 'Dancehall', in *Darkness and Delights* or in the selected poems. It's a naturalistic piece, it's definitive: the saxophone, the sweaty palm, the young men at the door; and it only starts to labour when it turns to darkness at the end – but I'll leave Lit. Crit. to someone else. He's very good on the girls flocking like sheep, and how when you manage to separate one – you work like an eye dog, he says – she must find her way, quick-stepping, back to her friends or else she's lost.

Tony Jameson was the first to succeed. He had the quickest tongue and the most attractive looks. His girl came back to the tent with him. We had to wait outside while they did it. That was far too public for me: I looked at her with horror when she came out. But she was off-hand with us and did not seem to know that she was lost, or used, or sluttish. She strolled away, yawning, with Tony in tow; but went off with another boy the following night. It set us all back.

Mark, poor Mark, never got a girl. Mark hardly even got a foxtrot. He drank a lot, down in the sand dunes, and spied on couples – but today he's a big-family, rich, suburban man, the only one who made it. (Tony Jameson had boiling water poured on him by his wife. These are Rex's friends. He kept in touch. Boiling water as a marital response gets into the poems twice.)

My girl and Rex's – I'm suspicious of possessives – were Diocesan sixth formers and once they had opened their mouths Rex and I concealed our Loomis vowels. Sarah fell to me. She was a lively pug-faced girl. I fell to Sarah, and I'd like to hear the adjectives she would choose. Some relatively-pleasing-in-the-face word, I would guess, but never lively. Rex danced with her then moved in on her friend, who had just refused a dance with me. They tipped us at each other, and that was our good luck, for later on, down in the sand dunes, although we didn't do it exactly right, Sarah was just as pleased as I. (It wasn't quite her first time.) We walked on the beach afterwards, back and forth. She told me things about being a girl I had never suspected – that they were individual not collective, for a start. I made better sense of them after that.

I told Rex I had never known you could talk with girls. It was nearly dawn. We sat cross-legged on the flat-topped hedge. The lemon-squeezer tents lay all below us and the sea washed and gloomed beyond the dunes. My nightful of achievements was nothing to Rex. He shone, he twitched, with what had happened to him.

She, the lovely one – and she was lovely, I don't remember her name but remember her face – had let him go nearly all the way. Some detail is called for after all. They peeled off from Sarah and me and found a place (the dunes accommodated dozens of couples), and there, for a long while, they kissed and stroked and fondled. I did not boast about my completed act but Rex did about his preliminaries. His assumption was plain that his girl counted while mine did not. She (the pretty one) let him put his hand there after a while – a good long while – and gasped and kissed and carried on and gave him all her signals to persist. He put his weapon (it's not his word and isn't really mine) in her hand and she raised her head to get a sight of it and ran her palm along and back as though the shape and size were much as she had expected. But when he tried to open her legs wider – 'Jesus, Jack, she started to cry.'

There's more, a good deal more, of no, please, don't, and lots of tears, while she continued to hang on. It ended with Rex not persisting. He believed, or so he seemed to say, that he had shown compassion.

Very few men would be able to turn back from so close; and here was a boy of eighteen . . . But a man, I think, would have read it differently and known he was meant to carry on. She held on to him all the time and reached down and showed him how to work his finger. All this he told me, on top of the hedge – Rex large-eyed and shining at his triumph over self. He stopped kissing the girl, put off her hand, withdrew his own, and helped her pull her scanties (his word) up. No wonder she ran off and would not say good-night.

He swam in the mouth of the estuary; detumesced; and now, hours later, was swollen up again, with moral pride. I listened to him tell it, and tell it again in better words; and I sat smiling to myself. I had words of my own, but no need to say them. I was contented.

I did not often do better than Rex. And let me add to that night at Orewa, Sarah's refusal to make love a second time after our walk on the beach. I shrugged and smiled, was disappointed, then recognized her sense (which became my own) of enough. I was schooled in moderation, after all. We kissed each other kindly at her door.

Those girls went home next morning and we never saw them again. And I wonder if Rex remembered, when he wrote 'Dancehall' in his early thirties, that his girl, thanks to him, had not been 'lost'. (And nor was Sarah!) It's fair to use the word all the same. Later on, in the unsuccessful poems he was writing in his final years with Alice, 'lost' came close to being a stock response. 'Lost' was Joy, and all those things time and circumstance had robbed him of.

Notebook: 5

My hand wants to come down heavily and I can't prevent it. I want to make sense; control by means of finding significance. I want to make moral assessments. That's the source of my irritability, the itch in my mind that I scratch all the time.

I'll resist. One method is to lay words flatly down, set memories out like plates on a table and make a neat three-sided box: knife, fork and spoon. But those are places set for someone else – a place for John Dobbie and the ones who come after him. It's my table and the meal is mine. What I must do is serve plain food. For a start, I'll avoid metaphors.

Rex went to university with a credit pass in Scholarship (I had one too). He worked in the freezing works at Westfield before term. Although my mother did not want me doing manual jobs I put in several weeks at the city markets, bagging grain, stacking crates, stuffing fowls into sacks as the slaughterman wrung their necks. It was 1949, the year of my book, the year Joy drowned. One of my poems is about the fowls. Their wings still moved and the sacks lunged and stumbled as I tied their mouths. Another is about my half hour on the auction table. I snapped the wires on the crates of fruit with a jemmy and levered back the lids for the buyers to see. The auctioneer sneered, Chinamen watched, as I bungled it. My jemmy speared a tomato. Rex said they were my two best poems. A pity though, he said, that I had spelled out meaning at the end. Description was meaning, why couldn't I see that?

I still have a dream in which a blind sack flaps bonily, and I'm inside. I dream of tiered Chinamen slanting down. I asked Rex once if he dreamed about his poems and he said no, writing them got them out of his system, right out. I don't believe him.

He wrote from the age of sixteen. Before that he could hardly spell his name. But I must avoid smartness. There are those who belittle Rex. I'm not one of them. Before the age of sixteen he showed no real ability with language. Then some sac of interest in him broke and carried him away on a flood of words. (So much for avoiding metaphors.) He began, quite simply, with describing; and he kept that up all his writing life. But there are ways and ways. If you want to find out some of them look at John Dobbie's bibliography, which will refer you to articles in *Landfall, Islands, London Magazine, World Literature in English, Australian and New Zealand Studies in Canada*, and a dozen others. Rex is taken seriously all right. But because he kept himself apart and shows few influences he's not easy to pin down. He has never been a fashionable poet.

John Dobbie: 'Petley's hard core of independence remained impervious to influences. He refused to take sides in the celebrated Auckland/Wellington struggle of the fifties. He would not, as he put it, be "a Curnoid" or "part of the flatulence from the south". All his life he remained innocent of theory, but was knowing to an almost encyclopaedic degree about the ways of practice, about the ways of words; and this I put down to the hard attention he paid physical things in his youth.'

The Elf is on to something here. Rex paid that hard attention, but in a natural way. He was never trying. Concentration, assimilation, were functions like breathing. Description began as a natural act. When we started writing verse I dealt with what I saw and how I felt about it, and what my feelings meant; Rex with what he saw and what he saw next. If he played a part it was usually to go away and leave things as they were. An example: in our first year at university we would meet in Albert Park and eat our cut lunches on the grass by the fountain. There were flower beds, Moreton Bay fig trees, and a statue of Queen Victoria enclosing us on three sides. Sunny hours after morning lectures; girl students all about in their summer frocks: we could not avoid writing about it. But I laboured at meanings – I made meanings up. The girls were moths in their season; their youth the flame they fluttered about; the spreading branches age and death; the queen our puritan history. Her marble eye put their fires out. It might have worked better but would never have worked well. Those half hours on the grass lose their nature in my meanings. Rex on the other hand . . . And it's most unusual. Don't boys and girls of that age want to know the reason, and don't they want improvement passionately? I was puzzled by his freedom from 'why' and 'where to', and later on I resented it.

My poem is the last one in *First Fruits*. Rex never published his. He showed it to me and I complained that nothing happened. I kept on waiting for the telling blow – just one word – and it never came. For six months, in 1949, I was the poet. Rex stopped showing me his writing, but he was keeping on and I allowed myself to encourage him, and could not understand my fear that he would move past. My abilities were so much greater than his. Rex was not very clever at all.

But oh how he could integrate. That too came as naturally as breathing. The woman in the kitchen shifts the damper. The chimney roars. She pushes the stewpot to one side and lifts the ring and drops a lump of axe-split tea-tree in. Down in the orchard the child runs home. He has an eel-hook in the ball of his thumb. The woman turns her husband's work socks on the drying rack. The child . . .

How do these few details come together and create a family; an inside place, an outside place, and, if I can use the phrase, a system of values? Without saying any of that? I would have said it. I'd have underlined; and the physical things in the poem would have lost their substance and faded away. These days I see Rex's mind at work; I see connections made. He was more than just a piece of recording equipment. But even his subtlety and his balancing skill were a part of his gift. (Yes, I believe in gift, just as I believe in work, fifty-fifty.) The family gathers round and looks with horror (Rex doesn't say horror, I say that) at the black hook in the child's white hand. The father takes it by the haft and with a thrust completes the circle. The point and barb break out the other side. He gets his pliers; snips. Quick and delicate undraws the circle . . . it's all there, the increase of pain for the cure of pain. Then the reversal and the hook without a barb. The welling out of blood. All the bits together. He makes them larger than their sum.

The simplicity of his poems made me angry. I felt he could do better than that. I believed that I was shining and Rex took some of my lustre off. It seemed a betrayal of mind not to look for meaning. I was, too, in something of a state about betterment. Rex had chosen Loomis and that was a shocking retreat from the world; from possibilities for useful work and self-enlargement. Yet I could see that some of his poems worked.

70

We both had a sense of other lives. We could both see and take in multiplicity. But he had a centre, I had not. While I strove to make mine (oh this second-hand language) he rested safe. Because of that safety he was able to roll particularities into a ball and then beat it flat and gaze at the variously-beautiful stretched-out surface. I did not have sufficient calmness for that. Yet later on – no, leave it. In 1949 he stopped showing me his poems because he saw it was a waste of time – and there was the waste in my spirit too, perhaps he saw that. Then came Joy's death and he stopped writing for several years. When he started again 'lost' was the sub-text in his work, 'lost' was the flavour. But even that does not mean his centre was gone. His centre was darkened, that is all. He could not have written if that had been lost too.

Rex dropped two of his second-year subjects and took a job as a postman. John Dobbie is accurate about his financial hardships and his struggle to educate himself. He let his credit-pass money go – it wasn't much – and gave up his plan of being a teacher. What would he be? He did not know, he wasn't worried. He might stay a postman all his life. 'The mail must go through.'

Dogs caused him trouble on his walk. He carried a two-foot length of reinforcing steel in a cloth scabbard on the side of his bag and was in trouble once for smashing a bull terrier's leg. 'It was him or me, Jack. The bastard was going to have me.' He was elated by the speed and effectiveness of his blow. Rex enjoyed violence, he believed in confrontation between the world and Petleys. Perhaps his length of steel set the balance right in some way after Joy. The supervisor confiscated it so Rex stocked up on dead light bulbs, which he smashed on the pavement to scare advancing dogs. But he hankered after his steel club and pinched it from the supervisor's desk after a while. 'You should have heard that bloody thing squealing.' He threw back his head and made the noise of a terrier in pain. I gritted my teeth and covered my ears. 'You think that's something, Jack? Wait until I catch up with an Alsatian.'

His exaggerated hatreds began at this time – dogs and the people who own them, bureaucrats, army officers, club-joiners, Christians, people with unearned incomes, people who talk too much, radio announcers, film actors, music-lovers (music played no part in his life). Bus drivers and tram conductors too. All this was a tightening of the wall around Petleys. I could still pass through but he wouldn't let me in very far. If his mother or sisters touched me – they were a family for touching – he would frown and get busy; rattle the cups away to the scullery. 'Come on, Jack, time we got moving,' and we'd head for the Loomis pictures or drive off in the Willys to a dance. He made his sisters furious by running their boyfriends down – and nearly ran down Melva's in the truck one night; tipped him off his bike into the gorse. 'Get yourself a light, you stupid bugger,' he yelled. 'Just about had him,' he said to me.

John Dobbie accuses me of running away from Rex's 'fight' with the bus driver. 'John Skeat quickly absented himself.' I could probably sue him for that. I was there almost until the end. It wasn't a fight either, John. Nor was there 'a principle involved'. You try too hard to turn him into a hero. Stupidity, irrationality, ego-strutting, weakness, in both the squabblers made me walk away. And Rex was tuppence short on his fare not just a penny. 'His strong sense of justice was called into play.' What rubbish! I will say though that he stood up straight. He looked noble even though his ear lobes turned red. The driver was a small man, hungry as a stoat. I think I would have backed him if the 'fight' had turned to blows.

'Loomis,' Rex said, tumbling coins into the tray.

'Tuppence short.'

'That's all I've got.'

'This isn't a charity, sonny. Off you get.'

'I'll pay,' I said, leaning round Rex and dropping a threepenny bit into the tray. Rex snared it, quick-fingered, before it could lie down. He flicked it backwards past my face and it ran into the gutter.

'Is tuppence so important to you, sonny?' he asked the driver.

I went back down the steps and found my threepence and leaned round Rex again and put it in the tray. This time the driver was quicker. He slid it with his finger over the edge. 'I want the money from this joker here.'

I won't go through the stages of escalation; simply note that Rex cried: 'I'm going to teach him people are more important than money.' (This is the Elf's 'principle'.) He marched down the bus and sat in the middle of the back seat, a prime place for keeping up the struggle. The driver made his declaration too: 'This bus doesn't move until you're off.' And there they sat, while the passengers got angry and took sides. I absented myself. I walked down to the ferry buildings and watched the boats and caught a late bus home. Rex asked me angrily next day: 'Where the hell did you get to?' – and must have told someone of my defection for it to reach John Dobbie's ears; but I'm happy with my behaviour. It was a fair piece of criticism. I'm only sorry that I wasn't there to see Rex resisting passively as two constables carried him off the bus. He was fined ten pounds and got a ticking off from the magistrate. As far as I know he's our only poet with a record.

It wasn't the ticking off that changed his ways. I suspect he recognized absurdity; and the Beezer helped. It cooled him down – wind in his face, rain in his face. The white road zipping back under the wheel carried his rage into the past. He had a rested look in his eyes when he took his goggles off after a spin.

The BSA motorbike was his final word to tram conductors and bus drivers. It worried Lila sick, she believed he would kill himself, but the rest of the family loved it and 'the Beezer' became an essential part of their lives. Remember 'Love Objects', John? It's a clever poem, although it's only a list. The cumulative energy, the longing, the enjoyment; and not a single adjective around. You don't know how he does it, no one does (I don't), so you worry away about 'referents'. And once you're 'quite in the dark' about a meaning. I give you 'the Beezer', no charge. He bought it second hand (although it was probably fifth or sixth) and coughed it home and spread all its parts out on the lawn and when he fitted them together it ran like a dream.

We learned Auckland on the Beezer. I sat on the pillion seat like a girlfriend but kept my hands behind me like a man. We rode north as far as Warkworth and Leigh and south to the Waikato heads. We went to the hot springs at Parakai and along the Whangaparaoa Peninsula to the army base (where Rex had some hard things to say about what he called 'the military mind'). French Bay, Green Bay, and the following Sunday down the other coast through Miranda to Ngatea, and I formed the impression I still hold of the Auckland isthmus drowning in mud. A little rise in temperature and we will have crocodiles basking in the mangroves.

We drove thirty miles up Muriwai beach, with the dunes on one side and slow green rollers, half a mile apart, on the other. Rex wound the Beezer up and we seemed to run on a mat of air. The wind got in my cheeks and blew my face up like a soccer ball. It whipped my chewing gum away. If we'd hit a patch of soft sand the bike would have stood on its nose and somersaulted and we'd have bounced along the beach and crackled with the breaking of our bones. 'You've been a hundred miles an hour,' Rex told me when we stopped.

Westwards became our direction. I fight the urge to become adjectival. The coast out there crushes language flat. South of Muriwai is Anawhata. Then Bethells Beach, Piha, Karekare, Whatipu. That says enough for me and it's enough for Rex, although if you look at his poems you'll find words that mean the same. We came at a walking pace down the twisting roads, with the Beezer ticking and creaking, and an expectation in our minds of sea and cliff and sand – movement overturning on itself, height leaning in and leaning out, the body overturning, the mind starting to fall – desire, revelation, perhaps death. This becomes far too explicit. Rex can do this sort of thing without coming out. (See 'Bethells Beach', see 'Comber'.) We lay on the hot black sand and body surfed in the waves, and went out several times in winter and stood as close to the surf as we dared and climbed on the rocks and asked the seventh wave to take us. Once we swam, midwinter, all alone at Bethells, naked in the waves that overtopped us like walls and we came out like old bait, with the blood washed out of us, and trembled and stood bent long after we had pulled our clothes on. Our wrinkled hands could not tie our bootlaces up.

He took his sisters there, one by one, and would have taken Lila but she refused to ride on the bike. A kind of fatalism came on her when he was driven home one night skinned from his wrists to his elbows after a fall. Lumps of skin were nipped from his kneecaps and his ribs. I talked with Lila at the gate. 'I can't do any more, Jack. I can't care any more or I'll go mad:' She kept on caring, of course, but damped down her ways of expressing it, and went a little mad in a self-denying way.

Rex took me riding on the Scenic Drive, Swanson to Titirangi and halfway back, the night before I caught the Limited to Wellington. We stopped at the lookout and Auckland lay spread flat, winking its

74

lights. 'Jesus,' I said, 'Wellington' (which I had never seen), 'I must be mad.'

'What does your old lady say?'

'She wants me to be a lawyer. Even doctors aren't good enough.'

'It's only a year, eh. Then you can come back.'

'If I come back I've got to live with her.'

'Who says?'

'Wellington's the only way I'll ever get away.'

He lit a cigarette and flicked the match away – down to Loomis, under the hills. 'I'm leaving home too. I'm getting a room in town.'

'Why?'

'Time is.' He grinned. 'I'm not going to stay too long like you.'

'You've got more than I have,' I said bitterly.

'That's just the way it turned out.'

We plunged down Forest Hill Road into Loomis. I was drunk with leaning over when we reached my gate. Light-headedness, and falling locked together, enclosed in our hard cell of light, made me say, 'I know how you feel, Rex.'

'Yeah?'

'My father and your sister, eh? It happened to us both.'

'Shut up, Jack.' His words came easily. But I had seen a pulse, a contraction, in his eyes, more than the street lamp could have made. He was enraged at my claim for equality; and then he was calm and put me off, tapping with his gloved fist on my shoulder. 'Take it easy down there. Keep in touch.' He pulled his goggles on and rode away.

It was six months before I saw Rex Petley again.

Escaping from the Barbecue

Alice Wilkey is sixty. She asks her friends and family to help her celebrate. Harry and Jack do not know why they are invited. Harry has not laid eyes on Alice for twenty years. Jack has kept in touch, visiting her several times on archival trips to Auckland. He finds afternoon tea with her a bit like tea with the Queen but he hangs on from a sense of uncompleted business. He is surprised on her trellised path by the smell of steaks. A barbecue is not like Alice at all. He takes his tie off and puts it in his pocket.

'Harriet Edwards,' Alice smiles. Though unemphatic it's political. They greet each other by touching cheeks, Alice bending down and Harry rising on her toes. 'And Jack.' She takes both his hands and lets him decide not to kiss her.

'Happy birthday,' Jack says. 'Harry brought a present. From us both.'

It's a Bellringer and Edwards, in paperback, and Harry apologizes for seeming to blow her own trumpet. 'It was Jack's idea.'

'Better than chocolates,' Jack says. 'It looks as if you like ferns anyway.'

'I like their modesty.' (Which makes him blink.) 'Thank you both. Now come and meet some people. And I do apologize for all this chops and sausages and alfresco business. It's really for the youngsters. We older ones are going to sit inside.'

Jack does not like being classed as an older one. If he had known about a barbecue and swimming he would have brought his togs along and dived off the board. Looking at the youngsters, he holds his stomach in and pulls his shoulders back.

'That's my grand-niece, Veronica. The other one is an exchange student from Denmark, at her school. I'm afraid we had to tell her not to sunbathe with her top off.'

'It gets Leon excited,' Stephen Wilkey says. 'Hello, Jack. Nice you could come. Is this your wife?'

'It does nothing of the sort. It makes him cross. It's bad for him to get upset.'

Stephen winks at Jack and shakes hands with Harry. Jack likes Alice's husband, he feels easy with him, and understands why Alice chose him after Rex. He has few appetites but is inquisitive and amused. (Demanding though, decisive, in business, Jack has heard.) That must be restful for Alice. She had little rest with Rex.

They climb steps to a stone-paved patio where children are sitting on iron chairs round a table, eating cake and drinking through straws. 'Grandchildren,' Alice says. 'Not all of them are mine.'

Jack tries to identify those who are, for they are Rex Petley's, but he doesn't know what features to look for. Noses and mouths change, eyes change too, with growing up. Ears should stay the same. He looks for ears. Alice guesses what he is up to but is wrong about his method.

'See, on the far side. There's no mistaking that forehead is there?' (Alice says forehead the English way.)

'Brain box,' Stephen adds. (He had once been chased half the length of a street by Rex, but he bears no malice.)

Jack can't see it. The boy has a dome, with none of Rex's squaring off. 'The little girl with the ponytail?' he murmurs. 'Around the eyes?' – concealing that her ears, over-large, give her away.

'Good heavens no, she's a ring-in,' Alice laughs, 'a neighbour's child. There's Simon' – the boy with the 'forrid' – 'and Luke and Amanda. And Peter and Terry and Cathy and Rex by the pool. There are plenty of Petley genes around, though I must say I'm just as pleased about the Pittaway ones.'

Jack looks at the youngsters by the pool but is confused by running and splashing and flopping down. A boy seems to have Rex's length of leg and his knotty joints; a girl – poor child – his nose; but, on the evidence of the neighbour's child, Jack is likely to be wrong. He gives it up and watches the Danish girl. She has ease of movement, physical charm. Her mind is probably in better order too, judging from the adult way she looks back at him. That does not mean she has a better mind. He's prepared to back the Petley genes, which may be gawky now but will come on strongly before long.

'Which one is Rex?'

'There. The boy on the board. Fiona's oldest.'

It is the long-limbed boy. His dive breaks into angles and water sprays as far as the flower beds. One of his great-aunts died under water, Jack remembers, but he finds the connection strained. He smiles at the boy when he comes up and meets, for a moment, Rex Petley's young dismissive eye. That connection comes with the straightness of a blow. Jack turns away and walks to the end of the patio. Below him, on the lawn, men work about the barbecue and carry plates of food to women sitting in the rock garden. These are the sons and daughters (and the sons- and daughters-in-law) of the Pittaway girls. Features have set into more or less permanent shape – they'll last through middle life – and he does not have to work hard to see Rex in Fiona as she turns up her face: that strength of bone, rounded and scaled down to a feminine shape.

'Jack, how are you? Come on down.'

'I've been ordered inside with the oldies.' But he stays grinning at her. 'How's it going? How's the counselling?' – knowing he is liked, and liking her again, instantly. Once he had not known whether he wanted Fiona for his son, David, or himself.

'Better grab a steak, there's not much left,' says a man in an apron that surely does not have the approval of the Pittaway girls: hairy-fingered male hands grab female breasts from behind.

'There's ham and chicken inside,' Alice says from the door. (Harry has gone in.) 'And a friend of yours,' she adds, with a meaningful look.

Jack knows who it will be. 'I think I'll have some steak first.' He pretends not to see her annoyance and goes down narrow steps at the side of the house; kisses Fiona. Her hand takes him on the curve of his shoulder and holds him close and he catches her elusive hot-metal smell that he had learned one night in his car, parked on the sea front at Island Bay, many years ago; when she had told him about her parents' marriage and why she could not stand being with them any more. Other things had happened on that night, kisses more than friendly, but he had argued himself into reverse, quoting their ages and his wife at home; and they had been distant for a while after that. She was, he had realized, not nearly so excited as he. And she had been barely eighteen.

'What have you been doing? I thought you would have come to visit me.'

'I would have. I've been getting Harry set up. Skylights in the ceiling, that sort of thing.'

'How is Harry?'

'She's fine. She's doing another book.'

'With the campanologist still?'

'Oh yes.'

'And the children?'

'They both live overseas. David's in Geneva. He's married to a Swiss woman years older than him.'

'Is that bad?'

'It wouldn't be if she didn't try to scare us off. Jill's OK. She did a nanny course and she's in Switzerland too. They see each other.'

'You sound as if you don't like nanny courses.'

'I can think of more important jobs.'

'Poor Jack, still tangled up with right and wrong.'

She introduces him to her husband. Jack is pleased it's not the man in the funny apron. Eating steak, he listens while Tom Pringle talks about his work as a Justice Department psychologist, and then hears Fiona on marriage counselling. They have the patience of mechanics but no high expectations of success. Is that what cements them? – for they are close, they run together. A perfect seamless couple. Familiarity with lives gone wrong makes them hold fast to what they have – is that a fair summing-up, leaving all their complications out?

'You still go off in dreams, Jack.'

'I'm sorry.' Leaving out their affections too? 'Which is Martin and Rob? That's Martin with the bald spot, isn't it?'

'And Dad's big ears. Don't mention Dad.'

'It's still like that?'

'I'm afraid so. Rob's OK. We're talking about you, Rob.'

He comes across with a glass of beer, and a sausage in his other hand. Rex Petley watered down, walking in a pigeon-toed way. Rex with his voice gone furry and his manner uncertain. 'Can't shake hands. Ha! It's good to see you, Jack.' He had once played Thomas Cup badminton, but could not foot it with the Indonesians. Rob had none of his father's pouncing quickness . . .

Jack cries enough. He sees that this is close to being diseased, introducing a dead man at the party and using him to measure his offspring by. He stops trying to stare Rob down, he blinks his eyes and chats about nothing; eats his steak – tender and bleeding and delicious – and after a while sidesteps off to look at the view. He had not realized they were so close to the edge of a cliff. A camellia hedge makes a barrier but he sees how children could slide through – have slid already judging from earth worn smooth between the trunks. Risk is part of childhood, cliffs and creeks; but a little bit of wire-netting . . . Jack stops himself again. He doesn't like his reflex of foreseeing sudden death. His father and Joy Petley had set it off all those years ago. But he should be able to control himself now; accept a percentage of deaths. He opens a gate (child-proofed) in the hedge and walks with a forward stoop to the cliff edge. Unagitated sea down there, making perfunctory foam on the rocks. He smiles at the words he controls his danger with, but moves back several steps all the same.

'Don't jump, it's not so bad,' Fiona says.

'I'll fall if you sneak up like that.'

They look at the view together but when he uses that word – view – Fiona says it gets in the way. This is the place she lives in, not looks at, and admiration isn't the right response. 'I hate seeing Rangitoto on postcards.' She steps to the edge and looks down. 'There used to be a path down there but part of it's fallen in. I wonder if I could get down now.'

He cannot stop his hand. He nips her blouse in his finger and thumb, and feels her shoulder blade underneath.

'Joke,' she grins. 'I'm too young to die.'

He understands he loves her, but it's easily contained and will not operate when he's away. It must show in his eyes for she stops her grin. She steps back from the edge and kisses him quickly on the mouth, then gives a little push on his chest to move away. 'We should have done it in the car that night. That was the time.'

'No,' he begins. He must let her know that all he does is love her. There is no need to possess. But Jack, who can put things exactly, cannot find the words for this. It's too simple and will take too much explaining.

'It's under control.'

'Keep it that way. I think Tom could get very jealous.' She seems to have just discovered it, and looks surprised. 'He might throw us both off the cliff.'

'Psychologists don't behave like that.'

Fiona shivers, then she laughs. She takes his arm and walks with him back to the gate. They lean on the outside looking in, with the sun striking their backs and barbecue smells drifting by; and Harry and John Dobbie smiling at them from the patio.

'I don't really care for that little man,' Fiona says.

Jack salutes him casually. 'Nor do I.'

'He was round here like a ferret as soon as Dad was dead. You could almost see him salivating.'

'Your mother didn't give him much.'

'She played the poet's wife. She's good at that. You know Dad's still the biggest thing that happened to her? He's the biggest thing that happened to Stephen too. But you're right. He wanted the inside stuff and Mum just gave him the party line.'

'I didn't see your name in the acknowledgements.'

'Or Martin's or Rob's. We've got an agreement. No talkee. People like John Dobbie are grave robbers. I'd tell you.' She angles her hand and taps him on the wrist. 'Dad told me once he warned you off his sisters.'

'I wasn't after them. He was wrong.'

'Is he the reason you couldn't make love to me?'

'It's a long time, Fiona. Let's leave it, eh?'

She turns her back on the house. 'You told me once Harry was switched off. Is she switched off now?'

Harry is laughing. He cannot pick her sound out from the party. Her distance from him stretches and he's on a road that bends away, and bends again, like in a dream. He wants to reach her. She'll turn with cool acceptance and she will help him out. 'We're all right. I'd better go and save her from the Elf.' Marriages are more interesting than affairs.

He ushers Fiona through the gate. Tom Pringle hooks her arm. Jack leaves her there and climbs the steps to the patio. He shakes hands with John Dobbie and admires the high polish of the man. He keeps himself so perfectly that hours must be taken up with grooming. He is five foot three but his silver hair gives him several inches. His pouter-pigeon chest increases him too.

'John.'

'Jack.'

Harry smiles into her hand.

'Sorry I couldn't get to your launching. I had a rather nasty sinus attack.'

'That's bad luck.'

'But it looks good. It's a nice book to handle.'

'Yes?'

'I like the cover photo. That's real Rex.' He is not going to say he likes the contents of the book.

'I found it in the Turnbull. Uncatalogued,' John Dobbie says. 'He looks like a despatch rider, don't you think? Until I found it no one knew he rode a motorbike.'

'I knew. I used to go for rides on the back.'

'Oh?'

'It's a pity his knee hides the name.'

'Yes? What was it?'

'An old BSA 1936. The Petleys used to call it the Beezer.'

John Dobbie blinks. Two little spots of red show on his cheeks. 'Of course,' he says, 'dredging up the facts can go too far. One needs, I think, to stand a good way off.'

'Sure. That's why I didn't bother you. I've got all sorts of stuff like that, but I think Rex liked a bit of mystery.'

'His sisters didn't say they called it the Beezer.'

'You saw them, did you? How are they?'

'The oldest one drinks too much, I can tell you that. I'm afraid she got sentimental. She wasn't much use.'

'Did you get to see Tweet?'

'Yes.' The Elf is quick to show he knows the name. 'All she wanted to do was talk about Rex getting hidings.'

'He did get plenty.'

'Frankly the sisters were disappointing. And I'm not sure the brothers can even read.'

Jack is the one under attack. He is sorry that he started this game and would apologize if he could find a way. The Elf can be hurt and is capable of sharp little punches in return. He has not got his range yet and Jack would like to stop him before he does. Surrender would cost him nothing, but he will not do it in front of Harry.

'What was Tweet's real name, did you find out?' He knows the answer, it's in the book – and he realizes, too late, that now the Elf will think he has not read it.

'Myra,' Harry says brightly. 'It's in chapter one.' She gives a sly grin. Harry had got no further than chapter one. (She did look in the index though, to see if she was there.)

'With a name like that,' the Elf says, 'it's no wonder they called her Tweet.'

'Wasn't it a family name?' Jack murmurs.

'A maternal grandmother.' The Elf shows off, talking of Petley forebears in England and Australia. He knows much more than Jack about this. 'One of them may have been a bare-knuckle fighter. I suppose the father's violence comes from there.'

'Yes, maybe.'

'And he married a woman who was a prostitute for a couple of years. I thought of putting that in an appendix.'

'Why didn't you?'

'I'm keeping it for the full biography.' He flashes his teeth. 'Alice has given me the go ahead.'

'Alice was only the first wife. What about Margot?'

'I think, you know, she was just a mistress. There were several of those.'

'He married her.'

'Yes, in the end. That was just to give the child a name.'

'So this full biography – you've started work on it?'

'I'm getting ready. It's a huge job, four or five years at least. The memoir will fill the gap nicely until then.'

'Well, you can put the Beezer in.'

'The memoir, you know, was really a preliminary sketch. I just wanted to get the feel of Rex.' He is fully restored and he glitters away, eyes and teeth, and polishes his fingernails on his lapel. Behind him Alice watches from a window. Jack wonders if she set him up for the Elf, and set her children up as well.

'Now,' John Dobbie says, 'the real job starts. Alice is going to let me use the papers. She wasn't very cooperative at first, but she liked the way I handled some of the more delicate stuff, you know, in the memoir.'

'And you want me too?'

'Well, Jack' – the Elf laughs – 'you're a great repository. This thing of mine will be definitive. I don't think you can afford to be left out.'

'How do you know I'm not writing my own book?'

'Ah Jack, you can't do Rex. Not without Alice. She's got a whole mountain of papers in there.'

'I can do a memoir though, like yours.'

'Rita Bullen said the same. I don't think Rex will support an industry. Major poet though he undoubtedly was.'

'Was Rita Bullen one of the mistresses?' Harry asks. She is giving Jack time to collect himself.

'That'd be telling,' the Elf says. 'I've got to keep some secrets.' He smiles. 'You knew him too, didn't you? I remember you at that party.'

'I never took much notice of Rex Petley. His poetry seems overblown to me.'

'Surely not the mid-career work? And the early stuff?'

Harry sighs. 'Poetry and I don't get along. And what I read I like hard and clean.'

'Well, hard and clean – that describes Petley exactly.' The Elf recites a stanza.

'Jesus!' says Martin Petley, walking by.

But Jack feels a prickling on his skin. The Elf does it well, and chooses well. There is the creek, and if not hard and clean then deep, dark, mysterious, exact. He wants to recite a stanza too but Harry stops him with a frown.

'I think that creek did Rex some damage.'

'Well, his sister drowned there,' says the Elf.

'No,' Jacks says, 'the other one. The creek on the other side of town.'

'That can't be right.'

'Good heavens, does it matter?' Harry asks.

'Yes, it does.' He goes into the house. Alice Wilkey beckons him but he turns the other way, down a passage. 'Toilet?' he asks a child, lying with her legs up the wall, reading a comic called – can that be right? – *Strontium Dog*.

'Along there.'

He finds the door ajar; and Leon Pittaway at the louvre window, peering at something through a crack. His head swivels round. 'I was here first.'

'Are you all right?' He's wedged between the wall and the pan, leaning off balance. A bottle of lavatory cleaner drips green blood from the cistern to the floor. Jack sets it upright.

'I could charge money for this,' Leon grins.

There's nothing left of his patrician loftiness. Age has ruined his face: rolled down his lower eyelids, made yellow bowls of his cheeks. Generic face, it lies on pillows everywhere. Yet Leon puts some life in it. 'Saw me,' he cackles. 'Little bitches.'

Jack slides into the gap on the other side. Veronica and the Danish girl are sunning themselves on a private lawn at the back of the house. Veronica is angry but the Dane is cool. She makes a bored face at Jack and does not hurry putting on her bra. She leans back on her arms and turns her face to the sun.

Jack mouths 'Sorry', trying to show he's not a peeping Tom. The girl is beautiful and there's no harm in looking, but it shouldn't be done from a lavatory window.

'Come on, Professor Pittaway.' He lifts the old man back on balance, but skids on the green liquid and they do a foxtrot turn in front of the pan. It gives Jack a tearing pain in his Achilles tendon; and Leon stamps his stick down on his toe. 'I hate you bloody poofters,' he says.

Jack sits him on the seat and backs away. 'Wait there.' He goes down the passage, steps over the child, and finds Martin Petley in the kitchen, lifting six-packs from the fridge.

'I think Professor Pittaway's in trouble in the toilet.'

'That's all I need.' Martin looks at Jack with dislike and pushes by him into the hall. 'Beat it you,' he says to the child, who takes no notice.

The lavatory door is locked. 'Come on out, Leon. What was he doing?'

'Spying on the girls through the window. He spilled the lavatory cleaner on the floor.'

'And now he's probably jacking off. Open up, Leon.' He bangs the door. 'Hey Leon, there's some sausage rolls left. I've got one here.' He turns to Jack. 'No point in you hanging round.'

'Well – '

'There's a dunny off the wash-house if that's what you want.'

Jack is pleased to get away. He uses the outside toilet, then goes down wooden steps into a yard surrounded by bougainvillaea in bloom. It's like being put down in Tahiti. The over-weening purple, its super-abundance, threatens him and he advances quickly, through and out; turns a corner, finds the girls on their patch of lawn.

'We don't like being spied on,' Veronica says. She's a pouty prickly girl and her dislike does not bother him; but he's hurt by the way the Dane turns her head away.

'I'm sure you don't.' There's no point in explaining, he sees how he would grin, ingratiate, and earn more scorn, so he steps by, eyes front, making for a wrought-iron gate that seems to open on to a side street. Out, away, escape the barbecue, with its literary elves and mad old men and disturbing younger generations. He crosses the road and hurts his Achilles tendon again, going down a grass verge on to a footpath. Best to shuffle for a while like an old man; but Leon persuades him against that – a face so dry and fractured that one hears crepitations. And the pink wetness of eye and mouth: pink is the colour of health – see Veronica's milk-drinking mouth – but in Leon it is what remains when red is soaked out and washed away.

Jack does not stride but achieves an uneven lope, decelerated. He does not know where he is going in this street of barbered lawns and sweet-orange trees. There's a white Mercedes on a tiled drive. There's a woman kneeling on a cushion, asking her roses to say ah. 'Burglar beware' the gate post says. Perhaps he should put on his tie. But when he takes it out he seems like a strangler and he stuffs it quickly back in his pocket.

Once around the block. Then he can drink another glass of beer and eat a sausage, and hook his arm, Tom Pringle-like, round Harry and drive home. He does not want to go inside the house. He does not want Alice Petley in her room of books; or her tame literary man; or the sanitized Life. But nor, for the moment, does he want the true past. Last time he visited Alice she had horrified him by pulling a rusty-stapled pamphlet from her shelves and asking him to auto-graph it. He had believed *First Fruits* long dead, and had stepped away with his hands held up in denial. But Alice lassoed him, led him to a chair, opened the thing at its title page, fitted a pen between his fingers and thumb.

He does not want to be in the same room as that signed copy.

The houses change from exclusive to desirable but the neighbourhood retains a grammar zone air. Large not small Japanese cars shine in the driveways. He turns right and the gulf lies ahead, inviting him to step down and walk across a tin floor to the inner islands. The view – no, that is banned – the prospect satisfies his desire to travel out and away. It's enough to do that with the eye. But a path with a motorbike barrier at the mouth angles down beneath pohutukawa. He favours his sore leg; and is jealous for Wellington that the descent is made in a back and forth way. That sort of dropping down is for the southern city. He finds a little beach between promontories, with houses set hard against the cliff. A path of pot-holed seal runs above the sand and he sets off along it for the further headland. Cliffs and rocks, meetings of land and sea, always attract him. He likes the change of element, which makes him feel he's close to knowledge and a source – although he's then dissatisfied not to find his way on from there. The cliffs are tame here though, and the sea is tame. Auckland-in-the-east has never invited exploration, even with Rangitoto sitting bare at the harbour mouth. One has to go west to the big cliffs and big sea for that.

Jack sees someone he knows. 'Hello,' he says. The man nods curtly and carries on watering his plants; and Jack walks on blushing. Television actor, elementary mistake. The fellow grins and prances in half a dozen ads and was a caning teacher in a witless comedy. Jack rubs his face, getting his foolishness away. He picks up a Coca-Cola can and places it neatly against a picket fence. A man in a dinghy, nosing in to shore, says, 'Gidday, Skeatsie.'

Jack stops. He leaves the path and walks down the sand. 'Skeatsie' puts them way back and he's not sure he wants to go there. He's disturbed, too, not to recognize someone who has known him at once. The man has grinning teeth in a sun-browned face. He steps into the water and heaves the wooden dinghy one-handed on to the sand. 'Got you beaten, eh?' Bare legs, tattered shorts; and a welt of scar tissue down the side of his neck, opening like a fan on his chest. There's a puckered nipple at the rim.

Jack looks into the man's face and makes his eyes go keen. But it's the scar that tells him. Rex had put that 'pink hand' in a poem.

'Tony,' he says. 'Tony Jameson.'

'Long time, Skeatsie.' They shake hands.

'Forty years, I guess. Almost.' He matches Tony Jameson's laconic style, although 'almost' is Skeatian. The time is thirty-eight years.

Tony reaches in the dinghy and takes out a box of cross-wound lines, with silver hooks safe in the cord. He stands with it under his arm as they fill each other in on what they have done. Jack draws his head back now and then from the smell of bait.

'Archives, eh? That's papers and stuff. I heard you were some big wheel down there.'

'Not so big.' He laughs modestly. 'How about you?'

'Done everything. Kinleith. Kawerau. I was on an oyster boat out of the Bluff for a while. Hard yakker, mate, but bloody good money.' Jack finds oyster boats difficult to believe for the pretty boy who got the girls. He's not pretty now – nose off centre, scaly head where his combed hair used to be; and the scar.

'Then I had a concrete-laying business for a while. How about you? You retired?'

'Yes.' It seems like a confession of failure. Tony says, 'Not me. I gotta keep on working or I'll curl up and die.'

'What do you do?'

'Collect garden rubbish. "Greensack", that's me. Two days a week. The rest of the time I make trellises. In the back yard there. Not a bad lurk.'

'That's your place?' A cottage with white walls and blue window-sills.

'Yeah. I sold that bit of land my old man had at Oratia. I couldn't have got in here otherwise. It's Round Table country, man. The rates are something fearful. We make out.'

'We?'

'Me and Pip. I got married again. It didn't take the first time, nobody's fault. How about you? Wife and kids?'

'Yes. Two children. Grown up and gone.'

'Come and meet the wife. Have a beer.'

'No, I can't.' He's pleased with this Tony Jameson, the man and his boat and his wife, after the girl-chasing youth and the boiling water. 'I'm at a barbecue up the hill. At Rex Petley's first wife. She's sixty.'

'That Alice sheila? He divorced her.'

'No, she divorced him, that's the way it was.'

'I met her once. You'd have thought I was the night-man. I had to meet Rex in the pub after that. Show 'im me scar.'

'He put it in a poem.'

'Cheeky bugger, he sent me a copy. Pip liked him OK though. See him on the telly, with all this book prize shit, she reckoned he was still a hooligan. Alice lives up there, eh?'

'Mrs Wilkey.'

Tony's eyes go click. 'That Wilkey?'

'Yes.'

'Big money, eh?'

'There's a fellow up there writing Rex's life. He'd probably like to have a look at your scar.'

'How much will he pay?' Tony grins; then waves the joke aside. 'Margot was the one I liked. There wasn't any bullshit. I still go out and see her. She makes a fair sort of red wine.' He bangs the dinghy with his foot. 'She gave me Rex's boat.'

Jack's mind drums like the dinghy. 'This one?'

'Yep.'

'I thought it sank.'

'The police launch found it, towed it in. She was swamped. Imagine an old pro like Rex getting caught.'

'A lot of people die out there.'

'Yeah, whole families.' He touches it with his toe again. 'Good little boat. Margot didn't need it. I've got to watch the weather though, she's no good when the waves get up.'

Jack looks at the spindly outboard on the back. 'Is that the same motor?'

'Yeah. It goes all right. I make sure I take a pair of oars though. Want a ride?'

'No thanks.' He wants to step back from the dinghy. He wants to get away from it.

The bait smell is the smell of Rex's death.

Notebook: 6

I forget which writer became convinced of 'the implanted crooked-ness of things'. It sounds like all writers to me; or like anyone who sees things straight.

From Auckland to Wellington was falling down a chute. One rattled down, bruised by the Limited, and came through the tunnel with aching joints and unwilling eyes and an ugly taste in the mouth. The Limited subtracted intelligence, and smoke and itch and shifting edge and downwards motion seemed the whole of life. Then out of the tunnel and Wellington burst like a bomb. It opened like a flower, was lit up like a room, explained itself exactly, became the capital. Wellington convinced me, for a while, of the straightness of things. It never became, in forty years, my home. I was an outsider, and some of the magic comes from there; the enduring strangeness comes from there. But I had a sense of growing up, of doing the adult thing I had not believed in for Jack Skeat. At last my life has started, I said.

The implanted crookedness came back, but Wellington kept itself free.

Auckland was never like that. Auckland was home.

1953. I was a primary colour and I used myself in combinations, all of them new. There's either a great deal to say or nothing at all. I hold these notes strictly to their subject or I let them follow their nose, which will it be? Rex came down, and I can bring him now, but is it Rex I want to write about? Don't I want to write about me?

I can say, he turned up on my doorstep late at night, soaked to the skin, stunned and stupid with cold – almost hypothermic, in fact – and I rubbed the grinning zombie down and got the girl out of my bed and put him in and poured hot drinks in him, and called a taxi for Brenda, but the last word is the one that interests me. She had a name, she wasn't just 'the girl', and I damage myself in calling her that; she was Brenda Littlejohn and I cared more for her than for

Rex. It does not matter that we made love only once. Her boyfriend was at Cambridge and before he left the modern fellow gave her a packet of condoms to emphasize he had no property rights; which offended her so deeply that she used them – only once. I worked this out later, getting over my rejection, and I'll admit I might be wrong. Her beauty over-excited me – it's no fun being beautiful – and I was too quick. That might have been a factor. But we had an interesting talk, waiting to try again, and I would have done the second one right; except that Rex banged on my door. And Brenda told me, next day, that she had decided to be faithful to Ben. They married, but it didn't last, and I lost track of her. She was, for many years, in the game men play, the best looking one of the ones I've had, although I worried about the style of having, did it count? But good looks and having fall into minor places and Brenda, what I know of her, is the point of writing this down.

She convinces me that I should confine myself to Rex.

He had hitchhiked down, coming a roundabout way through Taranaki to see a girl who worked as a journalist in Hawera. His last ride, from Foxton to the bottom of the Ngauranga Gorge, was on the tray of a truck. He climbed down so frozen he could barely stand, and walked along the shorefront to Thorndon and somehow found my three-roomed flat in Tinakori Road. Icy rain slanted into him all the way.

'You bloody moron,' I said, rubbing him down, 'don't you know this is Wellington?' I spiked his hair up straight and moulded his frozen skull and felt the limitations of what he carried in that squared-off container. Rex was short of common sense. Sandshoes and shorts and a football jersey, in August in a Wellington southerly. Numb-lipped and thick-tongued, he said he was sorry to take my bed. I was more than sorry to let him have it. On the other hand I felt a certain pleasure. Real life, crookedness, was confirmed. Also, I was shown to have a past.

I kept the gas fire on and lay in my sleeping bag in front of it and listened to him wheeze and snort and shiver through the night. Perhaps pneumonia was setting in and Rex would die in my bed. I grieved for him in a long dark dream, then both of us were savaged by dogs, and we climbed a tree that slowly bent and offered us.

Blood poured out like water from a tap . . . I woke to hear Rex saying, 'I'm bloody frozen, Skeatsie. Have you got another blanket?' It was four o'clock so I laid my sleeping bag over him and made a cup of tea, favouring my back where the worst bites had been, and we talked until morning. He had finished with university, he told me, and finished with getting stuff from books. Life was going to be at first hand now. As a programme this was not original. I told him we all got it first hand, whether we wanted to or not, there was no escape; and books, I said – the new librarian – didn't stand outside life but were a part of it. Don't insult all those dead writers, save it for the live ones, I said. Rex laughed. 'Looks like you've learned a thing or two, Skeatsie. Who was your girlfriend last night?'

I would not tell him. I asked about his parents and his sisters and got him back to what he meant to do.

'See the world.'

'That's hardly Wellington.'

'It'll do for a start. Is it OK if I stay for a couple of nights? Till I get a job and a bit of money?'

What had gone wrong up there, some woman trouble, some post office trouble? I asked. But he denied anything was wrong. It was time to branch out, that was all, and why not start with Jack in Wellington? I was pleased, although I did not believe him and told him so.

'I can't keep still, Skeatsie,' he said.

He had a great capacity for stillness, as I've said; for suspending movement, both intelligent and physical, while some new thing was planted in his brain. I took his complaint to mean that things were changing in his family. And when I asked about them again he was caught between his need to speak and the aggressive privacy I knew; so he advanced and then retreated, he began confessions and cancelled them with a rough movement of his hands.

Melva married the boy Rex had tipped into the gorse. A February wedding, just after I left for Wellington; and a June baby. 'She wanted me to hold it, but I couldn't. It made me feel – I don't know . . .' No rough gesture this time but a curious shrinking in his face. It was not the baby's earliness that upset him, but the baby. He found himself unwilling – unable – to open a door admitting it. His closed world had no room for new generations.

'Dulcie got engaged last week. And Mum's gone clucky, Skeatsie. I used to be able to talk to her.'

He had to leave in order to retain what he had. Coming to Wellington was self-preservation. In Wellington he kept still – although we rushed around to pubs and parties – and froze into shape, cemented in place, that perfect construct I have named 'the Petleys'. ('Petley' will do.) It became the template of his moral and emotional world, and left his intelligence free, up to a point. The ways in which it was enough, and then not enough, can be read in his poetry, if you know the language. For a while, because of it, there was nothing he could not look straight at, with a clear eye. Nothing, out in the world, was too much for Rex Petley.

I left him eating breakfast and went off to Library School, where my fellow student Brenda Littlejohn told me her decision. She was kind, which made me savage, and I replied she was a bloody coward – pleasing her more with this than I had in bed. In the afternoon we sat a cataloguing test, which I began intending to fail. The library trade was, quite suddenly, for second-raters. But taking up my *Sears List of Subject Headings*, which cuts the cloth of life and knowledge into neat little strips, I passed into countries of impossible relevance. ETHICS, I found, and then found HELL. Found JUSTICE, JOY AND SORROW, FUTURE LIFE. HONESTY, DUTY, SEXUAL ETHICS, BEHAVIOUR: everything was personal and adapted to me. FUTURE LIFE was not after death but how I would conduct myself tomorrow. HELL might be tomorrow too. LATITUDE: I knew I must not give myself too much. So I passed the test. And going out, smiled wisely at Brenda Littlejohn – which shows that HONESTY had some way yet to go. In fact my BEHAVIOUR was not much improved. I was, though, open to improvement, if not sure exactly where to find it.

SEX: I did without it, of necessity, for a while. I concentrated on FRIENDSHIP instead.

Rex had bought beer and steak, and some warmer clothes. 'I've got a job as a hospital porter, starting in the morning.' (That was how it was with jobs in those days.) He would ferry new patients to the wards, and from the wards to X-ray and theatre etc; and take the food trolleys out, collect the dirty laundry, turn patients too heavy for the nurses; change the oxygen; and now and then deliver bodies to the morgue.

He had the sort of job I would like.

'I thought you said all life was first hand, Skeatsie.'

'Yes, but for a couple of months – '

'I got the last vacancy.'

He did not want me there; possibly because he had decided to live with me. 'There's some filthy rooms around. Cockroaches like bloody Sherman tanks.' In the second-hand shop where he had bought his clothes he had also found a horse-hair mattress and a camp stretcher with a fractured leg. We splinted it and bound it with wire and Rex was my fellow tenant until Christmas. I let him have the sleeping bag and one of my pillows and he lay rigid on the narrow bed with his arms crossed on his chest like a crusader. Mutterings and groans and heavy breathing. Although he claimed not to dream I think he had whole zoos of night creatures in his head. Sometimes he laughed. Sometimes he seemed not to breathe. Dead silence. In the dark nights I came to think that he was dead. I rose on my elbows and strained my ears; I sat with my eiderdown turned back and my feet on the floor; I crept close and leaned over him. His eyes gleamed like fish in a pool. 'Are you going to kiss me or cut my throat?'

'Jesus Rex, I thought you were dead.'

'I was thinking.'

I scuttled back to bed.

'I like to think at night. There's nothing gets in the way.'

'There's monsters in the night.'

'Not for me. It's like dominoes.'

But when he slept again I heard groans and sighs and only the sleeping bag and the narrow bed kept him from ending the night in the shape of a St Andrew's cross.

He brought me a cup of morning tea and left porridge bubbling on the stove. Good housekeeping came from his mother. He folded his bed and mattress every morning, he cleaned the bath after using it, and he dusted in high places I had never thought to look. It offended me that Rex believed I did not wash enough. I answered sharply that I didn't wear second-hand clothes; but he showed me they were barely used – look at the cloth – and lectured me on the immorality of

94

waste, which was catching me on my own ground. So I shut up; and I washed again as frequently as my mother had taught me. I took up Rex's practice of striking a match after using the lavatory. I still do that. You'll find an old saucer of dead matches in there.

Our kitchen was big enough for one and I soon stayed out. Where did he learn to cook? Men cook today – they even do quiches, sauces, salads and desserts – but you've no idea how rare it was to even stir the stew in 1953. Rex, I think, tasted things in his head before he mixed them. I'm in the dark here. If I'm shown how to make a plain thing I can do it, but I don't dare add even a pinch of salt. I can follow a recipe. But making things up, experimenting! Is that why he was a poet and I'm not?

One or two of his pieces for children are recipes in disguise. The best known, 'Porridge', was written as I watched. Is there any New Zealand child who has not had it read to him (or her)? 'Her' should be the pronoun, for Wells – 'Porridge: for Wells' – was a girl. This is another thing I know that John Dobbie doesn't – 'the mysterious Wells, undoubtedly a child, probably a girl-child, but who?' Margot, John, who became his wife. 'He met Margot Stiles, a smallholder, in the mid seventies and married her in 1979, several years after the birth of their child.' I won't comment on 'smallholder' (where did you get the word?), but 'mid seventies', you are out by twenty years. She was our landlady's daughter in Tinakori Road and was nine years old when he wrote 'Porridge' for her. You'll have to go to Margot, John, you can't leave her out. Her Rex is the most important of all.

'Margot from Wells Fargo,' he said to the sandy overweight child at our door. Zane Grey must answer for the name. She was pleased with it though, after Rex had explained, and answered to Wells willingly. There are no more poems to Wells, and none to Margot; but then, there are none to Alice either.

I am not good with children. I change my voice for them and smile too much and pretend to interests I don't have. Some behave as though I'm touching them indecently. I was good – well, not too bad – with my own, but I've learned to turn away from other people's. I'd sooner offend the parents, for I like children. I watch them from the corner of my eye. That can seem suspicious too.

Margot did not like me when she was a child; and does not seem to like me very much now. I think she loved Rex from the start. She brought her homework in and he helped her with it: full stops, capital letters, addition, multiplication, things she really didn't need help with at all. They did the work together, for the fun of it; for the game they played of pretending not to know and getting wrong answers that were better than the right.

Overweight Margot. Freckled Margot with the crooked teeth (that were never put straight). Wriggly, screechy Margot. I soon found our flat – it was really just a bed-sitter at the back of a house, with a bathroom and a kitchenette attached – found it too small and I looked forward to the hour, increasingly delayed, when Mrs Stiles would bang on the permanently-locked connecting door and do her own screech: 'Margot, time for bed.'

'Nice kid,' Rex said, when she had gone.

'Does she have to come in every night?'

'Yes, she does. She's close to something pretty nasty, Jack, and we'll never get her out if she goes in.'

I did not know what he was talking about. The child was all bounce and flop, all puppy-play and loud unformed response. Something nasty? Where? What?

'Have you had a good look at that bastard who lives with her mother?'

'Sidgy?'

'Little Sidge.'

'He drinks too much but that's no crime. Are you trying to say . . . ?' Indeed he was, and I did not question it. I might be less observant than Rex but I was just as quick in understanding.

'Did she tell you?'

'She didn't need to. All you do is watch the two of them.'

'Have you told Mrs Stiles?'

'There's no point. Sidgy's what she's got and she's not going to risk letting him go. What she'd do is give the kid a hiding.'

'Yes, she would.'

'I'll have a talk with Sidgy, that's the way.'

'Yes.' Even though he might be dangerous. He was fat-faced and round-headed, with over-fine unhealthy cat-like hair and a grinny mouth. There were things to make you uncertain in his face. And his body, though small, seemed to have large stores of energy. He had short arms and legs with the muscles bunched-up hard, more complicated than muscles were meant to be. His sleeves were rolled up tight into his armpits.

'I'll come too.'

'No need. What I reckon is, he's probably done this sort of thing before. So if he knows someone's on to him . . .'

'Can't we tell the police?'

'They'd start asking Margot questions. She doesn't even know it's happening yet. I'll tell him to keep his hands off, OK? With any luck he won't stay around.'

'He'll go and do the same somewhere else.'

Rex had one of his spells of stillness. 'Maybe I'll just have to cut his balls off.' He did this sort of tough talking now and then and I was never sure it was an act, even though he put on a James Cagney voice. Sidgy though was more like James Cagney than Rex was.

I told him to be careful. In fact, I was terrified. My imagination went to work on Sidgy, equipping him with cat-feet, butcher knives, and a malevolence and cunning that, in the small hours, reduced our superiorities (they weren't only moral) to nothing at all. Coming through the yard, climbing the concrete steps beside the house, I kept away from shadows and took the corners wide.

But our superiorities worked well enough. 'The slimy little bastard,' Rex said.

'What happened?'

'He loves her like a daughter. I tell you what though Jack, he wasn't surprised. He couldn't keep his indignation going. Lots of little sneaky looks, trying to work me out.'

'He probably thinks you want her for yourself.'

'Jesus, I never thought of that. Anyway, now he knows, so he's not going to try it again. He reckons keeping Francie happy is a full-time job. He wanted to shake hands at the end.'

'Did you?'

'Sure Jack, it's experience.'

The next night he wrote that bubbly jingle about porridge, sitting with Margot cross-legged on the mat by the heater, on a page unstapled from her exercise book.

'Mum always forgets the salt.'

Rex put that in.

97

'Write "to Wells".'

He wrote 'for Wells'.

'Now it's mine.'

But when she had gone ('Margot!' Her mother, jackal-voiced, ruined her name) he took a notebook from his bag and copied the poem from memory, in the italic script he was teaching himself. He made improvements.

'How long have you been writing again?'

'A couple of months. Influence of Wellington,' he grinned.

The notebook was half full – you can see it (full) today in the Alexander Turnbull Library, where Alice deposited the drafts and manuscripts (she would not let the letters and the personal papers go) – and was three-quarters by the time I was able to sneak a look. I was looking for myself, for praise of me, however indirect, for signs that I was valuable to Rex, and looking, too, I have to admit, for his falling short. I was not ready for him to succeed where I had failed. But I did not find myself, except in a note – 'Jack's unwilling jaw' – and I found little falling short: found Rex Petley, found the poet. Not all the pieces succeed all the way and only two find a place in his *Selected Poems*. 'Porridge' is one. The other – it hollowed me out when I came on it, and made the hairs prickle on my neck – is 'First Visit to the Morgue'. You remember, he wheels the trolley in and takes off the lid and lifts the corpse, warty and ugly, on to a table – the jelly looseness of the limbs – and arranges it, and the nurse borrows Rex's comb and combs the dead hair, and it's only when he turns to leave that he sees, through a connecting door, the perfect child laid out ready on a post-mortem slab. It works, God how it works. There's nothing else. Nothing is needed. I read it and I groaned, 'No.' This was followed by a flash of joy. Rex was a poet.

I told him so when he came home. For a moment he was close to striking me. He grabbed the notebook from the table, where I had left it, and rammed it hard in his duffel bag, and might have walked out then. But he stood measuring my rights, and found them sufficient. 'You're a cheeky bastard, Skeat. You bloody wait until you're asked next time.'

'Yes, I'm sorry. But that's a marvellous poem. You've got to get that published.'

'I don't want it published. Not yet.'

'Merv Soper would take it.'

'Shut up, Skeatsie. See what I bought?' He picked it up from the floor, a black woollen overcoat with black shiny buttons. When he put it on its flared skirt almost reached his ankles.

'You're not going to wear it?'

'Good cloth. You feel.'

'You look like Jack the Ripper.'

'Who cares how I look? At least I'll stay warm.' He grinned at me. 'Second-hand, Skeatsie. Only five bob.'

'I'll walk on the other side of the road.'

Rita Bullen called it his rhyming cape, but that was in the following year when she discovered he was a poet. John Dobbie has a bit of fun, meant to be affectionate, with Rex as poseur. 'His poet's coat.' I'll go on record as saying that he wore it to stay warm. As soon as winter was gone (in Wellington it keeps coming back) he left it hanging behind the door.

I was his friend, with private knowledge of who he was. I didn't walk on the other side of the road but went along, matching steps with him, at his side. I grinned to myself in the company of minors and poseurs, and waited for him to come out. He was in no hurry.

'Rex is the only poet here,' I said, drunk.

'Sure,' he said, frowning, 'I write dirty limericks,' and turned it away. In his coat he looked as if that's exactly what he would do. 'You shut up about me,' he said, walking home.

'You've got to get those published, Rex. You've got to.'

'When I'm ready.'

He had written 'Cancer Patient' and 'Ward 10'. And yes, he had done it, picked the naked dry-stick man up from the floor, looked in his bright terrified eyes, put him carefully on his bed, wiped the shit off him – it is not made up. He had smuggled lipstick to the mad girl in Ward 10 and let her for a moment put his hand on her breast. It's all true but it wouldn't matter. The Elf – I'm tired of him and this is the last time I'll describe how he is wrong – concludes that the girl is Andra, because the poem is 'for Andra' and she spent time in Ward 10. He has done a bit of detective work and is right about 'this lovely troubled Estonian girl' but wrong in suggesting that she and Rex were lovers in the winter of 1953. I wanted to be her lover and I missed, then Rex came along and was her friend.

99

I see them at a party, in a hallway, she standing close and talking up, while her fingers twist the buttons of his coat. She seems to stand under his curve, like someone in a rock shelter keeping out of the rain. Easy for people to conclude that they were lovers. Or they're on the path out the back, in the half-light. She holds his lapels and wipes her face across and back, getting rid of tears. Rex jerks his head, sending me away.

When Margot went home Andra came in. I could not call the place my own. Yet I could not object for her grief was like something offered on the palm of her hand. Not everyone responded. Some people said that she whined. There was, too, a lot of anti-American-ism around, McCarthy was at his worst – most powerful – and hatred of the Russians was unfashionable, at least in the circles we moved in. Hungary was three years up ahead. Estonia? We did not even know where it was. I found it hard to understand how she could grieve so deeply for a country that seemed made up to me.

'That little Ruritanian,' Rita Bullen called her. Rita and Rex were lovers – but not yet, and it was only for a month. Lovers? No, they went to bed. Before that, though, Andra had made her two withdrawals from the world.

'Where is she?'

'In Ward 10.'

'What happened?'

He looked at me as though it were none of my business, but when I cried, 'She's my friend too,' he told me that she'd swallowed every pill she could lay her hands on; washed them down with milk; but had been found in time and pumped out and locked up in Ward 10.

'In time,' he said.

'You sound as if you want her to die.'

'She's dying anyway. She hasn't got a chance.'

I did not believe it. I thought he was romanticizing her. If she really wanted to kill herself she'd do it in a place where no one would find her. I still think that. I think he didn't read Andra right. And I think he loved her, in a way; a love that had, as part of it, acceptance of her death. There was something of the lurker in the shadows in Rex.

We watched her sail away on the *Wanganella* to her fellow Estonians in Sydney. We waved from the wharf, Rex did a scarecrow dance, and Andra smiled down prettily from the rail. She was on her way to another attempt. No one found her. Rex was in London by then. I see him keeping quiet, with his new friends. He turns away and wipes his hand across his eyes: I won't test the fiction, let it stand.

I would have given her a plainer sort of love, much faultier. I sometimes believe I could have saved her.

In December we had northerlies. I don't like that wind. A southerly comes from the Pole, bringing icy rain and sometimes snow, and cutting to the bone, numbing the bone. You bend into a southerly and fight back. It's an honest wind, the true Wellington wind. The northerly comes behind your back and punches you. It pushes you this way and that and puts a knee in your groin. It doesn't even make you decently cold and won't bring its rain in honest loads, but wets you and then, hypocritically, dries you out. It seems to have no source and no direction. Thumps the house, and leaves it still, then gives a sneaky heave and seems to push it out of square. All my days in Wellington I hated the northerly. In Tinakori Road it found a leak in our kitchenette and dripped discoloured water into a basin, through Rex's last weekend, day and night, off and on.

We visited Rita Bullen on Sunday afternoon and he told her he was leaving for Christchurch the next day. He made no attempt to soften it and just for an instant she looked as if he'd kneed her in the groin. But Rita is no softy, for all her displays of super-sensitivity. That's a game. Rita expects to be hurt and she does not make a fuss about it; even in poems; especially in poems. There's a very funny recent piece, 'Rough Trade', and I'm sure the man is Rex, although he wasn't quite as muscular as that. She's a great old backwards-looker, and not too inaccurate some of the time. Rita fights back.

We drank sherry and she drank too much, but it made her harsh not maudlin and she showed us 'callow boys' the door. Rex grinned all the way home. 'She's a bloody good poet, old Rita.' (She was thirty-six at the time.)

'Have you showed her any of your stuff?'

'Nope.'

'It'd be a bit tough for her.'

'Her stuff's pretty tough.'

We walked along in a break from the rain, with his coat crow-flapping about him. I asked him why he was heading south, what was there – colder places, smaller cities, that was all?

'Just for a look. I'll be back home for Christmas.'

'Here?'

'Auckland. Loomis town. You going up?'

'God no.'

'And then, in February, I've got a ticket for London. On the *Castel Felice*.'

'What?'

'An eight berth cabin below the water line. The Castle of Happiness.'

'Let me come too.'

'No, you stay here Jack, this is the place for you.' He patted me. And what can I say, I was comforted, I felt my solidity and worth. It seemed to me I had the better part. Was that his doing? Was it the sherry? Or just a lull in the wind?

'This town suits you.' I knew it was true. It was a town for clean bones and moral certitudes. It was platonic. Singapore, he said, as we walked along, Aden, Suez. In the grey streets I wanted none of them. It lasted only five minutes; and I grew loud in envy and declarations of coming too. But there was no desire in it. Tinakori Road seemed full of promise.

He had tried a Wellington poem, he said, but it wouldn't work. Leave them to Rita. She had some new ones that were great, they got Wellington the way no one else had managed – the houses and the hills, the crazy steps and zigzags, the crooked roads with treasure at the end (in Rita's case a mouth to be kissed). 'Not for me.' He didn't like the way the valleys wouldn't let you out, or the way things narrowed under the hills and left you with nowhere to go. 'They push you in the harbour. You end up walking on a slant.'

His not liking Wellington made it all the more mine. It was a place he would never have, and I would have.

Margot was sitting on our doorstep. 'Mum and him are doing it.'

'Tea and biscuits, Wells. Come on, you make it.'

She put the kettle on and laid out cups and sugar and milk and emptied the basin of water into the sink.

'Why do you have to go?'

'I've got to see the world, Wells. How can I know that you're the best unless I go and look at all the others?'

'Are you going to help them with their sums?'

'You're the only one I help with sums.'

'They'll be grown up. You'll marry them.'

'You can't marry more than one, it's bigamy.'

Their nonsense would not flow. She wanted him to see her pain, which was older than her years. Everything she said came out with an ugly childishness.

A door banged in the other part of the house. 'That's him going.'

'Without his tea.'

'I hope a car knocks him over.'

'I'll buy a car one day, Wells, we'll knock him over together.'

'You won't.'

'Wait and see.'

'You won't.'

'Pour the tea, it's going cold.'

'She won't get up for hours now.'

'Stay and eat with us then. Beans on toast.'

'Ugh!'

'Pancakes and golden syrup.'

'Yeah.' She had a smile that showed all her crooked teeth and made her innocent and beautiful.

We had pancakes and syrup, Rex cooking round the drip. Then they knelt on the floor and played knuckle-bones. She beat him although he tried to win. Real bones were best, he said, and the vertebrae of a small dog best of all. He told her how his sisters had dug up their fox-terrier to make a set. 'You're pretty good, Wells. You would have given Tweet a run.' It was the only time I heard him speak about his family to an outsider.

'Margot,' shouted Francie. (They don't broadcast wool auctions any more but if you've heard one of those wool buyers, that's her voice.)

'I've got to go.'

'Big smile, Wells.'

She tried. 'Will you write me letters?'

'I'll send you postcards. Ruined castles, how's that?'

'And the king?'

'Kings, queens, princesses, trained fleas, you name it.'

'Trained fleas.'

'Good choice. Shake hands, Wells, or is it a kiss you want?'

'Both.'

They shook hands gravely and kissed on the lips and she went to the door; where she turned and looked at him.

'Sidgy says wait until you've gone.'

It had stopped raining. In the silence a drop fell in the basin, plink!

'What do you think he meant by that?'

Her eyes slid away. 'I don't know. Give me some hidings I suppose.' But her sliding eyes had told the truth. She knew what Sidgy meant, she knew even better than Sidgy knew. Some part of it had happened before and she had put it out of her mind. Now it came back.

We've got to keep her here, I thought. But I was not in the conversation, I was not even in the room.

'Don't worry, he won't touch you, Wells.' He went to her and tapped her cheek. 'No hidings.'

They spoke in private, deeply: in tongues.

'Promise?' she said.

'I promise.'

She sighed. It seemed to me she almost went to sleep by the door. Rex opened it and put his hands on her shoulders and walked her out and sent her away.

'Jesus Christ,' I said, 'what do we do?'

'The dishes for a start. I'll wash, you dry.'

'I'm serious.'

'So am I. Keep out of it, eh.'

I badgered him, got angry; but kept quiet in the end when I realized that I was trying to give myself a place in the event. Moral place. And what event? I didn't really want to know.

When we'd done the dishes he looked at the leak. 'I'm buggered if I'm going to sleep another night with that.'

'I'm giving notice tomorrow. I'm leaving this place.'

'Good idea.' He got the broom and a yardstick and a wooden spoon and lashed them together and jammed the contraption between the ceiling and the sink, making a track for the water to run down.

'My old man couldn't improve on that.' His family were present on that night.

'What are you going to do about Sidgy, Rex?'

'Dunno.' His voice went flat, his eyes were flat. 'I'll see him in the morning. I reckon I'll have an early night.'

We both had an early night. Wind thumped the house, rain started up again, but Rex's anti-drip device allowed me some sleep. Feet seemed to pad on the lino. Doors seemed to open and close and draughts move down the walls and up from trapdoors opening in the floor. Haunted nights come with the northerly, I was getting used to them, and I burrowed in my blankets and tried to sleep. Woke with a lurch into the dark.

'Rex?'

'That bloody drip started again. I had to get up and fix it.'

'What time is it?'

'How would I know? Go to sleep.' He got back in his bed. I heard the canvas creak. 'Fucking Wellington.'

I made no answer. I heard him fit his back and buttocks into the mattress and cross his arms and breathe hard as though clearing bad air from his lungs. Why did I think that, bad air? Why was I so fully awake?

'Hear that?'

'What?'

'People talking.'

People shouting. Someone ran up the concrete steps beside the house and banged on our door.

'Your turn,' he said.

It was Francie, in her nightgown, with her wet hair plastered on her skull. 'Sidgy,' she shouted. She ran away and ran back. 'Sidgy's fallen down. Come and help.'

We went out and found him at the bottom of the steps. Two men knelt beside him: rain on spectacles, rain on an oilskin, beating hard. They held a fibrolite letterbox lid to shelter Sidgy's face.

'Don't move him,' as I bent down to see.

Blood thinned by water. Sidgy's nose and mouth scraped raw by the ragged concrete.

'Get some blankets. Get a pillow.' Someone had gone to phone for an ambulance. I ran up the steps and ripped a blanket from my bed and pulled my coat from behind the door, and took Rex's too and flung it at him where he stood holding Francie back.

'Right down the steps,' a neighbour said.

'Dumb bastard,' said another, 'stopping for a piss on a night like this.'

I saw what he meant: a gaping fly, a yellow penis. No one had been willing to put it away, but now they could hide it with my blanket. I had not brought a pillow so they eased a folded jacket under his head.

'It's my fault,' Francie sobbed. I can't remember any other time when she was quiet. Rex put his coat around her, then lifted it to shelter her head, and she stood like a little fat grieving prioress. He bared his teeth at me. He wanted someone to take her off his hands, and soon a woman came out with an umbrella and pulled her under it and held her tight.

'My fault.'

'Hush, love.'

We knew what she meant. On his pub nights, which were most nights, and on Sundays when he went to his after-hours place, she would not let him use the lavatory, he splashed the floor. So he stood at the top of the steps and pissed in the arum lilies before going inside. He believed he did it quietly but Rex and I heard his urine drumming on the wall. It was one of the reasons I wanted to shift.

'Where's Margot?'

He turned and looked at the house and I saw her there high up at the sitting-room window, with a yellow bulb behind her shining like the sun. I could not see the expression on her face. Perhaps I just imagine that she smiled.

Sidgy lost his footing, the coroner said. He went head first down those fifteen steps and suffered this and that, and that proved fatal. No witnesses. He had a word or two to say about the dangers of drink. Rex was gone by then and I was in my new flat. He got his coat back and I got my blanket.

'Bye, Rex, keep in touch,' I said at the ferry.

'I will.' He looked flatly at me and I looked flatly back. I hid my horror and my admiration.

His coat was wet already when I snatched it from the door.

Does my silence make me an accessory?

Notebook: 7

I am always careful on stairs. I slide my hand on the banister and if there isn't one I count to help my concentration. When I see young people leaping down as nimble as goats, back-chatting one another, hands in pockets, humming tunes, I'm tempted to stop them and point out the danger. I've known two men who died on steps so my nervousness is understandable. I don't like people walking behind me, coming down. I always stop and let them go past.

Wellington has flights that should be closed. There's one in Ngaio slimed by overhanging trees, with treads that slope downwards and risers of unequal height. It saved four minutes on the walk to the station so I went that way, never though without a sense of risk. But I was young and bounced down hand in hand with my new wife, and never fell. I must not exaggerate the dangers or let myself be thought a wimp. It is not a common death. In fact I know of only Merv and Sidgy, and Sidgy was pushed.

But the eye is lifted up or dragged down in that city. One stands at the top of a flight like standing on a cliff and sees little figures, saucer faces, down below, or one looks up and sees long torsos shrinking into flat worlds; and life is always up or down. Getting there, in Wellington, requires risk and strain.

When I opened *Landfall* I felt as if I'd been pushed down a flight of steps. There he was: 'Seven Hospital Poems: Rex Petley.' 'First Visit to the Morgue', 'Ward 10', 'Cancer Patient', and the rest: 'Barium Meal', 'Autoclave', 'DOA', 'Trolley Race'. (Later he added 'Fractures', 'The Dying Politician', 'Little Nurses', 'Oxygen', to make that sequence of eleven everybody knows and Rita Bullen claims he never improved on.)

He had gone south to see Charles Brasch and lay the poems in his hands. We know about the visit from the letter Brasch wrote him later on, that John Dobbie got his hands on and reproduces almost in full. ('Lay the poems in his hands' is pure Elf, it has the reverential tone that 'the oeuvre' and Brasch and *Landfall* and anyone judged 'major' will bring out. There's a curious self-abasement in Dobbie. He forgives Brasch for turning down his poems.)

I am putting off my hurt. Rex should have told me. He wrote the poems in my bed-sitter and should have told me where he was going and, later on, that Brasch had liked them. I felt myself tumble headlong down. Then I leafed through, one to seven, desperate to see 'for Jack' on one of them. That would save me. That would put me at his side for the world to see – but there was nothing: only 'for Andra' on 'Ward 10'. And there was never to be 'for Jack', or 'for' anyone again. Only Wells and Andra got poems from Rex and they were people he passed by and knew only for a month or two – although, as I've said, Wells came back. And none of his books has a dedication. There's not even the usual 'for my parents' on the first. That should make me feel a little better – but the hospital poems are part mine, I insist. He should have known.

His biographical note said: 'A young Auckland poet at present living in London'. I saw how right, how just, that was – free from boasting, free from modesty. It made me blush with shame at my *First Fruits* posturing. Others were having trouble too. Rita Bullen telephoned me at work.

'Why didn't you tell me?'

'He wouldn't let me, Rita. He didn't want anyone to know.'

Have I said that once or twice, by now, I'd been in Rita's bed? I'm not going to say how we got on. She doesn't say. I'm not rough trade and I didn't hurt her so my passing in the night (it was afternoon though, she did not want her young men hanging round after dark) is not recorded in verse. But Rex, damn and blast him (Rita's oath), spoiled that too. She never asked me back after his hospital seven came out. And she did not forgive me for laughing at her decision that they had been written in the several weeks of their affair. She was sensible enough not to make the claim again, although I've heard she hinted here and there (Rita was quite a poet-starter, started off two or three, I've heard). She doesn't change her opinion that those *Landfall* poems are the best he ever wrote.

I sent my praise, concealed my hurt, and he replied on cards. I don't know how he lived in London. John Dobbie tells us but I don't trust him. The young poet in the drab and dirty 1954 metropolis, drinking in pubs, going down to the dole office in a gang of 'young antipodeans' for the weekly handout (yes, the British gave out money to colonials for a while), and partying on rotten-hulled houseboats, and making paper darts of poems and flying them off Battersea Bridge (I don't believe that one, I've read it before, about someone else), and finding the place where John Keats lived and reciting the Chapman's Homer sonnet there (don't believe that either) – the Elf puts it all in; but I remember Rex saying, 'Jesus Jack, I just say the first bloody thing that comes into my head.' There's no documentation of his London year. There are just a few odd things he told journalists now and then. I have not been able to find a single reference to his time in England in his poems, and nor has the Elf, although he tries harder. Once he mentions swans, but we have those, and lockgates once, and Guinness, and he uses the unlikely adjective 'serpentine' – but who cares anyway, I certainly don't. It's much more interesting that he went to Spain and saw the Goyas in the Prado. Goya was his hero all his life.

He posted me a card from Madrid – 'The Execution of the Defenders, 1808' – 'Have a look at this, Jack. Who needs words? Good wine here. Good olives. Come on over.' It was one of the few invitations he ever made me.

This is chatter, this is gossip, I'll stop. He passed out of my life for another year – no more cards. When I took Harry to Loomis to meet my mother (my biro is struck with paralysis at that) I ran into Lila in the street and found that he had been back in Auckland since May and was living in Devonport and working at the Chelsea sugar-works.

'Don't be offended, Jack. He doesn't see anyone very much.'

Falling down steps, I almost did it again, but Harry was there to hold my hand. Before we visit Rex we'll visit her, we'll visit me. I'm tired of putting him in the centre all the time.

I saw her first as I walked down steps. There were two young women side by side, sunning themselves, and I have to say (and Harry knows it) that I noticed my future wife second. If I go for closer honesty, then I barely noticed her at all. (She doesn't know that.)

I had taken a bed-sitter in Kelburn, just past the string of shops now called 'the village'; towards the bridge over Glenmore Street and close to the steps where Merv Soper was to die. I walked down town each morning to my work in the public library: along Upland Road, up the steps, down the steps, into Central Terrace, and down the dizzy flight to Glasgow Street, through the university, across The Terrace, and down, always down, the paths and steps of Allenby Terrace. That last plunge was (still is) a grotty back way, past the windows of half-furnished rooms, past rotting aerial ways into kitchens, and the sharp right turn where if you chose to go straight on and make a running jump you would land on the roof of Saint Mary of the Angels. Allenby Terrace, with students springing up, gazelling down: that is where I saw Harry second.

It was a Saturday afternoon. I was on my way to a cricket match at the Basin Reserve – walking all the way because I did not really care for cricket all that much. Late March, 1955. I wanted to pick my life up and run with it somewhere. Nothing would quite end and nothing begin. Don't mistake me, there's no angst. I was beginning to be uncomfortable with my mediocrity. To buoy my spirits up I whistled myself down. I whistle well, with good mobility in my lips and tongue. I can, if you want them, do bird calls. (I do the tui with a glottal stop.) But I was whistling something gypsy from Dvořák on that day.

Valmai Dunn was sitting (with her friend) on a lean-to roof level with the top of the wooden fence. It covered the kitchen of the flat she shared with four other students (Harry was one). Valmai: offered on a tray. Her back was to the second-storey wall, her face was slanting to the sun, her hands rested on the closed book in her lap, her skirt was pulled up to bare her legs (her long long legs), and her toes played piano as I came down. Her eyes were closed. (Harry, at her side, was, I think, watching me.)

Her loveliness (Valmai's) took my breath away; it dried my mouth. Dvořák fell silent; and Valmai's toes fell still. She opened her eyes with a frown. They fixed on me, they penetrated, sliced into my skull. Then I had to pass below the wall.

I could not let that ice-blue gaze be cut off from me. So I smacked the steps with my rubber soles. I flicked the Penguin from my pocket into the gutter. I cried out sharply, thumped the wooden fence with my palm. (A piece of rotten wood sprang from the top.) Then I sat groaning, with my hands wrapped around my ankle and my torso bending with the pain.

They took their time coming out. A man who had seen my performance went by with a curious smile. Then the wooden door scraped on the path and Valmai, with her skirt down, edged out.

'Are you all right?'

'I think I've sprained my ankle.'

From the way she bit her lip and looked back through the gate I should have seen I would get nowhere.

'Harry,' she said.

There were thumps on the wall. The gate jerked open another foot. I expected a tanned giant to appear but a little glittery dark girl walked out. She looked at me measuringly and I turned away. 'I'll be all right,' I gritted at Valmai.

'You'd better come in, I suppose.' I let her help me up, which she did slack-handedly, while the other girl went ahead and opened the kitchen door.

'What do you do for sprains? A bucket of hot water or something?' Valmai said.

I took off my shoe and sock and lowered my foot on to the lino. 'Ow,' I said. 'I'm Jack. Hallo.'

'I'm Valmai. That's Harry.'

'What are you, students? Besides nurses?'

Harry gave a grunt of annoyance. She left the room. And Valmai, beautiful, lethargic, and already uninteresting – desirable though, like cake – fetched a basin of warm water and put a towel and bandage in my lap.

'It isn't swollen,' she accused, when I took my foot out.

'It will be by tonight. You wait and see. I'm lucky I didn't break my ankle.'

I was looking for Harry to come back, because that was where interest lay; and I would have to get on with her while going about an elementary task with the lovely Valmai. (So I think of her, and thought of her then, almost instantly – formulaic language, making her less than she was; and I must apologize, and resist 'poor Valmai' too; 'poor' because she was not happy, never was, and because she died of cancer in her thirties. I wonder who she really was; and I regret the chance I missed to know her. It has been that way all my life, I stop off at exteriors.)

Valmai watched while I bandaged my ankle. She made no move to help, although she put her finger on the knot while I tied; and she did not put the kettle on.

'What subjects are you doing?'

'English and history and French.'

'I did those. I did my degree in Auckland.'

'Oh yes.'

'I work at the public library now.' The male librarian seldom rouses much interest in a woman; not by naming his trade. 'I'm a poet too. A bit of a poet. I see you're reading Wordsworth.'

'We have to.'

She shocked me with her lack of enthusiasm; the narrowness of the mental space she seemed to occupy. So I went back to exteriors, I watched her move, which she did with no energy but some grace, and I looked for animation in her face but saw only beautiful modelling there. (I was never to see that flash of blue in her eyes again. It was almost impossible to startle Valmai. She did not want anyone to find out who she was.)

I put on my shoe and thanked her, and said I would come back and say thanks properly one day; and I went into the yard, and there was Harry on the kitchen roof; plump and plain and sharp-eyed, measuring me.

'How did you get on?'

'Sorry?'

'With Valmai? How did it go?'

'She gave me a bandage.'

Harry grinned. 'For your sore ankle. Don't forget to limp.'

'What do you mean?'

'You left it too long before you bumped the wall.'

'No,' I said; and then gave up. 'Are you going to tell her?'

'I'll just watch. It might be fun.'

'Can I come up and sit in the sun for a while?'

'You'll dent the roof.'

'No I won't, I'll stand on the joists.'

She did not know what joists were and I explained as I climbed the bank and balanced my way across the plank that served as a bridge. I sat with my back to the wall on a cushion with Valmai's dent in it.

'Where did you learn all that?'

113

'I worked as a carpenter's labourer in my holidays.'

'Where?'

'In Auckland.'

'I'm from Auckland too.' She turned her sharp eyes on me and I saw (perhaps saw later, I'm fooling myself if I claim to be accurate and truthful in all this) – I saw a willed aggressiveness, a willed projecting of herself, that hid her desire to be still and quiet and know her natural shape. (Yes, that sort of understanding must have come later.) We sat in the sun and talked about Auckland, her part, the North Shore, my part, Loomis, and agreed that we missed mud and mangroves, sub-tropical rain, summer humidity, still days – this in the middle of a hot still Wellington afternoon – red volcanic soil, city beaches, flat land, ferries, Queen Street, orchards and vineyards and Dalmatians, Muriwai and Piha, yachts and Rangitoto and the gulf; and although I began to argue for Wellington then I could not produce a list coming near to that. She would not allow Wellington any attractions at all. The harbour, which I had come to love – 'It's so dramatic' – she called a puddle; and the city, which I loved too – 'A real city, not just a glorified main street' – was 'all scrunched up, the hills are squashing it. I hate the hills'.

'What about the mountains?' waving my hands at the Orongorongos, resting in the sun like a herd of elephants.

'They're all right. They're good. They make you think the city shouldn't be there at all.'

'I don't suppose it should be. It's the wrong place for a city, that's why I like it.'

'I'm going back to Auckland one day.'

I knew that I would not let her go.

I've never seen before how like a romance it is – one of those teenage things my daughter Jill read for a while (and I leafed through to find out where she was). He fakes an accident to meet the lovely blonde and meets instead the quiet little friend. (It's called, I believe, 'the cute meet'.) I can't find an adult component; but it led soon enough to adult things – if that's the word for marriage, babies, and a life together.

But I must say, first, who she was. I'd found out 'Harriet' with a question, straight off, but it sounded like some husband-hunter in

Jane Austen, she said, and she didn't let anyone use it. Her father was a dentist who had joined his brother in practice in Palmerston North several years before – so Harry lost Auckland. Her parents would not help her through university unless she stayed within visiting distance of home, so here she was, in her last year of a BA, stuck in Wellington.

'I'm going back next year though, I'll be free.'

'What will you do?'

'I don't know. Training College, I suppose.'

'Don't do that.' I quoted Shaw, 'those who can' etc. Harry told me to mind my own business.

'Go and tell Valmai. She likes it here.'

'I'm finished with Valmai,' I grinned.

'That was quick.' Harry grinned back.

'She looks as if she needs an extra joint in her legs.' I betrayed the poor girl – let 'poor' stand – and Harry laughed, doing the same. (And ever after I was put off by Valmai, her long legs seemed unnatural.) She looked out shortly afterwards and saw me using her cushion, and went inside and did not come back. But her afternoon seems as interesting now as mine; I can never know it – and I mustn't let this complex molecule, Jack Skeat, lock on to her by speculation or else every other will join too – a monstrous explosion – and I'm not equipped to speak about that. Just me and Harry. We talked for an hour or two and I called for her that night and took her to the pictures, kissed her at the door, and was back on Sunday . . .

Harry, what am I doing with this pen and exercise book? Can I write down how we went on? Whose business is it anyway? I can answer that. It has turned into story. It's story's business. If you ever read this don't tear it up or burn it. Add your version, make corrections, be selective, disagree. You'll start to see what has happened then. You'll see that what I write is no betrayal.

Long before I left that day the places were reversed – Harry (Valmai).

And now I come to that midwinter night when we made love for the first time. When I think of it I'm joyful, and we must not leave joy out, there's too little of it anywhere. Memory sometimes seems the important thing – after, of course, the event. Their magical interdependence is our condition of good health. Neither can exist without the other. Without memory there is no event.

Wind and sleet, Wellington weather. The flatmates stayed in so out we went, in oilskins, and gumboots for Harry, and turned our backs to the southerly and climbed by way of Salamanca Road to the botanical gardens. We splashed in running gutters and skated on the grass and Harry sat down and slid. I took her by the legs and ran with her and when she had enough speed let her go and she went a hundred feet on her back, turning slowly, sliding quick, down the hill towards the trees. I thought I had killed her. She went between two trunks, curving fast, with her legs crooked upwards and her oilskin flaps between her thighs, and gave a dying shriek – what was it, pain, delight? – as the flat ground slowed her down. I ran after her and spun off trees, skinned my palms, and overtook her as she came to a stop. She lay in the dark with her white face shining at me. 'I want to do it again.' Now isn't that better than sex? But we didn't do it again, we turned to that. In a shelter rocked by wind I put her hand inside my outer layers, guided it.

'I just want you to know it's there. We don't have to use it.'

'I know it's there, I'm not silly – why can't we use it?'

'Where?'

'Have you got an Alphonse?' (Now Harry, that will embarrass you. Alphonse was french-letter in girl-talk that year.)

'Yes, but we can't lie down.' Puddles on the asphalt floor. (And at my place a landlady guarding the door, beside which the rules were tacked, no alcohol, no noise, no visitors – meaning no girls. The roofs should have blown off some of those Wellington houses with the suppressed pressures inside.)

'Valmai told me once she did it against a wall.'

Valmai had long legs though. 'You're too short.'

'I'll get some bricks.' And because I was unable to stand down she went into the rain and fetched them in, one at a time, four trips, and placed them properly – so far apart, a little further, loving it – and stood on them and we were matched; and coupled; and complete; and very pleased with ourselves, though dressed, uncomfortable and wet.

That is all that story asks.

'Your bum's cold.'

'So's yours.'

We covered up and ran to Allenby Terrace, against the rain, and I ran home.

And we were lucky. Harry would agree. All sorts of things go wrong in beds. There's nothing much can go wrong in a shelter on a wet and windy frozen Sunday night. Standing upright. In puddles. On bricks.

Our first time was memorable.

That's summer and winter. Leave autumn for the moment and come to spring. (The seasons are not significant.) In spring I took Harry to Auckland to meet my mother. I had visited Palmerston North and been approved (more than that, I had liked her mother and been liked) and now it was Harry's turn. Her examinations were over; she had to sit a more demanding one.

We travelled by air, a first for both of us, and I was able to show her Loomis as we came towards the airport at Whenuapai. The west coast beaches lay in their bites of land, the ranges, patted flat, spread a grey-green bush-stain down the valley. Paddocks, orchards, vineyards, made sharp and shallow angles and contrasts of green. The creek was a tree-line, bending lazily, and the town a little pasted-paper game. I found our house but was not quick enough to show Harry. She was straining to see her side of the harbour, the North Shore.

We used the Loomis taxi. My nervousness had made Harry nervous. Stained and damp and malodorous we faced the straight cold lady in the door. I kissed her cheek and smelled her chilly dryness; and pulled myself together, for Harry's sake and mine; and winked at Harry as her kiss was checked and she was made to shake hands. Though shake is wrong. Flat palm, no finger-curl, and quickly ended – that was my mother's way of meeting. She made no alteration for her future daughter-in-law.

Later, when Harry was out of her slacks and wearing a clean dress, and had brushed her hair and washed her face and put fresh lipstick on, and we were drinking tea in the living-room, my mother said, 'I'm afraid I shan't be able to come to the wedding.'

'Why not?'

'Palmerston North is too far away.'

'You could fly.'

'I think not. I'm sure Harriet will understand.'

And Harry, with a cool smile, Harry pulled together, like me, said, 'It is a long way, Mrs Skeat. I do understand.' But could not resist: 'As long as Jacko gets there, that's the main thing.'

Friendship between them had never been likely. The joke, the name, ended any thought I had of it.

'My husband and I chose "John" carefully,' my mother said, 'and I do think that in my house . . .' She let it trail away. Genteel incompletion was one of her ways of showing dislike. Harry heard beyond the murmur and saw beyond the smile.

If her cheeks went red there was a chance of cut and thrust. I would have preferred her hot to cold. But Harry is strong and she managed the harder way.

'I've made a choice too. In certain circumstances Jacko is right. Although perhaps not drinking afternoon tea with Mrs Skeat.' That's most impressive for a girl of twenty. It pleases me still. Her tiny smile mirrored my mother's and her teacup made only a single chink as she put it down.

So it was cool exchanges and gloved antipathy. Harry punished me a little as we walked in Loomis in the late afternoon – called my creek a ditch and laughed at the war memorial gates – but she held my hand as I talked with Lila Petley and bounced the swing-bridge when we crossed that way. We went into a vineyard and bought a bottle of sherry, and met, blanket-clad, in the summer house that night. We drank and made love, drank and made love, marvellously; without Alphonse, without thought – unless it was the thought of my mother in the house. Harry, I suspect, would have liked her to have known what was going on.

I have never been sure she didn't know. In her own house she knew everything.

My 'accident' in Allenby Terrace brought about another 'cute meet'. By roundabout ways I discovered my work.

This is the autumn of that *annus mirabilis*. I was shelving books when a voice said at my shoulder, 'I hope you've recovered from your fall.'

I faced a clean white gentleman with a rosy face and hair as light and soft as a baby's. The stirring in the air as I turned made it lift. He wore a perfect tie and a summer overcoat and shining shoes and only his smile was unorthodox.

'I would have stopped to help you but I thought . . .' And seeing my incomprehension: 'In Allenby Terrace. Oh, about a month or two ago.'

'Ah. Yes.' It was the man with the curious smile. 'Some girls in the flat came out and helped.'

'So I noticed. Nice girls, were they?'

For a horrible moment I thought he was a pansy. (I use the term for historical accuracy.) But a woman approached, a clean little lady to go with the man, and they stood together, so beautifully normal (although antiseptic) that I relaxed, I put myself perhaps too much at ease. And soon the man, Euan Brightmore, wanted me.

'It would only be for three months. And I could pay, oh, what you're getting here. I'm sure as experience it would stand you in good stead.' He picked a book from my hand. 'These are a product. In your profession I'd look for the source.'

'Well – '

'Chaos and order, my boy. A system is a kind of philosopher's stone.'

'Don't confuse him, Euan,' his wife said.

But I was not confused. My base metal was changed by Euan Brightmore. Not by his talk of systems, there were plenty of those in librarianship. By 'source'. By 'chaos and order'. Some of the processes would be moral.

And I was excited by opportunity.

I left my job and worked for Euan Brightmore and turned myself into an archivist. He was, as he said with a smile, not unknown. He is just about unknown today. What little fame he has rests on the papers I put in order in those months – they turned out to be six – I worked for him. He could, of course, have done it himself but was 'too lazy'. I defend him from the charge. He worked eight hours a day on his huge and still unpublished autobiography. It has since been added to the Brightmore papers in the Turnbull and is a prime source of information about literary life in 'the Dominion' between the wars. I am there, towards the end, in the dull post-World War Two part: 'my intelligent and industrious archival clerk'. There's no mention of *First Fruits*, I kept it secret. There's mention, there's praise, there's alarming praise, of forgotten poets (and 'poetesses') of the teens and twenties and thirties of this century; there are panegyrics on Homeward-looking novelists; and diatribes on Mason, Glover, Fairburn etc. Anyone now judged good is damned. Indeed there's a law that operates – cultural, aesthetic, historical – and it gives the Brightmore papers their value and fascination. A new age and outlook grates along the edge of the old. The wincing and the screeching and the anger and the pain – the shrinking, the sadness, the turning away, and the forgiveness now and then – all are there, in letters – how they wrote letters, how he wrote (and made copies) – and in his journal, in his notes, in his *Articles of Faith: a Life in Literature,* in his novels (published and unpublished), in his verse.

What a kind little man he was outside the giant anger and the pain. Euan had intended to be 'great' – they believed in 'great' – and was on his way until a 'clique', a 'coterie', sometimes even a 'congeries', of 'avant-gardiste poseurs' betrayed him. He could not see it was the times, the age, it was New Zealand. Poor dislocated fellow, he stayed on his wrong angle for the rest of his life – in, of course, plentiful company.

I kept very quiet and worked on the papers. I saw how valuable they were. I found my trade. Preservation became an absolute and put me in a moral workday universe.

Notebook: 8

We walked down Alma Street with Lila Petley and she gave us tea and pikelets in her kitchen. Les was not at home but Lila opened his workshop door and showed us a bench of freshly painted ambulances and fire engines and trucks. They were unfussy, functional; white and red and yellow and blue; and they made me wonder if Les had returned to some primary state and left his anger behind. But when I asked Lila how he was she shrugged and said, 'He doesn't change. Maybe he's not so rowdy I suppose. He's gone to the footy with the boys. He needs one on each side to keep him out of fights.'

She had pikelets made in minutes – a whisk, a sizzle, butter, jam – and they were delicious. I asked her what she thought of the hospital poems and a look showed on her face as though she had opened the oven and found something perfectly risen inside. It quickly passed. She said, almost wearily, 'Good. They're very good. Do you think so?'

'Yes, I do.'

'We don't worry about Rex any more. Les wonders how he's going to make a living, that's all.'

'Poets go hungry. It's part of the job. Maybe there'll be some sugarworks poems.'

'Oh, there are. Tweet went over to see him last week. We go there. He doesn't seem to like coming to Loomis any more.'

'He doesn't want to disturb it, that's the thing. In his head.'

'Don't romanticize him, Jack.'

She saw him, I think, as shifted into a world with different laws from her own; where he would suffer pain, and do his work, and earn rewards she would never know about. She was convinced of him, convinced of 'poet', and was prepared for sufferings consistent with that. Lila, not I, romanticized him. Her weariness, her switching off, were a way of acceptance.

I felt sorry for her. I praised him extravagantly, careless of Harry, who had found the hospital poems cold and cruel. Lila smiled a moment, then yawned.

'Dulcie's got a baby, did you know? And Melva is expecting again.'

A rattle of wheels on the doorstep and Melva backed in, with her pushchair laid on an angle and her child off balance, grabbing the air. I had never seen a woman so huge in front, I could not see how she kept herself from toppling forward. She cried my name and hugged me and I felt lumpy parts of baby inside and made up my mind I would never put Harry in that condition. Lila took the child from the pushchair and hugged it as hard as Melva was hugging me.

'He's dirty, Mum, watch out,' Melva said.

We smelled him. I gave a sickly grin at Harry, who gave a false one back. No babies! This was the one – called Tod from the time he had toddled, nicknames in that family had a way of holding on and I never learned his real name – this was the one Rex had not been able to hold. I did not blame him. There was something too raw and greedy there. A baby could throw fine balance out with its gross life and importunities. Meaning might not survive a baby. I understood how fragile 'Petleys' might be.

We said no to more pikelets after the dirty nap, and said goodbye and Harry bounced the bridge; and the next morning, after our summer-house night, we went, alive and yawning, hand in hand, by bus and ferry and foot, to Devonport to make a careless visit on Rex. Harry did not mind if she met him or not. She was happy just to be on the ferry, slanting across-tide to the Shore. I had promised her we'd go to Takapuna if there was time.

Lila had said he might not be home. He spent a lot of his spare time fishing from the wharves and from the rocks between the beaches. You could still catch snapper in those days. He had sent a twenty-pounder, scaled and gutted, home with Tweet, together with a note on the best way to cook it. (Lila sniffed.) He had a net too that he set across the mouth of a creek and once he had dropped in with a box of flounder that kept the family eating for a week.

We walked from the ferry to Albert Road, where he had a room in the basement of a house. 'If he's not home we'll climb up there,' pointing at the grassy sides of Mt. Victoria. It was almost sheer, with terraces that seemed designed as handholds; and it made me think of Harry, breasts and hips, and making love. Her mood was different, she had arrived at childhood places and did not need me. I've had to learn this – there are many times when Harry does not need me. She wanted to get down to the beaches and tuck up her skirt and walk in those little Sunday waves that pass for broken sea on the east coast. Cheltenham and Narrow Neck were just around the corner. When I touched her in the way that had become our sign she said sharply, 'Don't do that.' (There has been, in our marriage, a fair amount of 'don't do that', and much repositioning, not all of it from me.)

I was, then, more pleased than she to find Rex at home. He had the use of half the lawn at the back of the house and he lay there on a towel, with his head in the shade of a lemon tree, reading a book. (For those who want such things, it was *The True Confession of George Barker*. Someone else can work out if it influenced him.)

'Mum said you might show up.'

He got to his feet. There was a reluctance in him that put me off balance. 'Show up' seemed less than welcoming too. He touched me on the shoulder – and I realize now, from the well-known 'touch no one' in his poem of that time, 'Me. Here. Now.', that he was giving a great deal.

'Gidday,' he said to Harry, and I introduced them.

'Did your mother phone?'

'Yeah. Tod swallowed a threepence. They had to take him to the hospital.'

'Is he all right?'

'I guess so. She would've rung again.' He had a bottle of beer newly opened and he went to his room for two more glasses. I never saw the inside of that room but John Dobbie has a description from a woman who claimed to have visited him there. It was, she said, 'clean, bare, sterile, a table and a chair and a bed'. He had the use of a bathroom upstairs. 'A hot plate,' she said, 'and a plunger in a pot.' She hints (she's unnamed) that she stayed all night. More people claim to have known Rex than he ever had the time to know.

His hair was ragged, longer than was thought masculine, and he had a two-day stubble on his chin. What else did I notice? His toenails were uncut. They bent like yellow caps over the ends of his toes. He was muscular and carried no fat. 'He could be quite good looking if he tried,' Harry told me later.

'I liked the hospital poems,' I said when he came out.

'Yeah, you wrote.'

'Why didn't you tell me you were back?'

He poured a glass of beer for Harry.

'I dunno, Jack. I was sorting out a few things. I was busy.' He grinned with the side of his mouth. It was either false – Harry said false – or honest. I say honest. It settled me down and I was at ease with Rex again. I understood that he would move all the time, and reposition; and that he would alter but be the same for me; that I was unshiftable, I was in his life, although he might ignore me most of the time. I was part of 'Petleys', and nothing would change. I wanted, though, to find out what had happened to bring him here – bring him into his curious state.

A wooden-bodied Bradford van stood on the side of the lawn. One of those that rot away by hedges, under trees. Rusty in its metal parts, eaten in its wood, with most of its green paint flaked away. I was afraid Rex might end up like that.

'Want to go down the beach? Want a ride?'

'Yes,' said Harry.

'Don't tell me that thing goes?'

'Sure it goes. Drink up. We'll go to Takapuna.'

Harry rode with him in the front. I sat on his folded net among his fishing lines. Neither of them talked and I was too much assaulted by the thump and slew of the van and the smell of fish to make conversation. We parked down the road from the Mon Desir – a modest place in those days in spite of its name – and Harry walked off quickly to find the house she had grown up in, leaving me to follow with Rex.

'She's kind of sudden, isn't she?' he said.

I was jealous of his finding a word I'd been looking for. Harry was, is, will ever be, sudden – although I have other words for her too. It seemed that Rex had reached down and found it with no trouble; and there Harry was, exact and true. (But he did not know her complications. I was coming to know those.)

The tide was low and the water far away, silver and calm. We walked on the hard sand, watching her. She had an eager lean, as though she were on something's trail and set to grab it, and I saw, I almost felt, the blow when it fell. She broke her step, slowed, then ran, and stopped and turned around, looking for me. Her mouth made a silent screech, and I understood the house was no longer there.

'Knocked it down, I'll bet,' Rex said. He was quick.

'It's gone,' Harry said. Her face was white and shocked. But another thing about Harry, she will not be comforted. (Nor does she want apologies, she will not take 'sorry'.) She had looked for me, that was enough. I did not touch or hold her as we came up.

'Which one was it?'

'There.' Brick and tile and wrought iron, in place of weather-boards and sash-hung windows and a tin roof that storms roared on louder than the waves on the beach. We had exchanged childhoods, I knew the importance of what she had lost. Later I would argue that it was not lost.

'It's Dad's fault,' Harry said.

'Suburbia at the beach,' Rex said, and she looked at him dismiss-ively.

'I'm going for a walk,' and left us there. Ten yards away she hooked her sandals off and changed direction for the water, and when she reached it tucked up her skirt and waded knee-deep towards the south end of the beach. She never once, that I saw, turned to look at the new brick house.

'You going to marry her?' Rex said.

'Yes, I am.'

'I reckon you'll have an interesting time.'

'Yes.' I watched her slow down and felt her gradual easiness and was easy myself. 'How about you? Any ladies?'

'No.'

'How about England?'

'Sure, there's girls, there's always girls.'

'England though? How did you like that?'

'Not much. There's nothing we need there.'

I laughed. 'That's most of our history gone, like that.'

Rex laughed too. 'What I mean, there's too much stuff, all you need is your own bit.' He looked at Harry, far off, as though it were something she might know. But he seemed to feel he had said enough, for he changed direction down the sand. 'Wonder what the water's like.' I followed. I did not say what was in my mind, that he seemed to be keeping clear of his own bit, which was Loomis. He went in to his thighs, keeping a distance between us, and surged along. I took off my shoes and rolled my trousers up and paddled like an Englishman at Blackpool. 'Cold,' I yelled.

'You get used to it.' He came out and stripped off his shirt and shorts and threw them to me. I caught them inches clear of the water. He ran high-footed in his underpants, then threw himself forward and swam straight out, heading, it seemed, for Rangitoto. He had a powerful stroke and must have been fit for he went a quarter of a mile, and I thought: He's mad enough, it is Rangitoto.

Harry came back. 'How far's he going?'

'God knows.'

'He'll get drowned if he's not careful. I'm going to Thorne's Bay, I won't be long.'

'Where's that?' I did not want her to go. I thought it was time for us to be together again.

'Round there. Round the rocks. It isn't far.' She saw my unwillingness and smiled. 'You can come, leave his clothes.' But she was being kind, and was not ready for me, so I said, 'I'd better wait. We'll catch you up.'

Rex turned and started swimming back. Although he was coming towards me and Harry moving away I seemed to stay equally distant from them both. Their singleness put them out of reach – the girl (the woman) I had thought to possess intimately, by intense communication, mental and physical, over six months, and the man (friend) learned over almost twenty years. Each was wrapped in self, impenetrable; and that knowledge was suddenly the defining edge of me – it elated me. For a moment interest in them seemed enough.

She put her sandals on to walk over the reef to Thorne's Bay, and went from sight. Rex swam towards me, head sleeked by sun and water, arms making a crescent advance; an insect-jawed eating of the space between us. He came at me, utterly strange; and stood up and lolloped in, too familiar suddenly to be interesting. He dried himself with his shirt and pulled it on; pulled his shorts on over the underpants that sagged with a weight of water in the crotch, showing hairy parts that were out of keeping, too adult.

'Where's she gone now?'

'Thorne's Bay.'

'What for?'

I could have given half a dozen answers but gave none. My sense of loyalty was engaged. Also, I wanted to be private from Rex. I found no need to explain Harry, or 'us', and that gave me a feeling of great stability. We went across the black volcanic rocks. (Harry told us, on the way back, that the reef was a lava flow.) I asked Rex about London, Spain, the sugarworks, and why he did not go to Loomis any more, and must have seemed merely inquisitive; but swimming had opened him and made him less remote.

'I do go. I was over there a couple of weeks ago.'

'It's not enough for your mother.'

'She's all right. All she's interested in is the babies. There's no need to go out there any more.'

He was not, he said, writing any poems about Loomis. That, it turns out, isn't true. His notebooks show attempts and failures by the dozen. But he cannot look in at that place yet. He has other ground, there are good poems from that time, but there's no facing Loomis and 'Petleys' from the positions he can take. He can't be still, he can't be steady. Rex has a Loomis obsession, but not a subject yet; and when it becomes a subject it is savagely exclusive. Room for me – I'm a little annexe – but no room for those who marry in and for the babies, and no time after the death of Joy.

It's intellectual as well as emotional. He would not have got there without his intelligence. And it does not stop at poetry. The working out is in his life as well – but getting those two things apart is too big a job for me. They're locked in ways too intricate to unpick and have such a multiplicity of particulars that any will I have to start is soon reduced to impotence. All I can do is repeat: he rolls those particularities into a ball and beats it flat and studies the surface, and goes on to make his poetry. In some easiness at last he moves into the long middle part of his life.

I asked, with some delicacy, how he felt about Sidgy. (How do you ask your best friend if he has committed murder?) 'Do you think about Wellington?' I said.

He was readier for that than for questions about Loomis. 'Sure I do. What do you think?'

'Has anybody ever asked?'

'Why should they?'

'Do you keep in touch with Margot?'

He shrugged. 'Cards. Why not?'

'And what about Sidgy? Did he have any value, do you think?'

'How the hell can I know that? How can I know about value? I dream about the little bugger sometimes.'

That's – let me count – five questions from me and five from him, and only at the end a bit of information. There's no very great readiness there. We walked along a strip of sand and climbed another reef.

'Your overcoat was wet when I got it from the door.'

'Yeah, I know. I had to wait a long time. There wasn't much shelter.' Then more information. 'I'll always see him going down those steps. It was like flying.'

'Yes?'

'The second time his head hit, it made a different sound, so I knew it was smashed. It was softer, Jack.'

That was more than I wanted. It had the hard focus of some of his poetry: as if the only way to discover is to state, and let feeling follow on from there.

'Let's shut up about it, eh? – Have you still got your coat?'

'I left it in England.' He shivered. 'You need those bloody things over there. And Wellington. There's your girlfriend.'

'She's Harry.'

'Yeah, Harry. What's she found?'

We approached through the rocks. She was kneeling where they cluster and reach high and seemed to be looking at herself in a pool. She cupped water in her hands and splashed it on her face, then shook herself and sent drops flying everywhere. She grinned at us as we came up.

'Fresh. You can drink it if you like.'

'It can't be fresh.'

'Go on, try it.'

I scooped into the pool and sipped the water. 'That's impossible.'

'It's running,' Rex said. 'It's a spring.'

'There's half a dozen. It's seepage through the lava from Lake Pupuke. It seeps under the road and under the houses.'

'And comes out here?' Rex was kneeling. He took water in his hands and tasted it. 'Bloody amazing.' He washed his face.

'Pupuke's a maar,' Harry said. 'It's a single big explosion and fresh water filled the crater.' She smiled at me. I saw how she liked impressing Rex, and also how she did it for me. She stood up and took my hand and pointed out to sea. 'There are springs out there too. You find them when you're swimming under water. It feels like a fish under your foot. And when you get down close the sand is dancing.'

Rex stood up and faced out. I hadn't seen his dopey-looking stillness for years. So Harry made him a gift, and it finds a place in his poem 'Memory': grains of sand lift and dance, fresh water turns invisibly in the salt, making an upward pressure on the face and a clean taste in the mouth. No meaning is ascribed. The reader will find it for himself.

It's one of his better poems. It makes me angry that it's not 'for Harry'.

Visiting with the Second Voice

Jack Skeat's recent entries are a confession then? He makes it clear that he took part in a murder. His role is not as minor as he'd like it to be. Written down, the memory frightens him. Is there a statute of limitations on murder? There's no limiting the horror of the act. No limiting of responsibility.

He wants to know more about Sidgy. Writes his full name down: Cyril Reginald Morley. He wants to fill in that life too. Wants to know Sidgy's intentions about Margot. And how he got that way and if his life was as ugly as it seemed. How it seemed to him. And wants to know what Sidgy felt as he flew down the steps. The things there are to discover about a person are endless: would judgement remain possible if everything were known? If not, where does it leave him, with his ingrained belief in a moral basis for behaviour – in a morality defining us as human, in a way? He will lose a good part of his life if he is not able to pass judgement.

He passes judgement on himself with 'Cyril Reginald Morley'.

Jack keeps two sets of books: those and these. He writes in the morning when Harry, upstairs, is at work: those in Olympic 1B5 exercise books, in black biro, these in blue in Warwick 1B5. Blue seems to flow more easily. On the other hand, he prefers the back cover of the Olympic, where cartoons and text teach water survival: three people cling to an upturned dinghy, a boy clings to a log, a boy and a girl to a chillibin – all looking woeful but all safe. On the back of the Warwick there are only measurement tables.

He's interested in how long it takes to fill a page. Sometimes it takes a few minutes, sometimes a morning. Does taking time get him nearer to the truth? Does scratching out, second attempt, improve accuracy or does it move him further off from things that are painful? Closer definition does not always lead to the meaning of an event, or to an understanding of Rex, and of himself. There's a struggle going on between lost content and survival; but it may be that survival of another kind depends on getting where he shouldn't go.

Guessing can be useful as a way of breaking in, but too much invention isn't allowed. Where does imagination stop and invention start? He could not even attempt the thing without imagination. And he could not do it, could not carry on, if he was forbidden to leave out. Leaving out, it seems to him, is part of imagining.

He could not do it, either, without his second voice. There's a ragged emptiness between then and now and he stands differently on that side from this.

His mother has had a stroke that leaves her with very little right side awareness. Only half the world is left, and it is left. They have put her in a new room with the door, the visitor's chair, her bedside cabinet, in the half that is now her whole. Unfortunately the window is on the right, so the world out there does not exist.

As a side effect (he means no pun) her paranoia is cured. That part in which John Skeat and Harriet were demons is closed down. Jack prefers to see it as banged out – it's a black ball on the table and an accidental red has cannoned it into a side pocket. Mrs Skeat becomes a sweet old lady.

He holds her hand while he talks to her. The Maori nurses, she tells him, are nice, they are almost like New Zealanders. The food is nice. Everything is nice. It amazes him. Nice is a word she has never used in this sense – she's one of the few people he has heard use it correctly – and the concept one he would have thought her unfamiliar with. Lovely, she says when she doesn't say nice. They've cut her hair, leaving it two inches long all over. She looks like a wrinkled little man; she is tired and brave and patient. Jack is confused. He has never known this person. Has she been there all the time? Is she the companion of the lady talking to herself in the summer-house?

She even laughs, and when she laughs she wets herself. He hears the trickle of urine under her blankets. 'Ooh, the water,' she says, but she's not uncomfortable because she wears kanga pants now. Sometimes she sings, or tries to sing, in a sugar-candy little-girl voice. She knows many tunes and some first lines, and lines from the middle or the end, and sings them sweetly and tries to hum the rest.

'Oh Danny boy, the lights, the lights . . .'

'Are burning,' Jack suggests.

'Oh Danny boy, oh Danny boy . . .'

'That's good. Your voice is good.'

She watches him, or seems to. Perhaps she's watching something in her head.

'Show me the way to go home . . .'

'I'm tired . . .'

'I'm tired and I want to go to bed . . .'

'I had a little drink . . .'

'Show me the way to go home . . .'

Is she singing or trying to tell him something?

'Quiet down there,' Mrs Donald in the other bed cries. (The new room is double.) The matron looks in and straightens her. 'Get your filthy hands off me.' Mrs Donald.

'All right over there?' the matron asks.

'Yes thanks.'

'Ooh hallo,' Mrs Skeat trills, and gets a smile in return. 'That's one of the owners. They're the ones who sell us the fish.'

'What fish, Mum?'

'The fish . . . the fish . . .'

'Did you have fish for lunch?'

'No-o.'

So it goes on, but it's easier now. It's easier and harder: he cannot go away. He cannot take refuge in the injustice done to him. He has to see a mother here. She says it's lovely to see him and he believes it, but who does she think he is now? He feels unreal. Where has the poisoner gone? The poisoner had more substance than the loving son. But at other times he's grateful, he thinks it's nice, to be holding hands with a little old lady who may not be exactly sure who he is but who seems to love him all the same. And now and then he gets a double beat of his heart, a physical and a psychic kick, and he swells with emotion: this is my mother. He wants the knowledge while it lasts but when it goes away is pleased to be rid of it. He resents it. The ease with which she takes him back after sixty years of denial

. . . what is it? Monstrous! Can he tell the little old lady, the little old monster, she gave away her right to hold his hand long ago?

Harry comes in. She has waited in the car and comes to fetch him at the end. She cannot play the game of smiles and pats but will stand and say, 'Hallo, how are you?' and 'That's good.' (Not 'that's nice'.)

'Ooh. It's . . .'

'Harriet, Mum.'

'It's Mrs . . .' Starts to laugh at her failure to find the name, and wets herself.

'Skeat, Mum. Same as you.'

'It's Mrs Skeat. How are . . . how are . . . ?'

'I'm very well thank you.'

'How are you going to get home?'

'We've got our car.'

'Is she . . . ?'

'What, Mum?'

'Is she the one who sells us the fish?'

'No, Mum. She's my wife.'

It goes that way until Harry has done her five minutes and they can leave. Jack kisses his mother on the brow. She smiles at him. Her eyes shine; and perhaps, hidden away, is knowledge and surprise. 'I love your kisses.'

'How can she say that? How can she dare?' Harry says in the corridor.

'Daring doesn't come into it. She means it, that's all.' He does not mention his own rage – it was only a flash – that she should give him now, so easily, things he had sickened from wanting as a boy.

'Where have you gone to?' Harry asks. She's in that state he thinks of as dry. If he touched Harry her skin would feel like sandpaper – finishing grade, there is nothing coarse about Harry.

'Climbing mountains,' he replies; and when she raises her eyebrows: 'Mt. Duppa.'

'Pull over Jack and let me drive.'

'I'm all right.'

She switches on the radio. 'Listen to that and keep your mind on the road.'

133

They're advertising mufflers and they finish with a Woody Woodpecker laugh.

'Find some music.'

She obeys. 'Why Mt. Duppa?'

'I don't know. The view. Remember that little basin right on top?'

'Jack, that light was red! For heaven's sake!'

He pulls over and walks around to the passenger side. Harry slides across. Businesslike, she adjusts the seat, which makes rapid gunshots as it brings her under the wheel. He does not like the way she must sit, it puts her against the oncoming traffic. He takes the lumbar roll from behind him and fits it at the base of her spine, but would sooner fix it somehow across her breasts to protect them. If Harry dies it is his fault for thinking of his death.

He tries to imagine long happy lives for them. The difficulty comes with filling in the time. He must do it with activities and travel and occasions; and he looks for a way to make quiet and stillness count.

'Now what?' Harry says.

'You'd think when they advertise mufflers they'd be quiet.'

Harry drives through an amber light, intentionally although a little late. He says nothing. There are no more lights now on the drive to Green Bay.

'I liked her better the way she was,' Harry says.

'Maybe.'

'I like her better against you than for you.'

Now he feels a flash of rage at Harry. The huge revolution in his mother's life seems no more than tactics to her. Can't she understand that now, at sixty, he kisses her like a son for the first time, and has her love? But his rage passes and leaves him aware of loss – Harry gone? He rejects it. She's still there – but Harry with a new part revealed. He wants her to turn it away from him.

'You'd better not come any more.'

'Suits me.' Her pointed feet stab at the pedals. 'I just hate her doing it to you. After sixty years of bad behaviour . . . '

'I know.'

They turn around houses and the harbour lies in front. He's pleased to let his eye go speeding over the mudflats, and wants to send his mind out there too and let it rest. Naked water, naked mud: nothing lies between it and the weather and the sky.

Jo Bellringer's house, like Alice's, stands on a cliff, but it looks out on the unfashionable harbour; with the sewage farm on its southern shore; where the shellfish, healthy in themselves, poison human beings who are foolish enough to eat them. Yet the heads out there, clenched and tall, are washed by clean weather and beyond them surf crashes on the bar. Give this harbour a year or two without human use and it would emerge newborn.

He says to the woman at his side, 'It looks good from up here but down there it stinks.'

She shifts uneasily. 'I was just thinking how beautiful it was. Those silver currents on the blue.'

'They look like stretch marks,' says the clever one, next along. The clever one is the one he prefers. She's foxy and dangerous and he's happy to have the beauty-seer between him and her. If he felt more energetic he'd want her away and he and Miss Foxy would construct a conversation like a bridge over an abyss. If he was ten years younger too. He has not engaged in that sort of thing for a number of years. It is easy for him to forget how women see him. He is grateful suddenly for the neutrality of sixty.

'Are you Harriet Edwards's husband?' the nearer one says.

'Yes.'

'Mr Edwards,' the foxy one says with a grin.

'Skeat, actually.'

'I wish she'd do more children's books. I loved *Henry Hedgehog*.'

'She likes the sort of thing she's doing now.'

'*Henry Hedgehog's Happy Holiday*. My children adored it.'

The other snorts. '*Morris Maggot's Marvellous Meal*.'

'She didn't do the story,' Jack says.

'*Emily Eel's Elongated Evening*.'

Jack looks at her with more dislike than she has earned. Beth Simmonds wrote the story. He tries not to think about Beth. She's the precedent that, in its inverted way, legitimizes his pursuit of Jo. Harry's collaborators lie within his sexual purview.

But of course he doesn't pursue Jo except in his mind, and even there he's intermittent. Worse, he's bored. Jack realizes he can stop. He understands how badly he wants to stop – and in that instant Jo

135

is gone, out of his mind. He smiles with pleasure at the foxy lady; who thinks it is her wit that pleases him.

'*Abi Amoeba's Artless Appetite.*'

'No,' he says, 'that one doesn't work,' and he walks over the lawn to the lopsided table beneath the sun umbrella, where Harry and Jo spoil Jo's party by talking shop.

'Shall I bring out more drinks, Jo? Otherwise your friends will all go home.' Rest easy, he wants to say, it's over now. He would like to tell her too that he does not mind her feeling for Harry being less than pure. Harry will not betray him and will never betray herself. But surely there is something she can do, even if it's just to say, Stop it, that's not on.

'I don't mind being waiter,' he says.

Jo gets up – heaves up like a bullock. Has she heard something suggestive in his offer? She turns the narrow way out of her chair to cancel him and sends it toppling on its back. Jack picks it up, avoids her eye, and sits down while she lumbers to the house. Her warmth on the chair seat would have thrilled him a moment ago, now he finds it unpleasant.

'Why does she behave as though I'm not there?'

'It's chemistry,' Harry yawns; and he is angered by her laziness.

'It's more than that and you know it.'

'Don't start now, Jack,' she says.

'If I can see what she's after surely you can.'

'Oh, do be quiet. Hallo. Yes?' She smiles with false brightness at the woman advancing over the lawn.

'I just wanted to say . . . I hope I'm not interrupting?'

'No, of course not.'

'How much I like *Henry Hedgehog*. My children adored it.'

'Thank you.'

'Especially the part where he lets the baby snail go.'

'I didn't write the story,' Harry says. 'Beth Simmonds did that.'

'Yes, I know – '

'It was poor old Beth's only book.'

' – but I meant the illustration. The look on the little snail's face.'

'Excuse me,' Jack says. He crosses the lawn towards the path. The foxy woman darts at him – '*Nellie Newt's Naughty Night.*' He sidesteps and walks down the path to the gate. Escape from parties will become a habit. He gets into the car and finds the wheel in his lap. 'Ah, Harry,' he sighs, and moves the seat back. Ping, ping: she shoots him. 'Harry.' He loves her but there's no language for it and behaviour is impossible to find. Keeping it secret makes it nearly secret from him.

Anger is less troubling. If she had not left him on that last 'sabbatical' he would never have looked at Beth. And Beth would have got busy with Ronald Rat and Percy Possum and maybe would have progressed to large animals by now; instead of being nowhere, doing nothing.

Jack is angry with Beth too. He drives towards Titirangi, and turns away; plunges down Pleasant Road into Glen Eden. Too many women, he thinks; including the half one.

Where has her other half gone, and should the creature left be considered whole, affectively? It makes him laugh. He feels a huge sad lost affection for his mother.

Glen Eden has changed but is the same. There is simply more of it, closer cramped. As a Loomis and New Lynn poor relation it has never been remotely paradisal; but if one imagines earlier times, pre-European, pre-Maori . . .

He stops in a street of middle-aged houses and the short way Lila has travelled depresses him. The house a little bigger, a little newer, the town or suburb held between those two where she had lived all her married life. He wishes she had chosen somewhere else.

But the house, of course, belongs to Tweet. He has not seen Tweet for thirty years, although they have spoken on the phone, and the Harry-like woman who opens the door has no resemblance he can find to the teenaged girl.

'Tweet? Myra?'

Quick and cool, she knows him. 'It's Myra these days, Jack. Or are you John?'

'Jack will do. I didn't think you'd recognize me.'

'Of course I do, I'm good at faces. You nearly lived at our place anyway.' She hesitates. 'Come on in.'

She leaves the front door open and leads him into a living-room. 'I always know it's someone from way back when they say Tweet.'

'Does the rest of the family still use it?'

'Melva does.'

He apologizes for calling without warning, and wonders at the awkwardness – unwillingness to have him, perhaps? – behind her ease. Secretarial ease? He wishes he had stepped forward and hugged her at the door.

'Is this a bad time?'

'No. No. I'll take you in to see Mum in a minute. The thing is Jack – it's better if you don't mention Rex.'

'All right.'

'And Melva too. Just talk about what you're doing now.' She gives a half bad-tempered smile. 'It upsets her.'

'Melva – is Melva . . .'

'She drinks a lot. She's not very well.'

'I'm sorry.'

'It's not your fault.'

Jack had not, of course, meant that. 'How are the rest of them?'

She tells him briefly. All OK.

'And Lila?'

'Getting old. She's still pretty sharp though. Be careful what you say.'

'Yes. Tweet, I think you should know . . .' He tells her that John Dobbie is writing another book; a big one this time.

'Drat the man,' Tweet says; and the old-fashioned slang makes him smile.

'Would you like me to steer him away?'

'Tell him to wait until we're dead. Three generations.'

'That's a long time.'

'It's our lives, Jack. No one's got the right to make it public property.'

'No –'

'There's too much damage. Rex would have known.'

She has stepped sideways, gone somewhere, and thinks he knows something he does not know. He leaves too long a pause and cannot ask.

'Come on, she's in the sunroom.'

'Do you look after her fulltime?'

'She doesn't need looking after. But I stay home with her. Would you believe me if I said it's a pleasure?'

He knows that she is married and divorced and has no children and has been a nurse and travelled all over the world – worked in Australia and England and Saudi Arabia – and trained as a midwife and was prominent in the fight to legalize home births. He cannot see her staying at home all day with an old lady.

'Do you still deliver babies?'

'When I can. Here's someone to see you, Mum. Someone from Loomis.'

The old lady is peeling an apple with a pocket knife and she puts it on the plate in her lap and holds out her arms. 'Jack.' Takes him with damp fingers, hooks him in. A little off balance, he kisses her cheek, and stays leaning forward, supporting himself with his thighs on the arm of the chair as she holds her face against his. Her skin is papery and cool, but her fingers, holding him, are as strong as wire.

'How are you, Lila?' She lets him move back and he can say, 'You're looking well.' She is sharp and birdlike and alive. She does not look like someone who is frightened of talking about a dead son.

'What a lovely surprise. What a lovely thing to come and visit me. Did you bring your wife?'

'She's at a party over in Green Bay. I'll bring her next time.'

'And I'll make some more pikelets.' Her memory astonishes him. 'She's a little thing, isn't she, like Tweet?'

'Not as tall as Tweet.'

'And clever too.'

'She illustrates books. Flower pictures. I'll bring you one.'

'Sit down, Jack. Over here,' Tweet says. 'Would you like some tea? Or a glass of beer?'

'Tea please. I've got to drive.'

'Jack, now let me think, you're sixty,' Lila says. 'And you were the National Archivist. Is that important?'

'It depends on whether you think we should keep records or not.'

'Louder Jack, she's a wee bit deaf,' Tweet says. 'And not too much past.' She leaves the sun porch to make tea.

'I always knew you'd do well, whatever you took up. How are your children?'

He tells her, speaking loud – where they are, what they are doing – exaggerates their abilities and happiness. Lila takes her apple up

139

and peels. The skin bounces like a spring and he pauses to see if it will break. 'You're very good at that.'

'I've always had quick fingers. I used to make Plasticine statues when I was young. With ears and fingernails and plaited hair.' She stops her smile and looks at him sharply. 'I told you that.'

'Yes. Sitting on the swing-bridge.'

'I try to cut apples as thin as paper. I can't chew too well nowadays.' He is not sure that she has refused the memory but knows that something has gone dark in her. Does the swing-bridge mean Rex and Joy?

'You told me you put them in shop windows.'

'Yes. I made a knight in armour once and his lance was so thin I had to put a darning needle in to keep it straight. The dragon had tiny beads for eyes.'

'I'd love to have seen it.'

'Now look at that. Have you ever seen an apple sliced as thinly as that?' She offers him a piece. It melts on his tongue – not enough to bring out his rash. He lets his eyes go round the room and notes flowery curtains filtering the sun; crochet work lying on a table; a day bed with fat pillows; but is looking for Rex Petley's poetry. There had been a stack of travel books in the sitting-room; and here, down on the floor, is a shelf built like a trough to slant the spines. He has to lean out of his chair to read the titles.

Lila, slicing apple, smiles. 'They belonged to Les.'

'*The Roaring U.P. Trail. Riders of the Purple Sage.* I never thought I'd see those again.'

'This was his favourite.' She back-bends her arm in a young woman's way to fish it out. 'He really should have been Buck Duane.'

Buck Duane gets beaten to the draw. Jack has not forgiven Zane Grey that. 'My favourite was Brazos Keene. I was in Texas once, at a conference, and we crossed the Brazos River. I couldn't believe it. I kept on looking for a man on a horse.'

'He was reading that the day he died. He died quickly, Jack. It was like someone walking up and punching him on the jaw.'

'KO.'

Lila nods in a satisfied way. She gives Jack the book and eats more apple. He leafs through, near the back, not looking for the gunfight but wanting to discover if the blush – was there a blush in this one? – travels up or down. It's an interesting question and should be checked physiologically.

'What are you looking for?'

'Oh, the love scene,' coming on it. And he laughs. ' "What is this madness of love?" I'd forgotten what a bad writer he was.'

'What's wrong with that? Les and I were like that. He swept me away and there was nothing I could do.'

'No.'

'My parents didn't like him. My father hated him. I was my father's little girl and along came this man without a tie, and no collar even, and mortar splashed on his trouser cuffs. He held me by the back of my neck while he talked with them. One big hand right around the back of my neck. You should have seen how white my father went. But what could I do? I just packed my suitcase and went away with him. Imagine if I hadn't, Jack, if I'd stayed at home.'

'Yes.'

She appears to imagine. 'Love is a madness. If it isn't then it isn't love.' She stabs the apple to the heart and puts it on the plate. He closes the book. Now is the time to talk about Rex. Surely Rex can find an entrance here.

'It was a great genetic mix,' and sees from the movement of her eye that she understands (the same alertness Mrs Skeat had had when her poisoner came). It makes him turn his words aside. 'Bricks and mortar,' but what he means – and she hears, she's preternatural – is the rough building of poetry. 'And then all the fine work. Knights and dragons. And lances that don't droop. And beads for eyes.'

Her eyes are hard and bright. They have a beady glitter, and she's lifted as though on a welling-up of light. Jack is appalled by what he's done. He has fiddled with a box-lid and snakes come flashing out. But all she does is send a glittery shriek out to the kitchen: 'Tweet, what's taking you so long?'

Tweet comes running, with a tea-cosy in her hands. She utters bird-like cries as she lifts and pats her mother into place. It is like combing a child's hair and washing its face and getting it ready for play-school. Lila's mad glitter is snuffed out.

Jack picks up the cosy Tweet has dropped beside his chair. If he puts it on his head and sticks his ears through the holes will that amuse Lila, will that help her to forget? But he sees from Tweet's sharp elbows and narrow back that she wants him out of the way so he goes into the kitchen and fits it on the pot, then walks out to wait by the car. He leans on the mudguard and looks at the Waitakeres. There's a road in the bush there, in the shade. He and Rex dropped down it on the Beezer, leaning until their elbows almost touched the ground. He refuses to let Rex be snuffed out. There's too much of his own life in the gravitational dance.

'How is she?' he asks when Tweet comes out.

'She's all right. How did it happen? What did you say?'

Jack admits his miscalculation. He says that he is sorry and he won't come again. He can understand Lila, he says; but how sad it is she can't enjoy Rex in her old age.

Tweet grows angrier at this. 'You keep out of it. And keep that Dobbie man away from us.'

'Yes, I'll try. There'll be others, though. He's going to get more and more important.'

'How? Why?'

'As a poet.'

'God, there's another world, can't you see?' She starts for the gate, but turns back. 'You book people can have him. Just leave Mum alone. Melva too. And all of us.' She goes on to the path and locks herself behind the pickets. 'I'm sorry to be rude. But I can keep her going if people from outside will just –' Makes a pushing movement with her hands.

'Yes, all right.' He tells Tweet to look after herself.

But there's a dislocation, a mystery. Too much is made of Rex's death; even when Joy is in the sum. Are they saying Joy became too much for him? Forty years must have smoothed it down: a pebble in a creek, time works that way . . .

Are they saying Rex meant to drown out there? He broke a basic rule of water survival: cling to your dinghy – every Auckland boatie knows that one. And he left his life jacket on the bonnet of his car . . . but his work, his life, his poetry, were built on confidence . . . The coroner was satisfied, although he gave a warning . . .

Jack drives to Green Bay. He can't stop arguing. What do Tweet and Lila know? What must he find out? He wants to step away from mysteries and confusion and spend his time where everything is plain.

Jack needs to be with the two young men.

Notebook: 9

After Thorne's Bay I did not see him again for more than a year. I heard about his marriage to Alice Pittaway with something between alarm and amusement, believing that the shaggy Loomis boy and the daughter of that patrician house would reach accord only in a transitory passion – consume each other for a time but in the end violently repel. She might insist that he cut his toenails but would not change his way of looking at the world. Loomis not Epsom would come out on top.

I bored Harry with my analysis. She had no interest in Rex, and Alice was simply a name. Perhaps, she said, they were in love. That would overcome my silly dichotomies. It might do that, I agreed, with anyone but Rex, but he was – her scepticism made me overstate it – a wolf in the dogpack, running singly though he ran with them, and sooner or later he had to go off on his own. I knew his nature, I had watched him from the start. That wasn't true, Harry declared, I had simply grown up with him. 'Best friends' wasn't watching, it was a kind of blindness.

Now, of course, I have to agree. My watching of Rex was retrospective. It only began when I knew he was a poet.

Harry and I rented a villa in Ngaio. We tried to buy a house in Worser Bay, where the wind and spray – but I've said all that. We walked from Ngaio in good weather, across the gorge and up to the railway line on the other side, and down looping Upper Wadestown Road, under the black pines of Tinakori Hill. Twenty minutes from a waterfall creek and cliffs of rock, from tawa and fern and supple-jack, to the main street of the capital city – even Harry began to see that Wellington had its attractions. Then we bought a house in Kelburn, on the wrong side of the hill, and Harry, pregnant, walked to work with me through the gardens but travelled home at night by cable car. She had a job in the Health Department and I in the Turnbull Library, in the old brick house in Bowen Street. I was in charge of manuscripts, high under the roof, in a room where the maid must have slept, if Alexander Turnbull had a maid. Rex and Alice called on me there when they got off the Christchurch ferry after the Writers' Conference, 1957.

I heard her voice come winding up the stairs – dove notes increasing almost to a honk. Beautiful Alice, English Alice, Alice with her V. Woolf liquid eyes and V. Woolf hair. She cultivated the resemblance and when it was mentioned said with a laugh, oh but she was *manquée*, she was afraid, in everything else – which no one believed for a moment of course. I was bedazzled, and failed to get Rex properly in view. When I managed it I was impressed and disappointed – impressed more at first but disappointed later on. Corduroy jacket and white silk scarf and suede leather shoes. And a beard. I had not thought he would let Alice dress him up. Or that he could be so poet-like and spectacular. His beard had streaks of ginger. Les Petley's red was coming out. It was close-trimmed, jaw-hugging (Alice would not tolerate shagginess) and – it's odd – it made me see Lila, thrown into relief somehow, in the bones of his upper face.

'Auckland comes to town,' I said. 'You're not going out in the street dressed like that?'

'Same old Jack,' Rex said. He was pleased with me; but Alice, in that moment, knew that I would never do as Rex's best friend. She had someone else lined up for that anyway – and in he came, following his little pouter chest: John Dobbie, the Elf. He had a flamboyance I would never have – and (she recognized it, I am sure) an inveterate subservience. John wanted to be second, wanted Rex to be first. It satisfied him deeply, allowed him an importance that would not be out of control. He too had a wife, Evelyn known as Eve; with marble throat and limbs and a farm-girl face – Olympian and Waikato. She was thoroughly ill-matched with the Elf. Several times she held his hand but that made him look like a schoolboy with his mother.

'I read your piece in *Serpent*,' I said to John, 'it was very good' – although I meant 'quite'. (The thing I respect most about him is that he grew up in Helensville and so has some knowledge of mangroves and mud.)

145

'We've been reading poetry on the ferry,' Alice said. 'In the dawn, coming over the strait.'

'Up on deck,' Eve said. She was always uncertain and usually came in late.

'New stuff?' I asked Rex, but he said, 'John's. Out loud,' and I recognized him again and knew that Alice had not changed anything between us. Two words, dead-pan: the whole of our past was back in place. Beard and costume were a game he played. Was marriage a game that he played too? He could afford to let Alice dress him up. Under the beard, under the scarf, Rex from Loomis went about his work in his old way.

I showed them politicians' letters (how casual we were in 1957). 'I want to spoil the bastard's view,' McKenzie wrote, approving an unnecessary road between Buller's house and the lake. Rex loved it, but Alice was perturbed. For all her displays of unconventionality, she believed (continues to believe) in face value and official truth.

I gave Rex my key and sent him and Alice to Kelburn by taxi. (The Dobbies had friends of their own.) Harry pulled faces when I met her for lunch; behaved almost as though I had put her in danger. She grew private in her pregnancies, self-communicating in some way, and her brightness when she had to mix with others had a clockwork precision that made me listen for the breaking of a spring. I was ready to step forward and catch her when she fell. But this was Rex, not just anyone, I argued as we ate our filled rolls in the cemetery. Rex and his new wife. 'You'll like Alice,' – on speculation. 'I wouldn't mind betting she's pregnant too.' (She had thrown up on the ferry, halfway through John Dobbie's poem.) But other women's pregnancies were an affront to Harry and she forbade me to mention hers; although anyone with half an eye . . . She said she would cook tea and do her best but I mustn't expect any poetry talk from her. She did not like Rex's poetry. Some of it was cruel, she said, and not for any good reason. And it always turned to violence and the dark. No woman who was having a baby wanted that – which he had better learn if his wife really was pregnant. But it wasn't just optimism Harry needed. She liked things hard and clean and definite. Although she could admire the particularity of Rex's verse she didn't like the way the edge was blunted – so she said, I don't see it – as though it hit against something hard that knocked all the point and sharpness off.

'Go on,' I said. She had never talked in that way before.

'Everything gets cloudy. There's too much blood.'

'But he's absolutely clear, and anyway blood's a part of it,' needing her to see the Rex I saw.

But all she would say was, 'He's yours, not mine, so don't ask me to like him. I'll cook tea, that's all.'

She did not have to do that. He had left a note on the kitchen table that said Leon Pittaway was in town and was giving them dinner at his hotel, and later on there was a party at Rita Bullen's – 'You and your wife are invited' – and Leon had his car and was driving them to Auckland in the morning. All they needed was a bed for the night. 'Goody,' Harry said, and flopped down on the sofa with a grin.

I felt I had been pushed into the margins again; but that was more than made up for by being at the centre of Harry's life. She had me put my hand on the baby to feel it move, which was my first acquaintance with David: a flick like a cockabully's tail. It churned me up so much with elation and fright that I could not eat the extra piece of steak – Rex's piece – Harry gave me for tea.

'We don't have to go to this party.'

But she would like to sit and watch, she said – as long as she could come home as soon as she'd had enough. Rita's house was only a quarter of a mile away. We walked from our gully to Central Terrace, and insulted Barton Rymer with a bottle of cheap sherry at the door. 'No need, no call for that.' He put it behind him, out of sight. Barton was the husband Rita had at the time; a lawyer, and 'well-to-do' she had said while considering him. She liked especially his family house and harbour view; and found him 'nobody's fool' and 'more fun than you'd think'. And how could she resist being Rita Rymer? His flattened melancholy lower lip suggested to me that he had been broken in too fast to Rita's ways. Barton played the flute beautifully, but the flute, Rita said, was for later in the evening. Right now he must see that everybody had enough to drink.

Rex and Alice and Leon arrived late, which made Rita snappish. Merv Soper sat quiet, drinking more whisky than he was used to and saying ha-ha and golly now and then (on the last night of his life). Harry liked him best of anyone there, she said next day, but I don't honestly think she noticed him. And I did little more than nod across the room. I'm sorry to say I talked with John Dobbie and admired his conversational trick of self-reference and his way of mounting on his toes when being clever. We were both waiting for Rex. As soon as I realized it I pulled out of the game, dismayed at myself. I did not need to be subservient, I did not think second was an important place to be or that reflected light made one shine with interesting colours. I could stand aside from Rex and have his friendship. John Dobbie was not able to do that.

I sat with Harry and told her who was who as they came in: Laurie Sefton, Rita's protégé, whose first poems had just appeared in *Serpent*; the Training College poets and the coffee shop hobohemians (Rita hadn't invited the second group); Len Mooney, the short short-story writer, wearing his Marxist armour and looking for a fight; tall private-schooled Ray Candy, the abstract painter, who gave him one out in the garden (and married Mooney's girlfriend before long, that is what it was really about); a woman I thought was Ngaio Marsh, but who turned out to be the next door neighbour; some students selling copies of their poetry magazine.

James K. Baxter didn't come.

It wasn't a brilliant party. It needed Rex Petley and Leon Pittaway. John Dobbie remembers it as brilliant, although he can't prove it other than to say that when Rex stumbled on the steps coming in and bloodied his nose and bled into his hands while Alice ran off to find a towel, Rita said snidely (how did John miss the snide?): 'The great poet bleeds into the chalice of his palms,' and I said, 'Does anybody happen to have a wafer?' What was I doing with that remark? I can't recall. I like to think I was getting at John Dobbie for his elaborate concern and fussy importance.

Why doesn't he ask how it came about that sure-footed Rex should stumble on those easy steps?

Alice and Rita laid him on the king-sized bed in the master bedroom (laid meant just to lay down in those days) and he came out after a while with a plaster Aliced on his nose. 'Golly,' Merv Soper said. 'My boy' – Leon Pittaway.

'Lovely timing. Get him a drink, Barton,' Rita said.

I don't remember Rex in any detail at the party, perhaps for the reason that it wasn't him. He was an artefact, he was Alice's. I remember shifting between dismay and complacency. Complacent in my knowledge that he would be moving on, that he wasn't living this, he was *doing* it. Dismay was real all the same. His way of conversing with Leon upset me. It was nudge, wisecrack, smart-arse, all the time. Perhaps this is what the Elf calls brilliance. I understood, after a while, that it was Rex's way of keeping his distance and letting Leon have no foothold in his life.

'Hey Leon, here's one. Arbuthnot and Bottomely are drinking at the club and Arbuthnot says to Bottomely, "I say old man, have you heard about Ponsonby-Ponsonby? He's living with an elephant at the zoo." "I say! A male elephant?" "Good heavens no, a female one. There's nothing queer about Ponsonby-Ponsonby".' Leon cackled gleefully.

'I don't like Rex much this way,' Rita said.

'Nor do I.'

'I liked him better in his coat.'

'Yes.' (But please, everybody, forget the coat. The coat is in London, on the other side of the world.) 'I don't think Alice will keep him dressed up for long.'

'She'd better not. I didn't get him started for nothing.'

I grinned at Rita. It's impossible not to like her. 'The sugarworks poems are pretty good.'

'Not bad. I wish I knew what he's hiding from.'

'Nothing, Rita. Not in his poems. Right now he's hiding from his father-in-law.'

She disagreed on both counts. 'I'm the one who's hiding. The lecherous old toad.'

'The Pittaways are a special case.'

'Not in my house. His poetry is awful muck, you know.'

'Yes, I do.'

'I hope Rex realizes it.'

That was something I would have to find out. The damage would be real if he had come to think that poetry was made in the Pittaway verse factory. (Have I said that Alice wrote too, and that Merv Soper had turned down both her and her mother?)

But all this gossip counts for nothing. Remembering becomes an act of cleverness. I want to stop and let important things uncover themselves. Other important things I mean to keep to myself: Harry, and walking home with her in the night.

The fight in the back garden – it was hiss and grapple and rolling on the ground. The sensible Ngaio Marsh neighbour turned the hose on them. Out in front, as we left, Barton Rymer was playing his flute under a doctored cherry tree. He sat on one end of a wooden bench and Merv Soper sat on the other. I thought if one of them stood up the other would tip off.

If he had given all his time to it Barton could have played professionally. The flute, with its succession of monotones, its portion of breath mixed in each note, its furry shaking free into a penetrating clarity, has always been, for me, the instrument that best expresses body/mind, and pre-vocal wonder, and transcendence. It speaks, inevitably, of death. We stopped and listened as Barton, improvizing, told us that nothing mattered here, that doors were opening and arrival was at hand. I was, I suppose, made susceptible by drink. I wanted to 'cease upon the midnight', and Harry to cease with me, and urgencies to stop. I felt that we might float away, over the sparkling city at our feet, over the cold harbour and the starlit hills, and simplify to a molecule and have no need of bodies or of knowledge any more and become our own single point.

Harry tugged me out of the gate. 'I don't like that man. I can't stand his mouth.'

'He's marvellous on the flute.'

'All that phoney sadness. Anyone can do it.'

I did not try to say what I had felt. Harry and I slipped into accord and walking home in the wind soon became the best part of our night. I don't forget Barton's music though, and regret never hearing it again; although I heard him play several times before Rita ran away to live with Laurie Sefton.

'I feel sorry for Rex,' Harry said in bed.

'Why?'

'He seems younger now than when I met him.'

'He's playing games. Alice is a game.'

'Yes. Someone should tell her. She's mad about him, Jack. Did you see the way she comes up and sort of sinks against him? She'd get inside him if she could.'

'She's tough all the same.'

'She'll need to be. I wish she didn't look so much like – who did all those pictures?'

'Burne-Jones?'

'I suppose that must be what Rex likes.'

They came in not long after us but we kept our door closed and breathed softly; and giggled and clutched each other as they made love – grunts from Rex, flat and focused and definite, and little whoops and female barks from Alice.

'Phew,' Harry said.

'Bloody Rex. He's got to be the best at everything.'

'No he's not. No he's not.'

'Noise?' I whispered.

'We can be quiet. They can't.'

There was, in that, transcendence and repose. (And no little Skeat creature perched himself on my shoulder.)

Rex left Alice sleeping and called softly at our door: 'Jack. Jack.'

I thought his voice was beside my ear.

'It's him,' Harry said. Had she been awake?

'Bugger him.'

'Jack.'

'You'd better go.'

'What does he want?'

'Go and find out.'

I opened the door and slipped out, keeping my bedroom private. He was dressed.

'Sorry, mate.'

'What's wrong?'

'I can't get to sleep. I thought you might feel like a walk.'

'What's the time?'

'I dunno. Three o'clock or something. I'm off in the morning. It's not a bloody visit at all.'

I went back into the bedroom. Harry knew how tightly we were bound. 'Put on something warm.'

The lumpy northerly was waking the trees and letting them rest and waking them to frenzy again. Something in their heads seemed driving them insane. They resented us walking under them on the asphalt paths. I tried that out on Rex but he said, 'Lay off, Jack, I get enough of that sort of thing at home.' We went down through the gardens and by the begonia house and through the cemetery to The Terrace, which was a street in those days, not a canyon.

'Where to?'

'I don't know. It's your town.'

I felt easy, in command, and I led him (at his side, seven league steps) down Boulcott Street, past St Mary's, across Perrett's Corner by the George, along Manners Street and Courtenay Place, pleased with my deserted town that blew grit in our eyes and flipped pie bags in the air and boomed its iron verandas, and then ached with quiet, under speeding clouds that tipped the buildings sideways. I took him into Oriental Bay, where the waves smashed themselves on the sea wall and the wind drove spray in our faces. Petone over the harbour showed half a dozen lights, like a fishing fleet riding out a storm. Rex wiped his face. He found the plaster on his nose and ripped it off and threw it in the sea.

'Jesus Jack, I can't just get up and walk out on her.'

'If that's the way you feel I think you'd better.' But I heard my glibness and decided to keep quiet. We squatted behind the wall and lit cigarettes.

'Why did you marry her?'

'Wouldn't you?'

'I've got Harry.'

'Yeah mate, sorry. You've done all right.'

He threw his half-smoked cigarette over the wall but the wind blew it back and ran it, trailing sparks, across the road. He stood up and faced the sea. The cut on his nose was bleeding. He felt the moisture, tasted it to see what it was.

'I guess I got careless.' Did he mean Alice or his fall on the steps? 'I got greedy.' It was Alice. He laughed. 'There's a lot of things there it's nice to have.'

'Harry says you seem to have grown younger.'

He looked at me sharply. Harry would be told to mind her own business. But after a while he said, 'I guess I got free entry to the cake shop.'

I told him Alice had to be a bit more than that. I said I liked her.

'Yeah, she's all right, she's likeable, under it all. I can hurt her, Jack. I can crumple her up like a paper bag.'

'You can't do that.'

'She depends on me. You ever had anyone in love . . . Yeah, Harry. But I've got to do it her way, she tries to run me. She wants me to write novels. Bloody novels. And then we'll go to London and I'll be some sort of big wheel over there.'

'I don't see you as a novelist.'

'Of course I'm not. Jack, I can't write poems any more. Alice is doing better than me.'

'It'll come back.'

'You know what I am. I'm part of bloody Pittaways now.'

I tried to find ways of telling him he was not. I said that Loomis was pre-Pittaway. I said that there was no harm in taking a rest from it, and anyway inside his mind there must be a place . . . and he said, yeah, yeah, he knew all that; but when you lost a part of yourself it was gone for good. The idiom, the boyish phrase, convinced me that Rex was still there. My agitation started to die down.

'I don't go on your father-in-law much.'

'The bloody old prick. I can handle him.'

'What about this Dobbie joker?'

'Yeah, him too, the little greaser. I wrote a poem about him squatting on the dunny ceiling watching us shit. Alice made me tear it up. Can't say I blame her.'

'What's he up to?'

'I dunno. He's one of those blokes, he can be a big man as long as he comes second.'

I grinned at the way I had anticipated him. 'It'll all come right. You wait and see.'

'I'm getting a job when we get back.'

'What as?'

'Anything. I might be a postie again. I might go back to the sugarworks.'

'Alice won't like that, will she?'

'She's going to have to like it. First thing Jack, I'm going to shave this beard off. In the morning.'

'Not in my house, please.'

'Bloody piker.'

We went back along the wharves and climbed the iron gates by the station. The wind flung Rex's scarf up like an arm and then let it trail down his back. We walked up Hill Street to Tinakori Road. The narrow-shouldered houses were drawn up against the hill.

'Do Francie and Margot still live there?'

'They've gone up to the Hawke's Bay. Francie got married.'

'How's Margot?'

'She's OK. I haven't heard for a while. I think she doesn't need me any more.'

We stood over the road and looked at the house.

'If you got a crowbar you could tip it into the street.' He wiped his cheeks; but the wind in Wellington does that, blows moisture from your eyes across your face. 'You know the worst thing? He was still pissing. I should have let him finish, Jack.'

I could feel no regret for Sidgy. I still felt an awed respect for Rex. He had seen what must be done. (And had he seen what must be done when the time came for him to die? I must be quiet. I must not speak in that voice when I write in black.)

'Come on, we've got wives in bed.'

'I'll swap you, Skeatsie.' It was not crude and not belittling. He simply meant that Alice was his mistake. He meant, I think, that he had wronged them both, him and her, and knew that he must hurt them both in repairing it.

'Harry wouldn't have you,' I said.

'And Alice wouldn't have you either, mate.'

The wind was dying, as it does towards morning. We plunged into the gardens, taking the low path by the creek. Although the sky was lightening, down in the gully dark held on. It had a spongy quality and the air seemed as if it might become too thick to breathe.

'I wouldn't want to come here by myself,' Rex said.

The gravel whispered. We felt our way round corners and crossed a faintly-drumming wooden bridge. Further on I slowed him, pressing with my hand. 'There might be glow-worms.'

The little colony shone privately.

'Quiet,' I whispered, 'or they'll go out.'

We stood and watched. Far off, a car went up to Northland, changing gears. A shuddering in the trees recorded a gust of wind.

'I wish we'd had some of those in Loomis,' Rex said.

It's the only time I heard him wish. I scuffed my foot on the path and the worms switched off. We climbed the hill into the light. It was like swimming up from the bottom of a pool. We ran on the paths and Rex did one of his scarecrow dances. The hills over the harbour shuffled up a step.

'You'll be in Auckland tonight,' I said, satisfied with what I had.

'Yeah, thank God.' His mind went there; went south. 'Caxton's doing my book. That's why I went down.'

'When? Congratulations. What's it called?' Not telling me earlier was a sign that he was well and that his troubles would pass. I knew without him saying that he hadn't told John Dobbie.

'*Hospitals*. I nearly called it *Bedpans*. Pretty tame.'

'It's all right. It doesn't puff it up.'

'*First Fruits*.'

'Yeah,' (I borrowed his 'yeah') 'tinned apricots.'

'It might be the best one I'll ever do.'

'Bullshit,' I said.

'Merv asked me for some poems last night.'

'Send him some. It wouldn't hurt.'

'I told him he'd have to take some of Alice's too.'

'Jesus Rex, you can't do that.'

'No.'

'You'll have to send him something now.'

'Jimminy Skeat. OK, I will. Poor old Alice.'

We ran home and made our wives strong tea and heard each other through the wall waking them up. Harry cooked breakfast and we got ready for work. Leon, not subject to anything so boring as an arrangement, drove up late. Just before he arrived, Rita telephoned to say Merv Soper was dead.

'This bloody town,' Rex said. 'It'll kill us all.' He did not blame himself, and why should he?

But here's what I think. Merv came to the party, probably as publisher of Rita's new young man, and no one talked to him, in the usual way. Rita gave him whisky and left him alone, Jack Skeat nodded from across the room, Leon let his eyes brush past and did not know him (the man had refused to publish his wife), and Rex insulted him, carelessly – another party for the Serpent, at the end of which he sat on a bench in the garden and heard Barton Rymer playing his flute and let the music shift him from a place he had stayed in too long. That is it. I've only worked it out in describing

155

that night. I heard Merv open and close the gate. He followed Harry and me along the path to Upland Road, and turned the other way, and a while later, when he reached the steps to Glenmore Street, he let the wind push him through another gate . . .

Well all right, I'll leave it there. I've no proof. As I've said, I know three people who died from falling, my father, and Sidgy, and Merv. Each of them fell in a different way.

Merv's death is the one I'm closest to.

Notebook: 10

I waited for news that he had left her but heard instead that Fiona was born. 'Well mate, we're in the deep end now,' he wrote on the card. There were never any poems about fatherhood. 'Deep End' though is one of his better pieces. Specific as ever, it's the memory of a visit to the Olympic pool in Newmarket, but it means fatherhood to me because of the card. He chose it as the title poem of his second book – which also (at last) contained the first of the Loomis poems. I have said enough about those. I'm disappointed he never managed a poem about Fiona. Every child should have one, if the father happens to be, well, even a versifier. Rex pleases and disappoints me still and it sometimes seems that all I have to do is get on the phone.

I was on the phone to him when David was born, and later on with Jill, and on the second occasion heard that Rex and Alice had a second child too – no time wasted. 'I'll race you, Jack. First to three.' I was offended and he laughed at me. 'It's fun mate, it's no bloody mystical happening.'

'How's Alice?'

'Bearing up,' and laughed at his pun. 'She hasn't told me yet but I think there's another one in there.'

I don't care for that sort of humour. I very nearly put down the phone. Instead I asked him what he was doing for a living.

'I'm a fisherman.'

I thought he meant that he had gone back to netting flounder and catching kahawai off the rocks, which would mean Leon Pittaway was paying the bills; but, in fact, he was on wages, on a boat that worked in the Hauraki Gulf, catching snapper; and he stayed there for three years, and loved it, and only left when he tore half his index finger off in a pulley – that comes later.

'Alice can't stand the smell. Fish smells sexy though, don't you reckon?' I understood that Alice could hear and that Loomis set the rules. You'll find some phrases in the Elf about the 'quiet courage' of poets' wives. Unlike Rex, he is not specific. I daresay he'll spell it out in the biography. They lived in Mt. Eden, off Balmoral Road. Rex had a little car and drove away each morning in the dark, leaving Alice and her babies in the asphalt suburbs. I certainly don't quarrel with 'courage'. I wonder though how quiet she was. I can't believe that 'Pittaway' found no way of fighting back. I heard a door slam after Rex made his remark about fish. It got him off the phone – 'Someone at the door, Jack. Got to go' – and I was more sure than ever that the marriage would not last. How they had complicated it with babies though. It seemed to me, and seems still, that writing poetry does not exempt one from duty. (Harry laughed and patted my cheek when I said that.)

He turned up in Wellington again with his half finger. I stared at the stumpy thing wrapped in its bandage. He seemed in some primitive condition – Viking, Mongol warrior – and ready for a sudden homicide, some joyful skull-splitting with an axe. He still had his beard, now untrimmed. His corduroys were bald and stuck with fish scales here and there. The smell of fish invaded my tidy room of manuscripts. Stop changing shape, I wanted to say.

'Knock off for the day. Come and have a beer.'

In those casual times I could obey. We went into the public bar at De Bretts and I drank slowly while he drank fast, telling me about his job (which he intended going back to) and his car laid up in Bulls with a broken axle. 'I think it's a write-off. I might ring up and tell them to keep it.'

'How's Alice?'

'She's back in Wonderland. Ma and Pa. I'll tell you Jack, Alice is a good woman but she had her expectations wrong. I put the signs up in neon lights but she wouldn't read. Now she's having a bad time.'

'With three babies.'

'Sure. But the Pittaways make a nice soft landing place. You know the worst thing I did to her?' He poked his bandaged finger in the air. 'A mutilated hand is working class.'

'She knows where you come from.'

'She's censored it out.' He drank some beer. 'It bloody hurt getting that ripped off.'

'It's your typing finger.'

'Yeah, that too. I owe it to her and the bloody world to be a poet. Now,' he grinned, 'I can't even hold a pen. It's the perfect answer.'

I became a little nervous of him. He was making moves I could not keep track of. I could not try this new Rex against the old ones in my collection, or against the ur-Rex each of them looked back to. As student, as postman, as hospital porter and sugarworks labourer, he rose out of Loomis naturally. I was not troubled by him, although anxious for him now and then. As a literary man trying out life with the Pittaways, he had also been recognizable. That was 'passing through', 'Petley' behaviour. Now where was he? I could not see connecting lines. Minus half a finger? Other subtractions had been made, and additions too, and unless I became familiar with them Rex would get away from me as surely as he'd got away from Alice. I had my own things to do and did not particularly want him as a job; but a stance had been taken, an interest declared – so that shared boyhood came to seem – and both of us were in danger if we failed to carry on. I did not put it that way in De Bretts. It came to seem a simple thing of duty and affections. We ought not let each other go – I am sure Rex felt it; and that he too heard in 'ought' meanings apart from obligation.

By this you'll understand that we got drunk. (But drunk does not invalidate – or validate either. Drunk is simply useful in opening jammed doors, although it can't be used more than once.) We were almost in a fight because of Rex's beard. You wore one at your peril in those days. Men shouted 'Professor' across the street and a certain type of woman looked at you with disgust. The young fellows in De Bretts accused us of being poofters but when Rex unwound from the bar to his full height and they saw his lopped finger they backed off. He would have punched with that fist, and torn his stitches out – and I would have punched with my archivist's hands, and broken them possibly, and felt good about it; but seeing them turn and mumble off was enough.

Taxi home. And Harry was pleased with me in some obscure way, but not pleased to see Rex, which she showed by absenting herself in his embrace. He would not have tried embracing her if he had not been drunk. She asked after Alice but not the children. Harry was not interested in children (although interested in her own; interest, in fact, over-rode her other feelings, except that now and then a

159

mothering lust came over her and she bewildered them with attentions: perhaps I'll go into that later, perhaps not). Alice was a puzzle to her. She wanted to identify the woman behind the manners. How did Alice behave domestically? But Rex could not hear her questions; coldness was all he registered.

'I'd better find somewhere else to stay.'

'No, it's all right. It's me she's mad at.'

'I'll make the spare bed up after tea,' Harry called from the kitchen. 'Rex, do you eat lambs fry?'

'Yeah, love it. Hate the bloody stuff,' he whispered at me.

'You'll eat it and like it. There's always a price to pay.'

'Don't stop drinking on my account,' she called.

'I can go to Rita's.'

'Laurie Sefton's moved in. You can hear old Barton on his flute from here.'

'Rex, if you want to have a shower before tea . . .'

'Do I have to?' he whispered.

'It might be best.'

'Does she mean I stink?'

'Let's just say there's a fishy aroma. Did you bring any clothes?'

'My bag! I left it in the pub.'

I started to laugh.

'It's got my notebooks in it.'

'I'll get the car.'

'No you won't,' Harry said from the door.

'His bag's in the pub. It's got his poems.'

'He'll have to write some new ones then, won't he?' – with a nastiness insufficiently masked.

I started for the door.

'Not while you're drunk. Stay and finish the children. I'll take him.'

'God, Jack.' He was frightened of her and frightened for his poems.

'Go on, she can drive.'

I stayed and 'finished' the children – David at the kitchen table, Jill in her high chair. I sobered myself up and put them to bed. I floured the lambs fry and laid it ready for the pan. Then I sat and waited, and they did not come. I stood on the front porch and listened for the car;

160

imagined assaults and accidents. Imagined them running away together, up and over the Rimutakas into the Wairarapa. Harry's dislike was a pretence. My best friend had run off with my wife. I ran up to the gate and looked each way – and ran back to the phone and didn't know who to call. My life was overturned. Then, seeing the peeled potatoes and the meat, I put stupidity aside. I sat in my chair and folded my fingers. I had better believe that Harry meant what she said or Rex would overrun me in my marriage and ruin it.

I heard the car – a cheerful toot – and climbed to the road again. Harry, grinning, beautifully coloured-up and sharpened-up, came swinging from the garage in her small-woman stride. 'Got it,' she said, and gave me a hug. 'We had to go to Naenae and then back to town.'

Rex came from the garage. 'By God she can drive.' Fresh blood showed on his bandage. He held up his bag. 'I'm not sure it's worth it.'

'Now I deserve a drink,' Harry said. She poured a glass of sherry, while Rex lowered himself into a chair and nursed his hand.

'Sore?'

'Yes.'

'Let me look. How did it happen?'

'I had to grab this bastard by the collar – '

'He tackled him. You should have been there, Jack. We were great.'

I fetched scissors and a fresh bandage and doctored him while Harry sat complacently sipping sherry. His blind finger made me wince. The loss of the nail seemed a worse mutilation than the loss of two joints. I sponged away the leaking blood and freed the popped stitch, which made him hiss and stiffen his legs.

'Sorry.'

'Go ahead. I deserve some pain.'

'You'll have to get a new stitch put in.'

'Not tonight. Bandage it up.'

'We had to chase him all the way to Naenae,' Harry said.

'Who?'

'The man who took the bag.'

'Pot-bellied bloke,' Rex said.

'We saw him getting into a taxi by De Bretts. He was halfway along the Hutt Road before I got close. We just thought we'd follow and stop him when he got out. But we lost him when the taxi turned up a street in Naenae. Then Rex saw him outside a house. He tackled him when he tried to run.'

'Shit,' Rex said as I wound the bandage on.

'But the poems weren't in the bag.' I had never seen her so gleeful. 'Only a pair of trousers and a shirt. He left the dirty clothes and the notebooks in the taxi.'

'So you didn't get them?'

'Yes we did. We went back to town, to the taxi depot. They called up the driver and he'd put all the stuff in a rubbish tin by the station.'

'Don't tell me – '

'Yes we did. I did. I even got his dirty underpants.'

I looked at her delighted face. 'You'll have to come more often, Rex. What was in the notebooks?'

'Just some stuff.'

'Worth going through rubbish tins for?'

In fact they contained some of his best Loomis poems, as well as the first half dozen of the *Work Songs* – and Harry does not even get a dedication there. I handled the notebooks several years ago and found a greasy stain on the cover of one. Fish and chips from the rubbish tin? Nobody outside us three – two now – knows the story of that near loss. Though surely he kept his new poems in his head. I kept every line – every 'Oh' and exclamation mark – of *First Fruits* while I was putting it together. But there, I'm not a poet. Poets are forgetful. And ungenerous.

I'll ask Harry some time if she'd like to sell her story to the Elf. He's intrigued by *Work Songs* – wrong about it too. 'Plebeian sojourn' – what a phrase. It needed no stepping down for Rex to go where his father had been all his working life. He did not take manual jobs and haul nets on a fishing boat to collect material for poems. He lived his life, he went his ways, out of complexities of need and his poetry rose from where he happened to be. 'Poet' though, that condition? – it's too hard. His poetry, in some way, may have needed his behaviour. I'll leave it to the Elf to sort that out, he'll find a way (which will probably be wrong).

'Ring Alice. Tell her you're here,' Harry said.

'No.'

'Then I will.' She had spare energy to use.

'I'll go somewhere else if you do.'

'Keep out of it, Harry.'

'Go and put the dinner on, is that what you mean? I hope you did some onions for the liver.'

'If you've been going through rubbish tins shouldn't you have a bath?'

'Don't start quarrelling over me,' Rex said.

'Whatever went wrong, I'm on her side. She's got three children, don't forget. And so have you.'

'You think like you drive. We're having a break. I haven't said I'm not going back.'

'So it's your decision?'

'It's nobody's decision. We'll just let it turn out, that's all.'

'Oh ho, the lazy way. In the meantime you get drunk and lose your poems while she stays home and washes the naps.'

'Jesus!' he said. I felt sorry for him. 'Have you got any Aspros?' His face had gone grey and I think he was close to passing out. I was sorry for Harry too. Some buried part of her was jolted free and, it seemed to me, was hurting her. But she leaned sideways to see his face and went off to the bathroom and came back with Panadeine. 'These are best. Don't take them all.'

'Lay off him, Harry.'

'OK. I'll get back to the kitchen where I belong.' She smiled through the servery, hamming sweetness. 'Call me if you need any more driving.'

He stayed three nights with us and on the third Alice came knocking at our door. She seemed to me more beautiful than ever – more bones, interesting declivities, in her face. Knowledge in the place of satisfaction. She was, though, perfectly presented: not just any fisherman's wife.

'Is he here?'

'Yes, he is. He's out at the moment. But he's here.'

'Can I come in?'

I showed her into the living-room, where Harry embraced her with great warmth. (I smelt Alice's perfume on her cheeks that night.)

'Where is he?'

'He's round at Rita Bullen's, he shouldn't be long. Put Alice's bag in the bedroom, Jack.'

I lugged it away – even when pursuing a runaway husband Alice was not one to travel light – but left it on the stripped bed, not the one Rex was sleeping in. I did not know exactly where I stood.

A little of my story must find a place. I was entering the long middle portion of my life that can be described as prohibitive. I had been active morally; more 'do' than 'don't' in the way I went about things. Nothing went wrong dramatically – fear began to creep in, that is all. I suppose it has to do with uncertainty, my long apprenticeship in drawing back. Arms at sides, feet together – there's some certainty in that. One offers a cheek to be kissed. But a cheek alone is not enough. Nakedness must be offered too. Vulnerabilities must be exposed. And death is seen then, standing by at the side of love.

It was more than I could handle. I became afraid. More and more I found myself taking care; and from this grew a Skeatian code of 'don't'. I went inside and closed a door behind me.

This, with some propriety, becomes self-exposure. It is also an over-statement of the case. Harry still loved me. I became afraid that she would stop. Instead of trying harder – which probably wouldn't have worked anyway – I did less and less, drew my arms in closer to my sides so that she would find nothing to take exception to. But there was no salvation there. She loved me a little less each day: when she found that I had started knotting my shoelaces double; when she heard me tell David to stop behaving like a four-year-old. He was four at the time. Her pleasure in seeing me come home drunk is not, as I have called it, obscure.

Now here I was wanting to interfere in Rex's marriage. I saw where his duty lay. He should go back to Auckland and take up his role, honour his contract, as husband and father. Yet I wanted him to be free. Loomis was my possession too, Loomis put a roundness on me, unpinched my mind. Harry was no enemy of it. I cannot untangle the knot, but I believe that creek and town and Petleys made it possible for me to come out and meet her now and then. Alice, though, was the enemy of Loomis in Rex. Nonsense, I argued with myself, there's plenty of good verse gets written in the kitchen;

the back garden; the marriage bed. There's a chance that Alice will make him human and wash away the blood. But this, I saw, would diminish him. It would destroy him. Alice would break the artefact of his childhood and whatever Rex might write after that would have no animation, no privacy. He understood. That was why the fishing boat and the labouring jobs. It even explained his lopped-off finger.

I calmed down, I smiled to myself (although I left the suitcase where it was). Rex knew the danger. Rex would not be hurt. He might go back with Alice, but would not go back in the way she wanted. He would stay married and stay free. I trusted him to keep Loomis safe – and approved of him, in the same breath, for carrying out his duties as a husband.

But with beings as large and complicated as Alice and Rex one cannot stay in a fixed position. I was no sooner back in the living-room than Alice was dominant again. She would wash him in Persil and hang him out to dry.

'I'll look at the kids,' I said; but closed the door softly after kissing them and went out the back door and up to the footpath and slid along underneath the trees to Upland Road. I whistled to drive my sneakiness away. Rex answered from the steps to Central Terrace. I put my fingers in my mouth and gave the ear-splitter we'd used up and down Loomis Creek. He echoed it, although without the shrillness I had achieved.

'You were never any good at that.'

'Wrong hand, Jack. Had to use my left.'

'Alice is here.'

'Yeah.' He smiled calmly. 'I didn't think she'd be long.'

'What are you going to do?'

'Go home, I guess.'

'You can stay with us as long as you like.'

'Thanks. But I've got to go. I've been missing her.'

'I suppose Harry must have rung her up.'

He shook his head. 'She knew where I was. She goes home to Daddy, I just head for Jack.'

'Any time.' I nearly wept with love. (It came and went, all my life, along with other feelings – but never so strongly as this.)

'It lasts fifteen rounds, Jack. This is just round two.'

Alice stood up when we came in. They looked at each other

without smiling. Then she raised her arms and they embraced. The meeting could not help seeming rather badly acted.

'Sneaky sod,' Harry said to me in the kitchen. She was pleased with me again. Our contest over Rex and Alice's marriage was one of the things that brought us together. We made tea and took it in and went off to bed. I woke hours later to hear them making love. The duet was more restrained that night. Perhaps they were just getting older.

He must have had to keep his finger out of the way.

Three Visitors and a Dwarf

There is no pain, only discomfort, which stops when they take the catheter out. Then it's just a holiday, with visits from his wife.

She's fascinated by the technology: a resectoscope inserted through the penis, the spongy collar round the urethra trimmed with a cutting current. It must take such fine strokes, like shading in the hidden parts of a flower.

Jack is pleased that he interests her. There's a sparkle in Harry, a flick of eye and finger, that he has not seen for years. He does not mind being weakened if it restores her. He wonders if anyone has told her that when they resume 'marital relations' his performance will be 'only marginally impaired'. Why have all his doctors, here and in Wellington, told him that without being asked? He can't remember showing anxiety. And Harry will not be anxious, merely interested, in her way. Orgasm without ejaculation. Jack will have a scientific value.

Although his sexual parts are interfered with he thinks very little about sex. He tries not to think about micturition, although it comes frequently to mind. Blood in the toilet bowl unsettles him. He does not like the mixing of vital and waste fluids. Some essential barrier must be thinned. What if a rupture takes place, an appalling inrush . . .? He moves with care, starts nothing suddenly.

Harry is fascinated by the elderly progress of his hand to his water glass. 'You're like one of those South American sloths.'

He sees himself hanging upside down from a branch. How pleasant it would be to have one's natural movements proceed at that pace. Thought, care, anxiety slowed down? Curiosity creeping like treacle. What happened on that day – out in the boat – on the gulf . . .? How . . .? Why . . .? Answers lying motionless as one creeps slowly over them.

'That boy across in the corner bed had a gangrenous appendix. He thought he was going to die.'

'He looks fit enough from here.'

'The old man next to him is dying. He's going home this afternoon. He's got marvellous hands.'

'How do you mean?'

'Big long bones. They look as if they could hold the world.'

'You're not going to get religion in here?'

'The chaplain left a pamphlet. See. A rose. They've got good symbols.'

'Roses belong to everyone.'

'The best things in life are free.' He half sings it and laughs, which stabs him above his pubic bone. 'That thing they scraped out of me looked like a rose. You should do anatomical drawings.'

'I like subjects that stay still. Oh, I brought you . . .' Slides into her bag and lifts out a bundle in a napkin. Unwraps it on the blanket. Broad bean pods, glossy, immature, each one knobbled like a spine. She cracks one open – how quick her fingers are – and shows him the tender beans in their beds of satin. 'Hold out your hand.' Thumbs them one by one on to his palm. He eats them like jelly beans. Sweet and bitter, they wash his mouth. They take all the stickiness out of his mind; and he loves his wife. He's sharp and clean and definite.

'How's your work?'

'Nearly done. A couple more days.'

'You'll be finished by the time I get home.'

'It fitted in nicely. Jo's going to be late, as usual.'

'You should team up with someone else.' Then thinks, No, you can't just dump her like a sack of rubbish; and is pleased when Harry says, 'I couldn't do that. She needs me, Jack. It isn't just work with her, you know.'

'I know. It's a problem. I guess we've got her for keeps.'

She is pleased that he includes himself. Opens another bean pod. 'Aren't they beautiful. Like pearls.'

'I grow good beans.'

'You do. I'm sorry they hung weights on your penis.'

'No, they didn't.' He laughs and hurts himself again. 'The weights just held the water bag in place. I had a bag of water inflated . . .' He explains and sees her sparkle at the cleverness. It makes him proud of his operation. He feels as though he's done it himself.

She puts the beans in his cabinet, drops the empty pods in the waste. 'I went to see your mother.' Grimaces. 'Two hospitals in one day.'

'How was she?'

'A bit of paranoia coming back. Not for us. For the Asian nurses. She thinks she's been kidnapped to Singapore. And the swords. God, the swords.'

'What swords?'

'They had a troop of Scottish dancers in. Can you imagine? All the old ladies in their chairs and these girls in kilts hopping over swords. Your mother thought they'd come to murder her. Who's Georgina?'

'Georgina?'

'She thinks the woman in the other bed is someone called that. All the Scottish girls were her daughters, I think.'

'Georgina's daughters?'

'You'd better get well, Jack. I don't want to go back there again.'

'No, don't. Has Alice phoned?'

'No.'

'What about John Dobbie?'

'Not him either.'

He asks her to telephone John. For the first time in his life he wants a visit from the Elf.

'I thought you couldn't stand him.'

'I can't. But if he's going to do the book I'd better see he gets it right. I'm not going to tell him everything.' There's very little he will say, in fact. 'I might tell him how you saved the notebooks, remember?'

'You'll have to say he was running away from Alice. She won't like that.'

'It's not her book.'

'What does it matter, anyhow, that old stuff? No one's going to sort that marriage out.'

'I won't say much.'

'Let her be – what do they call it, dressed in white?'

'His muse. She wasn't that. Nor was Margot.'

'Who cares? It's nobody's business any more. He'd better leave me out.'

Jack gets out of bed, sloth-like, waits for a stab, and walks up the corridor and back with his wife. Her thin arm, hooked in his, holds him up. She smiles at him, enjoying his weakness and her strength. No one is going to sort out this marriage either – least of all him. And it's definitely no one else's business. The sister in her office thinks that they are Mr and Mrs Skeat passing by, but they're a good deal more than that.

Harry tucks him in and fills his water glass. She kisses him on the mouth and goes away. A flick of her skirt at the door, rubber steps in duet with the dinner trolley. Usually she kisses him on the forehead. Usually, when they walk, she goes along half a step in front – and sometimes makes a two-footed jump on to the kerb. Once it had embarrassed him. Now he hopes that she will jump, or take one of her long elastic steps, into the lift. She will go clickety-clack on the door to make it hurry.

A piece of broad bean skin is lodged in his molars. He works with his tongue, patiently; gets it free; crushes it between his incisors. A delicate bitter flavour spreads along his tongue. 'Thank you,' he whispers. How like drunkenness operations are, they make you come out and say it. 'Be careful, love. Remember your seat belt,' he says.

He does not tell John Dobbie that the enlarged gland reminded him of a rose, but likens it to a cauliflower. 'Don't be scared when your turn comes. It's no worse than getting a tooth pulled out. The worst part is the pre-op stuff. Doctors poking round up your bum. The loss of dignity is the worst part.'

'Do I necessarily have to have a turn?' His stuffiness hides fear.

'I don't know the percentages. But you should have one, John. It's a male experience. A man isn't a man until he's had his prostatectomy.'

'Rex didn't.'

'But his father did. In the days when they did it by incision. Rex used it, remember, in "Unkind Cuts".'

'Yes, I know. It isn't one of his best poems. In fact it's rather bad.'

Jack is disappointed. He prefers the Elf one-eyed. 'I asked you to come . . .' But he finds he can't get to it without preliminaries. Enquires about the book and hears that it is early days, the actual writing is still years away.

'I don't think I want you just yet. One has to be organized. I've got my lists, and of course you're one of the first on his boyhood one. It's going to take a lot of your time, I hope you're ready. And a tape recorder. Just taking notes isn't any good.'

'What if this thing turns into a cancer?'

The Elf draws his breath in with a hiss. He really is afraid. 'Don't joke about it.'

'Touch wood.' Jack touches his head but the Elf leans down and touches the skirting board. 'Anyway,' Jack says, 'it's not only Loomis I know about. My wife saved *Work Songs*, you know. And some of the Loomis poems.' He tells the story, tells it well, and is astonished to see that the Elf does not believe him. It's fisherman Rex he rejects as much as the events of that night. There's no place for dirty clothes and bleeding fingers in the authorized biography. 'Ask Harry if you don't believe me.' But Harry is rejected too. Jack is furious. 'There's a grease mark on one of the books, from the rubbish tin. Go and look in the Turnbull if you don't believe me. Jesus, do you want Rex or not? He was running away from Alice. He was clearing out.'

'Perhaps he realized how upset she was by the loss of his finger and made himself scarce until it healed. He didn't go back on the fishing boats. He'd got all he needed from there.'

'Did she tell you that?'

'It wasn't an ideal marriage, everyone knows. But it lasted for twenty years, until that woman broke it up.'

'That woman as you call her – ' But he stops. He'll give away nothing about Margot. The Margot part of Rex's life must come from her.

The Elf, meanwhile, says, 'The world came very close to losing Rex. If it hadn't been for Alice, against enormous odds . . . If I've got an idea of him now it's because of her. And I do have him, up here – ' taps his forehead – 'after huge amounts of work. There was so much to *pull around* and *get in shape*. And Jack, with respect, I don't want you interfering. I don't want people chipping in. All I want from you is some details about his boyhood.'

'You'll have to talk to Margot, though.'

'Yes. It won't be pleasant. I'll face that. But she's not going to alter Rex for me. What you forget is, I knew him too. I was his friend, I was at his shoulder . . .'

You were squatting on the ceiling, watching him shit. And now you're busy inventing a Rex who doesn't have a lower bowel at all.

He lies back on his pillows and closes his eyes.

'I'm sorry if I've made you tired. I'll go,' John Dobbie says.

'No, hold on.' He takes two or three deep breaths. A present for the Elf . . .

'One night we rode our bikes over to Te Atatu, when it was all farms there and no motorway. We had home-made flattie spears, number eight wire filed sharp and lashed on tea-tree poles, and we went after flounder on the mud flats. Rex's father had lent us a kerosene lamp and we went along in water up to our shins . . . There were hundreds of them. We got a whole sugar sack. We got tired of spearing. But what I remember most, Rex put his foot on one and he got such a fright he dropped his spear. So there it was kicking under his foot – bare feet you know – and him yelling at me to pick up his spear. But what I did, I stuck my own spear in, so close it went between his toes, it grazed the skin. There isn't any poem, but remember, "The muscle kick beneath the sole, the spear between the toes" – '

'In "Dangers".'

'That's right. That's where it comes from. It's not obscure as long as you know.'

'Jack, this is good. This is the sort of thing I want from you. As soon as you're out we'll make a time – '

'We made tin canoes out of corrugated iron. Filled all the holes with pitch and sawed paddles out of six by one.'

'I'll bring my tape-recorder.'

'We launched them at the back of Rex's place and paddled all the way down Loomis Creek to the sea. You're from Helensville, you know about mangroves. The tide was coming in and the wind was blowing. We ran into waves and we got swamped. He was in front, I saw him go down, then I went down. We had to swim. That was the first time he sank in a boat.'

'Jack – '

'I suppose he thought about it out off Tiri that night.'

'How can anyone know?'

'Harry and I were overseas. I didn't know he was dead until Jill wrote to us in Athens.'

172

'I'm sorry, I would have written – '

'Tell me about it, John. I went back through the papers but there wasn't much.'

'It's in the book. It's in the memoir.'

'Yes, I know.' And quite well done: his passion for fishing, his love of being alone out on the sea; and the fishing lines, the tub of bait, the torn shorts, the old green and black Loomis football jersey. The clinker-built dinghy and the antique motor. But why did he go as far as Wenderholm when usually he started from one of the East Coast bays? And what about the easterly, the rain and heavy swell; and the time of day? How could an experienced boatie like Rex get halfway to the Barrier, in bad weather, in the dark, and then have his motor run out of fuel? Why don't you ask those questions, John? Instead of going on about the tragedy?

'Have you ever thought Rex wanted to die?'

'No. Absurd.'

'He didn't have a life jacket. He didn't have any oars.'

'Rex was careless, you know that.'

'He wasn't careless on the sea.'

'And over-confident. He went for those long swims. He probably thought he could swim ashore. I never met anyone less suicidal.'

'John – '

'Anyway, the coroner went into that. I've got the report. He wasn't very pleased with Rex – but it was carelessness. I suppose living with Margot would make one like that. And I must say, Jack – '

'For God's sake, you can't blame Margot.'

' – I'm surprised to hear you, his supposed best friend – '

There's a roaring in Jack's ears. He'll strike at the Elf for that 'supposed'. He'll strike for Margot too, if he can reach out fast enough.

'Hey, hey! Nurse! Good God!'

A sloth-blow. The Elf should have been away and halfway up the wall instead of being anchored in his chair, holding his shoulder in that disbelieving way.

'That hurt.'

'I meant it to. I'm tired of people getting at Margot. She's worth a dozen of Alice any day.'

173

'I've a good mind . . . you could . . .'

'She's probably got a stack of manuscripts, John. And you'll never get your hands on them.'

He sees that the Elf knows and is unshaped by it: grotesquely swollen on one side and withered on the other. He's hurt far more badly than by an inept punch. Jack should have seen it earlier and not let dislike and jealousy carry him away.

The Elf moves his left arm. He moves his legs and feet. He's like an insect on the pavement, trying to cross spaces too huge to comprehend. Jack wants to comfort him. Console him. Repair him.

'I'm sorry, John. It's just that people getting at Margot – '

'I know she must have manuscripts. If you've got any influence–'

'I haven't. I haven't seen her since Rex died. I'm sorry I hit you.'

'I'll have a bruise. Did you try to hit me on the jaw?'

'Yes. Rex always aimed for the jaw.'

'It's not funny. I could charge you.'

'Please don't. I'm sick in hospital.'

'I'm going.'

'John.' Stops him at the bed-end. 'I will help. We'll make a date as soon as I'm out. I've got lots of stuff.'

'I think you should. It's up to all of us – all of his friends . . . We've got to see that Rex is properly' almost says 'done', but manages, with a stutter, 'appreciated.'

'I agree. Massage it, John. Get someone to rub liniment on.' Does he still have a wife? 'Thanks for coming. Good luck with your work.'

'I never knew hospital visiting was so dangerous.' The Elf gets out of the room with a joke. Jack is happy that he manages it. He is still unhappy with himself. Punches at sixty! And no answer to his question. The question bungled thoroughly in fact.

There are not many people he can turn to now.

Has weakness, medication, the knife (the electric current), pulled him so much closer to the surface of his feelings that he strikes at a man he does not like? What will happen (what happens) when a woman he likes, for whom in fact he has a guilty love, pays a visit?

'I'm not sure,' she says, 'that it's proper to call on a man in your condition.'

He takes her hand. Tears start in his eyes. He hopes they remain invisible. 'Fiona. How marvellous.' The long vowel threatens to get away.

'You don't look sick.'

'It's not really a sickness – '

'You look like a little boy wagging it from school. Can I kiss you?' On the forehead. Sisterly.

'Who told you I was here?'

'John Dobbie came steaming in to see Mum. I'm staying there for a couple of nights. What's this about Dad killing himself?'

'I don't want to talk about that. How are you, Fiona?'

She turns her head, turns back. He wonders about tears in her eyes – a tear-flash? She says brightly, 'That sounds like more than just a polite enquiry.'

'It is. You're my might-have-been. Everybody needs one of those.' This is what weakness brings: sentimentality. Fiona is only a little pleased. She takes her hand away and rummages in her bag.

'I brought you something. Yoghurt. It's only from the dairy across the road.'

'Thank you.'

'It's still cold. Eat it now. Have you got a spoon?' She goes away, finds the kitchen, comes back with a teaspoon. 'You've got John Dobbie very upset.'

'What about Alice?'

'She's interested. She's not quite sure how it affects her.'

'What do you mean?'

'As first wife. How it affects her standing. I think she'll probably come down against it.'

He finds this repugnant. The yoghurt, too, is not to his taste. Although there are lumps of peach the sweetness is synthetic. He puts it aside. Fiona, with her tanned face and large eyes, seems both tough and vulnerable.

'Don't you want it? I'll finish it.'

He would have wiped the spoon, even with a woman he loved. But there's something over-emphatic, perhaps a little frantic, in the way she digs every last bit from the carton.

'What's wrong, Fiona?'

'Nothing's wrong.' She holds it over the basket and drops it like a bomb. 'Bull's-eye.' Over-bright. 'I think you're wrong about Dad. I know he was supposed to be good in boats, and what he did was so bloody stupid. But I don't know, maybe he got drunk.'

'Booze was never a problem with Rex.'

'Maybe he had a fight then, with what's-her-name. And forgot all his boat-drill or something.'

'Maybe. Can't you say her name?'

'Oh, I forget. Margot, is that it?'

'Did you ever meet her?'

'I never got the opportunity. Or had the desire.'

'You would have liked her.' But that is more sentimentality. Fiona brushes it away.

'I know poets are always killing themselves. It's an occupational hazard, isn't that right? But Dad – he was far too tough, you know that.'

'I'm sorry if I've upset you.'

'I'm not upset. If he did I want to know. In the cause of truth.' Sarcastically. 'Though I'm not sure I want it written down in that little man's book. Have you talked to the Loomis lot? What do they think?'

He tells her about his visit to Lila and it seems more than ever to him that something has been hidden. But he's disturbed too by Fiona's phrase, 'the Loomis lot'. It hurts him to think of her locked away from them on the wrong side of Auckland. 'Rex used to take you out there now and then.'

'Oh, a few times. Lila's birthday. I never even got to call her grandma. You were there. Sliding in the mud.'

'At Moa Park.'

'Hundreds of them. Enough to start a colony on Mars. And all their names. Tweetie-weetie. Toddy-woddie.'

'They never said that.'

'It seemed like it. You've no idea how I envied them. At home we all rattled round – peas in a can – but they were squashed up close, like strawberries.' She frees herself with cleverness. 'Anyway Jack, I think you're wrong. I just think they can't stand death if it comes too soon. Dad was only fifty-eight. And somehow they'd lost him sooner than that. He died before they could get him back.'

He's startled by the insight, and wants to know how she arrived at it. But suddenly she's had enough of Rex. 'We're going to have him breakfast, lunch and tea for years now, with this stupid book.'

'Are you going to help?'

'I suppose so. I suppose I've got to. I've even said I'll try to get the other two to help. Mum's got so much invested in it. It's her book really, she'll just about write it. The first one was Dobbie's ego trip.'

'Is that why you're staying at her place?' He knows she wants to talk about it. There had been a pause at the start – a coin upon the ground that he might pick up if he cared. Now she decides to be evasive.

'How do you like retirement, Jack? What do you do with all your time?'

'I work in the garden. I grow broad beans.'

'Is that going to keep you occupied for the rest of your life?'

'I go for walks. I drive down to Takapuna beach and walk along it and walk back. Long Bay too. Long Bay's longer. When I'm out of here I might walk North Cape to the Bluff.'

'While Harry works?'

'Harry might come. She's nearly finished her book.'

This time it's more than a tear-flash. She makes no attempt to conceal it. He's tired now – five minutes, a change of direction, can tire him – but he knows the duty laid on him. Is she grieving, or despairing, or just sad? He keeps a pack of Snowtex by his pillow; pulls one out, offers it. She slashes at each eye. It seems a way of saying that she has no value.

'Harry makes sense. I'd give anything to be like her.'

'You make sense. Your work's just as important.'

'How does she stay so – all together?'

'She's not. You'd be surprised.' He does not want to talk about Harry. 'What's wrong, Fiona?'

'Remember at Mum's barbecue? How I caught him watching us?'

'Your husband? I wouldn't say caught.' He feels a little stab of pain – alarm – in the place by his pubic bone.

'I never knew until then I could make him jealous.'

Is that what she is doing now, coming to visit? 'Fiona – '

'Don't worry, it's nothing to do with you.'

He is relieved to be dismissed – although he doesn't like it. But she is close to giving up confession and going away. He sees her flash of anger, no more tears.

'Sorry, I'm a bit confused. Marriages are hard to understand.'

'Mine isn't. Mine is simple.'

'Yes?'

'I found out I don't like him.'

'Nonsense, Fiona.'

'For God's sake.' She stands up. 'Is that all you can say?'

'I'm sorry.'

'I might as well have stayed at home with Mum.'

'Sit down. I'm not used to people telling me things. Come on. Sit down.' She obeys. 'Now, what happened?'

'No fights. No kitchen knives, none of that. I was just so sure of him, that's all. And when I found out he was jealous I started looking at him again. I saw all sorts of things I didn't know. Like, I saw he was cheating. Not just with women – although he's doing that. I mean in conversation. Pretending to care. Pretending to care about me. He's jealous just because I'm his, that's all. He doesn't really want me except as part of his territory. And the children the same. All it is is "my kids". He doesn't even like them.'

Jack wants to say she imagines it. But she leans forward as though she's now about to say the worst thing. 'Jack, he doesn't care about his work. He's just been saying all that too. Pretending to be – pretending he knows what people are. But what we are – me, the kids, his job, we're a kind of fuel he pumps into himself to keep on running.'

Stories, he thinks. Everybody has one. Marriages: each one the same, and different. 'He must like the children. I can't believe he doesn't.'

'Do you think I'm saying this for fun? Jack, it was like unzipping him, a zip fastener right down his middle – you saw how pink and fat he was, and pleased with himself, and everything – and out stepped this, I don't know, black little dwarf.'

Jack shivers. Not just story. He seems to see the dwarf in himself, and feel the track, the metal itch, of a fastener from his forehead to his shrunken penis. He lets Fiona talk on – go for nouns and verbs and bend them crooked. She'll get there; arrive at a place she'll recognize; she will find out what to do. He thinks she may recognize the dwarf and come to like him. Look how he's shaken up her comfortable life. He thinks perhaps she'll start to look for unsuspected things in herself. Unzip herself.

And isn't that what he is doing too? His retirement work? Pulling himself open from his brainbox to the soles of his feet and finding out what's hidden by the pink exterior.

Did Rex do something like that, out in his boat?

Jack has given himself an added task. It is strange. Unwelcome.

He had thought he knew the dwarf in Rex already.

Notebook: 11

Moa Park. Lila's birthday, 1964. How did I get there?

There's a long middle journey and few large events on the way. My father used to tell me: 'The happy man lives in the Land of Steady Habits.' I came to believe in the wisdom of this. (For many years I thought he had invented the name but found out it belonged to Connecticut, where moral rectitude was bred in the bone.) I tried to turn my marriage into that place. Safety lay there. I made a little world like Rex's one that I've called 'Petley'. The difference is that his imagination was set free, the place generated poetry, while I, in my Land of Steady Habits, wrapped myself so tightly up that no light was able to escape. I was free from pain and danger and believed that Harry and David and Jill, locked up with me there, were also free.

This is not my story. I won't describe how I struggled out – part way out, there's a claw fixed in my ankle yet – but at those points along the way where I intersected with Rex I'll indicate what my position was – and that way of putting it gives a good idea of Jack Skeat in 1964.

My place at the picnic was outside. I did not want to be there. I did not want to be in Auckland, which had become dangerous; and I was not surprised that it spawned this fry of Petleys. They had crawled up from the mud; they had webbed feet and a slimy skin and were from mouth to anus a simple tube, ingesting, excreting, non-stop. (The only children I could accept were my own.) There were – there must have been – twenty grandchildren there. Of Lila and Les's eight only Tweet (and Joy) had failed to multiply.

I was welcome. Lila kissed me and Les pumped my forearm as though trying to dislocate my elbow. Melva, a widowed mother of five – her husband, Scahill, had been knocked off his bike, fatally this time – hugged me as though I were a God-sent replacement.

I was more welcome at Moa Park than in my mother's house.

There, again, at the door, she offered me her cheek while her body arched away from contact. She was selling the property and had written to say that I might have 'some memento of your father if you wish'. She would send it down – but I, with my instinct for neatness, had travelled up for a final look at the house, for a final sleep in my narrow bed. Even before she opened the door I began to wish I hadn't come.

My bedroom, stripped of all sign of me except the bed, drove me into a corner, where I wanted to sit down and hide my head. I had no place to occupy and felt reduced, as though by some process of skinning and drying. I had slept in the room on my visit with Harry – and she in a spare room, miles away – but had not been concerned with numbering then, or weighing parts.

'When you've washed I'll take you to your father's study.'

One washed after travelling, it was ordained. In the bathroom a ball of soap made from ends and slivers seemed to hold the meaning of my mother's life – but not my own. It was no better in my father's study. The room had not been used since his death. She had not turned it into a shrine, nothing like that, but had simply closed the door and turned the key. Now there was a grating in the lock and she had to rise a little on her toes to force it open. Daylight rinsed out the room but a puff of dead air in my mouth made me want to clear my throat and spit.

She crossed to the windows and opened the curtains. 'There's very little here, but take what you want.' She horrified me – horrifies me still. In any room that has not been entered for twenty years one cannot simply walk in and pull the curtains back and walk out again without looking round, without turning the head, however briefly, towards the desk or chair or the pictures on the walls. It's inhuman. I realized how badly my mother had been damaged and wanted my dry father to explain. But he could not – cannot. So I'll add 'hurt'. There must have been hurt as well as damage.

She left me and went to some other part of the house and I stood like a lost boy in the room where my father had smoked his pipe and delivered his cramped-up homilies. The ebony desk, with its leather surface mummified and lifting at the edges, the wooden chair angled to the right, holding its high arms in a shrug, the glass book-cases empty of books – empty of the bones, polished stones, trophies, souvenirs, the old postcards and letters, the ashtrays and paper-weights other non-book-reading men might have filled them with – made me shiver. Could my father's life have been so empty? How could one die and leave only a dead room behind? A dead wife?

I hunted for his pipes as though I might save Walter Skeat with them. They lay in the top left hand drawer, stems criss-crossed like Pick-up-sticks. Their bowls were narrow and scraped clean, no trace of ash, their mouthpieces discoloured from sucking. One had teeth marks bitten in. Perhaps it was a cheaper pipe – or had he clamped his teeth in a moment of high feeling? All were straight stemmed and wooden bowled: no eccentricity in material or shape. Strong emotion seemed unlikely too. He had, I recalled, smoked a mild blend. A leather pouch, with click-buttons instead of a zip, lay at the back of the drawer. I felt a wad of tobacco in the corner and thought perhaps a little of its aroma would be kept, but when I emptied it on my palm it was lifeless – no moisture, no colour, no smell. I closed the drawer. If my father had left false teeth, a hair-piece, an appendix in a bottle, I would have taken them. But it seemed to me that his pipes were instruments for jabbing at life with and keeping it at bay.

The pictures on the walls: two of them, framed photographs of coaches and horse teams and ladies in Merry Widow hats being helped by coachmen up the steps. He had probably bought them at a junk shop or snaffled them when some tourist office was closed, because a room must have something hanging on the walls. Snaffled – one of his rare joky words. A word might be all I would find to carry away.

I found his Gladstone bag in a cupboard by the bookshelves. The leather at the hinges creaked and split as I forced it open, releasing an aroma the tobacco had lacked. Inside were three books held in a perished rubber band. They surprised me: two by John Buchan, one by Sapper. My father, to my knowledge, only read the newspaper. I had brought home books by Buchan and Sapper – and found their English heroes less convincing than Buck Duane and Brazos Keene.

Dad, although he had picked them up – it was part of his job to know what his son was reading – had only tapped their covers and nodded his head. He recognized them as British stuff but showed no interest in reading them. Years later he was, it seemed, a fan of Bulldog Drummond and Richard Hannay – or had he brought the books home for me? I rejected that. He had never brought me anything except at the proper times, why should he have started on the day of his death? I looked at them to see if they might be first editions and came across the name 'G. Feist' written on the fly leaf. My father had a friend he borrowed from! It was like learning that he jumped from moving trains. Or perhaps – yes, yes – he had bought them, like the pictures, in a second-hand shop. The mystery was why they were alone in his bag. But wouldn't my mother have sent his business papers to his office?

I put them back. I carried off the only other book in the room, a *Webster's International Dictionary*, 1907, and I have it still, six kilograms – no, thirteen pounds as it was my father's. When I got it home I discovered how he passed his time, sitting in his study smoking his pipe. He read the dictionary and marked words on a scale of plus to minus five. There's nothing systematic in his progress, he didn't start at 'aam' and work on through – never graded aam at all in fact – but opened the pages at random and marked the words that struck him, that's my guess. It was more than a game. Why does 'pawky' earn plus five? And why 'love' minus two? With love perhaps he was being clever. But why give cunning and slyness such high marks? Unless he marked the word for its sound? He marked for sound now and then. 'Paxwax' on the same page gets plus one. But plus five (+5) is excessive for pawky. Remember that my father was a moralist.

Here are some of his words, in no order, pp.852–3: lily-livered, −3; light-footed, +5; ligustrin, −2; Lilliputian, −3; like-minded, −5 +3; lightsome, +3; likerous −3; liliaceous, +5.

I can't work this out. Is it a commentary or was he trying to write his life? Now and then he underlined a particular meaning. For 'Lilliputian' it is not 'the diminutive race described in Swift' he is marking but 'a person or thing of very small size'. For 'liliaceous' it's 'like the blossom of a lily in general form'. And for 'ligustrin' it's not the chemical substance that gets the mark but the 'bitter principle' it's extracted from. There are too many contradictions, yet my father was not one to be pulled in opposing ways. If he gave 'like-minded' both plus three and minus five he must have been applying it to more than one person – correction, one couple or company. (One has to be alert.) Perhaps he meant himself and my mother, then himself and me. But who was 'lily-livered', and why? 'Lilliputian', 'lightsome' – which is used of women, isn't it? – and 'likerous'? Perhaps he marked likerous for sound.

Words that have two marks make it almost certain that he had people in mind, or situations. As for 'bitter principle', it must apply to his marriage. 'Principle' (p.1138); the meaning 'fundamental substance or energy' is the one underlined. He marks it twice, plus and minus five.

'Light-footed' makes me glad. He must have loved his Friday jump from the moving train.

I learned none of this on my visit. I left the *Webster's* lying on the floor beside my bag and walked around the section, looked in the summer house, looked in the toolshed, where I found the tools thinner in the blade but sharp and clean. My mother had hired a man to keep the section straight, but fired (dismissed) him when he left the spade out overnight. She used schoolboys after that and found them 'more amenable and cheaper'.

I said to her at dinner: 'Who was G. Feist?'

'It's not a name I know.'

'It's written on some books in his Gladstone bag.'

'I saw them. They're not books I had any interest in.'

'What went wrong between you and Dad?' My voice had a starved sound and seemed to plead rather than question.

She stopped her small-mouthed chewing, looked at me with still eyes, laid down her knife and fork; she swallowed. She patted her dry mouth with a serviette.

'You have no licence to ask me questions.'

Anger would have pleased me. I had thought there might be outrage or denial. But my mother informed me that I had no licence. She did not say I had no right. It was not even a principle. She picked up her knife and fork and went on with her meal. When I think of it I wonder why I did not take her by the shoulders and try to shake some natural feeling into her. I can see her head flinging back and forth, out of time. Or I could have jumped up from the table and left the house. A son require a licence! And she, the wife, the mother, she hears for the first time the question that splits her open and shows her huge sick part and all she does is dab her lips and fork a piece of carrot into her mouth. But perhaps she had another room in her head, behind her face, where she sat, like my father in his study, and asked the question, answered it – and wished herself dead? She could not be confined to this woman at the table.

'More water?' Poured some in my glass.

'Thank you.'

She offered, perhaps, an apology? I cannot say. With my mother I'm not able to trust myself. All I can say is I had to put my serviette (must say table napkin) to my eyes. In a little while I offered to stay in Auckland and help her shift but she said she had hired a firm for that and I must go on Sunday as I'd planned; and I agreed, I must go home.

Getting through Sunday was difficult. I walked into Loomis and bought a paper and read it on the back lawn, avoiding the summer-house. Distantly I heard the front door bell but thought it must be someone come to talk about the shift. I wasn't prepared for Rex when he appeared round the side of the house.

'Gidday, Skeatsie.' How wrong the greeting sounded. It belonged in other places, other times.

'Rex. Who told you I was here?'

'Sniffed you out. You can't come to Loomis and keep away from me.'

He was wearing shorts and sandals and an unbuttoned shirt. The sun had been at him, colouring and oiling his long muscles and solid joints. He looked as if he could pick me up and carry me away under his arm. He squatted and shook hands and kept a little springing in his knees. Dulcie had seen me walking home with my paper, so Rex had jumped in his car and come to get me. It was Lila's birthday and they were all at Moa Park having a picnic.

'No – '

'Mum'd never forgive you. She's fifty-five. Hey, the old man's sixty-three, how about that?'

'No, I can't.'

'I cleared it with your old lady. She's OK.' He widened his eyes. 'She calls me Mr Petley. It's like we've never met.'

'No one's met my mother.' Harry was the only other one I would say that to. I folded the paper and took it inside, I told her I would be home by mid-afternoon (did I say 'home'?), and I drove with Rex to Moa Park. And there they were, as he had promised; more Petleys than I could handle.

'Man, can we breed,' standing by the car. A girl in a blue pinafore dress ran to him and he hoisted her, looped her in his arms, glued her for a moment to his front, then spun her to face me in two hands. 'This one's mine. Fiona. Fee.'

I saw nothing of Petley, nothing of Rex; she was smooth and glossy and delicately made. She was a scaled-down Alice and I saw why she would run from the barefoot Petleys, in her party dress, in her white shoes. 'Where did you go?'

'I had to get Jack. Say hallo to Jack. He's my ole mate.'

'You shouldn't have.'

'Hallo, Fiona.'

The girl would not answer, she squirmed to turn around, she wanted him. He put her down and she leaned into his waist and hooked her fingers in the band of his shorts.

'Have they been ganging up on you? Tell me which ones and I'll dong some heads.' But he freed himself and took me to Lila and flopped down on his elbow at her side. He wasn't at ease – hard in his movements, grating in his words, with a kind of brutal defensiveness. He was fleshy and loud – made, made-up, for an occasion.

I gave Lila my news – dressed up my life for her, told her how settled and contented I was and how I went ahead at my work. None of it lies. Melva, Dulcie, Austin, Gareth, Verna were all there (Tweet was overseas), with two husbands and two wives and an offspring horde. The adults sat on rugs under the trees, drinking beer, while the children homed in, or went shooting out, the older ones to the creek and the kiosk, the younger to the nearby swings and slides. They seemed to come back by affective attraction, collect their pats and kisses, clutch their lollies and cherry cake, hold up a nose to be wiped, and then be repelled by an adult force (benign). A diagram of their shooting off would be like a batsman's century. The getting up and sitting down, the panting in and screeching out, the sliding of faces across my vision, the rolling on to an elbow and rolling back, the gobbling of lumps of cake and the slap and splash of beer and sentences half finished and pet names called out, made me dizzy. I did not know what was going on. The hugs, the ruffled hair; mock insult, friendly punch; the filled nappie by the birthday ham; red throat, floppy breast, missing pre-molar; and Les and Lila like the hub of a wheel, Les and Lila radiating. This was a family all right, but I longed for the quietness and stillness of mine.

Lila confused me; and disappointed, even as I sat admiring her. Once she had made Plasticine maidens with plaited hair; had cried for lost Lilas on the bridge. Now here she was red-faced and meaty-armed, screaming with laughter as Les amused a baby with his false teeth. When the child got them in its fist and dragged them dripping from his mouth, she fell over backwards, delight had so exhausted her.

Rex became easier. He was quick-eyed and didn't miss a thing, and although he didn't laugh he grinned. He winked at me. We took the child, Fiona, to the seesaws and I asked him what he was writing. She sat on one end and he levered her up and sat on the other, kept the movement going, up and down, elastic-legged. 'Nothing much. Words are getting bloody hard to find.'

'I thought it got easier the older you got.'

'Bad verse is easy. Always was.'

'Higher, Daddy,' Fiona cried.

He made the board bump on the tyre and nearly shot her over the handlebar. 'Ow, ow,' she cried. I lifted her down.

'I hurt my thumbs.' At eight she was too large for cuddling so he hoisted her on to his shoulders and massaged her thumbs and soon she stopped dropping tears in his hair and sat looking happily about as we walked along the river bank. He told me he was writing two poems, side by side, a domestic one – trying to be a husband – and a (he hesitates) 'a kind of confessional thing'. He made no gloss on that. Neither was getting very far. 'I don't know, the real thing keeps sliding out of sight. I can't seem to get hold of it. So I just write something to show I can still do it. "Something" comes out not too bad at times.' (And of course there is a poem of that name, though

I'm not sure it's anything he referred to on that day. It has a lovely surface and is very popular but try and find out what it means and it slides away. It's a clever piece of self-criticism, in my view.)

We met Les coming out of the lavatory. 'I used to be a bloody sluicing hose, now I drip like a tap.'

Fiona bent forward and looked at Rex upside down. He evaded her by crossing his eyes, then pulling her forward and flipping her on to her feet. That got them past Les. She climbed Rex to have it done again.

'She's Alice's proxy,' he said as she ran about, but I saw how he loved the girl. He told me he had taken a job as a proof reader at the *Star*, not for the money, there was no shortage of that now that Celia Pittaway had died (the Elf will no doubt tell the tale of that complicated inheritance), but because he had to have some reason for being with people. He could easily go bush, he said, even though he knew that by himself he would go mad. I was unused to confession from Rex and wanted to pat him on the shoulder. I was embarrassed by the affection I felt, and I said, 'You'll never go mad while you've got a safety valve.' I meant his poetry. 'I'm the one who'll end up in Carrington.' Madness in Rex would be a breaking out, it would end in expression and leave him clean, himself again – if it came at all – while in me . . . Why was I thinking of madness for me? Why the image of dark branches turning towards a centre and tangling about some pale thing there?

'You all right, Skeatsie?'

'Yes.'

'You don't look so hot.'

'I'm having a hard weekend with my mother.'

He asked about Harry and the children and I told him, told him evenly, and pulled myself together. I recovered my certainties.

'You still don't want to teach the world how to behave?'

'Not any more. I just want to keep my family safe.'

'What from? Jesus, stupid question. I don't know how anyone gets through a single day.'

I knew. One gets through by vigilance, care, foresight, knowledge, rules. Neither of us, on that day, mentioned love, although we felt, I believe, an odd sort of love for one another.

He said, 'Look at her' – Fiona, fifty yards ahead, watching cousins

188

paddling canoes in a side creek – 'one day something's going to pick her up and break her in half, and what do we do?' He meant 'I' not 'we'. There was no one he could bowl down a flight of steps. He did not mention love but loved the girl.

We reached the side creek and I saw how it was that Petleys drowned: four children in two canoes, the youngest no more than six years old, rocking, splashing, barging, in muddy water ten feet deep even at half tide, and no adults anywhere in sight.

Fiona looked at Rex appealingly. 'You want a ride? Get your shoes and dress off.' She could not do that. She wanted Rex to order the other children out and let her paddle by herself.

'They won't bite.'

'Daddy, ple-ease.' She Aliced him and he gave way.

'Who do they belong to?' he shouted at the children.

'Mine. My father,' one of the girls said.

'Well, bring 'em in. I'm going to have a turn.'

'We're using them,' said the older boy.

'Quit answering back, Scahill, bring 'em in.'

But these were Petleys, these were tough kids.

'Come and get us.'

'Chuck Fee-only in, see if she floats.'

'Cheeky young buggers,' Rex grinned. 'Want a ride, Jack?'

'Not me.'

He fished in his back pocket and pulled out a pound note. 'Here you are, five bob each. I'll hire them for half an hour.'

The children talked that over, safe in mid-creek, and it was the older boy who persuaded them. 'Only half an hour,' said the girl who owned the canoes. 'And don't lose the paddles or we'll bash her.'

'Button your lip.' He gave her the pound note and the older boy yelled at them as they ran to the kiosk: 'Five bob of that's mine. You save it, Charlene.' He was torn between his instinct to be where the money was and his need to see what Rex would do.

'Where are you going?'

'Clear out, we don't want you.'

'Are you going down the creek?'

'Yep, and you can't come, so don't ask. Get in, Fee. Don't mind your dress. That one's yours, Jack.'

189

'It's covered in mud.'

'You didn't use to mind mud. Get your shoes off. Roll up your trousers.'

He had a hard sparkle in his eyes. It was not Fiona's ride any more, it was his and mine. The boy touched my arm. 'I'll come in yours. I can paddle so you won't get wet.' He was, I guessed, Melva's oldest – the child in the pushchair, clutching for balance with his hands – but I asked his name and he answered, 'Tod.' He had a bit of young Rex in him – less height, but the same skinny, knobble-jointed limbs; less openness in his face, and a lightness in his skull bones compared with Rex's squared-off block; but a little of that innocence that made one want, and not want, to hurt.

'All right. Jump in.' I took off my shoes and rolled up my trousers. Rex had his canoe half in the water, with Fiona in front. He climbed in and pushed off from the bank, and frowned when he looked back and saw Tod in mine.

'I don't want to hear you open your mouth.'

'Yes,' Tod said. I took the paddle from him and nosed out of the side creek and set off downriver. He seemed content to sit in the cockpit and stay out of sight. Rex paddled with hungry sweeps. He knew where he wanted to go. But I did not want too much of recapturing. Boys in canoes on the muddy creek, between the mangroves, racing each other to the next bend – that was then, we were grown up now; and what's more I had a wet behind. Soon, though, I began to enjoy myself. The banks of mud rose with a beautiful curve from the water. They were pocked with crab holes in which the flick of withdrawal showed, swifter than the blink of an eye. If you looked ahead, along the curve, below the mangrove jungle, you were riding between glossy limbs, woman thighs. I wonder if Rex felt it too; and if we'd felt it all those years ago in our tin canoes.

'Your uncle and I came down here when we were boys,' I said to Tod.

'Yes,' he answered; a clipped sound. He had no interest in me but enjoyed himself in his own way, perhaps with some fantasy of Redskins in canoes, if boys still went for that sort of thing.

The water was khaki-green, as thick as serge. I paddled faster to catch up with Rex, who took it as a challenge and tried to stay ahead.

I only caught him in the end because Tod knelt and sculled with his hands. I handed him the paddle then and slumped forward, panting, and Rex said mockingly, 'You're not fit, Skeatsie.' His chopped-off finger shone like a blind eye. How different he was from me in spite of what we shared. Our canoes turned slowly, touching bows.

'Up there,' Fiona said, pointing at the mouth of a side creek.

'No, down. It opens out. You might see the sea.'

I wondered if he remembered that the way she had pointed narrowed into the fresh-water creek where Joy had drowned. We paddled on but the sea was further off than he had thought, so he ran the bow of his canoe on to a mudbank and let Fiona climb out. She pulled off her shoes and dress – no reluctance now – and climbed in her singlet and pants (a patch of muddy water on the seat) up the bank to the top and stood six feet taller than us, which pleased her tremendously. 'There's miles and miles of it,' she screeched. 'I can feel crabs with my toes.' They did not frighten her. 'I'm down to my knees.'

'I'm going too,' Tod said, and gave me the paddle. Fiona pelted him with mud as he glogged up the bank – and what came next? Mud wrestling until they were coated from head to foot and only their eyes and teeth flashed out. Then they made mud chutes and slid down the bank into the water, while Rex and I watched from the canoes.

'Head first,' he called to Fiona. He was straddling the stern of his canoe, legs in the water, bow up high. 'Not you,' at Tod, 'her first'; and down the chute she came, slick as an eel, and plunged out of sight with a kick of her feet, and climbed up his leg on the far side of the canoe.

'I'm going to try that. Coming, Skeatsie?'

'No thanks.' I held his canoe and back-paddled with my hand against the tide and watched him climb and slide and wear his chute deeper; come out with sopping shorts and scramble up four-footed, racing Fiona. The boy, although he slid too, might as well not have been there.

'These crabs are cutting me to bits,' he yelled, and showed his chest and belly marked with vertical red lines. Fiona was scratched too. She raised her singlet and showed him. I tried to persuade them to stop, but they were drunk with it and kept on climbing and sliding, until I started to be afraid the girl would not surface in the water.

'Cut it out, Rex, you're going to drown her.'

He took no fright but waited for her to come up: 'OK chicken, that's enough.'

'One more.'

'Only one. Your mother's going to kill me for those scratches.'

'She's exhausted, Rex.'

'Sure, but at least she's had some fun.'

He pulled the canoe to the bank and helped her in. She flopped, she was drunk with sun and mud and being submerged. Rex looked at her anxiously.

'We'll go home, eh?'

'Yes.' She would have lain down and slept if she had not been in the canoe.

Tod travelled back in the mangroves, keeping pace with us as we paddled against the tide. He slid and wriggled, flashing brown, he splashed in the leaves and angled his body through the branches, keeping up a Tarzan yell, until Rex shouted, 'Shut that bloody racket.' Tod was quiet then and tracked us silently.

I saw how Rex would not forgive the boy for breaking 'Petley' – and saw as we landed that Tod could not understand why he was disliked. Full of life, shining with it, yet he was subdued, and sent frowning glances at Rex, until I gave him half a crown, 'That's for paddling me.' Then he ran away to get 'the rest of my dough'.

Rex carried his sleeping daughter back to Lila's picnic.

'I'd better get her home, Mum, we can't stay.'

'What's happened to her?'

'Swimming. She's all right. She's tired, that's all.' And although his sisters crowded round and hissed at her scratches, he stayed impassive. He laid her on the back seat of the car. 'Jump in, Jack. Happy birthday, Mum.' We drove away.

I made him put me down outside the park. I was anxious for him to get Fiona home to her mother.

'See you, Rex. Thanks, eh.'

'Don't slam the door.' He looked at Fiona, curled up under her damp dress on the seat. 'She'll be all right.'

I nodded.

'One thing, she'll remember it.' He drove away, and we did not meet again for many years.

I met Fiona before I met him.

Notebook: 12

He came knocking on my door at close to midnight, in the rain, but we had moved from that house several months before. The new owners, culture wekas, recognized him and drew him in. They gave him a bath and a bed; told us about it by telephone next day, right down to the new cake of soap and the hot-water bottle. In the morning he was gone, after breakfast, who knows where? No word, no letter, to me. How nice he was, the woman said, how he made them laugh. Fancy him not wanting porridge though.

I saw him next on television, sailor instead of poet. He was the owner of one of half a dozen launches smashed in a storm. It was broken to matchwood, he said – as flat in his language as anyone else.

'Look how long his hair is.'

'He seems quite comfortable,' Harry said.

I read his two books of those middle years and thought them unadventurous and tired, although they had an evenness that pleased me. There was nothing about mudfights but much about kitchen and, with a strange politeness, about bed. About marriage. Some reviewers said about love, but they're mistaken. There are poems about children, and fathers too, and a painful equivocal love shows through there.

I wrote to him and told him I had enjoyed his books and said I approved of his new way of standing back. Poems at a low temperature, I think I said. He didn't answer, but later on sent a note to Harry saying he liked her Henry Hedgehog drawings, he liked the way the little bugger grinned on only one side of his mouth. There was a PS: 'How's ole Jack? Tell him to keep out his left.'

I did that but never used my right. No, correction: buying the house in Central Terrace was a risky thing. Harry worked hard on me, she persuaded me. I did not want to do up an old house, I was hopeless with a hammer and a paint brush, I said. 'I'm not,' she replied. 'You can lift and carry anyway. Jack, I want it. I'll go by myself if you won't come.' Persuasion! And Harry kept herself busy there for the next five years, Harry was a dynamo. She generated energy but no warmth, none for me. I don't blame her. Enough warmth for David and Jill; and made up with her carelessness for my anxieties. Harry saved us, saved herself. That is not for putting down here. But I must. I must tell some of it or there's a hole and no way of getting to the other side. I can't send only part of me to meet Rex when we meet again.

Quick and simple, bare outline. She would have gone. Not to Central Terrace, she could not have afforded it, but somewhere else. With the children.

Why?

Because I tied my shoelaces with a double knot. Because I said, 'Stop acting like a four-year-old.' Because I darted at Jill with a cloth every time I saw a smear of food on her face. Because I cleaned my teeth with salt and would not learn to use an electric razor. Because I closed the curtains when she changed even though nobody, *nobody*, could see. Because. Because I was afraid and started teaching nervousness and shrinking to my children. I said, though not out loud, that dogs were waiting to bite them, fire to burn, water to drown, cliffs to lure them to the edge. Men to . . . people to . . . life . . . Unless you stepped back and did not risk it. Don't do that! Be careful!

Don't try. That was it. Harry saw me start to make our children tiny. She saw me shrink and dry them. Dehydration. And while I was about it, saw me try to teach them what to do. When it wasn't a case of 'must not' it was 'must'. Behaviour was never neutral. Harry said, 'Why do they always look at you before they do anything?'

'What rubbish.'

'We've got kids who hesitate all the time. They never just get up and do.'

'I've tried to show them what's right and wrong.'

'Where did you learn it? How do you know?'

I knew, I might have answered, in my bones. I knew (and here I would have puffed my chest) from my sense of other people. As soon as there were two there was right and wrong. Two made murder. Two made love. Love, Harry would have scoffed, what do

195

you know about that? I knew she would accuse me, that is why I mumbled off in another direction. To myself I declared that I loved abundantly, and that love assaulted me in every waking hour – but I did not want to defend these propositions. I did not want particularity. Pain lay in that direction. Terror.

I was terrified for my children – of all the usual things. And terrified that they would grow without a moral sense. It never made me violent. I never struck David and Jillian, never once, or shouted at them; but nor did I hug them, devour them; tumble, roll, throw them at the ceiling and catch them inches from the floor. I kissed them lightly and touched them on the head. I pointed things out. When someone offered them a cake or lolly they would half put out a hand then look at me and I would nod my head, yes, all right. Or I would say, 'The other children haven't had a second one yet.' I was marvellously even. I was a marvel of evenness.

I chose straight (and strait again), denying crooked.

Meanwhile Harry . . . if only we could have kept the carefreeness of the night when we first made love. But wouldn't that be the common cry? We were not unique.

She kept me busy with the old house in Central Terrace. She kept a hold on me and did not let me slip too far away. I might be a monster of some sort now if it hadn't been for stripping and sanding and puttying and painting; for tearing down wallpaper and scrim and filling the skip; fixing gib board, plastering. My neatness and carefulness made me good at some things. My wallpaper hangs perfectly.

We were able to save the panelling and the tiled fireplace in the sitting-room but in the bedrooms had to gib. One afternoon I went into David's room to sand the plaster and found Harry drawing on the wall. She was using a hard pencil and making such delicate marks I thought she was writing. But as I watched a twig appeared, with a praying mantis on it, holding a fly in its jointed arms.

'That's a bit gruesome, isn't it?'

She printed 'Dinner' underneath. 'Would you sooner have butterflies?'

'Yes, I would.'

'Butterflies get eaten too.' She drew one for me though, settling on a rose. 'For Jack' she wrote. She drew a caterpillar munching a leaf.

Whatever her mood at the start, she was growing pleased with herself.

'A snail,' I said.

She drew one; then a stick insect.

'They're marvellous.' She sometimes drew frowns and smiles in letters to her friends but nothing like this. The tea-tree jack had a pent-up stillness. The fly, although it buzzed, had given up hope. If you touched the snail's eye it would retract.

Ten years of marriage and I had not known that she could draw.

'Why didn't you tell me?'

'You never asked.' That has always struck me as the most unfair of rejoinders. She used it fairly often at the time, in all sorts of ways. I was losing her, she was going private. Although she drew the snail and tea-tree jack when I requested, her parted lips expressed her privacy. She travelled down her arm, through her fingers and her pencil, into the fragments of a world on the wall, while I could only watch and admire.

'It's a pity to paper them over,' I said.

'Well, don't.'

She drew ferns, lilies, ants; a sparrow bathing in the dust. She drew wasps on an apple core. I went into Jill's room and sanded the plaster and while I worked, coating myself with dust, I had the idea of papering the children's walls white and asking Harry to paint pictures on them. I would, of course, want the right of censorship – no insects eating insects, no caterpillars munching at one end and excreting from the other. I thought of flowers and butterflies and birds. How comforting to go to sleep with a mother's pictures all around.

When I went back to suggest it I found her drawing tinily on another wall. (All her drawings were tiny, as though they were meant for a corner of the page.)

'What's that?'

'In the bush.'

It was more. Everything was angled, twisted, swollen, torn, reversed. Everything was greedy and malevolent. Creepers strangled trees; they cut deep grooves in them. Fat branches pushed starving branches down. Roots split boulders, which crushed ferns. Toadstools grew aslant rotten logs. Toadstools? Fungus of a sort,

197

squat and gross. Grubs poked out their heads, and centipedes lay bent and still, curved like scimitars. Water dripped. Gum congealed. Lichen crept. A little cowed animal, possibly a hedgehog, poked out its snout from a hollow under a log.

The picture crept across half a wall – tiny acts of terror and greed; images of pain and desolation and defeat.

All I could say was, 'Hedgehogs don't go in the bush.'

'Yes they do. It mightn't be a hedgehog anyway.'

I went to the kitchen and made a cup of tea and put hers on the floor beside her. I went outside to see that the children were safe. That is the order. I tried to look after Harry first. I've said she saved me by putting me to work on the house. Perhaps I saved her too, with a cup of tea.

When I went back late in the afternoon she had finished. Had enough. She had signed it 'Edwards', made – ironically? – with forget-me-nots. And gone on from there to draw isolated leaves and ladybirds. Clean and pretty. Washed with rain. Unreal perhaps beside her other world, but making a place for themselves by clarity and closeness and need.

She smiled at me. 'Your hair's gone white.' Attacked it with her hand and made a cloud of dust around us.

'They're nice,' I said, touching a ladybird.

'Aren't they just.'

I sneezed.

'Bless you,' she smiled.

'I was thinking . . .' I put my idea about the walls.

'No, it doesn't matter. I've finished now. Paper them over.' She put her pencil in her pocket like an office girl.

So we went on, and made our old house comfortable and clean; improved its value. We made it beautiful, as it had been before the time of yellow paint, partitions, lowered ceilings, and seventeen students crammed in. We restored the barge boards and the fretwork and raised new finials and all the while I felt that I restored our marriage and pulled off ugly bits I had tacked on. I thinned the trees and opened up the view. We looked across the city and Oriental Bay. We had the inner harbour on the left, and Somes Island, the eastern bays, the Orongorongos, the Tararuas. On the right, beyond the red-roofed flatlands leading to Island Bay, we had

Cook Strait. Its colours ranged from white to black as fine days and stormy days passed through. I've seen it basalt-coloured, green, blue, yellow, I've seen the white ships shine like icebergs coming from the south, while over beyond the entrance, beyond the reefs, the shelves of Baring Head, planed as smooth as timber and shining like fields of wheat, lay in the sun, an untouched, warm, impossible new land.

I can't do lyricism and shouldn't try, but the Central Terrace view moves me still, even though poles and insulators and sagging wires lie across the front of it.

Harry admired but never came to love it. She watched the changes, recognized the moods, and would run to fetch me – 'Look at this' – but it never became more than a spectacle for her. These were not the right hills or this the right sea.

The damage done was not repaired, not in those years or that easy way. She painted and she drew, she took extramural units from Massey; and raised the children – not only raised but broadened them – cured Jill of an obsessive hand-washing habit that I was responsible for in some way, I suppose, and worked through David's reading difficulties with him, although she never managed to get him reading books.

Now and then she had to go away. She had to have time by herself, with none of us. It happened only six or seven times and lasted from three days to more than a month. A month! Cards came or I would have called the police. She did not say where she was, simply that she was well and would be home soon and we mustn't worry. I read the postmarks: National Park, Taumarunui. She took outdoor clothes, walking shoes, a sketch pad, nothing more. Was she climbing mountains? Was she drawing in the bush?

Meeting a man? I did not ask, but when I said, 'By yourself? You did all that alone?' she knew what the question was, and was pleased by it and kind to me.

'I did a canoe trip down the Wanganui.'

'Not by yourself?'

'In a group run by a Latvian man. There was a doctor and his wife and a bus driver and an electrician. And two secretaries. And some students. Democratic. Seven days.'

'I would have liked to do that.'

'Poor Jack.' She patted my hand. 'Next time.' But next time was a week in a bach on the Mahia peninsula and she didn't take me.

'Who did you meet?'

'No one, Jack. I was all alone. I never spoke to anyone the whole of the time.' Her cheeks went pink from pleasure not from guilt. Her eyes shone at the memory.

'I caught crayfish in the rocks, with my hands, and let them go. There was a man' – so there had been a man – 'who left me snapper in a sack at the gate. He was sixty, Jack. Poor Jack. He was old.' Less pleased with me this time, giving some needle. She did not like me spoiling her time away.

Her sketch pads were always full and when I looked secretly at them – so bright, so private, so exact – I knew there were no affairs, no secret meetings and couplings in motel rooms, and knew that she met only herself when she went away, and that I held her by letting her go. So her escapes became a part of our status quo and her strangeness to me one of the things that kept us together. I had to enlarge myself in order to accept it. Small concerns began to drop away.

Neither of us had an easy time. And surely I deserved some payment for my understanding. I did not want a turn at going away – was filled with alarm at the thought: I would go mad – but wanted something guilty, something to hide. (And something to blame on her as well.) I wanted a woman. Unaware that I would please Harry by cheating, I went about it secretly; but I'd forgotten how, I'd forgotten the moves. The only women I came close to being unfaithful with were Beth Simmonds and Fiona Petley.

Poor Beth. Weeping woman. That's specific. She came into our lives with tears and went out with tears. Our sitting-room over-looked the neighbours' front garden. On the night of one of their dinner parties Harry suddenly crossed the room and turned out our light. 'Come here,' she said as I began to protest. 'Someone in the corner. Past the bird-path, by the hedge.'

'A woman?'

'Yes. I thought it was a man at first, having a pee.'

'What's she doing?' A car went by in the street and showed a gleam of tears on her cheek. 'Is she hurt?'

We watched for five minutes and she stood without moving, although she wiped her cheeks with her hands.

'I'm going down,' Harry said.

'Don't interfere.'

But she was gone: down our path and out the front gate. The woman in the shadows slid into an angle of the hedge. I thought that she might be a man after all, dressed in a skirt, she was big enough, and I threw the window up. But her movements as she stepped away from me, and from Harry advancing on the neighbours' lawn, were fugitive and panic-stricken.

'It's all right,' Harry told her, 'don't be frightened.' She tunnelled a whisper at me: 'Go away.' They stood close together in the dark. I could not see or hear, and returned to my chair, hoping Harry would deal with it down there and not bring her into our house. But like so many of my hopes . . .

'Where is she?'

'In the bathroom.'

'What's wrong with her?'

'She's terrified, Jack. She's supposed to be at dinner with the Perretts but she can't go in. It's some sort of social phobia.'

'Is she . . . Hadn't we better . . .'

'She's quite safe.' Contemptuous. 'But I'll go and get her. You can put the kettle on.'

So Beth, big and shrinking – mouse-bereted, gabardine-coated, square-shoed – Beth with washed red cheeks and weeping eyes, came into our lives; and we helped her and she helped us, for a time.

She was twenty-two, a kindergarten teacher, and she could talk to children but couldn't get a word off her tongue with adults – although she poured her life out to Harry and me that night. The Perretts' daughter, trying to help, had invited her, but terror struck inside the gate, with lighted windows shining down, and she scuttled into the dark beyond the bird-bath, where blindness, paralysis, suspension of breath . . .

'It's all right now,' Harry said.

And what did I say? 'No one can get you here.'

Beth became our baby-sitter and our weekend friend. She made hours of free time for Harry and me and learned to talk without getting ready or thinking our concentration was fixed on her. She learned that other people were central to themselves – and, working on from there, found them self-serving, even in their love. I could not argue her out of that conclusion.

'Who are you trying to convince?' she grinned at me. She was likeable when she wasn't afraid.

When Harry went off on her 'sabbaticals' Beth came to look after the children; and looked after me as well, with washing and ironing and cooking and cleaning. She was better than Harry at being that sort of wife. She sat by the fire in Harry's chair and held her breath in case the spell should break. I was a grumpy husband, but she remained, in all domestic things, a perfect helpmeet. I told her so, using that old word. She failed to hear my sourness and blushed.

I left possession to David and Jillian. They bullied her; demanded drinks and cookies in the night; woke and called and made her sit shivering on the bed while they drifted back to sleep, even when they were too old for that sort of thing. She took them to the pictures and the Easter Show and brought them home dazed with food and pleasure. I suspended rules while Harry was away. I punished her by letting Beth unfix our children, it served her right. I wished that they would stay unmanageable, bad.

'Which one was that?' when she came back to the sitting-room.

'Jill. She had a dream.'

'All she needs is the door closed and the light out.' Unconvincing.

'Well,' hearing it, 'she got a story instead.'

'One of yours?'

She went red.

'Tell it to me.'

'No, it's silly.'

'Come on.'

So she told me, and I thought it silly and still do; but I said, 'That's good. You should get Harry to do some drawings for that. She's good at hedgehogs.'

I had her tell Harry when she came back; and put in a recommendation: 'Don't have him smiling all the time.'

The pictures are better than the words. See the book. Amazingly, it's still in print. And there would have been others if Harry had not gone away south. This time she put the strait between us.

'I thought you'd finished with all this running away.'

'It's not running. It's a break.' She frowned at the inadequate word. 'Beth will come. You won't have to manage on your own.'

All right, I said, you asked for it. I think she heard, although I did not say it aloud. Harry is as much to blame as me. (I've learned not to blame but I'll leave it in.) We put Beth in the wife's chair one more time; and things had to turn out differently. David and Jill were thirteen and eleven and did not need her any more. Who needed Beth? Was she here for her own need? None of us fully understood.

It was not a cold night but I made a fire. We sat with our chairs right-angled to each other – or perhaps a few degrees more closed – and read and conversed.

'Cold?'

'No.'

'I'll put some more wood on anyway.'

'Yes.'

'I like fires.'

'Me too.'

'There, that's better.'

She made a cup of tea. Nine o'clock. Ten o'clock. Half past. The children were asleep. As a rule, Beth was in bed by ten. I heard her breathing – big-woman breathing, deep and even, through her nose. It should have been a calm sound but was not. There was a pent-up stillness in her, like the tea-tree jack. Beth had loved her situation with us. When had she discovered she loved me? It must have been when, by my own stillness, I signalled that I would take everything from her. What sort of battle did she fight? Or was she mine in a flash?

Eleven o'clock. At that close angle she started it. Must have waited for me and when I put it off, watched the hand until it reached the hour . . .

She stood up and went to the fire – embers, ash – and knelt in front of it on the mat. She put a block of wood on, carefully. Then she turned a look on me of such beseechingness that it forced me back in my chair; and, elastic, drew me to her side, kneeling on the mat. I kissed her softly, once, then long and deep. She had never kissed. Unpractised, bold, submissive, demanding, innocent – a kiss so complicated I don't know what to think. But I knew then. I must go ahead. For both of us. And I must be careful.

203

Memory is complicated too. I can be hard or tender; kind or cruel; coarse or fine. In each of those I can replace 'or' with 'and'. What shall I do? Not try too hard and let it find its way? That is best. Don't tell lies and don't be 'honest', Jack.

She wore a blouse buttoned down the front. I unbuttoned it and reached around and unhooked her bra while she watched as though she could not fully understand. It seemed to me that she forgot to breathe. I can't make the sound on paper that she made when I touched her breasts. (I make it, soft-throated, in my hole under the stairs, and Harry, passing, raps the door: 'Are you all right in there?' Yes, I'm all right, up to a point. It's just that I don't want to say how I behaved.)

'Lie down,' I said, and she obeyed as though no split-second must be lost. Smooth and full. Not just her body but her face. So plain, her face. She moves me with her beauty. I touched and kissed and played little games while she held me through my trouser-cloth. Then – calculation and excitement both – I unzipped her skirt and slid my hand beneath her clothes and touched her with more knowledge than she understood. She held me harder then. And with just my touch she came, crushing, devouring, my hand in her thighs.

It amazes me. So much readiness. So much need. I can be warm with happiness, thinking of the pleasure I gave, if I don't go on.

Beth's mistake was to want things properly done, and done with propriety too. She did not want the mat in front of the fire, and did not want Harry's marriage bed; but a bed was necessary, and we must go to her room and make ourselves safe in that narrow cell, in the narrow bed, with the door locked so the children would never know, and the Skeat house would never know. She gave me time to think of tomorrow and next week. 'All right,' I said, 'you go. I'll just make the fire safe and lock up. I won't be long,' and that is what I intended – but after the fire-screen and the front door I went to the bathroom and washed my hands. I felt a grating in my wrist where her thighs had crushed me (a nasty swelling the next day) and her passion frightened me. I did not understand the truth, which was, it's very plain, one night was all she was going to ask. She would have gone away, and not come back; given up the Skeats for her night of love. She had made a bargain. But I became frightened for my children, and for Harry, and myself. On the mat, it should have been, and nothing would have been lost – the big hungry woman, the doggy little man. And nothing would have been lost in her room. Her instinct to go there and make a cell of it was perfectly sound – but she did not know me and our pause was her mistake.

Fear and, of course, morality. I called on that. When Beth came tapping on my bedroom door – she must have realized by then; the courage of her walk along the hall – I opened it an inch or two and said, 'I'm sorry, I can't. I'm married, Beth.'

The desolation in her eyes as she saw me through the opening I allowed – I need not have spoken any words. 'Yes,' she said, and went away.

I lay all night wanting her. I even slid across the room and opened the door, opened it wide, hoping she would find it and come to my bed. But as I slept in the dawn she passed by and closed it. I heard the click. I heard her in the kitchen making tea, but it was only for herself.

She told the children breakfast was on the table. Then she left.

'Beth's gone,' they said.

'Where?'

'Gone home. She said you're looking after us until Mum comes home.'

'She was crying. Her nose was running.'

'I'm glad she's gone. I hate fat people,' Jill said.

'Me too,' David said.

I made them apologize – which they did easily, by rote. Apologizing had become like yawning to my children.

Harry telephoned Beth when she came home. She put down the phone and turned to me. 'What did you do?'

'How do you mean?'

'Something must have happened.'

'No, she left. The children don't need her now. I guess they let her see.'

Harry can look at me as though I'm a bug. She takes in my left side and my right as though getting me with a line or two. 'Don't use the children.'

'Eh?'

'Couldn't you even do that right?'

'What are you talking about?'

'You must have known what you owed her, Jack.'

I do now, and might have understood it then if Harry had not let me see that she had arranged it. Beth, though, knew nothing about that. Harry had recognized her, recognized her time . . . There's no point in going on. I don't object any more. I wish we could try again, all three, and do it right.

I raged a bit. Said I wasn't hers to give away. Didn't fuck fat ladies for charity.

'Oh shut up, Jack. Go and take a walk somewhere. Go and climb a tree.'

I did that. I climbed a tree in the botanical gardens. I went up high and sat in the branches and watched people walking on the paths; and enjoyed it, removed from family and love and right and wrong. Leaves on my face, wind up my trouser legs, darkness filling the sky. I hugged the trunk and felt the life in it, and felt the life in the moving air. I let tears blow slanting on my cheeks; then climbed down and went on with my marriage.

Harry and Beth met in town now and then. They talked about writing another book but never started. I don't know what else they talked about. Perhaps the Values Party. Beth was TV spokesperson in the elections of 1972 and 1975. She was quick and positive but never blinked her eyes. 'Relax,' I told her on the screen. She stood for parliament in 1975 and managed not to lose her deposit.

In later years I passed her several times on Lambton Quay and said hallo. She gave a stern little nod.

Where is Beth now? I must ask Harry.

Fiona is easier to face. I've only selfish regrets about saying no. Beth takes place in interiors. Fiona is in the open air, even though we sat in my car.

It seems as though it happened the next day. In fact more than six years went by and in that time Harry and I settled down again. For a short time, at our beginning, we had stood face to face and touched nakedly; then, like figures set on clockwork pedestals, had turned away from each other – not had eye contact any more, or contact much of any sort. House and children and Beth, in her way, kept us together; kept us, rather, in proximity. Harry drew, she straightened and broadened David and Jill, and went away on her trips, while I slowly untangled, unknotted myself, partly in apology and partly to survive. After Beth we turned, with a creaking of machinery, a squeaking of wooden parts, to face, almost face, each other again. Not quite. We were slightly askew, but could make our eyes meet without rolling them too painfully.

The metaphor works, almost works. I need it for then. I don't need metaphors now, for Harry and me. That is marvellous progress – and I'd like to come up here, into this time, but must stay back. All these extras push into the centre – I push – but Rex is my subject in the end. Fiona's importance, when she came, is that she told me about Rex.

'Someone called Fiona Petley on the phone,' David said.

She was staying with a friend of her mother's in Seatoun Heights and her father had told her to call and say hallo.

'Just hallo?'

'You know Dad.'

'Yes, I do. How long are you here? Can you come over?'

'I'd love to,' lowering her voice in a way that told me she was having a difficult time with her mother's friend.

I picked her up and drove her back to our place round the bays. Wellington was in shades of grey and I wanted to impress her, but she said, 'I've had enough of views. Sadie' – Alice's friend – 'keeps going on about it, how it "enlarges her soul". And then she talks about the *Wahine* on the reef. "Those poor creatures dying out there, while we watched from our picture windows. So sad." She never thought of going down to help.'

'There wasn't very much she could have done.'

'You can always do something.' An affirming and a cancelling mind. If I disagreed she would cancel me. People like that are hard to entertain. Harry and I tried but Harry went to bed when the clock said ten.

'I'm sorry, have I upset your wife?'

'She's got a headache, from eyestrain. She does all this very fine drawing, botanical stuff – '

'I keep on judging all the time. I know it makes people mad at me.'

'Why do you do it?'

'Because I want them to be – I don't know, just *reasonable*.'

'Is your father?'

'No.'

'What about Alice?'

'No, she's hopeless. Everyone is.'

'You too?'

'Me especially.'

David came in from badminton. He was sweating in his whites, and a bit too red, but not bad-looking – better-looking than I had ever been. I'd been hoping he would come and that I could put them together – but he was hopeless too, I saw from her glance, and I gave up for that night and said I would drive her home.

'I always do that,' she said in the car, 'turn people off.'

'I'm not turned off.'

'You don't like me though.'

'Yes I do. I remember you at Loomis, sliding in the mud.'

'You're like Dad, you always want to talk about then. What's wrong with now?'

'I like you now.'

'Do we have to go through the tunnel? I can't stand tunnels.'

So I drove round the Basin Reserve and past the hospital to Island Bay.

'There,' I said, 'Cook Strait. You look right down the side of the South Island and then there's nothing till Antarctica. Ice and snow.'

'I suppose that enlarges your soul?'

'No.'

'Can we stop?'

I parked on the shore front and we looked past the island and the fishing boats into the dark. The moon was in the clouds, invisible; no stars.

'What was that music when we left your place?'

'An old man three doors up. He plays his flute in the garden.'

'It sounded like dogs.'

'He has to be feeling pretty bad to go out on a night like this. He's calling his wife. She went away with another man.'

'You're putting me on.'

The first time I had heard that phrase. 'On what?'

'You're making fun of me.'

'Not very much. I'm cheering you up.' I wondered if it would amuse her to know that both her father and I had been bedmates of the runaway wife. (She hadn't run far, just to Brooklyn, the next hill. It's possible Barton really thought his flute would carry there.)

'Is that why you haven't asked about Mum and Dad?'

'Aren't they a cheerful subject? Is something wrong?'

She told me – and remember, this is second-hand.

He had left his job as a proof reader after more than ten years. He had bought a piece of scrubland out by Muriwai and put a bach on it and was living there, trying to farm.

'Mum goes out each weekend to see if he's ready to come home.'

'Is he?'

'He's never coming. She doesn't know.'

'If you do, she must.'

'No. It's changed. She's always let him do whatever he wanted' – not true, but I did not argue – 'because she knew he'd always come back. She doesn't believe any man could run away from her, whether it's Dad or not.'

'Are you saying she's had other men?'

'No. Just friends. They don't get far. It's only Dad she wants. But this time he's gone and she can't see.' Her eyes were wet but she wiped her mouth, coarse and hard. 'I'd better tell her to buy a flute.'

'Why are you so sure? Have you talked with Rex?'

'I don't have to talk, I can see. There's a woman out there with him. It's joint title. She lives in another bach but I know what they are.'

'Your mother must know.'

'She thinks it's just girlfriends. She's never been scared of them. But she's the wife now and Mum's not. It's more than sex.'

'What sort of farming do they do?'

'Crops and things. Berries and green peppers. There's grape vines too. He's trying to start a vineyard, he's gone crazy.'

I asked if Rex had had many other girlfriends.

'I don't know. I suppose. Mum says what they really like is his finger, they think it's sexy. She always tried to make him wear a finger-stall on it.'

I didn't like this freedom – have never cared for the way young people talk about sex – and I was relieved when she got out of the car and walked down the beach. I wasn't sure she wanted me to follow so I stood by the open door and watched her fade into the dark. Her pale clothing moved back and forth at the edge of the sea. Then she paddled. But the waves, even here, inside the island . . . I ran down. How would I tell Rex his daughter was drowned? To make things even worse, it started to rain.

'Fiona.'

She was up to her thighs, and had not bothered to lift her skirt.

'Fiona.'

She came in, and saw at once the way her wildness affected me – sodden skirt, wet sandals, hair glued to her face. She ran to the car and I followed, and how did she make it seem that I was chasing her? At the door she took off her skirt and wrung it out and threw it on the floor; climbed into her seat.

I got in mine. Started the engine. 'I'm taking you home.'

'I'm not ready.'

I wasn't going to be bossed by an eighteen-year-old. I saw that I must get her off my hands.

'No. Turn on the heater, I want to get dry. I'll go in like this, without my skirt.'

So I did as I was told, and wrapped us in warm air.

'Tell me some more about Rex.' How erotic that was, by chance, for both of us. She pushed her seat back with her legs and dragged her wet hair forward and parted it to let her eyes look out. She told me about growing up with Rex and Alice.

'Dad chased one of her friends down the street. He was having a drink with her, in the living-room, and Dad came home. There was nothing wrong, Stephen's just someone for company. He jerks away, you know, and gives a little yelp if he touches her. Anyway Dad, he stood there in the door and showed his teeth and growled like a dog. He made a step at Stephen, and the hair would have stood up on his neck if he could have done it. Stephen spilled his drink and tried to get behind his chair. Dad was only having fun, I think he'd had a bit too much to drink. He kept on stepping after Stephen growling, and Stephen kept on jumping back, and Mum was saying, "Stop it Rex, leave him alone", but you could see how excited she was. Anyway, Stephen ran out the door and down the steps and Dad chased him all the way down the street. Stephen didn't even have time to get in his car. But I've never seen Dad grinning so much as when he came back. "I needed a bit of exercise," he said. And Mum just said, "Oh Rex," and kind of flopped in his arms. They locked themselves in the bedroom. But I don't know, it wasn't Dad, it just wasn't him. It was like he was doing it with just his eyes and mouth. All the big important bit was gone away somewhere. He left soon after that anyway, with his new lady. I hope they are having fun. I hope they are. Fun's what we need, isn't it?'

Her gaiety was sadder than her sadness had been. So I patted, then I stroked, and then I kissed. And touch made me recognize the Petley in her. I had not seen it. The squareness in her head, which I had seen as round. Her nose and her jaw and her long mouth. I stopped and drew away from him – Rex in her face. There was nothing erotic any more.

'What's the matter. I've done it plenty of times.'

That did not encourage me either. I drove Fiona back to Seatoun Heights. She struggled into her skirt on the way.

'Has this girlfriend of your father's got a name?'

'Margot,' she sulked. 'Margot Stiles.'

Notebook: 13

After Sidgy, all those years before, it has to be seen as another cute meet. (Dangerous too. Remember that I'm an accessory.)

He was loafing in the sun in Albert Park on a seat by the Moreton Bay fig trees where he and I had read our early verses to each other when a woman eating sandwiches on the grass stood up and approached him with her lunch box and her greaseproof paper bundled in her arms.

'You're Rex Petley, aren't you?'

He said yes. He hated it when strangers told him that they liked his poems.

'Can I sit down?'

'It's a free country.' He was often clichéd when he was off balance.

She put her book and lunch box between them. 'I'm Margot Stiles.'

He knew before she said it. He beat her by – didn't say a heartbeat, wasn't as clichéd as that, but it must have thumped him in that sort of way. 'Her freckles, that was one thing.' But a complex of things: her directness, her adult voice in which there was a child, her breadth of face, the openness of her eyes . . .

People almost always say, 'Do you remember,' even when there's no way to forget. Not Margot. They talked about where they'd been for twenty-five years and what they'd done; then, after a silence, she said, 'Wasn't there any other way to stop him?'

'I couldn't think of one,' Rex said.

He told me that in a way it was like coming home. In that half hour on the bench he knew that he would never let her go. Cliché again, but I believe it. He spoke as if he'd hunted long and hard and found exactly the right words.

Her mother went to Napier and found the wrong man again. This one was a self-deceiving drunk who turned self-pitying when he couldn't fool himself any longer. Margot grew up with his decline. She liked him in some ways and stopped her mother scalding him with words when she could. The man began to use her as safe place, which she had to stop; and did it by leaving home when she was seventeen. She trained as a physiotherapist in Christchurch; worked in hospitals everywhere. She had seen enough of marriage and wouldn't be trapped, but she had the usual boyfriends: plenty of good times and a fright or two. When Rex met her again she had reached the end of that and had been alone for several years.

He told me about Margot, walking up Muriwai Beach and walking back. He had never said so much before. This was a new, open Rex. I'm tempted to say he was happy but the word has too absolute a sound. He was easier, more contented, than I had known him before, but it was conditional on Margot. He seemed to feel he did not know her yet although they'd been together for two years. He seemed to be saying that Margot was unknowable. His happiness was full but never still and never safe. It trembled on its surface like liquid in a bucket that vibrates. Margot was a current, was vibration, all the time. I'm straining for a meaning I can't find – and I wonder if I'm simply saying that the loved person can never be possessed and that Rex was finding it out. Indeed, that finding out he could not have her made him happy in some way? One can take pleasure, even delight, from knowing that the person one loves is free.

Five miles up and five miles back was enough for that. In fact, what I've written down wasn't always said. We talked about many things. I told him I had telephoned Fiona and she had picked me up at my hotel – my mother's unit had no room for me – and driven me to Alice in Mt. Eden, where, I said, I had had an interesting time.

'Dad wants a divorce,' Fiona told me. 'He wants to be the guilty party though. Mum got the letter last week.'
'What did she do?'
'She sat down,' an ugly grin from Fiona, 'and readjusted.'
I wasn't sure what she meant.
'Mum's – I don't know – she's kind of huge. She cranked herself round and now she's facing in a new direction. I think she decided he was finished. He's kind of – dead.'
'As a poet?'

'All ways. A man who walks out on Mum has got to be a zombie. Anyway, when his letter came that was it. Dad was done for. She's got it postmarked on the envelope, the time when Rex Petley ceased to be. She'll keep him up to that time though. No one's going to get away with the poetry he wrote married to her.'

I knew Alice well enough not to argue with that.

She offered me a cheek to kiss. Alice was being gentle and removed, but she could not hide her steeliness.

'Have you met this woman, Jack?'

'No.'

'She was always there, working away in the garden, when I went out. Sometimes she didn't wear a top. I'm not against that necessarily . . . but nakedness should be aesthetic, I believe. She hasn't the . . .'

'Her boobs are too big,' Fiona explained.

'Did you ever speak to her?'

'Rex introduced us. It seems to me there's a kind of coarseness – coarse-mindedness. Of course, Rex could be that way himself. But there's a whole substratum of fineness too and that's where he needs to go if he's to write. He doesn't have access without me. I don't believe he'll write any more.'

She did not want him to write any more. That's understandable; and, in a way, she's had her wish. He published only two more poems in what was left of his life, and they are ones he began while he was with her. 'Fragments 1 & 2.' Interesting. Elegiac. He said goodbye to her in style.

'Will you stay here, in this house?'

'No. Too many . . .' Almost said memories. 'Fortunately, I'm able . . .'

'Dad only took enough to freehold the property,' Fiona said.

'I don't see that our finances are any concern of Jack's.'

'Margot wasn't after his money. It's part of their thing to live off the land. Money in the bank is kind of cheating.'

'Besides which, Rex earned very little in that job. And almost nothing from his poetry.' Any cash around, she meant, was Pittaway cash.

She sent Fiona to the kitchen to make tea. 'Jack, I'm glad you

214

came. There's something you can advise me on but I need your promise that you won't tell anyone, especially Rex.'

'Well . . .' I did not like this. 'As long as it's . . . as long as it doesn't . . .'

'It won't damage him, trust me for that. I'm not vindictive. It will even serve him in the end. The fact is, I've got his manuscripts, I've got his papers. It's mostly drafts – and poems through all their stages. And notebooks. And corrected proofs. One or two talks he gave. That sort of thing. Some little prose pieces he did for me once.'

'Letters?'

'Rex never wrote letters very much.'

'I mean from other people. Other writers.'

'One or two.'

'Memoirs?'

'No, Rex kept his memories in his head. Or put them in poems. But what I need to know, who owns it all?'

'Well . . .'

'He would have saved nothing, Jack. He used to throw stuff in the rubbish tin. I took it out and he just laughed. He said if I wanted I could have it. That constitutes ownership, doesn't it?'

'Well, possibly . . .'

'He said to sell it to the Yanks. It was my insurance, he said.'

'Don't let the Yanks get it.'

'I won't. But then, later on, he said, "Burn all that junk. I don't want the thesis boys busy on me." And he meant it. So I said I would. But I kept it. And what I need to know, is it mine?'

Well, I said, the copyright, copyright stayed with Rex. Ownership, that was difficult. What she should do was keep very quiet; or she could leave it all with me –

'No.'

'Put it in the Turnbull then. Tell them to bury it. I don't think Rex would ever find out. The Hocken? The Auckland Institute?'

She shook her head at each suggestion. 'I want to keep them with me. In a way I'm guardian. He never – he never looked after himself, Jack.' She meant his reputation. And if she meant hers, who can blame her? Poets' wives come badly out of things. I was pleased with her. The archivist in me was delighted. I did not care where his papers went as long as somebody kept them safe.

'He's capable of coming here and claiming it all. And burning it. It goes with this simple life nonsense he's tied up with. She treats him like a labourer. Someone to dig drains and chop down trees. You'd think he wasn't Rex Petley at all. One of our best poets. Some people say our very best.' She wanted credit for him, she wanted her part known. That made the steeliness behind her front. I admired her more than I ever had.

'Just put them somewhere safe and deny that they exist. People are going to thank you one day.' I did not feel I was betraying Rex. I'll lie and cheat for manuscripts and archives. Preservation is a ruling principle and it makes its own morality.

'I kept a daybook too: where he went, who he talked to – visitors, dinner parties, that kind of thing. When he started poems and when he finished. I thought one day, for a biography . . .?'

'Yes. Good. What about things he said?'

'If they seemed' – she turned her head, removed herself a little – 'important. It's odd, he didn't say very much.'

She had survived the disappointment. I admired her even more; and wondered if her daybook recorded his meeting with Margot Stiles.

'There's an interesting thing he said about you.'

'Me?'

'He said – wait, I'll get it.' She went out; and closed the door in case I should see her hiding place. I looked at the paintings round the room – an Ellis motorway, some Hanly agitated molecules: she hadn't managed to hang Rex but she had some good things on the walls.

'Now – ' reappearing with a bundle of notebooks (hard-covered, octavo) held in a thick rubber band – 'what year did your wife draw that little children's book about a hedgehog?'

'1970. It came out in October. For Christmas.'

She found the book, and the place – the ideal archivist. She read: 'Rex brought home a children's picture book [*Henry Hedgehog's Happy Holiday*, by Beth Simmonds and Harriet Edwards, Sandpit Press, 1970] and said, "Who does that remind you of?" [the hedgehog]. I could not tell. "It's Jack. Harry's done Jack as a hedgehog. And look at the way she's split him down the middle. Poor old Jack, he doesn't know whether he's supposed to laugh or

216

cry. Or run away or go in boots and all. She knows a thing or two, that girl. I hope she never tries to draw me." '

'Can I look?'

'That's all. I hope you don't mind. But I tried to write down everything he said about books. Even . . . He really did admire it. We had it round the house for several years.'

'Can I look at 1971?'

Steady voice, steady hands. I knew the dates – late February, early March. And I knew what I would find. 'Rex was away all week, he won't say where. "In the bush." He says he writes best when he's close to water and he wanted to see some rivers "down south" where it isn't muddy it's clear. There don't seem to be any poems though.'

Fiona brought in tea. How neatly I drank – sip, sip – and nibbled my biscuit. I cupped my hand to catch the crumbs. Then I left Alice – Woolfish Alice – standing in the shade of her front hall and drove with Fiona to my hotel.

'What's the matter?'

'Nothing.'

'She can be depressing. If I was either one of them I think I'd leave the other. I haven't told you, Jack, I'm getting married.'

'Good for you.'

'He's a psychologist. Tom Pringle. We see things so much the same way.'

'Good for you.'

'He thinks both my parents are mad.'

A new, open Rex. I knew that he would tell me about Harry.

'How do you mean, interesting?' Rex is quick.

'I got the chance to check some dates. How often did you and Harry go away together?'

The sea turning over in long rows; thin water streaming up the sand. Far ahead figures moved in the sea-haze at the southern end of the beach.

'Only once. I met her twice but the first time it was an accident. She was in Taumarunui. She was going down the Wanganui River the next day. I was just – wandering around. I had to get away from Alice now and then.'

'And Harry had to get away from me.'

'Yeah, she did.'

'Did she tell you why?'

'We had some drinks. We talked a bit about it.'

'And went to bed?'

'No, mate, nothing like that. I guess we both just knew if we needed help there was someone we could ask.'

'And Harry asked? In nineteen seventy one?'

'Yeah, I guess. We said goodnight. She went down the river and I went – don't remember. I was getting out of Auckland quite a bit around that time. I nearly called on you once but you'd shifted house.'

'That was before Taumarunui.'

'Probably. Anyway Jack, no bed. Though I won't say it didn't cross my mind. I guess I like Harry as much as anyone I know.'

'She always told me she didn't like you.'

'She didn't. She doesn't. Except now and then. Now and then I guess I was OK.'

'So what about that note you sent about her book? Did you write that to let her know you were available? You went to bed the next time. I'm not a bloody fool.'

'Take it easy, Jack. I thought I saw something – so I wrote.'

'Saw what?'

'In the hedgehog. I thought she must be pretty desperate.'

There were moments, walking on the beach, when I wanted to kill him.

'Take it easy.'

I swung back and forth like a pendulum: hatred, love. You can love your friend who has made love to your wife. You can even love your friend who has understood her.

I asked him what had happened 'down south'.

'She sent me a card at work. It just said where she'd be, and when.'

'And where was that?'

'Takaka. We went across to Totaranui and stayed in the farmhouse. We went for walks up and down the coast.'

I would have liked to do that.

'What else?'

'Jack, these things, I don't know, they just kind of happen. It was a case of knowing each other for so long. No one betrayed anyone else.'

He did not say that it had happened six years ago. He understood that it was now for me. I turned to the sea. Tears ran on my face at Harry's need to get away, and to have me with her in Rex, whom she didn't like. I understood how passionate she must have been with him.

'If you ever write a poem about this I'll fucking kill you.'

'Sure, Jack. I won't write a poem.'

Even so, I did not see it as adultery. I saw it as Harry's deep need. I saw it as love in which, somehow, I was object. And it must have been like that, a little, for Rex: I was probably not central but off to one side. (I wonder where Alice was standing.) I'm not concerned with the sex part. There must have been an interesting chemistry between them. I'm not going to think about that. I thought about it for a while, then I turned it off. It's a part of Harry's private life. The loved person must be free to have a private life.

As for Rex and me, that chemistry – but I'll leave it. We walked down the beach to our car and driving back to Waimauku he asked me to come in and say hallo to Margot. She should be home by now. A man of simple states, Rex, this new/old creature, Rex. Our Harry conversation was all done; and he had a need of his own, which was to lay at rest the small last part of Sidgy's death I carried round with me.

I sat on a pile of bricks by her shack while he went into the vine rows to find her. Silence, except for the wind and the cicadas. Silence in me, a cold fog. Then, advancing through it, almost sub-aural, a chatter not of voices, of events – the rattle, the collisions, the agitation, of Harry's life and mine, our lives together. It grew into a roar. It rattled away down a chute and fell from hearing, and I was empty and must start again. All we had was our naked selves, facing each other and, perhaps, prepared to reach out and touch each other. I won't say that I understood it; but I came into a state – perhaps from the sky, the moving grass, the dusty road turning across the hill – into a position from which, sometime soon, understanding might be reached for and be found. I would survive. I knew that I had an 'I' to survive. I would increase. And Harry was Harry, it would happen to her too. I'm not talking about happiness, it's salvation; but happiness does come into it.

A dog ran round the corner of the shack and skidded to a halt; a nondescript dog of the sort you see on TV, working sheep. It looked at me and looked away at someone out of sight. Perhaps it guarded me, or kept me company, I could not tell; but its eyes and attentive nose and sharpened ears underlined me in my new position. I said, 'Gidday.'

Margot, when she came, underlined me too, with a close and wary look. 'Jack? No, don't get up.' She was stained jungle-green from tomato leaves, and smelled of them.

'Hallo, Margot.'

We shook hands.

Rex had known her the way you turn a page and know the first word. I could not make the connection. The whole long emptiness between – Margot now, Margot then; you take the easy step across; don't look down or you'll see the chasm falling away, and all that inner surface . . . False analogy. There's no similarity in the relations. Margot doesn't wear trickiness, she exposes it. I simply have to leave her life to her, and stand them side by side, the child and the woman, and treat them somehow as contemporaries.

The woman, I saw at once, was pregnant: no soft swelling, a hard lump. It was localized and muscular – the child held tight. I told her how much I admired their piece of land. It wasn't often you saw land used so intensively. Were they trying to live off it or did they go outside to work?

'I do,' Margot said.

'She's got some private patients,' Rex said.

'How long will you be able . . .'

Right through, she answered. Exercise was good for pregnant women, and good for the baby too.

'And how long before you'll be making wine?' I nodded at the vine rows on the hill.

'Years. We've got to learn how.'

'I got old Ivan Franich up to help me with the planting. God knows what we'll do when we get some grapes,' Rex said.

'We'll manage.'

'I'm sure you will.'

We finished topics quickly. I liked Margot at once but saw that she didn't much like me. Was it me now or me then she had trouble with?

'Would you like a cup of tea, Jack?' That, and a biscuit, she owed me. I wanted more. Hadn't I come to tell her that Sidgy might stay dead? I had walked through her gate and patted her dog and smiled at her. In a way I sanctioned her baby and I didn't want now just to nod and go away.

She had been a fat child. Now she was square and muscular. She had been freckled and sandy. She was freckled and sandy still. No mystery, no darkness, little curve (even with a baby on the way); no moist corners or fronded declivities. Her hips and pelvis made a footing for the foetal sac that rode inside. I nearly wrote 'precious load' for 'foetal sac' but there seemed to be none of that, just an immense practicality. A powerful in-turning. Nothing delicate or 'sensitive'.

Her face? Ordinary. Nondescript. Open, not mean; private, not loud. She would smile but it did not light her up, it simply made her available for a moment or two. She did nothing with her hair but keep it short. She did not hide her ears – lop ears are they called? – that jutted like serving spoons from the side of her head. Her hair had mostly hidden them when she was a child.

I did not need to mention Sidgy. They simply had to see me to know that he wasn't coming back from my direction. I don't think he bothered them much. He was a scar they carried on some part covered by clothes. Birthmark might be more accurate, in the sense that Sidgy was present in their beginning; but scar is deeper and more apt. They did not feel it any longer but probably noticed it now and then. Margot perhaps noticed more, being pregnant. She had needed to see me. After the cup of tea she needed me gone.

'And you still live in Wellington, Jack?'

'Yes. In Kelburn.'

'And you're married? With children?'

I told her. I said Harry's name and it sounded in me like a gong.

Then it sounded like a simple, clear, direct call home. Harry reduced Margot to her proper size. Margot and Rex. I did not want, or need, to be part of them. For the first time in my life I didn't need Rex. It was stunning, liberating. It was like a load of shingle sliding off a truck and leaving the tray empty, polished clean, and sinking easily to its proper place.

Such things do not last. He has troubled me again. He has been a load I bear; that I bear gladly now and then. But the moment when I stood free of him and emptied out, is – what? Valid state, absolute condition. That is me. As long as I remember it . . .

'Harry? Is that short for Harriet?'

'Yes.'

She sent a look at Rex and I wondered if he had told her. Probably had. They were not people who would hide earlier lives.

'I'll be home tomorrow. That will be good. I don't really like Auckland much.'

'I don't either,' Margot said. 'But I love it here.' That, with her marvellous directness, was for Rex. I saw why he loved her but I did not envy him. I wanted to get home to Harry.

'Does he still call you Wells?'

'Not now.'

'They use "Porridge" in schools, you know. "For Wells".'

'Yes, I've heard. I'm going back to work, Rex. I've got another three rows to do. Goodbye, Jack. Thanks for being kind to me when I was a child.'

'Rex was the kind one.'

'Yes. Come and see us when you're up again.' That was the only time she wasn't honest. She went back to her work nipping laterals and I haven't met her since, although I've spoken with her on the phone.

'Does Alice know she's pregnant?'

'No. Margot goes up the hill when she comes out.'

'She won't be coming out again, after your letter.'

'I guess not.'

'And you really live like this, separately?'

'It's the way she wants it. My place is over by the other entrance. Sometimes we don't meet for a couple of days.'

'Are you getting married?'

'We're kind of married already. Come and have a look at the place.'

Margot's dog came with us. He had been trained to keep to the paths – though now and then he peed where he shouldn't have – and he trotted ahead, keeping his nose to the breeze and possibly smelling Margot, working far away among the tomatoes. She had taken off her shirt and I saw the curved sweat-shine of her back – a curve in Margot after all.

We went up through the clipped vines on their wires and when I complained about the clay he told me grapes grew well in that sort of soil. The place had a micro-climate, it had a lid on it and a wall around. In a way, he said, it was displaced – half a beat outside time, a millimetre off the grid of the paddocks round about. I saw a little clinker-built dinghy standing on its stern against the back wall of his shack.

'You still do some fishing?'

'When I can. Margot doesn't like the sea. She doesn't trust it.'

'Where do you go?'

'Out on the Kaipara.' A sports car – Jaguar, or some conspicuous thing – stopped by his stall at the gate and he watched it with narrowed eyes until it drove away. He did not seem to care about selling. 'It's a bit too closed in though. I go across the other side. Off the Whangaparaoa.' He grinned. 'She likes the fish.'

'I thought they were all gone.'

'I know where they're hiding. You've got to work at it. I've been sitting out in the Hauraki Gulf for a long time now.' He was happy, he was pleased with himself, and his boasting was a part of it. The sea was not the reason, Margot was, Margot and this piece of land with a lid on it. He had found a place to stand better than 'Petley' – which, now, perhaps he could leave.

'Can you keep on writing?'

'Maybe.'

'Alice thinks you won't.'

'Alice is a bit out of touch.'

'Does the family come? The boys?'

'They've got other things to do.'

'What about Lila and Melva and the others?'

'They're still there in Loomis. I go and visit them. Margot's not too

223

good with families. Come up here, Jack. When you stand on top of the hill you can see right across to the dunes at the back of the beach. When the wind's right the spray comes up and makes it like a fire. You think it's all burning, twenty or thirty miles of it, on the other side.'

Don't ask questions, he meant to say.

So there's Rex, on his bit of land, with his 'wife'. Alice was to say 'he never married', but she was wrong. He did not marry her because she had no territory. Margot had a territory. He lived with Margot and their child between Muriwai and Waimauku, and learned to make wine that could just about be drunk. He sold produce at the gate and sent a few trays and sacks to market now and then. Margot kept a patient or two. There was never much money. He managed to keep his old car on the road and drove off to the Kaipara or the gulf with the dinghy on the roof-rack and the motor in the boot and came home with snapper and kahawai and kingfish.

Then he was drowned out there, past Tiri.

And how did that happen, Jack wonders, what went wrong?

But I don't wonder, not here. He wrote but never published, and Margot has not published his work of those last years. I don't even know whether she kept it or destroyed it.

I'm the only one who knows he didn't stop. (His 'maybe' meant 'yes', I have no doubt.) Alice does not know. John Dobbie does not know. I can't think of any reason to tell them. The poems are from that micro-climate. I can't be an archivist there.

We walked down to my rental car, parked by his shack. He fetched me some peppers from his stall. Margot raised a finger in goodbye. I thought of her turning away, in the lighted window, while Sidgy lay dead in the rain. I thought of Sidgy flying down the steps, with an arc of urine trailing behind. It seemed to me the murder was behind us now. We need not think of Sidgy any more. I almost sighed. I had not known how much he stayed with me.

224

Jo and Georgy

He learns to pee again. He exercises his pelvic floor. He writes three chapters in his notebook. While all this is going on Jo Bellringer dies. He discovers the truth about his father. Jack congratulates himself that he stayed calm and managed to keep on with his work.

He does not need to hide behind this voice any more but keeps it to make discoveries. It puts his pulse rate up and makes him lively. He's able to invent himself more. He eats better in the third person and present tense and he doesn't sneeze as much. Memory is not so important. Involvement is important. Consciousness too; and behaviour. (Memory is oil in the works.) 'He' not 'I' stands 'now' up straight and stops it slouching about. Everything gets a fair chance.

Harry says, 'I wish you'd get out from under the stairs. It's unhealthy.'

'I'm fitter now than I've ever been.' He almost says he's like a sluicing hose but his waterworks no longer amuse her.

'Use my room if you must keep writing. I don't need it for a while.'

She is in the garden mornings. Her drawings are with the publisher (and Jo has sent her text in at last). He thinks of asking her to illustrate his notebooks. She would find things he has missed. She would put a different look on people's faces. One more time he'll go back there, and perhaps invite her along. In the meantime, blue biro, Olympic 1B5 . . .

Harry becomes his helpmate for a while. (Helpmeet, he finds, is incorrect.) The eye in the ceiling has nothing to see. She brings him cups of tea and makes a cooked lunch instead of ramming bread in the toaster. Several times each morning she taps on his door and puts her head in. 'I'm walking down to the shops, Jack. Is there anything you want?' 'I'm putting some cabbages in. Is it too early, do you think?' When she had been busy he did not interrupt. He found his way around the garden alone. But he smiles, he's pleased

225

she needs him. If now and then he loses a word there are plenty of other words to take its place.

He writes about his father's dictionary and turns the pages looking for minus and plus. 'L' is a good choice. 'Likerous', 'liliaceous' are full of suggestion and won't keep still. Several weeks later he comes to Beth and she is plain. He knows what he should have done with her.

Harry taps. 'Jo's still not answering her phone.'

'Shall we go and have a look this afternoon?'

'I rang Sarah Cook' (their publisher) 'and she hasn't heard. I would like to go if you don't mind.'

Harry drives, and smiles at him, she is pleased to be out. Jack likes it too: the hump-backed bridge, the city squatting in the sun. The roads bend this way and that and make him feel that he and Harry have travelled a long way and have further ways to go. He is coming to like Auckland again, not just for Loomis. There's a humpiness in its spreading out that makes interesting bends and twists. It can't match Wellington for swoop and dive and exhilaration but it doesn't punish with vertigo. A carbohydrate city, short on vitamins, but pulpy and greasy and comfortable. When he's finished writing he'll grow fat.

They stop at Jo Bellringer's gate and he knows at once that something is wrong. Jo is an organized person. She would not go away without stopping her paper and mail.

'Jack?' Harry says.

'Her car's not in the garage,' which has the hollowed-out look that makes them so forlorn. 'At least it means she's not in the house.'

'Unless it's stolen.'

They have the same thought (confess it later): rapist, strangler, driving away in his victim's car. Jack knocks on the door and rings the bell. They look in the windows, shading the glass. It's no *Marie Celeste*. There's no food waiting to be eaten and no lights on. The bed – it's hard to tell with duvets – seems to be made. Jack hunts for a key while Harry takes the mail from the box and collects the papers.

'Tuesday morning. That's four days. I'm going to ask next door.'

The woman has been watching. She fixes the safety chain as they approach.

'We're friends of Ms Bellringer,' Harry explains through the gap.

'Ms' makes the woman tighten her lips. She has not seen Miss
Bellringer, she says, for several days. She drove away on Monday
afternoon. 'I didn't realize she hadn't come back.'

'Will you look after her mail?'

'I'd sooner not, if something's wrong.'

'Can we use your phone then? We'd better tell the police.'

'I'd sooner not be involved at all.'

They drive to the shopping centre and find a card phone, then
hunt for a shop selling cards. The police are polite and ask them to
wait at the address. They wait for an hour and a half.

'I'm going,' Jack says.

'No, they'll come.'

'You'd think that bitch next door would make us a cup of tea.'

'Don't get cross. Something's wrong with Jo.'

'Has she been depressed?'

'She always is when we finish a book.'

'She wouldn't do anything before it comes out.'

Harry finds chewing-gum in the glove box and gives him some.
Later on she gets out and sits on Jo's fence while he listens to 'My
Music' on the radio. He would like Harry to listen. These are not the
sort of jokes – they're puns and verbal turns – that can be told later
on. He feels he's getting something good that she refuses to share. Jo
has probably gone off the way Harry herself used to go. She's down
the Wanganui in a canoe or holed up in a farmhouse with a girlfriend
somewhere.

He apologizes. He apologizes to them both. He turns the radio off
and sits on the fence and makes up happy scenarios until she tells
him, 'Do be quiet.' The police car arrives at a crawl and a young
constable climbs out with a house-agent smile. He knows what to
do: hunts for a key, looks in the windows, finds the oldest paper –
brings himself up level with them. Jack tells him the woman next
door seems rather keen to help and the constable, Young is his
name, marches off there. While he's away a man crosses the street
and shows them a house key hanging behind a calendar in the
garage.

'Good place,' he grins. The calendar is nine years old.

They call the policeman and go into the house: dishes washed,
bed made, nothing out of order. A jigsaw puzzle – four thousand

pieces, the box-lid says – lies quarter finished on the dining-room table. Young takes their names, asks about relatives and friends, says these things usually have a simple explanation. He fits a piece of sailing ship into the puzzle. Keeps the key.

'I'm worried, Jack.'

'Me too.' He's worried about Harry. She seems to be grieving for Jo. Does she have special knowledge? Their minds have been bonded for many years.

Jack drives home carefully. Harry sits beside him with her hands in her lap. He reaches out and taps them to make them lie still.

He sees for the first time that her hands are growing old.

His mother laughs at everything he says. 'You're so funny. I don't remember you making me laugh when you were a boy.'

She is not supposed to use words like remember, even to complain that she can't. Memory, as a concept, is meant to be beyond her, but she won't obey the rules.

'You were such a stern little boy.'

She is not making it up and is not mistaken. What she can't remember, or won't remember, is her part.

Lightning flashes. Rain snarls across the window. The hospital is like a liner riding through a storm. Mrs Brockie, in the other bed (Mrs Donald died a month ago), yelps with fright and her visitor (daughter , by her face) winks at Jack. He bends his mouth, avoiding complicity. They'll be there soon enough themselves and should prepare for Duppa.

'Is that the train?'

'It's thunder, Mum. Did you see the lightning?'

'Walter got down before it stopped.'

He's proud of her. Connections are meant to be too hard. And he's pleased – he's delighted – that she does not disapprove. His father gets a nod from her at last.

'Do you remember him?'

'What a funny question.'

'I do. I often think about him.'

'So you should. You don't look like him. He was very handsome. She looks more like him than you do.'

'Who?'

'Her over there with Georgina.'

He looks around, looks back. 'Georgina?'

'They wouldn't let her bring her sword. I don't think she wants to kill me now.'

'Sshh, Mum.'

'She looks like Walter.'

'It's Mrs Brockie's daughter. There's no Georgina, Mum.'

'We talk about him all the time, how kind he was.'

She closes her eyes and seems to sleep, and he takes her hand.

'Your mother thinks I'm somebody else,' Mrs Brockie's daughter says.

'Yes, I'm sorry.'

'They all do that. Don't you, Mum? She thinks you're the doctor and you never look at her. It makes her cross.'

'Sorry.'

'What does she mean about a sword all the time?'

'I've no idea.'

'She thinks her husband and my mother, isn't it rich? That makes him your father, I suppose.'

Mrs Skeat shivers. Her hand tightens and her fingers creak. Is she dreaming? Are the Scottish dancers chasing her? Or perhaps there's another blockage, a t.i.e. They happen all the time now, warning of bigger things to come. She opens her eyes.

'Take your umbrella if it's wet.'

'Yes, I will.'

'And put on your – put on . . .'

'Galoshes?'

She smiles and runs her thumb along his knuckles; then looks at him sharply. 'You're not Walter.'

'No, I'm John.'

'Why do you say you're Walter if you're John?'

'I don't.'

'There's no good comes . . .'

He is shaken by the message she receives through her hand. How can he believe it? He never once saw them holding hands. He never saw them touch or pat or stroke or kiss at all. There's no good comes from lying, perhaps she meant to say; but can she, in her condition, lie?

229

Let her sleep. Let her hold Walter's hand again.

Mrs Brockie's daughter stops at the foot of the bed. 'It's nice your mother talks to her even if she can't answer back.'

He smiles and nods.

'Her name is Elsie though, not Georgina.'

'I'll tell her.'

'Your father must have been a bit of a dag.'

'No, no. All that's imagination too.' Go away, he wants to say. Senile parents don't form a bond.

'She made me show Mum his letter the other day.'

'What letter?'

'From Georgy. In her box. I wouldn't mind getting a letter like that.'

'Ah,' Jack says, sounding vague. Inside he is hideously quick; fits pieces into place with a flick and a picture lies, slanting from left to right, as flat as a glazed tile, on his mind. Walter Skeat and Georgy embrace. The Gladstone bag sits by Walter's feet. His hat is tilted back (James Joyce style) so the brim lies on her raised Edwardian hair – why Edwardian? Pipey mouth devours a soft pink mouth (Bullen style). It almost makes Jack retch with excitement and disgust.

'Ta-ta.' Mrs Brockie's daughter.

'Ugh!' His mother, in her sleep.

He swallows. He slows himself down in order to discover with maturity. The brooches in the box beside Roget are quality pieces (no beads, no bangles, that was not her style, and nor were rings, which cluttered up the hands; and somehow dirtied them, she seemed to say). They're pearly and filigreed but weigh the letter down. Why has he not seen it? Where has she kept it until now?

King George stamp. White envelope gone yellow; addressed to the office; and marked rather shyly: 'Personal'. The lady has a delicate hand; but – he unfolds the paper – she makes a bold start:

Walt my love,

Why did you leave without a kiss? I've dreamed of kissing you at the door. How proper you suddenly became in the hall. Does the world outside threaten you? Don't think of the world, think of the room and us two in it and our love. I will wait next Friday. We needn't go near that other place. Come to me here.

Our room, Walt. Dear Walt. Our bed.
Nothing can go wrong any more.
　Your Georgy

He reads the date: the day his father died. She must have written it
when he had gone; was writing it perhaps, while he rode to Loomis
on the train. Did she post it in a corner box as Walter Skeat
misjudged his leap and ran with smacking soles on the station
platform? On Monday it would have been delivered to his office.
'Personal': someone there had passed it on to Dorothy Skeat.

There's too much to take in. His neatness won't function any
more. The slanted hat, the Edwardian lady, zoom away. He's left
with pieces that won't fit. A woman, Georgy. A man, adulterer –
Walter Skeat. A wronged wife in her summer house; a son in his
room. Was there a baby? Was there only one time and did it frighten
him? Did it make him leap from the train too soon?

What made him leap on those other days? Some other woman, in
'that other place'?

Betrayal turns him into a judge. He's revolted by his father
suddenly: to poke with his pipe and weave his web of do and don't
and knot his son at the wrists and ankles, while all the time he jumps
from trains and walks free himself. While he has women. Jack has to
say it: 'While he lives and I don't live.'

His father should have taken him there; or given him some hint
there was a way.

He'll look up 'hypocrisy', he'll look up 'lies', and see what plus or
minus they score. As for the rest, 'likerous', 'liliaceous', they are not
a mystery any more. He'll look up 'fornication' and 'adultery'. His
father fornicated on Friday afternoons. With a liliaceous lady. And
came home to ask about their day and nod with another sort of
satisfaction that it had progressed so uneventfully.

Jack takes out his pocket notebook and slips the matchstick pencil
from its spine. He copies the letter with a steady hand. But 'Georgy'
is illicit; it is genteel and sexy and familiar and strange. He signs it
fast to get it down and out of the way. The looping 'g' and looping 'y'
almost make a circle, with 'e' and 'o' – what does 'eo' mean? – paired
inside. The lady should have Greeked them and put a row of kisses.

Jack slides the notebook flat against his heart. The letter rattles into place underneath the brooches. What should he do next? He smooths an inch-long wisp of hair from his mother's brow. He takes her hand and holds it again.

She does not wake. Her fingers tighten. And under her smooth eyelids – so young, so much like bean pods – her eyes move about. Perhaps she dreams of Walter Skeat.

He sees that at last his mother is doing well.

The storm has gone out past Rangitoto. It makes a shadow there, twinned with the Coromandel's hump. Jack drives to the station. He finds, to his surprise, that a train still goes out west.

'Harry. Listen. I won't be home for lunch. I'm going on a train ride. Yes, it's to do with Rex. No, not Loomis. I'm going to Mt. Albert to have a look at our school.' Lies. Lies.

He eats a pie and drinks a carton of juice. The straw, concertinad at the bend, looks like a piece of intestine. The world is changing too fast and he responds with grotesqueries. But the train, in spite of its diesel engine, comes from vanished times and almost makes him forget where he is going. It's mostly goods, with a single passenger carriage, and although everything is different – upholstery, panelling, windows – it's the same. The grit is gone, the sulphur's gone, the luggage racks you could hammock in, but the squalor is in place and he is blindly happy for a moment. Rex would understand. There had been some truth, after all, in his lies to Harry.

They pass Carlaw Park, they go through the tunnel, and there is no time, he sees, for even a rudimentary act of love, especially in that time of buttoned flies – although Seddon Tech boys were brutal and quick. Newmarket. Kingsland. He creeps up on Mt. Albert, reversing his father's line of approach. Ah, the lies. He had not even gone to Auckland on those afternoons. Had he got off at this station too before the train pulled up?

Jack asks his way; goes down the hill and along towards Fowlds Park; then has to turn left and cross the line he has travelled on. He lays his palm on the rail to feel if it is warm and would leave a ten cent piece to be flattened out if a woman was not watching from the other footpath. His father had brought him home a flattened penny once. It seemed out of character, but is in character now. It might have been done on this stretch of line.

He crosses the road to the woman. 'I'm looking for Verona Avenue.'

She points. He goes. A 1920s street of bungalows with an Italian city name; romantic name for Walter Skeat and his lightsome lady. Principle, bitter or not, must have been hard to keep in mind in this sunny hollow. Was it sunny on the day his father died?

He walks along the footpath reading the numbers and works out which house it must have been: bungalow, with a bow window, and a roof of decramastic tile out of keeping with the weather-boards. Georgy would not like it, possibly not even recognize it, if she were alive and came this way. Why does he think she had good taste? Is it the literary tone of her letter? She would know the Phoenix palm on the lawn. It must have been planted when the house was new.

He reads the number. Sees the name. Too many shocks. 'G. Feist'. He remembers the rexine-covered cheap editions rubberbanded in his father's bag. Georgy then is G. Feist; and G. Feist is alive, in the house where she and his father made love. It is more than Jack can understand. He walks on, stops; walks on again. Another woman looks at him. 'What's up? Lost?' she says.

'I was looking for . . . Is there a Miss, or Mrs Feist?'

'Yes. Georgina. Miss, it is. You've passed her place. The house with the palm tree. Name on the box.'

'Thank you.'

Now he must turn back. Must go in. He does not want to. He feels that Georgy, whatever she is like – Edwardian, Georgian, decramastic – will press him as flat as paper and crumple him up.

The woman is watching, bossy, bright, and he must go. He wants, of course, to look at Georgy, even if she strikes him throat and groin, even if she sucks the blood from him. (Jack makes up these feelings as he writes, although he's not sure he didn't feel them for too short a time to call back.) He walks up the path and knocks at the door. Does not press the worn bell his father must have pressed. A card thumb-tacked below it says 'Bell out of order. Please knock'.

Georgina Feist says, 'Good afternoon.' She is not liliaceous. She's a forgotten apple in a bowl, with its skin wrinkled and its flesh spongy and dry. But no, she is not grotesque, she is simply old; she's natural and full of years and knows how to smile. He is no longer afraid.

233

'Miss Feist?'

'Yes.'

'My name is Jack – John, Skeat. I'm the son of Walter.'

'Yes?'

'I wondered if I could come in and talk about him.'

'Well . . .'

He is used to strongmindedness in old ladies. 'Walter Skeat. You knew him in 1947.' He does not want to bully; he wants to get inside and hear her say what sort of man his father was. He wants to know if there was a child.

'Yes, I did. I remember' – Miss Feist swallows but seems more puzzled than afraid – 'Walter Skeat. He was an accountant. He did my father's books. But there's nothing – '

'Just a little while. I won't take much of your time.'

She allows him into the hall; opens a door, revealing a sitting-room, and a chair in which he may sit down. She does not smile but frowns at him, with concentration it seems.

'He died, didn't he, Walter Skeat, on a train?'

'He fell getting off a train. In 1947.'

'I'm afraid I didn't know him very well. He seemed a very nice man. Very helpful.'

'Miss Feist – '

'I think I might have met your mother too. On a tram. She had a small boy. That must have been you! Is she . . . ?'

'She's still alive. She's in an old people's hospital.' He understands her need to turn him aside. She has put it all away – has locked it up and starved it, probably to death. After more than forty years she has no wish to bring it back to life. He admires her smooth evasiveness.

'My mother found out in the end. If she'd already met you she would have known Georgy was Georgina.'

'I'm sorry, I'm not sure . . .' She's more alarmed than puzzled. Jack begins to feel alarm himself. He and Miss Feist are on different lines.

'He called you – my father called you Georgy.'

'Oh no.' She is cross. 'I never called myself that. Or let anyone . . . But I see . . .' She smiles; smiles nicely; makes a sweet old lady of herself. 'I never knew they'd met. Come along with me, Mr Skeat.'

She takes him into the hall and opens another door. A man is watching cricket on the television, with a transistor radio held to his ear. He turns unseeing eyes on them.

'Georgy, turn that off and say hallo to Mr Skeat.'

Georgy Feist is not much older than Jack. Georgy has not locked it up, he remembers it all. He is loquacious and precise, he's a happy man.

Miss Feist brings them lemonade and cake. She knows her brother, it would seem, and is amused and incurious. She gives him a yellow hairpiece, hooked on her finger, and nods to show it's straight as he puts it on. She pats Jack on the arm and goes away to the back of the house.

The screen flickers green and white and takes Georgy's eye frequently. He watches for boundaries and dismissals while he tells Jack who his father was. Politely, he has switched the radio off. 'I watch on there and listen here. It's a better commentary on the radio. Are you interested in cricket?'

'No.'

'Walt used to be. It was more than just the lads in their whites. We went to Eden Park and saw Bert Sutcliffe hit a hundred. And he was always going on about Doctor Grace. In fact so much we started calling him that.'

'Who is we?'

'Oh, everyone at Herne Bay. There was a man, his house was a place where we could meet. It wasn't easy then, you know, in fact it was dangerous. You could go to prison for a very long time. Anyway, he kept us off the streets, all us boys, and older men like Walt used to go. Don't get me wrong, it wasn't a bordello. But there was something just a little bit – sordid, shall we say? It got like that.' Georgy laughs and lets his memory slip somewhere else.

'The first time I went there I saw Walt, and all I wanted to do was run away. He'd been at our house a couple of times, looking after Dad's stuff – Dad had a biscuit factory, it's been bought out now, but Gina and I have got enough. Well, just enough. Anyway – oh he's gone, a yorker, middle stump. Walt didn't like that one, he called it the Geordie ball. Am I upsetting you?'

'No.'

'Where was I? Yes, we met. At Herne Bay. I was terrified. I thought my father had found out and sent him to get me, but he just said, "Well met, Georgy." He was expecting me, in a way. You can't keep it secret, not from an older man. Are you sure you want to know about all this?'

Jack isn't sure. But he can't not listen and can't not know.

'We only came back here one time. And that night he was dead. You're not inclined to see a judgement in that?'

'No.'

'My father would have. Divine wrath. This fellow will stonewall all day. And your mother, of course. I've always been curious about her. She must have known – I don't mean me – but she must have known.'

'She thought Georgy meant Georgina.'

'Oh, I see.' Georgy looks at him with speculation, but doesn't say what is in his mind.

'He ruined her life. He – devastated it. But she always thought you were a woman.'

Georgy looks away. 'Ho,' he says.

'I didn't come to talk about her. What was he like?'

'He was – it doesn't bother me if you disapprove.'

Jack shakes his head. Disapproval is way out of it – in another country somewhere.

'Well,' Georgy says, 'he was – gay.' Laughs. 'In the old sense. A happy man, man who was alive. He had a wonderful sense of fun. He made me laugh. He was – well, he was Doctor Grace. There was a kind of light on him. I don't mean that in a blasphemous way. He had a moral light in his countenance.' Georgy avoids saying 'face'. And Jack sees that his father has become a fiction. He decides not to criticize; or hear any more of it; and puts away that 'moral light' to look at later on. He wants the facts.

'Was he both ways? Was he bisexual?'

'Well, he must have been. Early on. But he made his choice. It isn't really a choice though. There's an imperative.' Georgy smiles.

'What did you do, together, here? Did you go all the way?' Jack knows some crude words and will use them if he must. Not to nail his father. He's not ready for his father yet. But he wants to fend Georgy off.

236

'I don't know that I'm prepared to talk about that.'

'At the house in Herne Bay, what was he like?'

'You mean, did he go with anyone? No, he didn't. Walt mainly went to relax. To be where he didn't have to pretend.'

'So you were the first?'

'I was the only one from there.' Georgy is fierce. And seeing this rag of passion, Jack smiles. He feels at ease, and out of Georgy's range; although not out of Walter Skeat's.

'Going home from here he fell over and killed himself.'

'There, I knew you'd blame me.'

'There's no blame. He had some books of yours. I'm sorry I can't return them, I think they're lost.'

'I don't recall . . .'

'Sapper and John Buchan.'

'Ah. I'd grown out of those. He took them for you. Extraordinary memory.' He taps his brow. 'Forty years.'

'I'd grown out of them too. Does a man' – it is more than curiosity now – 'doing what he did, still think of his family?'

'What a dreadful question.'

It is. Jack sees it. He has gone too far. But Georgy, somehow, is pleased.

'Walt reminded me of Richard Hannay. Very British.'

'Did your sister know about you?'

'Me, yes. Walt, no. She made up her mind to be outside.' He wags his finger high. 'Not above. Gina was before her time. I was a bit – sickly, so I didn't have a job. That's why – Friday afternoons. Gina worked. She never found out about Walt until now, with you poking in. And she's still outside. Good old girl. How did you discover it?'

'You wrote a letter. Someone at his office must have given it to my mother.'

'And she thought I was a girl, you say? I wonder.' He slips his finger under his hairpiece and scratches his scalp.

'What's your real name? George?'

'Good heavens no, not with Georgina. I'm a Gerald. I'd be Gerry. But I was a plump little boy before I got sick. Roly-poly. So – Georgy, from Georgy Porgy pudding and pie, and it stuck. Even when I grew up and got – willowy. I'm six foot two.' He stands up from his chair. 'I towered over Walt.'

Like a lily, Jack thinks.

'It's handy for theatricals. I did a bit of that.' He juts his crooked arms and hooks his head. 'Vulture bird.' He shrinks and creeps. 'Poisoner. I could do the male lead too. Nice and straight and manly. Gerald Feist.'

'Georgy Porgy pudding and pie, kissed the girls and made them cry.'

Georgy laughs. 'I beat you to that one years ago. I didn't run away though, when the boys came out.' Behind him the stonewalling batsman is caught in the slips but Jack does not mention it. Gives himself a little more command. He's on a plateau of satisfaction. His father makes sense. His mother makes sense – although if what Georgy has hinted at is true: that she had known who her husband was . . . But he'll tip backwards if he thinks of that. Jack stands up and is almost a head shorter than Georgy. Lilies wither though and turn brown; they shake hands like men of sixty-five.

'I hope all this hasn't turned you too much upside down.'

'No. It hasn't.'

'Your father was a good man. He was a lovely man.'

Jack will decide that for himself. He points Georgy back at the cricket. 'There was someone caught a moment ago.' Lets himself into the hall, doesn't disturb Georgina. But Georgy opens a window and puts his yellow head into the sun.

'Walt said we should call ourselves Valentine and Proteus.'

Jack is blank.

'The two gentlemen of Verona.'

'Ah. Yes.'

Until now he would not have been sure that his father even knew who Hamlet and Horatio were, or Lear and the fool.

He takes a bus to Symonds Street and walks to the station. He would like to tell Harry, and hear what she has to say, but knows he won't because he will complain. His father never took him to see Bert Sutcliffe make a hundred. (Buchan and Sapper don't make up for that.) But especially for lying all his life, with pipe and precepts and manliness. Worse than complain, Jack will hate. Even though – he stops on the footpath – Walter Skeat might have been steering his son into paths different from his own. There might have been love

238

in his behaviour. (Surely he could see I'm not like that, Jack complains.)

There had been no love for his wife. No mercy.

Already Walter Skeat is an interesting man.

Moral light? No. But a light of some sort Jack is willing to concede. The light of being natural at last? 'Never do more than take your share, Johnnyboy, but decide as quick as you can what it is and then insist on having it.' When he took his own share it turned out to be a Feist. (There's a pun Walter Skeat might have allowed.)

Jack gets into his car. Surely he should feel more than this. Perhaps he is in shock. The whole thing is, after all, rather like a car crash. He's trapped in the wreckage and twisted out of shape, but soon they'll lift him out and he'll start to scream.

No, he decides, no melodrama. He is confident he can handle it. Most of all he has a new father to get to know. And already Walter Skeat makes good sense. Doctor Grace. As for his mother – that's not easy. Jack should complain, he should do some hating, for her devastation, for her ruined life.

Georgy is right. She must have known. She was a clever woman, very sharp, and all those years with him, those years of Herne Bay, and of other places probably . . . Why hadn't she simply gone away? Taken herself and her son away?

But now, at last, she escapes. Georgy can be Georgina now. Her mind is working for her (what is left of it) and giving her a place to go.

She would have forgiven Walter Skeat if it had been women he liked.

So Jack speculates as he drives home; up and over the harbour bridge, along to Castor Bay. He will never love his parents, it isn't possible, but maybe he will come to understand them.

Harry runs out to the garage. 'The police rang up. They've found Jo. She crashed her car.'

'Where? Is she all right?'

'She's dead. She's been dead for more than a week.'

Her car ran off the road on the way to Whatipu. It lay crushed in a creek, out of sight, with Jo inside, equally crushed. Oil leaked into the water and when someone traced it back, there was the Deux

Chevaux lying on its roof, with Jo's arm reaching out as though to pluck a fern frond from the bank.

She loved the road to Whatipu. Harry had sometimes gone out there with her. She followed Jo down gullies and up and down creeks – up that same creek where Jo had died – and had come home with new knowledge (botanical) and a happy glow on her face.

'Jo was a careful driver.'

'Yes, she was.'

'She wouldn't have run off the road if she hadn't been unhappy.'

Harry is close to blaming herself but good sense stops her. She knows it was impossible for her to make Jo happy. Jack could have, should have, given Beth Simmonds one happy night but there's nothing Harry could have done for Jo.

Was there nothing Walter Skeat could have done for his wife?

Notebook: 14

I can know only small parts of Auckland. What can I know of Otara and the populations there? The conurbation out west, where Loomis, Massey, Swanson, Te Atatu used to be – I drive through and watch strangers from my car window. It is partly a matter of race and class. (All of us are New Zealanders, it's said, but anyone can see that we are two nations; three.) And it is partly fear; I'm still afraid. I fear my white face, my incomprehension; and, less justifiably, the burglar and the gag. Modesty of temperament also plays a part. I'm not a gatherer of all things.

I'll move about in my middle class suburbs. I'll stroll on Takapuna beach. And I'll visit Loomis in my head. It is old Loomis, under this same sky, that makes me feel I have come home after the long adventure of Wellington.

When David and Jillian left home we sold the house in Central Terrace and moved to a smaller place in Boundary Road. It's hard to shift from a house you've made with your own hands – where Harry has drawn pictures on the walls and you have lain on the roof, holding on with one hand and painting with the other; and leave rooms you've kept secrets in and spoken lies. You try a new start – tell, admit – but you can't change the story of a house. Deception, secrecy, are for ever a part of you.

I told her, in Boundary Road, that I knew about her and Rex. We were sitting in the garden enjoying the view – we'd not lost the view.

Harry said, 'I know you know.'

I had been angry, I'd been suicidal, at my failure to be devastated. I took it as proof of my inability to love. At times I had wanted to destroy (not kill, I never wanted to kill) Harry as the object of my failure. But the impulse went away, as these things do in people whose temperature is low. It went away fairly soon. My climate won't produce a lasting storm but makes long spells of grey cold weather. Those too come to an end. But Harry discovers what they mean. My secrets are not secret from her, even though she never lets them out. And when I do we don't talk about them for long, we just let them go away.

We readjust with a few words of confession, a smile or two. It's a way that seems to work for us.

Perhaps it would not have worked if I had not known they meant no harm – that they helped each other, and helped me (although that can't have been their intention).

'Have you ever been close to going away for good?'

'Once or twice. Rex stopped me from that.'

'Deliberately? The pair of you talked about it?'

'No, Jack. But we talked. He loves you, in some peculiar way. You're next after – whatever matters most. And after his new wife now, I suppose.'

'He knew you were going to stay?'

'He knew.'

That is almost all we said. She did not apologize. I gave her only one short-arm jab. 'Did you want our adulteries to be simultaneous?' Harry grinned. 'I was thinking more of Beth than you and me.' Seeing I had pleased her, I shut up.

So we sat in the garden holding hands – metaphorically most of the time – and talked about David and Jillian (hundreds of hours we spent on them now that there was little we could do) and my work and her work, and we read each other newspaper paragraphs and witty or ungrammatical sentences from books. We bought good wine, and Harry developed a taste for gin, but we never drank too much – just enough to make us relaxed. What did Walter Skeat say? 'Do nothing with immoderation.' I could not reach disbelief in that, but discovered freedom within those bounds. For her part, Harry believed in keeping a clear head and a steady hand.

We did a lot of walking in those days, in sneakers and sun hats and dark glasses, with little Swedish day-packs on our backs – a light parka, insect repellent, an apple, a sandwich, water, a packet of barley sugars, a packet of bandaids; and, for me, a plastic rubbish sack to pick up rubbish other people dropped. (I did not always bother.) We went to Red Rocks and Cape Turakirae to see the seals. We went to the Orongorongo Valley and climbed Mt. Matthews (the biggest of the elephants). No point in listing our walks and climbs and scrambles, our scrapes and falls; but in Nelson, on Mt. Duppa, we climbed through moss and fern, and limestone boulders in a net of roots, and I seemed to see the world Harry had drawn on the bedroom wall. She always knew a little more than I, a little sooner. Between Johnston's Hill and Mt. Kaukau, with the city and the harbour at our feet – a postcard, too lovely to approach – we came on two men fighting in a hollow. They were middle-aged, red, exhausted, stripped to the waist, and they whacked and missed each other with huge boxing gloves on their white arms. I wanted to watch, and stop them perhaps when they'd had enough, but Harry tugged me on. 'Can't you see it's private?' Later, as we ate lunch, they walked by, carrying their gloves, one behind the other, with something settled between them, it was plain. I recognized one of them, he was a third party politician.

Harry knew about privacy. We kept our own, each from the other, and I look on it now as natural. And even more: desirable. Confession, bleeding, shrieking, 'letting it all hang out' – is that the phrase? – I see as absurd, unnatural, promiscuous, among those not intimate, and between those intimate, as Harry and I were (are), likely to damage or destroy. There are all sorts of places to go, hand in hand, all sorts of pleasures to share, with the body or in the mind, and these acts of touching are like the pebble kicked along the path, that changes the centre of gravity of the universe. We love each other sufficiently when that has been understood.

But I should speak only for Harry and me. I club a broken tea-tree jack (as Les Petley had clubbed the broken-backed dog) and Harry takes me inside and makes me wash my face and sits me down with a cup of tea. I tell her when she wakes from anaesthetic that the lump in her breast is benign. I hold the basin while she is sick. And we walk downtown and climb home through Allenby Terrace after a movie that makes us laugh. I, she, we, in a thousand ways. Married people know all about it. There's a lazy gravity at work between these two that don't escape but never touch.

Arrangement and description has been my work. A&D; a moral principle. At the pick-up, disorder; everything is, by nature it can seem, and deliberately it also seems, discomposed. But inherent in it there's due order and we have systems to find it out. At the end, accessibility. The thing is preserved and available. Not always, but now and then, I feel that I have used my life well.

I would love to have been a literary detective: found the Boswell papers; the truth about Sir Thomas Malory; the true account of Christopher Marlowe's death. I visited the Public Records Office in London; and there I turned side on, I was thinned out by attraction and repulsion. Half of me wanted to rush in and the other half to rush away. I was overcome by delight and fear. So much treasure. So much life and death. I was afraid that I would find the attempt absurd. I stayed only a short time and I'm not sure what I took away.

Back in Wellington I was top man. I climbed the pyramid at last and enjoyed the view from my narrow seat. But sometimes it was like the wheel the Persian satrap sat Polycrates of Samos on to die. (That doesn't work exactly; and didn't work for Rex when he used the spike in a poem, standing for conscience. The mechanics, the anatomy, are wrong.) I learned bureaucracies and budgets and staff – how I learned staff – and how to overcome and enjoy difficulty, and how to stand aside and let the thing roll past that won't be stopped. But all the time I remained the reader who turns to the back of the book and judges it by its bibliography. And in Coblenz when the archivist put a letter from Heinrich Himmler in my hands I felt something dark uncoil in me; I had to find a washroom and soap myself up to the elbows. I retained that susceptibility.

Harry might say, 'Oh God, the whole family wiped out, because some drunken hoon had to drive his car.' Or: 'All of them drowned. Two little girls and the mother. She was pregnant too! And the poor father, trying to swim for help. Imagine what he feels like, Jack.' I could imagine. But I was interested more in deliberate acts. 'They tied him up and put him in the boot of the car and drove two hundred miles and threw him in the Huka Falls. The police think he was still alive.' I wanted the reports of it. I wanted the bloodied singlet and the ropes. For my archives. Beautiful things alone are not enough.

Archives bring a kind of control.

We saw Rex again on television, 1981. He was marching against the Springbok tour but it seemed to me that Margot was the one who was there and she had brought Rex along. She flashed her eyes at the camera and held her placard high while he had his attention somewhere else.

'I can't do that shouting by numbers. Margot can't either. That was the only time we went.'

'So, did you write a poem about it?'

'I don't write much poetry any more.'

'Dried up, eh?'

He looked evasive. 'We wrote a couple of letters to the paper.' (John Dobbie quotes from one, proving Rex had a social conscience. He fails to mention Margot signed it too. Perhaps she wrote it and he signed.)

I did not speak to Margot on that visit, but saw her working in the depths of a shed: bare legs, tartan shirt, that was all. I could not see her face but I think she smiled. She raised her finger in a small salute.

'Swim, Sal,' Rex called, and their child ran out. She was brown and shaggy-haired, and over-muscular for a seven-year-old.

'This is Jack. A mate of mine.'

The child unwound her towel from his arm and ran ahead of us up the hill. She flashed in the vine rows, climbed the fence, disappeared into scrub overlapping the ridge.

'We bought a bit more land,' Rex explained. 'There's a creek down the other side.'

'Good swimming holes?'

'Not as deep as Loomis, it's more stony. The water's better though, you can see the bottom.'

The scrub turned into bush halfway down. There were ferns and nikau palms and supple-jack: jungly bush, as much in its own climate as the vineyard over the hill. But the creek was wide and open to the air; it did not seem to me a creek at all. I save that word for gorge water, slow and deep and green. This, I told Rex, was a stream.

'Yeah, maybe.' We sat on rocks in the sun and watched the naked child swinging on a knotted rope and dropping into the water.

'Want to go in?'

'Next time. I'll bring some togs.' I took off my shoes and let the water run over my feet. Rex delved under the bank and came up with two cans of beer.

'Emergency supplies.'

'I thought you'd be drinking wine.'

'Margot hasn't got it quite right yet. We sell most of our grapes to Ivan Franich.'

He had moved from the active to the passive. He seemed not to go out to things, in his mind, but let them come to him, the way the creek or stream came, round its bend, over his square feet on the shingle; and let things go in that way. It was the same with past and future. He did not want to visit. As usual I wanted to go back; wanted the extra dimension. Rex had always been a door for me. I tried him with the Fun Doctor: our standard two room, Miss Warburton in the corner, all her sharp authority gone, and the old man – bow tie, crinkled Auden face – juggling dusters (little puffs of chalk dust from his hands) and balancing stacks of chairs on his forehead. And I tried him with junket, grated nutmeg sprinkled on top. 'A schoolteacher told me kids don't know what junket is any more.' Rex looked down the creek and yawned.

'Old Norman Tate. Remember the time the chairs came down and took the skin off his nose?'

'Yeah.' He picked up a pebble and lobbed it into the water. He lived in a capsule labelled 'here and now', and time slid by and the world slid by while he enjoyed the golden weather inside. Yet he had mentioned Loomis Creek without being prompted. Perhaps there were some pictures on the walls. And I had entry. I could visit this new creek (this 'now' creek) and watch the child swinging on her rope. I could come as long as I stayed simple.

Storing beer under the bank was as far ahead as Rex wanted to go. I could not see that sitting by the hole enjoying the sun, watching Sal fall and splash and swim to the tree roots and climb up and capture the rope again, was any better – healthier – than nosing obsessively down Loomis Creek and sliding in the mud chute with Fiona. I could not see that there was any fight left in Rex. And it was not until we went back to the house – they had a house and lived together now – and I saw his old Holden with the dinghy roped on top, and knew he had an escape from his thirty acres, that I felt my depression lift.

We had no conversation to record. And you can only say so much about an hour spent sitting by a creek. We went there. We did that. Then we walked back. The child vanished into the shed. I heard Margot hammering at something inside.

Rex and I shook hands. 'See you, Jack. Come out again.' That was all. A happy man.

Why was I uneasy as I drove away?

John Dobbie has trouble with those years. He likens Rex to a fish in a tank. It's effective as a simile if you don't know what I know, that Rex loved Margot and Sal and was happy there. Poetry stopped, spirit died in him, John says; and although he's right in the first part, as far as publication is concerned, he has no evidence for the second. He has, he says (but does not write), Alice's word for it that something shrivelled up in Rex when 'that unlit woman' came into his life. But Alice is constructing a story. She thinks there was a Rex within Rex, driving, navigating, and that she was the route he took. The Elf goes along with this and when he has done it will be official. It does little good my saying no. I've no more evidence than John – less, for he has Alice while I don't have Margot. I do have – we both have – the weight of those eleven years he spent out there. Some thousands of days go into the balance and the Elf will not be able to ignore them. But he'll find a way around the mountain. Alice is waiting on the other side.

I know what I know. But I have a question. Why did he go out in his boat when he shouldn't have? Why did he drown?

I'll have to visit Margot, there is no other way. But first I must finish this. I'll set myself square: stand Wellington and Harry and Jack Skeat in their place. Since he first came to Loomis school I've never ceased feeling Rex's gravitational pull but other things have worked on me too. Rex was not the whole of it.

A southerly and then a northerly. There was no rest. We called our bedroom Scott's tent. The wind whooped and moaned. It rattled tiles and bent the window glass. The rain sometimes came up from below. Great solid lumps of air, ninety miles an hour, banged at us day and night. The house inched round, we were sure of it. Window latches burst. Curtains fled across the room.

When I made our early morning cup of tea Harry called me Captain Oates. Another gust struck. 'Jesus!' I said. An earthquake now?

There were sunny days and still days but they are not a memory. I simply know that they occurred. How could our garden have grown without sunny days? But I remember the pine tree crushing the letterbox. And the bank lunging halfway across the street, as yellow and quick as a tiger. The picture window bulges and I put myself in front of Harry to save her. We criss-cross it with sticky tape. She is not against precautions now.

Downtown, the Quay bends left and right. Plaques set in the footpath show where the shoreline used to be. I am thrilled by that – by huge buildings standing where once there had been sea. Against my will I'm impressed by the beehive stepping into the sky. Politics can thrill me until I remember that those ordinary folk don't decide – they adjust, adjust, react, react, and the machine clanks and grinds and moves itself on another day in a direction that's changed only by a degree or two left or right. But the illusion is sometimes there, the thrill is felt, that one lives in an important place. (And lately there has been a turn – adjustment to the instinct of greed – that alters the way we go a little more than usual.)

I did my job; reported to National or Labour, in that over-designed unhappy building. Outlasted them: the frightened minister, the thick-headed minister on the political make. (Had a good one too, once. He reached out for the brand new book I carried and sniffed it and held it for a moment against his cheek.)

Harry perfected her art. Jo Bellringer was our guest for months on end, and while she loved Harry and hid her love I played my harmless game of lusting after her. Still it does not make me ashamed. Their books sold steadily and Harry was able to put money away. I published too – an article on archives here and there – and a book. Did I say at the start 'author of one bad book'? I have a good one too, that I was not going to mention. It's my *Bibliography of New Zealand Bibliographies*. A first class work that sits uneasily in the National Bibliography alongside *First Fruits*. I made some modest royalties.

In the mid eighties when everybody wanted to get rich we began to want it too. We did our sums on bits of paper, grew fat in our minds with figures like 30 per cent, 35, 40; and thought we might get close to half a million before long. So we switched our money from no-risk to risk, which was 'as safe as houses' in those days. What did we go into? RADA, Equiticorp, RJI, Lupercal. And we bought prosperity bonds, but not guaranteed, no, no, shares. In November 1987 – well, some of our investments didn't do as badly as the rest. But still, we were 'wiped out', that's the term, which I like because it takes on all sorts of meanings.

We grieved for our lost money; and were angry at other times and flung about looking for someone to blame; attack; destroy. Afterwards we looked at ourselves with a kind of shame. It hurts a little still, our loss I mean; but the knowledge hurts more that we could be greedy, that we had meant to stuff ourselves.

'Poor Jillian, poor David,' we managed to say. They would not have much more than the house when we were dead.

'What about our trip?'

'We can still go. I've got my leave and the tickets are paid for. We'll have to do it more on the cheap.'

So we went to Europe as we'd planned, for six months, and stayed in pensions and cheap hotels and youth hostels and bed-and-breakfast places, and ate off stalls and travelled on local buses and walked across cities instead of taking taxis. Got off the plane in Athens, zigzagged up to Norway, and had a month in England and Scotland at the end. We boast that we would not travel in any other way. How heavy our packs grew at times.

In Auckland, as we set out, I telephoned Rex, but Margot told me he had gone out fishing in his boat.

'Give him my, give him our love.'

'Yes, I will.'

Rex went out of mind then until Jill posted clippings from the *Herald* – his swamped boat was found – and the *Star* – his body found. The letter was waiting when we returned to Athens from the Peloponnese.

'That's the day – that was the day we left.' We clutched each other, fingers hooked. Had my face gone as white as hers?

We flew across Australia as Rex drowned. It seemed to me that I withdrew my love.

'I thought of him . . .' In the Peloponnese, at Nestor's palace. It had been the only time: the runnel and the basin in the clay, where the king had poured his libation – Rex would like that.

Then I thought, Clay is archive, poor old Nestor's only art; and I forgot. But it had been genuine, I had signed our friendship, running back. It saved me in Athens when I held his death in my hands.

I could not grieve. I was simply relieved to pass a test. For the rest of our trip I thought of him in faked ways: Joannina (Byron was here); the Stockholm archipelago (reeling in a fish); Battersea Bridge. It wasn't until our plane banked to line up the runway at Mangere and I saw the gulf islands sliding away that I understood Rex was drowned.

'You got my letter, Margot?'

'Yes, I did.'

'I couldn't take it in. Not properly. But I wanted to say how sorry I was.'

'Thank you, Jack. Sal and I appreciated it.' She did not apologize for not writing back. Lila had written back. I read her half dozen lines in Zurich.

'My daughter wrote and told us and sent clippings. I still can't . . . I telephoned just before we got on the plane. It happened on that same afternoon.'

'Yes.'

'So you couldn't give him – our – love.'

A silent wire.

'I'm sorry, Margot, I'm not blaming you. Where was – did many people go?'

'Quite a few.'

'The family?'

'Yes.'

'And – Alice and her children?'

'Yes. Them.'

'I'm glad.'

Silence again. She was not.

'Did any writers . . . ?'

'Rita Bullen came. She read some poems.'

'Hers?'

'No, his.'

'That's good.' I wanted to know which ones. (I know now, I telephoned Rita. And John Dobbie named them in his book. John was there.)

'I would have liked . . . I couldn't come back.'

'Yes, I know.' Tenderness in her voice, it almost seemed.

'There's our boarding call for Wellington. Margot, when I come up again, can I come and see you?'

'If you like. But you don't have to.'

'I will. Next time I come. Oh Margot – where . . . ?'

'On the property. We scattered them here.'

'That's good.'

'Alice wanted them. She came up to me and demanded them. Before he was even burned. She said she had the right.' (The Elf did not put that in his book.)

'What did you do?' Harry pulled my arm. 'Margot, I'm sorry, I've got to go. Next time I come up we'll talk.'

I telephoned Rita when I got home and she told me that Margot had simply turned her back. She and her daughter had climbed into their car – Rex's old big-banger with the roof-rack where the dinghy had been roped – and had driven away. Rita said she felt like applauding. A party, wake, for Rex was held at Alice's house but not many people went along. Perhaps John Dobbie had too much to drink and counted double.

I took retirement at sixty although my contract allowed me to stay until sixty-five. Harry was eager to be away. She could not settle down again after Europe. All those other places had told her that Auckland was her place. Part of Wellington is part of Harry, but her buried part, her deepest clay, is Auckland clay, and I had promised we would go. I wanted it. With Rex dead there was a space up there, call it Loomis, call it what you will, waiting for me to remember and occupy.

The Monday before we left we walked from Johnston's hill to Mt. Kaukau. We wore our little Fjallraven packs but she carried our water and our parkas. In mine I had a French loaf folded in two, some smoked salmon, olives, Esrom, brie, and a bottle of white wine, which was warmed by my back when I took it out. That did not spoil it for us; or the need to anchor our cloth with stones on the grass. We would have felt cheated if the wind had not come along. We lunched on a hilltop, with the city on one side and the strait on the other. The South Island darkened all its mountains seductively but Harry and I were heading the other way. Our eyes followed the Horowhenua coast, which seemed to climb. We thought we glimpsed Mt. Taranaki in a cloud. Mist lowered and streamed around us and we were like stones fixed on the hill. It was emphatic. Wellington made its play for us. But we stood up and folded our cloth and went on our way. We crossed the hill below the ghostly mast. It's been nice to know you, we said; and meant it too. Wellington had roughened our skins and damaged our eyes and slanted us; taught us up and down and hidden treasure, and 'danger' and 'impossible' and 'stupid' and 'brave'. We loved and hated it and were glad to be leaving. The mist slid away towards the strait, exposing Khandallah on its shelf, with ice-blue swimming pool and shining roads and busy cars, and women playing tennis and men up ladders painting walls. Two steps into the harbour, so it seemed; toy ships, containers stacked like blocks; downtown Wellington standing tall on land that once had been the sea; and a whisper jet, lower than us, sinking towards the runway by the golf course at Miramar.

Harry took a photo. I'll say this for myself, I don't need photos. We walked down, knee-jolted down, to Simla Crescent and took the unit into town, and had our last cable car ride home.

On the Quay Harry bought a street map of Auckland.

Notebook: 15

It is more now than filling in, it is finding out. Remembering has run its course but Rex's life isn't finished yet. I don't know which voice to use.

I have been in Auckland for a year. My promise to visit Margot is broken. I can claim of course that I've waited until the time is right. I brought her Rex when she was a child, at a time when she needed him, even though it was by accident. I can't remind her of it but I'll tell her there is something I must know and she'll understand I need him now.

I'm not knitted into one garment, seamed up tight. I haven't earned the rest and comfort of the past tense. There are things still left to do – Alice, Margot. But 'I' want to go. I'll insist on it. I don't want to stand off and call myself Jack Skeat. That has been a curious evasion.

Alice summons me in her grandest style.

'Jack, I need to see you. I'm free this afternoon if you'll drop by.'

I don't resist. Going to see Alice is required if I am to keep the balance right. So I leave Harry planting seeds and step outside; which changes to a stepping in as I drive away. Down the motorway to the bridge; along past the wharves and the railway yards; through that interleaving of land and sea where the joggers run; and up into Mercedes land. Here's regal Alice on her patio. Is she Alice Wilkey or Petley today? I must wait until she declares herself.

I tell her that she is looking well; and it's the truth. Good health prolongs her beauty; keeps Alice porcelain and fine. Will she come to stringiness and desiccation soon? That's the usual end of the long-throated, thin-handed beauty she cultivates. The open weave of her sun-hat brim drops flakes of gold on her cheeks.

'You're punctual, Jack.' She gestures at the tea on the iron table and sits down. 'Fiona said not to make it until you arrived but I said you always came on time.' She makes it sound common and I nearly apologize.

'Is Fiona here?'

'That's her swimming.' Up and down. I had thought it was a granddaughter under the mermaid cap.

'Is she . . . are they . . . ?'

'Yes. Do you have any influence with her, Jack?'

'No. None. I've no way of knowing what would be right for her.'

'There's only one right thing and that's going back. Families mustn't be broken up.'

One might disagree, in a case or two. Jack doesn't – I don't bother. I sit where Alice directs me and take milk not lemon to show her that I don't mind being common in the least – indeed, that I choose commonness. I watch Fiona through the wrought-iron railing. There's something defeated in her stroke. She does not reach far enough on the water.

'How are the children? Is it three they've got?'

'Three. They're fine. Tom's moved a new woman in. Men don't take long.'

'Can't she – can't Fiona get custody?'

'They're too old to be fought over. In any case, they want Tom and Fiona back together. They'll soon get this other woman out.'

'Is that what they're doing? Getting her out?'

'Why not? They're sensible children. They know who their real parents are.' There is some bravado in that.

'Are you frightened Fiona mightn't want to go?'

Alice pours tea. It gives her time. 'Fiona has got some sorting out to do. I hoped that you . . . You'd better not say anything foolish to her, Jack.'

'I won't say anything at all.'

Alice spoons the slice of lemon from her cup. She puts it in her mouth and chews, but seems to get no pleasure. She shivers like my mother sipping sherry (New Year's Eve, her annual glass).

'Fiona has some of Rex's' – she swallows – 'lack of courage.'

So, she is Petley today. It's not her daughter she wants to talk about. I turn away from her and watch Fiona; who climbs the silver ladder from the pool, peels off her cap and shakes her hair, drags on her towelling robe with long-limbed grace. I can't believe 'lack of courage'. There's nothing defeated in her now – unless the soap-opera gloss of foam-white bathing suit and tanned legs and straw-berry hair, with the sparkling pool and the gulf behind, is a retreat into unreality. It goes with the dialogue Alice and I have just completed. I turn the other way and find Leon Pittaway gargoyling at me through glass. A woman – hired nurse? – moves him back, sits him in a chair, wipes his chin, then stands with her face framed in the window, staring like a prisoner at the day.

'Hallo, Jack,' Fiona says, and sits down hard on an iron chair. 'Chlorine. What a foul taste.' She takes a slice of lemon and clamps it between her tongue and the roof of her mouth; extracts the juice, flings the slice into the barbecue pit. She asks how Harry is and how I'm functioning.

'Very well.'

'I hope my plumbing never packs up.'

'You seem fit enough. How many lengths?'

'I don't count. In either sense.' How quick she is. Unhappiness makes her crackle and spit.

'Sugar?' Alice says, ignoring her.

'Thank you.' The cups are so delicate there's nowhere for my fingers to go. I say how sensible the Russians are to drink their tea from glasses; but Alice isn't having pointless talk. Or pessimistic. Stops Fiona with a nail-tap on her hand.

'Jack, I've been thinking about this idea of yours.'

'Idea?'

'It seems to me you could well be right.'

I understand what she is talking about; but sip my tea. The Rex I am completing has nothing to do with Alice's Rex.

'He was careless about all sorts of things, but not about the sea.'

'It could have been a gamble, a sort of Russian roulette,' Fiona says.

'That's possible too.'

'Take me if you're ready. If not I'll turn round and go home.'

'Possibly.'

I am reluctant to enter this. I feel as if I might be sick, which is a reaction too extreme.

'It was your idea, Jack, not mine,' Alice says. 'It seemed odd that you should start a rumour of that sort – '

'I didn't – '

' – but then I remembered how well you knew him.'

'I didn't start a rumour. I just felt . . .'

She waits.

'I felt that something wasn't right.'

'Exactly.'

'But I don't want to go on with it. There's no point.'

'I disagree.'

'Rex's death is Rex's death.' And Margot's. And mine. I don't want her fitting it into the Alice story. 'There are all sorts of things we'll never know. His whole life with Margot, for one thing. And I'm not' – I stop Alice with a raised finger, the first time I've ever accomplished it – 'I'm not going out there asking questions. They kept themselves private and no one else was invited in.'

Alice sits upright and still. A breeze lifts the fine hair by her ear, which is as white and delicate as my cup. She pats either side of her nose with a folded hankie. Alice can be angry or she can seduce. Fiona too watches to see which she will choose; and we're both surprised. It is seduction by good sense.

'Why did his poetry stop, Jack?' Soft and calm. 'I'm not the only one who wants to know. He had a habit of speaking, didn't he, in verse? He worked hard – like a tenor improving his voice. It's not all gift. I'm the only one who knows how hard he worked. And how important getting that perfect tone and meaning was – and how happy he was when he managed it. It was the most important thing in his whole life. Not me. I came second. Writing poems. It *was* his life. He couldn't just suddenly stop.' She makes us wait. Alice is brilliant. Timing superb. 'Unless . . .'

'Yes?' I say.

'Unless something died in him. Something withered up.'

'How do you know he didn't keep on writing?' – but I'm unconvincing, even to myself. 'There might be whole piles of . . .' I'll trap myself into being sent to investigate.

'No.'

'No?'

'You tried yourself, didn't you Jack? To be a poet. And I tried. So we both know – publication is part of it. It's part of the process. There's writing and there's reading.' She touches her hand and eye.

256

'And one can't exist without the other. You don't know how eager Rex was for his poems in print. He felt they didn't have a real existence until then. It was just shouting in the wind.' She hears the effectiveness of that and lets it work. Then she lays her hand on my arm. 'There's no lost poetry, Jack. There's nothing to go and see Margot Stiles for. What we've got to work out is what she did to him, why the *poet* died.'

'Alice – '

'There's no mystery about why *Rex* killed himself.'

'You can't' – and she waits now – 'you can't say Margot Stiles. She was his wife as much as you.'

'No.' Gives a patient smile. 'I told you once that he never married. Remember? I meant he was married to poetry. So anyone, even me, turned into an enemy at times. But your Margot must have been his enemy all the time. Jack, you mightn't believe me, but I was something more. I didn't only have my domestic face. I turned about and I became a source of poetry.'

Fiona – we've forgotten her – makes a little splutter. Appallingly rude. Alice tells her to get dressed or she'll catch cold.

'She's not,' I say, 'my Margot. I hardly know her. And Rex knew her much longer than you realize. For most of his life.'

She thinks I'm telling her that Margot was the woman from his adolescent dream, taking flesh. An ugly red spoils her cheeks. Her tea-cup rattles in the saucer. I can't break Alice up like this. So I tell her about young Margot Stiles and Wells and 'Porridge'; but leaving Sidgy out cripples the story. I've got a plain fat girl in a cruddy bed-sit, whingeing and bumptious by turns, and a bored Rex amusing himself. It's wrong and only murder can make it right. I try sentiment instead: Margot the sad child, unloved by her mother, and Rex Petley being kind to her. Alice, very still, turns that over; accepts. She is not pleased, but can stand outside and not be hurt. She'll modify Rex and leave his essential parts untouched.

'Does anyone else know about this?'

'No.'

'Don't tell anyone. It's exactly the sort of new thing John needs for our book.'

'Margot mightn't want – '

'John can see her. It explains . . .' Alice calculates. She can't decide what it explains but will find something in the end. Margot then will be made to fit with Margot later; and suicide will round things off. 'Did he meet her again, after that?'

'Not that I know of.'

'No. You were in Wellington. It's up here that counts. Jack' – business now – 'there's something you can do for me.'

'I'm not going out to Margot's. I'm not fishing round for anyone.'

This is *lèse-majesté*. Alice closes her eyes to show how patient she can be. 'I'm not suggesting it. It's not your place, it's for John Dobbie. He'll have to make her understand . . . What I'd like you to do' – a tiny rattle on her saucer again – 'is go and see John and let me know how he's getting on.'

'Why, is he sick?'

'I don't think so. But I'm having trouble – '

'He's got some woman out there,' Fiona says, 'and every time Mum rings up she says he's not at home.'

'It might be his wife. What happened to his wife?'

'I tried once.' Fiona. 'She just said "Out" and slammed down the phone. She sounds like a female wrestler.'

'I've no idea what happened to his wife,' Alice says. 'After a while she simply wasn't there. I always assumed they'd separated. Wives' – a flash of bitterness – 'get put out of the picture.'

'She could be a housekeeper,' I say.

'Possibly. But I've got to keep in contact, Jack. At this stage it's important. He was coming over here to work on some papers.'

I agree to go and have a look. I'll do this for Alice; and not come back. I'm tired of being used. I'll wind her tame biographer up and get him jerking along; then I'll do something for myself. I'll carry on with my Rex and leave them with theirs. I'll warn Margot what she might be in for.

'Where does he live?'

'In Mt. Albert. Fiona, can you get the address? She was, anyway, unsuitable for John. She was just a big girl off a farm.'

I don't want to go to Mt. Albert. For a moment Alice, speckled with yellow sun, and Georgy Feist in his golden hairpiece, become one. They do not allow me to be myself. Then I shrug them off. I really have quite a hard, well-shaped self these days. It's not in danger. I don't have to drive around the edges of Mt. Albert.

Fiona comes back. She has changed into a skirt and sandals and brushed her hair.

'I'm coming with you. I need to get out.'

'Oh. Good.' I'm pleased to have the company of this woman I might have loved. Perhaps, I think, I can cheer her up. I am willing to help Alice too. I see how tired she is; and how much will goes into the making of an Alice for the world to see. She should rest but she can't for years. She has a senile father and an unhappy daughter, and shouldn't have the extra job of getting an ex-husband into shape.

I lift her hand and pat it, surprising us both. Fiona gives a twisted smile at what she takes to be another victory for her mother. We drive away in my car, heading for a street on the other side of Mt. Albert from Verona Avenue, not that it matters. As we zip high and easy over Broadway I make Fiona laugh with Newmarket tunnel.

'How long?'

'Less than a minute.'

'If you're young and keen enough,' she says.

I ask her – she smells of chlorine still – if she'll ever go back to her husband.

'I want to but I can't. I want to for the kids. But I saw Tom and we had a talk. It's just – I don't like him any more. It's very simple.'

'Have you tried – you know?' It would be indecent to say.

'Marriage guidance? That's the other thing that's gone down the tubes. How could I have been so simple, Jack?'

I remember that I'm cheering her up and I tell her about Rex arriving, hypothermic in the southerly, and spoiling my night of love with Brenda Littlejohn.

'That's sad,' she cries. 'That makes me want to cry. We need . . .'

Does she mean every night of love that we can get? She is open to desperation.

'I wasn't upset. I was always pleased to see Rex.' I mean that I loved him too, and giving him my bed was an act of love – but she doesn't hear it.

'Where did that girl go? Did you . . . ?'

'It never happened again. God these hills, look at them will you. We've got the cheek to say Mt. Eden and Mt. Albert. They're like pudding basins upside down.'

John's street is near the grammar school. He never went there, the poor devil had to go to Helensville District High. Some of the school bits in his memoir are wrong and I'll have to see he gets them right in the biography. The teachers' nicknames were, it's true, Itchy, Slimy, Snarler, Butch, but the teachers themselves weren't like that, not exclusively.

'I should have asked Margot before I told your mother about Wells.'

'It's too late now. I like that – Wells Fargo.'

I wonder if she would like Sidgy bouncing down the steps with his penis out. It mustn't be told – but one day must, when we are dead. When I am dead and Margot is dead. And what about Fiona and Sal, how will it affect them? Their children will be far enough removed to get some excitement, pleasure perhaps, from the knowledge that their grandfather committed a murder. Will it interest them more than his poetry?

But how it wrenches his life round when I say 'murder'. It makes him face in another direction. I shiver as I look at John Dobbie's house. How much will the little man find out?

There are bow windows, blind in the sun. There are two fresh-painted steps to a porch, where a stained-glass rose grows in a port hole. Everything is clean and clipped. The brass door-knocker is a lion with all his fierceness on display.

John Dobbie comes scuttling round the side of the house. He has a gnomish crookedness and lurch. Where is the Elf?

'Jack, don't knock. Come this way.'

'Alice sent us, John. Are you – '

'This way, quick. She'll hear.'

He takes us, plucks us by our clothing, round the corner and down the side of the house. A wooden shed stands by a vegetable garden with straight rows of everything that grows in early summer. He peers along the back wall at the kitchen and we see a hand in there, polishing a window pane with a yellow cloth.

'Inside. She can't see anything in here.'

'Who is it John? Alice has been phoning.'

'I phoned too,' Fiona says. 'Someone hung up on me.'

The shed makes us stand too close together. We breathe on each other, but John is so short his breath warms the base of my throat. He's not the John, the Elf, I have known for thirty-five years. I have never seen him without a tie, or seen his hair disarranged. It is thin and elderly and does not add three inches to his height.

'It's my wife. They've sent her back.'

'Where from?'

'Carrington. She's been in Carrington since 1973. They're – it's a new policy – they're making them go and live outside.'

Like Rex's his life is wrenched around. There has always been another Elf. I have been too lazy knowing him. Hair, tie, pouter chest, self-importance, pomposity – I've taken that as the whole of John and written him full of mistakes.

'They shouldn't do it, Jack, it's not right. There's a woman comes round and says how nicely she's getting on. But she's still mad. They don't see. I think they must have told her that she had to help, so she polishes things. That's all she does. She cleans the windows over and over, all the time. I can't work. I haven't done any work for more than a week. And I can't get out. She might burn the house down, she might tear up all my books.'

'John – '

'I can't telephone. She comes and snatches it and polishes it. She's big, Jack. She's bigger than I am. She won't let me answer.'

Fiona says, 'I'm going to see her.'

'No.'

'I'll be all right. I've been handling disturbed people all my life.' She walks along the path to the back door. The yellow cloth stops circling on the pane.

'Fiona knows what she's doing,' I say uncertainly.

'But Eve's so huge. She's huge, Jack. She nearly punched my eye out once, before they put her in Carrington.'

'They can't send people out if they're dangerous.'

'Yes they can. It's money. There's no money to look after them.'

I hear Fiona's voice, falsely cheerful; and listen so that I can run and fling my weight in there, against the woman I still see as tall and marble-throated, Artemis-like.

'She never talks. She doesn't hear voices except on the phone. They say I should introduce her to my friends. They're mad, Jack. They're as mad as she is. She eats flies.'

261

'What?'

'She hits them with the fly swat and picks them up and eats them. I told them. Do you know what they said? She's cleaning up. They said she'd stop if I . . . I can't be patient, Jack. I've got my work. This book is the only thing I'll ever do.'

'Get someone to watch her. Hire a nurse.'

'And pay with what? I haven't been on a fat salary like some people I know. I've still got a mortgage on this house.'

I tell him that Alice will help. If she wants her book she'll have to pay. She'll pay for a private nursing home if that is what Eve needs. Stephen Wilkey has got money to burn. I make these promises to keep from thinking about flies. 'When you're ready I'll come and talk to you. I've got all this stuff about his childhood you can have. But you'll have to see Margot yourself.'

'Do you really think she'll pay for a nursing home?'

'She will for the book. Get an agreement. Make it for the length of Eve's life.'

'John,' Fiona calls from the back steps. He goes out with some of his old bounce. I follow him into the kitchen and we find Fiona and Eve at the table, polishing the cutlery with Silvo.

'All she needs is company,' Fiona says. 'You've got to do things with her, then she's all right.'

'I can't – '

'You don't have to, I will.'

'She shouldn't have knives.'

'I'm watching her. Do that spoon again Eve, you've missed some Silvo on the handle.'

The woman obeys. I can't, for the moment, get closer than that. Her dress, her hair, say 'woman'. I can't see the farm girl, and can't see John's wife. There's a person overflowing the kitchen chair. She turns her collapsed face at me and turns it back. The knives and spoons on the table are too small for her hands, which have ballooned and rounded on their backs. Her nails are swallowed in flesh – but I won't go on: body, face. A catalogue of swellings and slidings-away and discolorations: no point. If she's anything she's more, she's other, than these ruined parts. I must believe in a continuity for her mind; in the presence of Eve Dobbie in some vestigial form.

'Hallo, Eve.'

She takes no notice, works on a spoon.

'I'm going to stay a while, until you get something sorted out,' Fiona says. 'She's OK at polishing but not at other things.' She means the dishes in the sink, the grit and dust on the floor, the filthy stove.

'She won't let me do it.'

'She will me.'

'Jack said Alice might pay for a home.'

'Is that what you want? How long has she been inside so far? She likes it here.' Fiona grins. 'She's got her own kitchen.'

'My book – '

'You can lock yourself in. The book must go on, after all. Or else you can take a taxi and work over at Mum's. She'll pay, don't worry. She'll hire a Rolls for you if you like.'

'You're not serious?' I say to Fiona. 'Staying here?'

She starts a smart answer, then sighs. 'I don't know. For a while. I need something to do.' Grins again. 'We can't have John going mad. One's enough, eh Eve?'

The woman is watching a fly on the sink. She reaches for the swatter leaning on the table leg. Fiona doesn't know about the flies yet.

'I'm going,' I say. 'I'll keep in touch. Bye, Fiona. Bye, John.' I give a skimpy wave and get out the door. She probably wants me to fetch her stuff, but she can phone Alice and have it sent around by Rolls. I've done all the helping I can do. Must get away. Find ways of containing Eve, with her diet of flies; and John, whose book on Rex Petley is all he'll ever do. Fiona too, who takes them on to cure herself, must be contained.

Although it takes me out of my way I drive through Verona Avenue. I've got my father and mother sorted out, they weren't too hard. They should have tipped me upside down and cracked me at least; but here I am enlarged by Walter and Dorothy Skeat (although perhaps only in proportion to the shrinking they once caused). So I'll manage these later ones without much trouble.

That leaves Rex.

Rex and Ralph Murdoch and Margot and Sal
(and Harry and Jack)

Margot said: 'Come this afternoon.'

I drove though Albany and Riverhead and through the forest backroads to Waimauku. The sea was half an hour away but when I wound my window down the smell of baked earth and dried-out ditches was mixed with salt. I wondered if Margot's wine had a salt flavour and if the creek ran deep enough for Sal. Heat shimmered over the dunes at Muriwai. The vineyard, concave on its hill, was green and tender. The micro-climate seemed to make breezes of its own.

Margot opened the gate and waved me through. I stopped in the yard and looked at her dogs.

'What are they?'

'Ridgebacks. You can get out.'

'I'm nervous of big dogs. I always expect them to attack.'

'That's how I feel about some men I have to pass.'

She was cheerful and hostile equally. It was up to me which would take control. I got out of the car and let the dogs sniff my trouser legs.

'Ben. Mac.' She snapped her fingers and sent them behind the house. We shook hands, looking at each other cautiously. She did not expect to please me or I to please her. She was brown, grey-blond, muscular. I liked the smell of sun and earth on her. I don't think she liked my suburban moistness.

'Come in, Jack. I want to talk before Sal gets home.'

'Where is she?'

'School. She's in the third form. She's thirteen.'

I had thought of the vineyard as not connecting with the world. School set me right. School blouses dried on the washing line.

'Hold on, I brought you something.' I reached into the car and took it from the seat. 'Halva. For you both. I don't know . . .'

'Yes. That's lovely. Sal's never had it. She's in for a treat.'

I walked behind her into the house. She wore shorts and a halter top and sandshoes. Her hair was cut level with the angle of her jaw. Nothing was designed for show. (I don't say there's virtue in it, just that she's congruent with her way.) She took me into a room that was kitchen and living-room both – sink and bench, table, chairs, settee, mats on wood – and offered tea.

'I'd rather have some of your wine. Just one glass.'

'One's all you'll get if you're driving.' The bottle had no label. I hoped she saved her best for the guests, but was disappointed when I drank – too fresh, too grapy.

'That's good.'

'It's getting better. I'll never be one of the great wine makers.' She did not take any herself but ran a glass of water from the tap. I would have liked some water to thin my wine.

'You're using labour now, though,' nodding up the hillside at a man working in the vines.

'Yes.' Flat. Dismissive. Not my business. I wondered if he replaced Rex with more than labour.

Margot slid her shoes off, using her big toe against each heel, and pushed them away. 'You're up in Auckland permanently.' She leaned against the sink and crossed her ankles. 'So I heard.'

'Who from?'

'Tony Jameson. He comes out for that.' A nod at my wine. 'He gets it cheap.'

'Ah, Tony. I met him on the beach. He's got – ' But I wasn't ready. 'I'm sorry I didn't come earlier. I've been writing some memoirs.'

'About Rex.'

'Mainly. Yes.'

'I had a phone call from a man called Dobbie, who wrote that book. He wants to come out.'

'When was that?'

'A month ago. I told him no. He said he'd ring back but he hasn't.'

'He's had a hiccup. He will soon. Margot . . .'

'There's all sorts of things to say. Take your time.'

'Alice is behind John Dobbie. It's a full-scale biography and she wants to make sure he writes it her way. Her Rex.'

'Yes, I know.'

'So you'll have to talk to him, and tell him you and Rex, out here . . .'

'No.' She shook her head.

'Otherwise they're going to get it wrong.'

'It doesn't matter. You talk to him. Make sure they do his boyhood right.'

'Margot, I told her. Alice. About Wells. I shouldn't have. But not' – seeing her face – 'about Sidgy. I'll never tell that.'

'Is he in your memoir?'

'Yes, he is. I had to, Margot. I'm not going to publish it. I had to get it down for myself. The whole thing.'

'Will you let me see?'

'If you like.' I smiled and swallowed from my glass. The wine burned and was truthful. Perhaps it was just my enormous relief – to know I had been writing for her too, that it wasn't solitary and wasted and turned in.

'I'm sorry about Wells.'

'It doesn't matter. Someone would have found out one day.'

'They can't find Sidgy.'

'He's in a lot of Rex's poetry.' She turned and looked out the window, past the corrugated iron shed and the vines. She tipped her glass of water over her hands and let them drip into the sink. 'So are you.' She dried her hands on a tea towel. 'He said you always wanted a poem, for Jack.'

'Yes, I did.'

'But you were there so you didn't need one, he said.'

'Margot.'

She was smiling privately. 'Mm?'

'There's something else they want to put in. Alice does.'

'About me?'

'It's about you both, more or less. She thinks, they think, Rex meant to drown himself out there.'

Margot turned back to the sink. She put her hands on it and rested her weight. Her calmness seemed unnatural to me. 'I can see how it would suit her,' she said at last. She sighed and went to sit on a chair at the table. 'I suppose you want to know too, Jack?'

'No. Well – yes. If you can.' I swallowed. 'It's my fault, all this. I told them I didn't think Rex would ever get as careless as that, on the sea. And then, Lila and Tweet were hiding something. I don't know.

Rex had no need. I know how happy he was here. But there are things that don't fit in.'

She listened gravely. She widened her eyes as if to see something she had not meant to look at again. 'You're right. He was never careless.'

'No.'

'Rex was a professional fisherman.'

'Yes.'

'He went out there to see if it would happen. To see if it had to, I mean.'

'I don't understand . . . I'm sorry, Margot. If you don't want . . .'

'He left me a letter. It's mine' – seeing me start – 'no one can see. But he said, "Jack knew Tod. You can tell him if he wants to know." I think he felt you knew about Sidgy, so this . . .' She shrugged. 'Everyone thought Rex was simple. They didn't know how complicated he was.'

I said, 'Tod? I remember Tod.'

'Most people don't. He's a shape-shifter.' We heard the squeal of a tap outside, and the sound of water. 'Come here, Jack.' She crossed the room to a side window and beckoned me. The man from the vines was at the rain-tank, letting water run into his hands. He was intent; and he was, somehow, breakable: bony in his shoulders and skewed in his neck. I saw his Adam's apple work as he drank. He had enormous gravity. When he had finished drinking he washed his face. He turned off the tap and stayed bent, letting water drip into the puddle on the ground. He rubbed his palms on his shorts and pulled his skin dry, forehead to chin. Then he picked up a cloth hat from the edge of the stand and set it on his head. The sun-flap covered his neck. It was like a cupboard door shutting him in. The ridgebacks watched. They moved several steps after him as he walked into the vines.

'That's him,' Margot said.

'Tod?'

'Ralph's his proper name.'

'He didn't look . . .' But that had been a skinny boy. I'd flipped him half a crown and taken little notice of his face. 'What's he doing here?'

'He works. He lives over there, in Rex's old shack.'

267

I watched him go up the hill and fit in among the vines and bend to his thinning. 'What's wrong with him?'

Margot had gone back to her chair. 'We used to say a breakdown, didn't we? I guess you could say he's broken in bits. And he's mine until . . . I inherited him. Until he puts himself together, if it ever happens. I wouldn't have him here without the dogs. Not with Sal.'

'You mean . . . ?'

Margot laughed, without humour. 'No, not after Sidgy. No little girls. Although I guess . . . You must know about him, Jack.'

'No. I don't.'

'Ralph Murdoch. It was in the papers.'

'Tod's name was Scahill.'

'His mother married again. The kids changed to the new name. Don't Alice and them know about it?'

'He kept the two families apart. And Tod was never in Petleys anyway.'

'Yeah, that's true. I wasn't going to talk about this, Jack. It was something else I wanted you for.'

I went to the sink and ran water into my glass. I would have liked to wash my face, like Tod. My need to know had broken a sweat out on my cheekbones.

'It isn't just curiosity.'

'Shall I make some tea?'

'Is this rainwater?'

'Yes.'

'It's good. We had tanks. So did Rex.' I tried to explain 'Petleys': how it was Rex's affective world, which he must keep safe, and how his poetry came from there, even when it seemed to be about something else. I demonstrated my right to know – and perhaps went on too long, for Margot turned away. Her eyes – blue, have I said, and too small for 'good looks', in a face rounded overmuch in the forehead and cheeks – had a watery sparkle. She said with some spite, 'He always said you talked too much.'

'Yes, I do.'

'You're right about it, though. About Petleys. But we had it too, out here, just as important, another world. It had nothing to do with all that stuff in Loomis.' She smiled sourly. 'Rex grew up.'

'Yes, I think he did.'

'But you can't put up walls, can you? There aren't any little worlds where you can be safe.'

All I could do was shake my head.

'The outside gets in. If we hadn't been so happy . . . Too much happiness, he said. There can't be too much, can there? You're mad when you think that.'

'Is mad what he was? Something came along and tipped him over?'

She turned away; and turned back as though accusing me. 'Part of it had to do with morality.'

The word made me shiver, which Margot did not see. She went to the cupboard and poured herself a glass of wine. 'He said you were a specialist at that.'

'No, I gave it up.'

'I don't think you can.'

'I gave up being a specialist. Margot, if you'd rather . . .' She alarmed me. The dogs too had picked up her distress and were whining at the door. She opened it and calmed them, then washed their slobber off her hands.

'OK.' She sat beside me with her glass. 'Tod. Ralph Murdoch. All the time we lived out here he kept on visiting. It wasn't often. Once or twice a year. The others didn't come, Melva and Lila and the rest, Rex went to see them. But Tod kept on turning up, we'd see him sitting in his car, grinning through the window, waiting for us to ask him in. He was by himself at first and later on with his wife and kids. Rex didn't like him. I couldn't see why, I thought he was harmless enough. But Rex – he didn't like people coming here. You and Tony were all right. It was like you were accessories. But Tod was trying to break in. Get an entrance somehow, get himself a place here, I don't know. And Rex wasn't having any. He'd send him away at first, when he came by himself. Later on it wasn't so easy, with his wife and the two little girls.' Margot drank. She was dry-eyed and quick in her voice. She spoke as though she were reading minutes.

'He seemed to think Rex had secrets. He knew something Tod had to know. I don't know what he thought it was. Maybe it was what you call Petleys, and Rex was inside there and Tod was out. But

God, Jack' – feeling at last – 'that was just an imaginary place, wasn't it? I mean a place for his imagination. Everyone else, Lila and the rest, were pleased with Tod. No one else tried to keep him out.'

'No.'

'But he recognized the – magic? – OK, magic, somehow. I mean for Rex. He saw how it gave Rex another life. Once he came out here with some poetry he'd written, shitty stuff, he knew it was shit, but he was telling Rex he knew there was a secret place, and special meanings. Rex wouldn't even read it, I did. I had to tell him it was no good.'

'What did he do?'

'Just grinned at me. He took it away. The important thing was, he'd signalled Rex. That was what mattered. God, he was like some black little bat with claws that wanted to hang on Rex's shoulder.'

'What was his job?'

'He worked with some investment place, doing – I don't know. He was one of those guys you see talking on two telephones at once, and watching the screen, and shouting at the girls with the chalk. He'd been some sort of whizz kid at first, I know that. He used to come out here in a flash sportscar. A Jaguar. But I think he must have burned out. They do that, don't they? You have to be a top executive before it happens or they dump you. Tod wasn't making it to the top.'

'What was the firm?'

'He changed a lot. Some fancy name at the end. The boss was one of those big wheels the government used to put on special committees, telling us how to reorganize and behave – you know, self-reliance, moral behaviour, and make sure everything makes a profit, nothing's free. Trim the fat. They were getting ready to knight him. I think he's coming up for his fraud trial soon.'

'Hopkins. Lupercal.'

'That's the one. Anyway – money was important to Tod. He had it for a while. And he couldn't work out why Rex had something he couldn't have. Then 1987 came. Most of his money was in Lupercal. Poof. All gone. And as well as that he'd lost his job. Lila told Rex. We didn't see Tod for a while after that. Not until after his wife and children got drowned.'

'Jesus.' I knew who Tod Scahill had become. I had read about him in the papers and had nearly wept for the brave young man. His runabout was swamped coming down from Leigh. He tried to keep his wife and daughters afloat, but later on he swam for help. He swam all night, in the waves, and came ashore at Wenderholm at dawn. Searchers found the family roped to the half-sunken boat, the two girls and the pregnant wife; all dead. Harry read it to me. We did not know who Ralph Murdoch was.

I went to the window and saw the man at work: his legionnaire's cap, his thin shoulders rising and dipping in the vines. 'That's him?'

'Yes.'

Expressions of pity would have been insulting. 'He doesn't look as if he could swim very far.'

'He's strong. He's one of those wiry skinny blokes.'

'I can understand a breakdown. But I can't . . .' I could not see how it tied in with Rex.

Margot said: 'You'd better sit down again, Jack.'

Now I must tell the rest of it, and not say what she did and I did: sipped our wine or water at first, stood up, walked about, looked at him again out the window, went pale with dread. (She told me I had gone as white as paper.) None of that. Tod's story, then Rex's story:

They started late from Matheson's Bay (not from Leigh as the paper said). If it was to happen it must happen in the dark. But it was not decided on, darkness would not decide. He put it on the weather so the choice would not be his. Weather was a dice he threw.

A light rain came up, and wind and waves. Everything was swallowed up in greyness. He made a game of it at first, skidding down the waves, and his daughters shrieked with delight, but were soon afraid. His wife, Janice, was afraid too, but she trusted him. He told her they would head for Red Beach not Murray's Bay, and go ashore there.

Then came his part, the decision was his. It was easy to seem to misjudge – to hit a wave the wrong way and fill up with water. He had wanted the boat to tip over but it didn't happen that way.

His younger daughter was washed away. Desley was her name. He swam after her and brought her back, hoping his wife would be

271

gone, but she was there, holding on to one side of the swamped runabout, with Jane on the other. So far it didn't seem like murder. He grabbed a fishing line (not rope) from the slopping sea in the cockpit and cut lengths with his pocket knife and fastened the girls to a rail. Then he swam around to his wife. She was weak already. It was easy to unlock her hands. He turned her away from him, touching lightly so she would not bruise. He pushed her under the water and sat on her shoulders. The ledge of her belly made a place for his feet. He wondered how long it would take for the baby to die. Soon he was able to slide off. He tied her body to the boat. Then he swam back to the girls. Desley had not been able to hold her head up. She was dead. He knew he should drown Jane, but found he could not. He did not think she would last very long.

'Hold on tight. Daddy's going for help.'

He swam away.

'All night,' Margot said. 'Some campers found him crawling up the beach at Wenderholm.'

And the papers got the story and tried to make a hero – tragic hero – of Ralph Murdoch. He would not talk to them and soon they were forced to leave him alone. The police left him alone too, after the questions they had to ask. He stayed in hospital for a week with shock and exhaustion. Then Melva took him home to Loomis and tried to ease him back into his life.

But Ralph Murdoch never came out of shock. ('A special kind of shock,' Margot said.) He seemed to forget how to talk. Words got lost. People got lost. His range of vision seemed too short even when they stood close to him. When Lila and Tweet took him to Glen Eden he sat in the sunroom in Les's chair. In front of him the curtains shifted in the breeze, but his eyes, open wide, never went that far. He watched something inside himself, unbelievable yet true, which he must keep his eyes fixed on. He seemed – not afraid – enormously grave.

One day he found his voice again. He told Melva and Lila and Tweet that he had drowned his family. They thought that he was taking blame: that holding under, swimming away, were a fantasy.

'Tod,' they cried, stroking him and holding him in their arms. He stood up and walked outside and did not come back.

No one knows how he got to Waimauku, but in the morning there he was, standing in the yard.

He told Rex. Rex believed him.

I could walk to the window and see Tod. I could see Rex almost as clearly. I did not need Margot to say, 'He said . . . he thought . . .'

They went to the shack and stayed all day, while Margot waited in the house, knowing that her family's safe time was at an end. Then Rex came back and told her everything that Tod had said; and that he had given him the shack, until they sorted out what the hell to do. He gave her a grin that was – Margot hunts for words – pale and afraid.

'He knew already.'

Someone else has a place in it. Sidgy was waiting at the end.

There is no getting past Sidgy.

Rex telephoned Glen Eden and told his mother and sisters Tod was safe. He sat inside next morning and wrote Margot a letter – explaining, trying to explain. (She'll never ask for help with it although she can't understand.) She worked outside with Sal, keeping busy in the vines, as though she might in that way keep them safe.

Rex walked up from the house and held her hands and kissed her. He kissed Sal. Then he heaved his dinghy on top of the car and drove away.

If he had come ashore he would have got past them, Tod and Sidgy, and stood on the other side, the Margot and Sal side, and been able to carry on. He must have expected to come ashore. He liked his chances. That's what I think; Margot too. He would not have left Tod with her otherwise. But he was almost sixty, he wasn't strong and wiry any more.

Tod, in his tipped pushchair, grabs the air. His mouth opens but he

273

does not cry. He follows our canoes on Loomis Creek, keeping pace. I see his sleek hair shine and his knees flash. His skinny arms spear in the mangroves and haul him along.

It was always going to be Tod, for Rex.

He drives to Wenderholm and heads out to sea. The waves are smooth at first and the wind is soft. But I don't need this. Not now. I have his end.

There should be more to say about Tod's wife and daughters. I can't say it. It has been hard even to write their names. (Was Rex trying, in some way, to bring them to the shore?)

And I have nothing to say about Tod. There he is. That is what he did. Like Rex I believe it happened that way. But I don't have to take it on myself. I have to carry it round with me for the rest of my life.

He came with no warning, although I should have expected him. Rex expected him, in some way.

So I had the end of Rex. But I did not have his proper dimensions. Margot had to say: 'Sometimes I hate him. What did he think he was trying to do? I needed him. Sal needed him. Why couldn't he see Sal? Why did he have to put himself first?'

'He loved you. He loved both of you.'

I sat beside her on the sofa, as I'd sat with Lila on the bridge. I put my arms around her and let her cry. Perhaps it was the first time she had cried.

'When he knew he was going to drown, he must have been – I can't bear to think about it, Jack.'

I asked her how long Tod would stay. She did not know. He understood where Rex had gone and what had happened to him. He had nodded his head and walked up the hill and sat in the sun. Margot thought Tweet would come and take him to Glen Eden when her mother died.

But what about now? I wanted to say. It was possible for him to do anything. He might tell his story to the police. He might go out to Muriwai and walk into the waves. He might decide that Margot and Sal had to die . . .

274

I looked at him again out the window. Still he worked.

'I think he's harmless,' Margot said. 'Anyway, my dogs . . .'

The thing he carries with him, though? What about that? Surely, surely, he should be locked up.

'No,' Margot said.

'But it's not your business any more.'

'Yes it is. Rex let him in. It won't be for ever.' She smiled at me. 'Crying helps.'

She got up and wiped her face dry.

I said, 'I'll have to stop Alice and John with their suicide story.'

'Don't bother. Do something else for me.'

She went into her bedroom and brought out a stack of exercise books – eight Olympics, my sort – and a folder bulging with papers.

'I want you to edit these and have them published.'

'What are they?' – although I knew.

'His poetry, Jack. He never stopped writing. There's more than ten years of poems in there. Don't read them now, take them home with you. Come back soon and tell me what you think.'

'Are these . . .?'

'The notebooks are his, the typing's mine. My transcriptions. I might have made some mistakes. Places he meant to start a new line, things he crossed out. Can you do it?'

'Yes. Yes. Are these the only copies?'

'I've taken some carbons, don't worry.' She smiled again. 'Each time he filled a notebook up he'd give it to me. I think that was his way of publishing them. Although he took them back sometimes and made alterations.'

'I should have come sooner. These are . . .'

'I knew you'd get here in the end. There wasn't any hurry anyway. I liked it when they were only mine.'

She came out with me to the car. Ben and Mac looked me over again. They are not dogs I would mess with. But it was Rex's poems, banging on my calf in a supermarket bag, that seemed to promise Margot and Sal would be safe. Tod, up the hillside, had crossed paths with them and now was moving steadily somewhere else. I'd like to say, in order to dismiss him, that he was in some anti-matter universe; but that won't do, he's here all right, he's in our universe, he is Margot's and Rex's and mine.

'Was there some insurance? Was that it?'

'No. None. But everything he had was all gone. He had to start again. He couldn't have them round his neck.' She shivered. 'He was trimming fat.'

I turned away from him. I cannot disbelieve in Tod.

I needed Sal. I needed to see her. She got down from the school bus at the gate. The dogs bounded to her and turned themselves into puppies. I waited in my car in the yard. Margot brought her to me and said, 'This is Jack. He was a friend of your father's.'

'I met you once. You were swimming in the creek.'

She did not remember. A girl in an ugly school uniform, with a name and telephone number inked on the back of her hand. She had her mother's Tinakori plumpness, and something of young Rex in her face. No single feature held it – eyes and nose, forehead, jaw: little bits of Rex here and there.

'Go and get changed, love.'

'Does she know about Tod?'

'No. God, no. She just thinks he's . . .' Circled her forefinger at her temple. 'She keeps out of his way. Thanks for coming, Jack. I won't give her the halva until tea.'

I drove back to Castor Bay with Rex's poems on the seat beside me.

Not all of them are good. In some plain statement fails from too much simplicity. But half, more than half, are almost as good as the Loomis poems or the hospital ones. If they are less good it's because they are less hard – but that is not to say that they are soft.

I mustn't measure in this way. It's not for me to judge but to present. Before that I've had to A&D. Not difficult, they were arranged already, chronologically. As an archivist I'll hold to that. As editor though, what should I do? There are forty-nine sonnets scattered here and there. (Several of the exercise books have the water safety cartoon on the back.) I'd like to bring them together, but did he intend them as a sequence? It's hard to tell. Did he mean those poems he does not title independently but calls simply

'Moments' – which in other hands might sound twee – did he mean them to stand as a group? I have asked Margot but she has nothing to say. It seems to me she browsed in the poems and chewed this and that one like a cud. No editorial problems for her. Did he mean 'Seasons' – there are more than four – and 'Years' to stand in groups? The only answer I can find is that he didn't mean them to stand at all, unless it was in Margot's mind. So I'll have to work it out for myself.

He catalogues the place from the road-edge to the creek, and fence to fence. He kept his sharp eye but lost his ear to some extent. Happy poems should sing, but Rex doesn't sing. Happy poems are hard to do. The less successful ones are not much more than a friendly ramble; unhurried steps through the grass, swish, swish. The fence wires squeak. He pants a little going up the hill. (How did he ever think he could swim five miles?) But the good ones are tight, hard, intricate in stepping in and out and round and down, they make music of a sort, and strike resonances, in me at least: I hear Rex Petley's voice and it is continuous with his Loomis voice. They are better – they're more interesting and please me more – than most of the verse he wrote when he was with Alice. But I won't get into that argument.

Margot is there: in work poems and kitchen poems – quotidian but never trivial – and in love poems too. It surprises me she did not hold some of them back. She's sometimes 'Margot' not just 'you' and 'she'. I'll have to decide whether to bring the love ones together. It might be best to publish half a dozen thinner volumes. And Sal is there. There's music in his poems about Sal – so quiet you almost don't hear it at times.

Each of the exercise books has a dedication – 'For Margot'. Perhaps he did go a little soft.

Happy poems. They won't please everyone. Some people are going to say, Where's the tension? Some are even going to say, There's nothing here, no content. But it seems like poetry to me, even though it rarely gets off the property.

One thing is sure, Alice and John will never make suicide stick.

It wasn't suicide anyway. Rex wanted to come back. He meant to come. Going out there was a thing he could not avoid. He could not, finally, keep Tod locked outside. As proprietor of his 'world' he took responsibility. So out he went, like his mother's Plasticine knight, to face – what? What did he find there? I don't know, although I could guess. But he was swimming westwards in the end; swimming back to Margot, and possibly to Loomis as well. The whole thing has the arrogance of his best poems, which never fail.

Tod does not invalidate the poems.

I'm going to make copies for John Dobbie. He'll have a problem. He's going to have to decide between Alice and the truth. I'll give him whatever help I can. But no Tod (and no Sidgy). Those parts of the truth he cannot have. I'll leave them in my notebooks, which will have an embargo of – fifty years? Someone else can finish Rex's life, if there's any interest in him left.

I brought the poems home and read them half the night. 'Have a look at these when you've got time,' I said to Harry. She is part of me and I of her; and Rex of us both. She liked some of them quite well. She liked them better than the hospital poems. Her favourite is the one that starts: 'Jack wants to talk about the Fun Doctor. I say no.' Later on he does talk about him – a line or two. I wish he had made it clear that 'crinkled Auden face' is my phrase, not his.

I've asked Harry to read my notebooks too, when I get them from Margot. (I took them out next day. Tod was still at work in the vines. The Ridgebacks kept watch in the yard.) I'll give Harry the Warwick ones as well, interleaving them, so to speak, with the Olympic. I hope I'm not making a mistake. But I feel there's a cure in what I've written and I want Harry to know about my health. Now and then fold into each other like the fingers of two hands.

I don't sneeze so much any more. I don't get a rash on my chest and my short-term memory is holding on. Perhaps I won't need to go to Duppa this decade. Last night, watching a foolish thing on television, I saw a man gagged and locked in a cupboard and I didn't have to get up and leave the room.

Harry is contented. She is doing a set of botanical posters for schools. Harry needs to work. When the weather is fine we walk on Takapuna Beach. If it rains – it rains a lot in Auckland but the wind doesn't blow like Wellington's – we run for our car, holding hands.

We bring home Chinese take-aways and eat watching the news (which isn't good). I'm beginning to see how Rex's poems should be arranged.

Morning tea time. I'll take a cup to Harry, with a scone, and she'll tap her finger on the desk to show me where to put it. I'm out of my hole under the stairs and do my own work at a desk in the sitting-room. I watch liners and container ships going in and out. Past Rangitoto is the Coromandel. The little yachts stand upright on the sea.

I've let my eye look inside and back. It's good to be able now to turn another way.